The Loyal Angel

Nathan Crocker

Acknowledgments

First and foremost, I thank God for all the blessings of my life, for providing me the inspiration for this book, and for convicting me to persevere in its writing.

Thank you to all those family and friends who read countless drafts and provided invaluable feedback and support along the way; Mom, Dad, Ganny, Lindsay, Ashley, and Emily. Thank you to my friends at work who did the same, especially John, my brother in Christ. Thank you for championing this cause.

Thank you, Rueben. You are not only my editor but also my good friend.

And to my wife, Tara, for her love, patience, and understanding when my work on this book tested all three. In other words, thank you for putting up with me.

The Loyal Angel

This book is dedicated to

Gordon and Bettye

Chapter 1

The Demon

A steamy fog rose above the crystal-clear water of the river, it's bubbling currents cascading over rocks to create miniature whirlpools as it raced by on its way to the Mediterranean Sea. To the east, the rising sun peeked out over the nearby mountaintop, bathing the Roman city of Philippi in a warm summer's light.

A crowd had gathered by the river that morning, men and women with their children sitting on blankets and cloaks spread upon the rocky ground. They had come to hear the words of a wise teacher, a traveler from the east, but they had not expected the tense confrontation now unfolding before their eyes.

"These men are servants of the Most High God, who proclaim to us the way of salvation!"

The Traveler, his brows furrowed, glanced at the young vagabond girl who shouted this statement, then back to his friend. His companion's face expressed an odd combination of annoyance and concern, and the Traveler understood why. The last thing they needed was a disturbance that would draw the attention of the local authorities.

Sitting atop a boulder, the Traveler gazed out over the multitude that had gathered to hear him speak and recognized the concern on their faces as well. Many of them were Jews, which meant they lived under a constant cloud of suspicion and ambivalence. Merely gathering together this way was likely to invite scrutiny. Still, the crowd was undeterred. These people represented the downtrodden of society, the poor, the destitute, the reviled. They had come that morning to receive a message of hope, and he was determined to deliver it.

The Traveler glowered at the young vagabond. She was perhaps twelve years old, frail and thin with dark hair and ghostly pale skin. Her face would have been pretty if it were not smudged with dirt and peppered with the scars of the pox. Dressed in old, dirty rags, she stood awkwardly, half bent to the side and teetered there, swaying left and right while she giggled and bit the nails of her hands.

It was not what the girl said that bothered the Traveler, for her statement was true. He and his companions were indeed servants of God. They had come to preach the gospel of Jesus Christ and show the people of this city the way to salvation. The problem was the motive behind her words.

She had been following them for the last few days, incessantly repeating the same mocking phrase over and over, interrupting the Traveler when he tried to speak and making the people uneasy. Now, her eyes bulged wide as she cackled and repeated her tiresome declaration.

"These men are servants of the Most High God, who proclaim to us the way of salvation!"

Taking a deep breath to steady himself, the Traveler squared his head and glared at the vagabond. The eyes that locked onto hers were icy gray against the weathered and sun-browned skin of his face. The balding crown of his head and the large hooked nose bespoke age and wisdom, while the taut wrinkles about the intense eyes bore witness to the potent vitality that fueled his relentless drive. This was a man who had traveled much and seen more, a man who had faced ridicule and threats, refusing to compromise his principles or his faith.

As the Traveler's gaze bore down upon her, unflinching and unwavering, a tense silence fell over the crowd. The girl hesitated, and perhaps unnerved by the relentless intensity of those eyes, her determination buckled. She took a step back, sat down, and wrapped her arms around her knees. A pained expression swept over her face as she began rocking back and forth, a soft mewing sound issuing from her tightly closed lips.

Satisfied for the moment, the Traveler turned back to his audience and broke the silence by clearing his throat. He resituated himself on the rock, pulling the skirts of his faded brown robe up and away from the dusty ground. Then he addressed the assembly once more.

"Men and women of Philippi, my companions and I would like to thank you again for your warm welcome."

A few of the gathering still eyed the girl, perhaps wondering if she would again interrupt the lesson. For the moment though, she remained quiet, rocking back and forth with her arms wrapped around her folded legs. Gradually, they returned their attention to the Traveler who smiled down at a middle-aged woman seated near the front.

"I would especially like to thank Lydia," he said, a smile growing on his weathered face, "who has opened her home to us while we preach the gospel in your city."

Lydia, a dye merchant who specialized in purple cloth, smiled sheepishly beneath her headscarf and gave a slight bow. She had attended this gathering the previous week and become one of the first in the city to accept salvation.

The Traveler turned from Lydia and gestured toward two men sitting off to the side. "I would also like to thank Brother Luke for introducing us to the community here."

Luke, a doctor and prominent man in Philippi, nodded in acknowledgment. The Traveler next indicated the man sitting beside Luke.

"Allow me to introduce Brother Timothy. He joined us in Lystra and accompanied us from there to Troas, where we received a vision from the Holy Spirit that we were needed here in Macedonia."

The small crowd murmured together at the mention of the Holy Spirit. Sensing the curiosity of the group, the Traveler explained how God had guided them on their journey from Judea in the East up to

Antioch and across Asia Minor to Greece where they now preached to the people of Philippi.

"The Holy Spirit sent me a vision," he said, "of a man of Macedonia who pleaded with me to—"

"These men are servants of the Most High God, who proclaim to us the way of salvation!"

The Traveler stopped mid-sentence, his mouth hanging open, and along with everyone else, looked over at the young girl who had stood back up and interrupted him yet again. He sighed, but then something behind the girl caught the Traveler's eye. He peered past her, further up the slope, to where a crowd of onlookers had gathered when the girl first began making a scene. These were people of the city, curious about the spectacle unfolding at the river.

A couple of men stepped out from the spectators and shuffled to either side of the girl. It was apparent that she knew these men, but she did not welcome them. She struggled as they took hold of her arms and hissed at them between clenched teeth, but despite her contortions, they succeeded in turning her back toward the city.

As the girl was led away, the Traveler turned back to his audience and said, "My apologies,'' but then the girl broke one arm free of her escort. She spun around and yelled back at the top of her lungs, "These men are servants of the Most High God, who proclaim to us the way of salvation!" followed by an eruption of maniacal laughter.

With this outburst, the Traveler lost the last vestige of his patience. He slid down from atop the boulder and advanced upon the young girl. Straining against the man who still held her by one arm, she leaned out toward the Traveler and grinned mischievously through rotten teeth, mocking him with a hissing laugh. The Traveler stopped only inches from her, and looking her in the eye, spoke in a clear, booming, and authoritative voice.

"I command you in the name of Jesus Christ to come out of her."

The girl's triumphant grin melted, her expression morphing into shock and horror as her jaw dropped and disbelief spread across her stricken face. A thick fog of silent anticipation held the onlookers' gazes as they waited with rapt attention.

Then she screamed.

The girl cried out in what seemed like pain and dropped to the ground, her back arching and her hands clawing at the air. Startled, the man holding her arm let go and stepped back as she writhed before him, convulsing in spasms. Then her head snapped up, and she screamed at the Traveler, a feral cat-like roar, all pain and outrage. The Traveler, unmoved, stood calmly over her and waited patiently for the fit to end.

And then it did. The girl's shoulders slumped, and she dropped her head as though the weight of it was suddenly more than she could bear. The dirty, matted locks fell to cover her face as she reached out her palms to steady herself upon the dusty ground. Quietly, she began to sob.

Gasps and murmurs from the crowd drowned out the sounds of her cries, but they were evidenced by the heaving of her shoulders as her whole body trembled. The Traveler, who only moments ago had rebuked her harshly, now laid a gentle hand atop her head. At his touch, her sobbing faded to a whimper, and she sniffed in a rapid staccato of sharply inhaled breaths.

The girl peered up at him through tear glistened eyes and whispered, "Thank you."

The Traveler nodded. Then he stepped back as one of the two men who had earlier attempted to lead the girl away took her by both arms, yanking her up to face him. He was tall and well-muscled, but exceedingly ugly. Scars covered his broad face, and his flattened nose was crooked, no doubt the result of countless brawls. She stiffened as he gripped her with his meaty hands and pulled her close to his mangled face.

The Brute leaned in, his twisted nose almost touching hers, and peered into her eyes as though searching for something locked deep within. She stared back at him wide-eyed and trembling, and he must not have seen what he was looking for because he abruptly released the girl. She dropped to the ground, crumpling at his feet, and broke into a fresh bout of sobs. Turning from his small charge to the Traveler, he pointed an accusing finger, his face a twisted red mask of anger.

"You've taken away her power!"

The Traveler frowned at the incensed man. Then someone stepped up beside him, and Luke's voice whispered into his ear, "She was a fortune-teller. This man is her master."

The Traveler nodded, a knowing expression passing over his face. To the Brute, he said, "She was possessed of an evil spirit. I have freed her."

"You've ruined her!" he spat back. "She's worthless to me now!"

The Traveler watched as three other savage-looking men stepped out of the crowd and glowered at him in turn. Their leader again jabbed a finger at the Traveler as he turned to address the onlookers.

"These men are Jews!" He spat the word with disgust and malice. "They spread their lies and mislead our citizens. Now they deprive us of our seer!"

The crowd murmured at that, clearly troubled by the idea. The Brute continued, "Who will tell us if the harvest will be good this year? Who will warn us of famine or plague?"

There were nods and sounds of agreement from the assembly as they grew more agitated by his accusations.

"No one asked these men to come here and press their foreign ways upon us. Hasn't the Emperor of Rome said that Jews are troublemakers to be watched and rebuked?"

People shouted their agreement. A few called for them to be expelled from Philippi. Others said they should be beaten, and some even cried out for their deaths. Finding himself suddenly the leader of a mob, the Brute glared back at the Traveler and grinned maliciously.

"We'd be within our rights to hang them from this tree, here and now!"

There were calls of assent, and one of the Brute's men took a threatening step toward the Traveler. Alarmed, Luke stepped forward with his arms spread wide.

"Citizens of Philippi," he said in a calm voice, "do not allow yourselves to be carried away to violence. Are we not a law-abiding society?"

The more reasonable members of the mob gave their agreement to this statement while others shouted at Luke to mind himself and be quiet.

"Brothers and sisters," Luke said, "You all know me. I am asking you to leave these men in peace. They have done nothing to harm you."

The Brute shook his head. "That's a lie! They've deprived us of the one person who can tell us the future." He paused before adding, "But as you said, we're a people of laws. We have magistrates and courts, so let's take these men to the authorities and let them pronounce judgment!"

At the Brute's order, his men stepped forward and seized the Traveler and his companions. Luke opened his mouth to object but was rudely brushed aside before he could say anything further. Turning, he addressed the one who took hold of Timothy.

"This man is a Greek, a citizen of Ionia."

The vigilante looked puzzled. "He's not a Jew?"

Luke kept both his gaze and tone firm as he said, "His father is Greek."

The man looked to his leader for guidance. The Brute had taken hold of the Traveler and seemed more concerned with securing his prize than dealing with this new complication. Uninterested, he replied, "Leave that one if he's Greek, but these two go to the authorities."

With that, the ruffians started toward the city, leading the Traveler and his companion away while the mob followed close behind. The Traveler could only hope his friends would be wise enough to make themselves scarce.

Chapter 2

Authorities and Magistrates

The Traveler stumbled. In the press of the mob, someone stepped on his heel, making him lose his footing. He nearly fell, but the Brute still held him tightly by the arm, and now he yanked up savagely. "Get up!"

The Traveler glanced around, trying to get his bearings. They were in the city center now. Stone buildings replaced the huts and cottages that dominated the outskirts, and he recognized the palaestra, the wrestling school, as they passed by. Now, the streets grew narrower, and the Traveler found himself jostled and thrust about by the mob as it flowed around buildings like the onrush of flooding water.

A sharp pain erupted in the Traveler's foot as his toes slammed against something hard and unyielding. He stumbled again, tripping over the lip of the unseen object. Then the soles of his sandals came down on ground that was much firmer than the dirt of the valley. Regaining his balance, the Traveler realized he now trod upon a stone roadway, the Via Egnatia.

The sounds of urban life enveloped them as they passed the public baths. Then the road widened, and the Traveler felt the pressure of the crowd release, the people ahead of him spilling out into the open area of the agora, the central marketplace.

The mob washed through this space, disturbing the normal activities of the shoppers and sellers and picking up curious onlookers as it went. People did not know why it formed or even where it was headed, but they joined just the same, not wanting to miss the rare excitement.

The mass slowed as it entered the forum, the city square, and the Traveler felt the pressure increase behind him as the trailing edge of the crowd caught up. People fanned out, edging closer to gain a better view of the anticipated spectacle.

The Brute still held tight to the Traveler's arm, and now he hauled him up a row of steps that led to a pillared stone structure at the summit of a hill overlooking the forum. As they topped the stairs and came to a stop in the courtyard, three men dressed in white togas exited the building. They were elderly but held themselves tall and rigid. These were proud men, accustomed to being respected and obeyed.

"What is the meaning of this disturbance?" one of them asked.

The Brute pushed the Traveler and his companion forward. Then he answered the magistrate. "These men, being Jews, trouble our city."

One of the magistrates, the eldest of the three, stepped forward to peer more closely at the two men. He looked back to the Traveler's antagonist, and knowing him, addressed him by name.

"Epaphroditus, are these the men who came to our city a week ago, the ones who have been staying in the house of Lydia?"

The irony of the Brute's name was not lost on the Traveler. In Greek, it meant lovely or charming. Epaphroditus was obviously neither of those things, although the Traveler doubted anyone would dare to point out the contradiction, at least to his face.

Epaphroditus replied, "Yes, Magistrate. They've been causing trouble since they arrived. They teach customs that aren't lawful for us Romans."

The magistrate nodded. "We know. Many good citizens have informed us of their activities, and we have learned much about them." Turning to the Traveler, he added, "You are called Saul of Tarsus, yes? And this is your companion, Silvanus?"

The Traveler stood up straight and looked the magistrate in the eye. "My name is Paul, and he is Silas."

The magistrate's face took on a bewildered expression, and Paul understood why. The magistrate was well informed, but he did not know everything about him. Indeed, he had once been known as Saul. He was a Pharisee, a scholar of Jewish law, and had once been one of the leaders of the Hebrew political elite. In fact, previously a zealous persecutor of Christians, he had been authorized to hunt down and arrest members of the budding Christian church.

Then one day, while traveling to Damascus, Saul had encountered a blinding light and heard the voice of Jesus Christ Himself, who asked him, "Saul, Saul, why are you persecuting Me?" In that terrible moment, Saul realized his life had been dedicated to persecuting the followers of the true Messiah. He had been working against God.

Blinded, he was led into the city of Damascus where he spent three long days without his sight while he neither ate nor drank. Finally, a man named Ananias, who received a vision from the Lord, came to Saul and laid hands upon him. Saul's sight returned, and he was filled with the Holy Spirit. From that moment on, he became a fervent follower of Jesus and preached the gospel wherever he went. He took the name Paul, the Roman version of his Hebrew name, as an indicator of his changed nature.

The Brute, Epaphroditus, seemed irritated by the confusion over his prisoner's name. Seeking to refocus the conversation, he said, "They are pressing their foreign ways upon us and used magic against my fortunetelling slave. We want them punished!"

The mob reacted to Epaphroditus' outrage with a surge of agitation and began shouting over each other in a confused cacophony. The magistrate glanced about in concern. With relief, he spotted a detachment of Roman soldiers entering the Forum. They pushed their way through the crowd and up the stairs. When they reached the top of the steps, they positioned themselves between the crowd and the magistrates with their prisoners. Seeking to calm the rising tension, the elderly magistrate folded his arms over his toga and addressed the two men in the loud voice of a practiced statesman.

"The Roman Empire is very tolerant of different religions and the worshipping of various gods. We take no issue with you practicing your traditions with those of your faith. But the Roman Senate has decreed that no strange deities may be introduced to the Roman people whose teachings are contrary to the customs of the Empire. You are free to worship your gods, but your proselytizing must cease."

Paul assumed the magistrate must have considered this the wise and measured course, a fair compromise that would restore order to the city. But Paul was not one to compromise his principles or his faith, regardless of the danger.

Raising his gaze, he addressed the magistrate. "There is but one God in Heaven. I have been commissioned to preach the gospel of the Lord Jesus Christ, and that is what I shall do."

The magistrate stared in appalled confusion, his face reddening. This Jew dared to defy his authority, and in front of the people no less! In a flash of sudden anger, the magistrate grabbed Paul by his robe.

"Take these men!" he commanded the soldiers. "Let them be beaten with rods for their defiance. We will not countenance their kind here!"

The mob cheered with excitement and surged forward, intent on carrying out the magistrate's order themselves. In response, the Roman soldiers stepped forward and formed a line between the crowd and the magistrates, raising their rectangular shields to hold back the mob.

The magistrate shouted at the people to stand back and allow the soldiers to handle the situation, but his words fell on deaf ears. The soldiers leaned into their shields, holding back the crowd, but the weight of the mob forced them backward. Then someone threw a rock that hit one of the soldiers on his helmet. Cursing, the soldier drew his sword.

Paul pleaded with the magistrate, "Take us away now before there is bloodshed."

The magistrate's eyes moved to the Centurion, the grizzled commander of the Roman garrison, and nodded. The Centurion acknowledged the implied order with a curt nod of his own. He took Paul and Silas each by the arm but hesitated before leading them away. They all watched as the magistrate stepped toward the crowd, his hands held high.

"People of Philippi, listen to me!"

He might have been mute for all the good his shouting did amidst the roar of the crowd. The mob forced the soldiers further backward, and the man with the drawn sword raised it in a threatening gesture. The magistrate's eyes darted about in dread.

Then a sound like thunder echoed through the forum, catching the attention of the mob and causing many of them to pause in confusion. The sound came again, and Paul was amazed to see one of the magistrates pounding a staff on the flagstones of the courtyard. The booming sound in the echo chamber of the forum managed to distract the mob just long enough for the leading magistrate to address the crowd once more.

"People of Philippi, calm yourselves!" he shouted. "These men will be punished, but they will be punished according to the law!"

Some of the crowd, those that worked for Epaphroditus, began to push against the soldiers again, but the madness had gone out of the masses, and they received no further support. Paul sighed in relief to see the fever fade from the faces of the people. The magistrate turned and addressed the soldiers, loudly, for the benefit of the crowd.

"Soldiers of Rome, take these two men to the jail and administer their punishment. Set them in stocks and confine them securely while we confer to decide their fate."

With the spectacle at an end, people began to back away, the energy ebbing from the moment. One by one, the soldiers made their way over to where Paul and Silas stood. The magistrate threw the folds of his toga over his arm and hustled across the courtyard toward the council building with his colleagues in tow. As they disappeared through the open door and into the solace of the building's interior, the prisoners were led away to pay the price for their insolence and stubborn faith.

Chapter 3

The Visitor

Sitting in the darkness of the cell, Paul groaned. He could still feel the sting of the rod as it snapped across his back. He had been determined not to cry out, but after the eleventh strike, the scream had been ripped from his throat against his will.

He did not know how many more blows he had suffered before he passed out. He did not remember being carried to the cell, nor having his feet set in the stocks. He had woken up to find himself surrounded by absolute darkness.

He did not know the size of the cell or if he shared it with unseen others. Nor did he know what had become of Silas. All he knew was the pain of the welts on his back and the deep black silence of the cell, broken only by the echoing sound of his own breathing and the occasional dripping of water somewhere in the distance.

Except, that... wait. There was something else. Paul held his breath and listened. The ragged, faint sound of breathing continued. What he had mistaken for the echoes of his own breathing was, in fact, the sound of another prisoner somewhere in the darkness. Paul focused on the sound; irregular, halting, labored. Whoever it was must be in far worse condition than he. He closed his eyes, ignoring the ridiculousness of doing so while in darkness, and mouthed a silent prayer for the poor soul who shared the cell.

He was still praying for the unknown prisoner when a searing white light erupted in the enclosed space. Paul threw his hands over his face and attempted to shut his eyes. Then he remembered they were already closed, which made the intensity of the light that much more alarming. Even with his eyes shut and his hands covering them, it was like staring into the face of the sun.

Then someone spoke. The voice was powerful, though not loud, with an odd musical quality that echoed strangely in the small space.

"My apologies," the voice said. "I sometimes forget how uncomfortable my aura can be for mortals."

The light assaulting Paul's vision faded until it settled into a warm, steady glow. Slowly, carefully, he opened his eyes and taking a deep breath, cautiously lowered his hands from his face, ready to bring them back up again if the light proved to be too much.

It was not. Paul squinted as his eyes adjusted to the now well-lit room. Then he gasped, his breath whisked away by what he saw. The entity standing before him appeared to be awash in brilliant white light, its outline blurry and indistinct. Faint variations indicated what might be a body with arms and legs, but whatever manner of clothing the being wore shined forth with the same powerful glow, washing out any perceptible detail.

Long, shimmering golden hair framed a beautiful and flawless face. So perfect were the features of that face, Paul could not decide whether they belonged to a male or female, if such distinction even applied to this apparition. And it had wings, like a pair of eagle's wings with soft white feathers, the outline visible behind the creature's back.

Paul blinked rapidly as he realized there was only one explanation for what he beheld, only one possibility. With a halting voice, Paul said, "Are you an angel?"

It grinned knowingly at him and nodded softly. Paul was struck by how human its expressions were. He found it odd, but then, what did he know of angels? Still, the being's mannerisms were surprising casual, an observation that made Paul more curious than afraid.

"Is that better, I hope?"

The voice of the angel took Paul by surprise, and he realized he had been staring at it stupidly. He shook his head to clear the fog from his mind, realizing as he did so that the angel was referring to the lessening of the light. Ignoring the pounding of his heart, he forced his mind to focus.

"Yes," he said. "Thank you."

The angel's grin warmed to a broad smile. "I'm glad."

But as it said this, it looked past Paul, and its expression shifted to one of concern. Paul turned his head to follow the angel's gaze. A body lay on the stone floor a few paces away. Like Paul, the feet of the man sat immobile within stocks, but unlike Paul, he was not conscious. He lay on his side, one of his arms thrust out past his head, the other out of view. Angry red welts covered his bare back, and Paul could not help but wonder if that was how his own back appeared. The unconscious prisoner's head faced the opposite direction, but Paul knew without a doubt who he was; Silas, his missionary companion, and friend.

He appeared close to death. Dried blood caked the back of Silas' head, the hair matted and crusted. His breathing was shallow, erratic, and a long pause between breaths caused the air in Paul's own throat to catch with apprehension. He looked back to the angel pleadingly.

"Can you help him?"

The angel's expression softened. Glancing up, it gazed at the ceiling for a moment. Then it closed its eyes, smiled, and nodded. Without a sound, the angel moved over to Silas. Paul could not tell if it took steps or just glided across the floor. Kneeling over Silas, it placed one hand on his battered back, and the glow from that hand grew white-hot. Paul turned half away as he squinted again. The glow faded, and as it did, Silas' breathing grew steadier and less labored. Withdrawing its hand, the angel stood and moved back to the near corner where Paul sat in his stocks.

"He will sleep while we talk," the angel said.

Paul looked around at the entire cell, now fully visible thanks to the angel's light. The room was much larger than he had at first supposed, and he now saw that they were not alone. Five other prisoners lay scattered about the cell, each with their legs similarly shackled. There was no way to tell how long they had been imprisoned here. They all either lay flat or sat slumped over the stocks, and none appeared to be awake, for none reacted to the appearance of the angel.

Paul indicated the other prisoners. "What about them?"

"They will sleep as well," the angel said. "Do you mind if I sit?"

What a ridiculous question, Paul thought. Did angels sit? If they did, this one certainly did not need his permission to do so. Overcome by the absurdity of it, he laughed, which hurt.

"Please," Paul said with a grin of his own and held out a hand in mock courtesy.

He watched as the angel lowered itself to the ground, and again, he could perceive no mechanical action from the movement. The angel did not reach out a hand to steady itself. It simply lowered, hovering, to a sitting position. One corner of the angel's mouth curled up into a sly grin.

"You know, I told Tannin not to antagonize you," it said, chuckling. "He was actually quite shocked when you banished him. I don't think he expected that."

"Tannin?"

"The demon you exorcised from that girl. I warned him to leave you alone, but he just wouldn't listen."

"You were there?" Paul said, astonished. "You spoke to the demon?"

"Of course!" The angel made a clucking noise and chuckled again. "Poor Tannin, always taking on more than he can manage."

"You know this demon?"

"Oh, yes! I've known him since before the rebellion, before the Fall. Since then, I have contended against him regularly enough here on earth. I'm sorry to say he's the reason you find yourself in this jail cell now."

"What do you mean?"

"After you cast him out of the young girl, he began whispering poison into the ear of that Brute, Epaphroditus. Tannin influenced him to rile up the mob and deliver you to the magistrates."

"I see," Paul whispered, and his eyes glazed over as he grappled with the implications of the angel's words. He found himself contemplating the possibilities of a world layered on top of this one, out of view and imperceptible. He had never considered the extent to which heavenly and demonic forces might contend with each other to influence the actions of humans, either for good or evil. As he pondered, the angel continued.

"Tannin has one of the slipperiest tongues in all Satan's horde. He is adept at sowing seeds of doubt, of whispering drops of poisonous suggestion into the ears of men." The angel's eyes narrowed. "Through his vile influence, he has caused many men and women to doubt the power of God's grace and turn away from Him." The angel waved a dismissive hand. "I wouldn't worry too much about Tannin though. While he is troublesome and capable of influencing the weak-minded, your faith is strong. And you have me to watch over you."

Paul stared in puzzlement at the angel. Its mannerisms and expressions were so casual, not at all what he would have expected from an angel. He assumed a member of the heavenly host would present a haughty, formal presence. Instead, this angel expressed an almost human personality. Perhaps perceiving his bewilderment, the angel grinned again.

"Paul, you look confused."

"Well," Paul said haltingly, "I have never met an angel before, but I would not have expected you to be so... normal."

The angel laughed. "It's interesting, isn't it, human imagination? You conjure up ideas of things beyond your perception and understanding. Then you're dismayed and disappointed when they don't turn out to be just as your feeble mind imagined."

"I meant no disrespect," Paul said. The angel chuckled again.

"Oh, I took no offense. If anything, I'm amused and perhaps a little flattered. I've been on earth for thousands of your years now. I suppose in spending so much time with humans, I've grown comfortable with your mannerisms." The angel nodded with decision. "Yes, I think I shall take that as a compliment. Now, if you were to behold some of my brethren in Heaven, you would not be disappointed. They are some of the least interesting creatures you would ever meet; all pomp and ceremony. Take Gabriel for instance. No sense of humor whatsoever. Yes, most of my fellow hosts would be just as you imagined; reverent, solemn, and exceedingly dull!"

Paul smiled. He could not help but like this angel. Still, its presence confused him. "If I may ask, what is the purpose of revealing yourself to me? Do you bring a message?"

"No message, although I can tell you the Almighty is pleased with your work thus far. No, I am here to comfort you in your time of distress."

"I appreciate that, and thank you for what you did for Silas."

The angel considered that for a moment. "I don't think the Lord meant for Silas to die this night."

"You don't think? You mean, you aren't certain of God's will?"

"Well, of course, I know His will!" the angel said with a touch of indignation. "We angels are not omniscient if that's what you mean, but the Lord does speak to me. He did so just now and granted me permission to heal Silas. I also receive constant updates on proclamations made in Heaven, not that much new has happened, not until fifty years ago."

"Fifty years ago?"

"When the Father sent His Son to earth."

"Ah," Paul replied in understanding.

"Now, that was an exciting time! After thousands of years of conflict, we finally dealt a decisive blow against the enemy."

"The enemy?"

"Satan and his demons." The angel's eyes narrowed as he spoke. "For millennia they have gained ground in the struggle, but now the tide has turned. Victory is at hand!"

Paul tilted his head as his mind raced to process what the angel said. "Pardon me for saying so, for I am no soldier, but I've known a few. You remind me of them, and you speak as though you're engaged in a war."

"Oh, we are!" the angel insisted. "We're combatants in the greatest struggle in the history of the world, indeed beyond this world. This war has raged since the Lord laid the foundations of the earth, and I have been at its center since the beginning."

Paul's forehead creased with contemplation. As with all Jews, he had been taught how Satan tempted man to sin, but he had never thought about it as an active conflict, a war between heavenly forces.

"So, you were there when Satan rebelled?"

"I was." The angel's countenance changed. The easy smile vanished to be replaced by a wistful expression. His eyes stared vacantly as though recalling past events. "I was there when Lucifer's pride led him to believe he could supplant the Almighty. I was there when he and his angels assaulted the Holy Seat and were cast down—"

"To earth," Paul said.

"Into the void," the angel corrected him, "although it took them little enough time to make their way here."

"So, it's for revenge then," Paul probed, "that Satan leads man astray? He seeks to pull us down with him to damnation?"

"Partly. Lucifer could not defeat God, so he seeks to hurt Him the only way he can, by targeting those the Lord loves. But do not underestimate your role in this matter. Mankind is not merely collateral damage in some heavenly power struggle. No, Lucifer holds a special hatred for your kind. You see, humanity was the catalyst for the Conflict from the very beginning, and he blames you for his fall."

"What do you mean? Can you tell me about this war and how it started?"

The angel paused, perhaps considering whether he should reveal the information. After a long moment, he nodded with decision, and the face changed, taking on the most serious expression Paul had seen up to that point, a fierce visage that reminded him this was a being of immense power.

"I have been sent here to comfort you," the angel said in a formal tone, "so if it will bring you comfort, I will tell you about the war, but be warned. This information is unknown to humanity, at least in so much as the details are concerned. This, therefore, constitutes a revelation, and as such, there will be a price."

"What price?" Paul asked, with some trepidation.

"That's not for me to say, but there will be one. Also, you should not reveal what I am about to share with you to any other mortal person, either through speech or the written word. You recently wrote a letter to the churches in Galatia, and I assume you will continue to write to others as your ministry grows?"

"Yes," Paul agreed, "if God allows me to leave this prison, certainly."

"In that case, I must insist that you do not disclose anything I share with you in those letters. In fact, it would be best for you not to reveal that I have appeared to you at all. Few mortals have received revelations of this kind, and none have heard the full story of the Conflict from one of the heavenly host. This will be a great burden for you to bear, and as I said, there will be a price."

The angel paused before asking, "So, Paul, do you wish me to tell you the story of this war and of humanity's place in it? Please be certain before you answer."

Paul hesitated only a moment before nodding. "I do. Please share your story with me."

"Oh, this is not my story." The angel grinned. "This is your story. As I said, humanity is not some mere proxy in the Conflict. You are the front line, and earth is the main theatre. The war started almost from the very beginning of this world, but to understand why it happened, we must go back a little further, to just before God created the heavens and the earth."

Part One

In The Beginning

"In the beginning, God created the heavens and the earth. The earth was without form and void, and darkness was over the face of the deep. And the Spirit of God was hovering over the face of the waters." (Genesis 1:1-2, ESV)

Chapter 4

Before the Beginning

I suppose I should begin with a proper introduction. My name is Malachi, and I am an angel. I say that not to state the obvious, but to place myself in the proper order of hosts. I mean I belong to the fourth order of angels created by the Lord, known as the common angels.

I did not witness the Lord bring forth the Archangels, the Cherubim, or the Seraphim. They were all created before me. For this reason, I cannot bear witness to any events that occurred before my inception. I can tell you of Lucifer's betrayal and fall, but not of his creation. All I know of that early time is based on legend and rumor.

Lucifer was the firstborn of the angels, created when Heaven was still bare and featureless, for God alone had dwelt there. None of us can say for certain how long Lucifer existed alone with God before the Almighty created the rest of the angels. It may have been millennia or mere moments. The point is no one, save God and Lucifer, knows for sure.

He was called the Morning Star, the brightest and most powerful of all angels, second in command to God, and the hero of all who stood in the ranks. I am, of course, speaking only for myself. I cannot say to what degree the other angels revered Lucifer, but I idolized him.

You must understand the danger inherent in that word, idolize. It is not easy for me to say, even now, but Lucifer was admired to such an extent that we placed him on a metaphoric pedestal right below God. Mind you, we did not worship him. It did not go so far as that. But we revered him, and Lucifer encouraged this behavior.

He enjoyed the status afforded him by his position and his proximity to God. He had existed before any of the rest of us, and as such, he shared a special relationship with the Almighty. He alone, aside from the Lord's Seraphim attendees, was allowed to enter the direct presence of the Father. It is no wonder then when he stepped out from the Holy of Holies, the other angels would gaze upon him with renewed awe and respect. This was the atmosphere into which I was created. From the first day of my existence, I was aware that Lucifer was the prince of Heaven.

Perhaps that is why I wanted so much to join his legion. Lucifer was the Captain of the Guard, an elite corps of angels who guarded the Holy of Holies, the very throne of God. Named after its captain, the Morning Star Legion comprised perhaps only a tenth of the angelic host. The other two legions contained far more in numbers, but not in prestige. Like Lucifer himself, the members of the Morning Star Legion carried themselves with an air of superiority. Their position, responsibility, and proximity to the Almighty made them special. And they knew it.

More than anything, I wanted to be a part of the Morning Star Legion, to join the elite ranks of the Personal Guard. I wanted to bask in the glory of being part of the elite caste. So, you can imagine my disappointment when, instead, I was assigned to Gabriel's legion. Of the three units I could have been attached to, Gabriel's was the one I wanted the least. I would have been happy in Michael's unit, for the Flaming Sword Legion was at least a corps of warriors. But no, I was assigned to Gabriel.

The Mighty Trumpet Legion. That is what it was called. Gabriel's unit was the Worship Corps of Heaven, a true choir of angels. While the Morning Star Legion bore the triumphant banners of the Holy City, and the Flaming Sword Legion carried its swords and spears, the Mighty Trumpet Legion carried its musical instruments.

Oh, I am being awfully unfair to Gabriel and his legion; please do not misunderstand me. The Trumpet Legion is an important unit in the Army of Angelic Hosts and fulfils a vital role, its sole mission to glorify the Almighty. While the other two units strutted, the angels of Gabriel's legion played the instruments and sang the songs which proclaimed the glory of God. It is an essential part of the Triumphant Processional and an honorable posting. It is just not what I wanted.

You may find it strange to hear an angel speak of what he desired. You must understand, angelic beings are not perfect. It should be obvious that we too possess the capacity for sin. Otherwise, how could Lucifer have betrayed God and fallen from grace? We are not so unlike mankind except whereas you were created in the mortal realm, we were created in the immortal plane of Heaven. We do not share the same carnal weakness of the flesh; therefore, we are exposed to fewer temptations. This does not make us better than mankind, only less susceptible. To forget that is to court disaster because heavenly hosts do possess one weakness, one inherent tendency which can manifest itself as sin if allowed to remain unchecked. Pride.

Pride is the one sin angels are prone to. This was the folly of Lucifer. His pride led him to believe he could ascend to the heights and displace God. His pride led him to claim equality with the Almighty. His pride served as the catalyst for his fall and that of his angels. Not all hosts succumbed to this weakness, but all have the capacity, and I was no different. My pride led me to grow unsatisfied with the role afforded me by the Mighty Trumpet Legion. I wanted to be a warrior. I wanted honor, prestige, and glory. I wanted to join the Morning Star.

My chance finally came on the day the Lord first began His work of creating the heavens and the earth. By heavens I mean the first and second heavens, the skies and stars. The third heaven is where the Holy City is situated, where we existed in the presence of God before the creation of the world, and where the souls of the redeemed go when they shake off their mortal existence. On that day, the Almighty began the process of creating what would become the earth as it is today.

I should mention, a day in Heaven is a somewhat loose term. Time works differently there than it does here on earth. In fact, it does not even proceed at a consistent rate. God is not bound by time. Therefore, time tends to stretch and contract in the Holy City. Some days in Heaven are like a thousand years here on earth while some days on earth are like a thousand years in heaven.

It would be difficult to explain to your mortal mind so I will not attempt it. You cannot apply your normal concepts of time to the realm of Heaven or to God Himself. It does not really matter how long a day is. When discussing the creation, it is enough to know that God created all and that He did it in six days.

That first day began like any other, with the Triumphant Processional. The Army of Angelic Hosts formed up in ranks and was inspected by their division leaders. Then the three legions formed a column, seven ranks wide, with the Morning Star Legion in the front, Michael's Flaming Sword Legion following, and Gabriel's Mighty Trumpet Legion in the rear. The parade began at the gates of the City. From there it proceeded through the shining streets of Heaven, up through the mansions and dwelling places toward the Holy Palace atop the Mount of the Lord.

In perfect order and synchronous movement, the angelic hosts marched, the thunder of a hundred thousand feet striking the shimmering ground in simultaneous rhythm and echoing throughout the streets of the Holy City. In the fore, the angels of the Morning Star carried the banners of the Lord with Lucifer leading the formation from the very front, dressed in his finery and shining like a beacon in the night. It was at this moment that his power and brilliance were most apparent, for his aura contrasted sharply with the other angels lined up in the Processional.

An angel's aura is the glow that shines out from our bodies. Some mortal men call it a halo, but few have seen it with their own eyes, so the account of our angelic appearance has been poorly described. The aura does not emanate only from the head of an angel. It pours forth from his entire body and manifests itself as a white-hot light, shining out from the core of our being.

Of course, you know this, for you have witnessed this light first-hand. Even now, I must focus much of my attention on keeping my aura at a level which will not be uncomfortable for you. Mortal men are unable to withstand the full power of an angelic aura, and without protection, you would be blinded, or worse.

However, the aura is not generated by, nor is it the product of any power inherent to the angel himself. It is a reflection of the power and purity of the Lord God Almighty, bestowed upon and shining out through His heavenly host. An angel shines because he reflects the light and power of God, just as the moon shines as it reflects the light and power of the sun. This is a fact Lucifer forgot, that angels are not in and of themselves powerful. Only through the gift of the Almighty do we possess any power at all.

Lucifer was created first and spent the most time in the presence of the Lord. Through that proximity, the Almighty's power grew in Lucifer until his aura outshone all other angels in Heaven. The rest of us were like fireflies in daylight, our feeble glows swallowed up by the overpowering brilliance of the Morning Star's potent aura.

Like the beam from a lighthouse, Lucifer led the processional through the winding streets of Heaven toward the Holy Palace, his legion following close behind in perfect order with banners held high. Following the Morning Star Legion, the archangel Michael marched at the head of his own unit, the Flaming Sword of the Spirit, though we rarely called it by its full name. Usually, we just referred to it as the Flaming Sword Legion.

Michael was an impressive figure in his own right. Although not as luminous or powerful as Lucifer, he boasted qualities that were superior to even the Morning Star. Where Lucifer was tall and thin, an aristocratic figure, Michael stood tall and strong, barrel-chested with broad shoulders and bulging arms. Where Lucifer boasted a high brow and well-defined cheeks, Michael had wide jaws and a strong chin. None in Heaven could best Michael in a wrestling contest, for he was the most athletic of all the angelic host, and he led a legion of warriors.

Each member of the Flaming Sword was equipped for battle, their auras lancing forth from the eye holes in their white gold helmets. They were clad in white lamellar armor, the overlapping plates trimmed with gold, and each legionnaire was armed with sword and spear. During the Processional, the swords were sheathed while they carried their spears upright along their sides. Each gleaming tip rose high into the air and swayed back and forth as the angels' arms swung in rhythm to their marching.

After the Flaming Sword Legion came Gabriel and the Mighty Trumpet Legion, the Worship Corps of Heaven. With trumpets blaring, drums beating, and voices raised high, we proclaimed the glory of God as the whole processional marched on toward the Holy Seat.

Gabriel was not as tall as Lucifer or as intimidatingly athletic as Michael. His features were softer and more epicene than those of the warrior caste. His golden hair shimmered about his delicate facial features as his beautifully clear tenor voice sang the praises of God. As I have said, I have been unfair to Gabriel. While he is no warrior, he is an archangel and possessed the third most powerful aura of all the host. It is true he is humorless and stiff, but that is because he takes his duty as the herald of the Lord extremely seriously.

The boom of the drums, the blare of the trumpets, and the harmony of angelic voices carried the Processional up the steps of the Holy Mountain and into the courtyard of the Palace of the Almighty. As the column approached the steps of the palace, Lucifer came to a sudden halt, and just as it appeared the angels marching behind might crash into him, the leading ranks abruptly changed direction, executing a perfect column left maneuver.

Once the entire column turned to fill the courtyard, and without a single spoken command, the angels stopped their forward movement as they marked time, marching in place. After a short interval, the entire Army of Heaven halted with a single thunderous clap as one hundred thousand heels crashed down as one upon the glittering ground. After another moment, the formation faced right, spinning on their heels to bring their chests to bear upon the palace.

The archangels, Michael and Gabriel, marched forward and lined up next to each other behind Lucifer, who had moved to the center of the formation. An instant later, as though by unheard command, the entire Army of the Lord fell to one knee, heads bowed upon their chests with their eyes upon the ground.

It was at this point that the mighty gates of the palace would open, sending a flood of light washing over the assembled host. The gates are guarded by two cherubim, one on either side, and as the doors to the palace swung open, these formidable warriors would step aside and kneel. Then God the Father would come forth upon His throne to accept the worship of His servants. Above the Lord fly the seraphim, six-winged angels who sing His praises without pause. With two of their wings, they fly while with the other two pairs they cover their faces and feet, for none may look upon the face of God.

I should pause for a moment to explain a point which might be confusing to mortal perception. The Lord God is omnipotent, omniscient, and omnipresent. He is all powerful, all knowing, and all being. He is everywhere, knows all things, and is in command of all things at all times. He is not restricted to any single place or time but exists in all places at all times and throughout time. In Heaven, His Spirit fills every space and manifests Himself as pure white light, the Light of the Lord. That is why there are no shadows in the Holy City. All light is evenly distributed as it emanates from God who is everywhere. The light shines forth from the angels as our auras, and there is not a corner of Heaven that is untouched by it.

I mention this so as not to cause confusion. It is a difficult concept to comprehend, but one which you must accept. For it is not that the Lord was within the palace upon His throne and only in that place. Rather, His presence was manifested and concentrated within that place for the benefit and purpose of fellowshipping with His angelic creations. Just as the Lord Jesus Christ, God the Son, was the physical manifestation of God on earth, His presence concentrated within the mortal shell of a human body so he could walk among men, so also was God the Father in this place.

As the Lord came forth, all would be silent, all except for the seraphim singing, "Holy, holy, holy, is the LORD of hosts: the whole universe is full of His glory!"

After inspecting the ranks, the Father would address His Captain of the Army of Angelic Hosts. "Lucifer, son of the morning, why have you come?"

At this question, Lucifer would reply, "To present to You, oh Lord, Your heavenly host; for You are the Almighty One, the Alpha and Omega, the Beginning and the End. To You is due all praise and worship. Holy is the name of the Lord. We worship and magnify Your name."

At that, all the other angels would speak with one voice, "Amen!"

The Lord God would bless His angels and command them to go forth in His name. The throne would move back into the palace, and the gates would shut. The cherubim would stand and move back in front of the now closed gates and resume their posts, stock still as statues. Lucifer would rise and give the host of heaven the command to do the same.

Afterward, the formation again would turn to form a column, and the entire Processional would repeat itself in reverse. To the thunderous beating of drums and the blaring of trumpets, the angelic host would march back to the gates of the city. Once there, Lucifer would dismiss his lieutenants, Michael and Gabriel, and they, in turn, would dismiss their legions. This was how every day began in the kingdom of Heaven.

But not this day.

On this day, when the Army of Hosts had arrayed themselves before the palace gates, when every head was bowed and every angel knelt in submission, the Lord God did not appear. Instead, the cherubim guarding the gate stood and stepped forward, and one of them spoke. His name was Ophaniel, and so strange was it to hear his voice, so accustomed had the angelic host become to this daily routine, that the shock of it caused many of us to raise our heads in confusion. I was one of these. At first, I was alarmed, but nothing appeared to be amiss, only unexpected and irregular. Then, curiosity overtook me, and I craned my neck to take in what the cherub had to say.

"The Lord God Almighty," Ophaniel's voice boomed and echoed across the mountain, "shall not inspect the heavenly host this day."

Lucifer leapt to his feet in an instant.

"What is the meaning of this?" he demanded. "Where is the Lord?"

"The Lord God has departed the Holy City."

A collective gasp erupted from thousands of angelic mouths. Never had any angel known the Lord to leave Heaven. Of course, He was still in Heaven just as He was also everywhere else besides Heaven, but never had the presence of God departed the Holy City.

"Where is the Son?" Lucifer asked next. "Where is the Spirit?"

Ophaniel did not react to Lucifer's anger. His countenance remained blank and emotionless as he said, "The entire Godhead has departed. The Lord has gone into the void."

Another round of shocked gasps erupted from the ranks at the mention of the void, and the angelic host began murmuring together excitedly. Spinning on his heel, Lucifer turned and glared at the Army of Heaven.

"Silence!"

Every mouth snapped shut. Looking back on the event, it is plain to me now that Lucifer was not angry because the Lord had departed, but because he had not been told. He was just as shocked and surprised to receive this news as the rest of the angels, and that was the issue. Lucifer did not consider himself to be just another one of the angels. In his mind, he should have been given prior knowledge of the Lord's decision to leave Heaven. It was now obvious to all present that he had not been informed. He was embarrassed and angry with the Lord for making him appear... common.

Turning back to the cherub, an indignant Lucifer addressed Ophaniel once more. "Do you know why the Lord has chosen to break with timeless tradition and disappear into the void without so much as a word?"

Ophaniel stepped forward and leaned out to look down upon Lucifer from the top of the steps. His figure appeared to grow, to swell, his aura brightening.

"I do not make a habit of questioning the Almighty, Lucifer, servant of the Lord."

The cherub placed emphasis on the word servant as though reminding him of his place. This was not the first time Lucifer and the cherubim had exchanged words. They were a separate class of angel and part of no legion, answering to none but God Himself. Lucifer did not appreciate there being angels who did not report to him, but as much as he might attempt to exert his authority over them, the cherubim had always stubbornly refused to be intimidated.

Lucifer could see he would get nowhere with the indomitable Ophaniel, so he spun back around once more to face the formation. For a moment, he appeared unsure what to do next. Then, with exasperation, he threw a hand in the air, seemingly willing the entire assembly of angels to just disappear.

With a sneer, he shook his head and said, "Dismissed."

Shaking out his wings, he rose into the air, and without so much as a glance back at the angelic host, Lucifer turned and flew away from the Holy Mountain.

Chapter 5

Let There Be Light

I was stunned, and I was not alone. Angels wandered about and gathered into small groups, debating the possible implications of this sudden change in routine. I had not moved since Lucifer flew away, my mind racing to make sense of the unprecedented event I had just witnessed. I must have made quite the sight, standing as though paralyzed while all around me angels moved frantically about, gesticulating wildly as they argued. They questioned each other about what had happened and what should be done now, but none of them had any answers.

Someone grabbed me by the arm. I blinked rapidly and turned to see Agiel, my friend and fellow member of the Mighty Trumpet Legion. Agiel and I had been created at the same time and viewed each other as brothers. We shared a similar desire to be free of the Trumpet legion and to join the ranks of the Morning Star. Every day we practiced our wrestling and swordcraft in the open space behind the Trumpet Legion dwelling house, preparing for the day we might be given the opportunity to achieve our goal.

"Malachi!"

I realized with a start that Agiel had been speaking to me, but that his words had not registered. His mouth moved, but it was as though no sound issued from it. As he shook me, the fog began to clear from my mind.

"Malachi!" he shouted again as though from a distance, "What should we do?"

"I do not know," I said, glancing around at the chaos. "I cannot think here."

My friend nodded in agreement. As usual, we were of the same mind and did not need to waste more words in affirming our shared conviction. Flapping our wings, we rose into the air. We flew down from the mountain, across the cityscape of Heaven, to the top of the wall near the city gates. The walls of the city were not there to keep intruders out, for none existed, but rather to mark the boundary of the Holy City for the sake of the angelic host. None may pass beyond the boundary and venture into the void, such was the Law of Heaven.

We descended and settled onto the glittering golden ramparts, our usual place for contemplation and discussion. Here, we would sit gazing out into the black nothingness, an oddly soothing vantage point, and dream of one day being counted among the elite ranks of the Morning Star Legion. We would play a game now and then, weaving a story of how that might happen. Perhaps we would find Lucifer in trouble and help him out of it, and in gratitude he would grant us entry. Or perhaps he would witness us performing some feat of bravery and skill, and recognizing our worth, invite us to join his legion. We had imagined a thousand ways we might find ourselves admitted to the Morning Star and worked them out while sitting on this spot. Now though, as we sat with our backs to the ramparts and gazed out into the void, we spoke of more immediate concerns.

"Why would God go into the void?" Agiel wondered aloud.

I shook my head. "I cannot imagine. There is nothing out there."

"There is nothing out there that we know of. No angel has ever ventured beyond the gates, so how can we say?"

"Only the Lord knows," I agreed. "What is more interesting is that the entire Godhead has gone. It is not necessary. Any part of the Trinity could go, and the full power of God would go with Him."

"True," my friend said. "What would make God want to take His three-fold presence away from Heaven and into that nothingness?"

At that moment, a flare of white light erupted far off in the void. The explosion was so intense that both Agiel and I threw our hands across our faces and started up at the sight of it. There was no sound from the brilliant explosion, but its power was evident from the intensity of the light and the rate at which it grew in the distance. A wave of energy raced outward in a circular arc with startling speed. It rolled through the void, expanding exponentially and picking up speed.

"What is that?" I exclaimed in shock and wonder. Nothing like it had ever been seen by angelic eyes.

"I have no idea." My friend pointed at the explosion in the distance. "Look! It is receding."

True enough, the flare of light retracted before our eyes, shrinking back in upon itself. Soon it would wink out of existence again.

Except that it did not. Just as the pinprick of light seemed like it must go out, it remained as a tiny white dot in the distance. We glanced at each other in confusion, then to the light and back again. I could not be sure whether I felt more excited or terrified.

My attention was gradually drawn away from the light by the sound of voices, low and muffled, yet sharply punctuated. With effort, I forced my mind to disengage from the spectacle in the void and focus on the sounds behind and below me. There were two distinct voices, and they were arguing.

I peered down from the top of the wall into the interior of the gate to see two angels standing there. One was Lucifer, wings outstretched to their full span, his face a mask of rage. His aura burned hotly and intensified as his temper grew. Opposite him, stood a cherubic gate guard whose duty it was to ensure that none left the Holy City.

"I am going out there!" Lucifer declared.

"No," the cherub said, quite calmly, "you are not."

"You dare to speak to me in that manner?" Lucifer's voice was icy as he glowered at the imperturbable cherub who returned the look with one of stony resolve.

"With all due respect, sir, you have no authority over me."

It only lasted the briefest of moments, but I was almost certain I saw a red glow flash in the eyes of the Morning Star. His aura intensified even further as his anger spiked.

"I may have no authority over you Cherub, but you likewise hold no authority over me. Now stand aside!"

The gate guard took a step back and rested his spear upon the ground.

"The Lord God Almighty left specific instructions before He departed. None may pass beyond the gates of Heaven, not you, nor any angel. That is my authority, son of the morning. That is the word of God."

Lucifer knew when he was defeated, but he would not admit it. Without another word, he spun on his heel and stormed away, back toward the city. As he passed under our section of the wall, he paused and flicked his eyes up, staring right into our faces. Reflexively, we jumped back with a jerk and crouched down. After what seemed like a long time, we peered out over the ramparts once more to find that Lucifer had gone.

We sat back against the wall and breathed a sigh of relief. Then, with a shock, I sensed a form looming over us. At first, I thought it was Lucifer, and my heart sank. He would berate us and demand our names. Our dreams of joining the Morning Star Legion would be dashed forever.

Then I raised my eyes, and with relief, saw that the host was not Lucifer after all, but the cherubic gate guard we had seen him arguing with. He stared down at us with arms crossed, a stern expression of disapproval etched on his marble face.

"You should not be here," he said without emotion. "Zadkiel has ordered all angelic hosts to gather on the training ground."

Zadkiel was the chief of the Cherubic Corps and the angel in charge of issuing orders and proclamations from the Throne. If he had summoned the host, it meant an announcement was imminent. Finally, I thought, we would get some answers.

"Yes, sir!" I said. Then we both stood and launched ourselves into the air.

The training ground was a large, flat area in the center of heaven, below the Holy Mountain. It was here that the heavenly host would marshal each morning before marching to the city gates to begin the Triumphant Processional. Four enormous buildings faced in toward the field from the four sides of the complex, forming a box. These were the headquarters buildings of the Army of the Lord, one for each of the three legions and another that served as the joint command center for the three archangels and Zadkiel, the head of the Cherubic Corps.

By the time we reached the training ground, it looked as though the entire angelic host had already assembled on the field. Tens upon tens of thousands of angels stood in their divisions. The Morning Star Legion formed up on the left flank, facing in toward the courtyard from the side. The Mighty Trumpet Legion, my unit, formed up across from them. The Flaming Sword Legion, the largest of the three units, completed the box by facing the main headquarters building, from where the proclamation would take place.

As I flew over the stolid ranks of the Flaming Sword Legion toward my own unit, I remember fearing that everyone must be waiting on us and that we would receive a sharp reprimand for holding up the announcement. Then I noticed a few more stragglers still coming to join the assembly, and I breathed a sigh of relief. Once we landed, Agiel and I quickly melded into the formation, taking our places without attracting notice.

I was still settling in when I felt the shock of sudden impact. A burly arm dropped across my shoulders, and I grunted in surprise as I was jerked sideways. But my shock disappeared, and I smiled knowingly as a chuckling voice whispered into my ear, "Now where have you been, little brother?"

I turned my head to the side and up, for the host who embraced me was a head taller than I. He beamed down at me with a smile that lit up his glowing face. This was Grigori, my self-appointed mentor. He had taken it upon himself to act as a big brother to Agiel and me, and we loved him. Grigori leaned his forehead down to touch mine and spoke in a soft, mock conspiratorial tone.

"Oh, do not tell me," he said with a chuckle in his voice. "I know where you have been. You and Agiel have been sitting atop the walls, staring into the blackness, have you not?"

A sheepish grin drew across my face. "You know us too well."

Grigori was the most cheerful angel in Heaven and embraced the mission of the Trumpet Legion with unabashed relish. His voice always sounded the loudest in song, a fact made possible by his incredible girth, for Grigori also happened to be one of the largest angels in Heaven.

"So," he asked, straightening up and giving me a slap on the back that sent me staggering forward, "do you think we will get some answers now?"

"We hope so," Agiel replied.

"Well, whatever the Lord is doing in the void, I am sure it will be glorious!" Grigori said grandly. "Even a small work would be grand if done in the name of the Lord. And do you know why?"

His expression changed, a mischievous smile creeping across his broad face. I understood Grigori well enough to realize he had happened upon a joke and was already laughing at it to himself.

"Why is that?" I prompted, unable to keep the smile off my own face. I glanced at Agiel to see that he too was grinning.

"Because," Grigori's eyes twinkled as he spoke, "we shall magnify His name!"

The ground shook as Grigori erupted in booming laughter. He wrapped his arms around his massive midsection and doubled over, thoroughly enjoying himself. I chuckled, for as thin as Grigori's jokes often were, his enthusiasm more than made up for any lack of wit.

A trumpet blast cut short the mass of chattering angels, and the entire group fell silent. Grigori winked at me before raising his eyes to a balcony that protruded from one of the upper floors of the main headquarters building. Zadkiel, a long rod in hand, stepped out onto the platform and gazed down upon the gathered throng below. To either side of him stepped the three archangels, Lucifer to his right, with Michael and Gabriel to his left.

"Hark, angels of the heavenly host!" Zadkiel's clear, deep voice boomed across the training ground. "Hear the word of the Lord!"

Not a sound followed these words. Every angel peered up in anticipation, for Zadkiel spoke with the authority of God.

"The Lord God Almighty, Creator of Heaven and its host has gone into the void," he announced. "There, He has begun a new creation."

A shudder swept through the assembled masses, and more than a few angels began whispering excitedly. Zadkiel brought the rod down on the floor of the balcony with a crash. The thunder of it echoed across the entirety of Heaven, and at the sound, the angelic host fell silent once more.

Zadkiel spoke again, "The Lord God has said, 'Let there be light' in the void, and there was light. He has separated the light from the darkness, and the light He has called day, and the darkness He has called night. As it is the will of the Lord..."

"Let it be so." Every angelic mouth, including the three archangels, finished the statement for him, as was the way of Heaven.

The cherubic captain continued, "For the next six days, the Lord shall remain in the void to complete His creation. He has decreed that none may pass the gates of the Holy City for that time, nor shall the Triumphant Processional take place. While the Lord is in the void, the host of heaven shall receive daily updates on His progress. As it is the will of the Lord..."

"Let it be so," every mouth intoned once more.

Zadkiel switched the rod from his right hand to his left, indicating he was done reciting the word of the Lord and that his next words would be his own. This was important, for it prevented the host from misconstruing a lesser announcement with the weight of a divine proclamation.

"Hark!" he said, implying the start of a new topic. "Let all the host of Heaven hear."

These words indicated an announcement from the command element of the Army of the Lord. Although not the direct word of God, it was still an important proclamation from one or more of the archangels.

"Let it be known that Lucifer, son of the morning, archangel, captain of the Elite Guard, Commander of the legion of the Morning

Star, has decreed that the ranks of the Morning Star Legion shall be opened for expansion."

Another rush of excited voices sprang up from the crowd. I felt a hand grip my arm tightly, and the voice of Agiel exclaimed, "Did you hear that?"

I was too stunned to speak. Had I heard correctly? Then the rod crashed down, cutting off the rumble once more. Agiel removed his hand from my arm as Zadkiel continued.

"Any angel wishing to be considered for acceptance should apply in person at the headquarters of the Morning Star Legion. Only those who demonstrate exceptional qualities and abilities shall be considered to join the elite ranks of the Guard."

The rod struck the ground again, and Zadkiel concluded his announcement. "You are dismissed."

To the accompanying sound of the trumpet, Zadkiel and the three archangels turned to walk back into the interior of the headquarters building.

Agiel and I glanced at each other, our faces a mix of shock, wonder, and excitement. This was the moment we had waited for our entire lives, the opportunity to petition to join the Elite Guard. I could hardly believe it, but now was not the time for hesitation. My eyes met my friend's, and again, no words were necessary. We turned and rose into the air, heading straight across the field to the headquarters of the Morning Star Legion.

Chapter 6

The Morning Star

We were not the only ones interested in joining the Morning Star. The entire sky was filled with wings as countless angelic hosts made their way to the legion headquarters building on the far side of the training ground. Because the Mighty Trumpet Legion formation was situated the furthest away from that end of the field, Agiel and I were nearly the last to arrive. A line had formed in the courtyard outside the headquarters building, and the doors were still shut.

As we touched down, we realized we would have a long wait. Still, we were here and about to be admitted into the headquarters of the Morning Star Legion. Never had we set foot in that honored space. In the entire history of Heaven, at least for the entirety of my existence, the Elite Guard had not opened its doors to new applicants. This might be the only time for countless ages to come, our one and only chance to fulfill our dream.

The line moved so slowly that it felt like we waited for an eternity. One by one, angels disappeared through the massive doors, only to re-emerge much later. Some smiled in jubilation while others wore the dejected, crestfallen expression of rejection and failure. As we neared the doors, my excitement gave way to apprehension. What if they denied us entry? What if we were rejected?

So engrossed had I become in my thoughts, it was not until Agiel grabbed my arm and urged me forward that I realized we now stood at the front of the line. The open doors gaped before me and the guards, standing at rigid attention on either side, eyed us with impatience. Regaining my wits, I hurried forward through the doors and into the interior of the legion headquarters.

I gazed about in awe as we stepped into the enormous foyer. A full quarter of the entire building must have been dedicated to this space. It loomed three stories high with multiple indoor balconies protruding from the floors above. Angels of the Morning Star gazed out from these balconies, down at the hosts who sought to join their ranks. Three short lines began just inside the foyer. Each ended at a small table with an angel sitting on the other side. This must be where the initial interview would take place. To gain additional consideration, Agiel and I must impress the angel who would evaluate us as candidates.

We moved to the end of the center line, and as we stood there, I continued to look about, taking in the scene. The interior walls of the room were covered with beautiful murals. On the high walls to the left and right of me were depicted angels of the legion in their full glory. They held their spears and swords aloft, gazing upwards toward the higher floors above, their arms stretching toward the ceiling.

There was a mural like this in the headquarters of the Mighty Trumpet Legion as well, the prime difference being that instead of swords and spears, the angels depicted there carried horns, lyres, harps, and drums. I assumed there was another one in the foyer of the Flaming Sword Legion also, angels with their arms raised in praise and worship to the Almighty. On the ceiling of the Trumpet Legion headquarters, the mural culminated in a beautiful representation of the three-fold nature of God. The Father sat upon His throne, the Son at His right hand while a fog, representing the Spirit, hovered about both figures. All the angelic hosts represented in the mural looked up at the Creator in praise.

I raised my head to look at the ceiling, and sure enough, there was the same representation of the Lord God, but something was different here from the mural at the Trumpet Legion headquarters. Standing before the Lord's throne, his wings spread, was an image of

Lucifer. It struck me as odd, but not because Lucifer was depicted in the mural. This was his legion after all.

I stared at it for a long moment before I realized why it seemed strange to me. In the image, Lucifer was not displayed with his back to us, looking up at the throne of God along with all the other angels depicted in the mural. Rather, he faced forward and gazed down at the angels represented below. From this perspective, I found it difficult to discern whether the angels depicted in the mural were raising their faces to God...

Or to Lucifer.

A chill came over me at that moment, although I would not fully understand why until much later. I was so used to the ways of the Mighty Trumpet Legion, a corps of angels dedicated to one purpose, the praise and worship of God. That was when I first began to understand there was something very different about the Morning Star Legion.

Before that kernel of thought could form into anything more concrete, I found myself in front of the interview table with Agiel at my side. A stern looking angel glanced up from the other side of the desk. At the sight of us, his expression transformed from bored disinterest to amused bewilderment. One corner of his mouth curled into a smirk, and he chuckled.

"What is this, a joke?" His voice dripped with arrogant condescension. "What do you two think you are doing?"

Agiel and I glanced at each other, confused as to why we would garner this sort of reaction.

"We are here, sir," I stated, trying to keep the irritation out of my voice, "to apply for admission to the Morning Star Legion."

He laughed.

Others in the hall glanced furtively at us now as the examiner guffawed at our expense. My shock gave way to embarrassment, then anger. Pulling myself up to my full height, I glowered at the angel who mocked us.

"What is so funny?" I demanded.

In his mirth, the examiner had thrown his head back and shook it from side to side, but now as he lowered his face to make eye contact with me again, the laughter died away on his lips. He met my determined gaze, and with one last chortle, his jocular demeanor morphed into scornful derision.

"You cannot be serious," he scoffed, leaning back in his seat. Then raising his arms to indicate the other occupants in the room, he said, "Look around you. All these angels are warriors of the Flaming Sword Legion, come to pledge themselves to the Morning Star. Return to your harps and lyres, Mighty Trumpeteers." He placed sarcastic emphasis on the last two words. "Perhaps if the day comes that the Guard sees fit to form a marching band, we will notify you."

I looked around as he suggested and realized for the first time that we two were the only members of Gabriel's legion present. This was glaringly apparent, for, while Michael's angels wore the lamellar armor of the warrior caste, we angels of the Trumpet legion wore flowing white robes. It dawned on me just how ridiculous we must have appeared in comparison with those majestic figures. I burned hot with humiliated rage.

Agiel stepped forward to vent his own fury. With a crash, he brought his fist down hard onto the table and said, "Malachi and I are just as capable and worthy as any of these and deserve no less consideration!"

"The Morning Star Legion is a unit of warriors," the examiner spat back, "the best of the best! You would not last one day in our training program!"

The hum of the other applicants' conversation and activity died away, and an awkward silence descended upon the room as every angel's attention was unavoidably captured by our conflict. If we left now, defeated and rejected, we would be mocked and ridiculed. There would be whispers and laughter at our expense. We could not retreat without at least proving our courage. If nothing else, we must defend our honor as angels.

"We will show you our worthiness," I said loudly, for the benefit of the crowd. "Agiel is the best wrestler in the Trumpet Legion, and I am a match for any of my brothers with a sword."

"The best in the Trumpet Legion," the examiner said in a mocking tone, "as though that were stating something of significance. The greatest of the least is still mediocre."

I leaned in toward him and was gratified to see a flicker of uncertainty flash across his hawk-like face.

"Test us then," I said in a quiet, yet intense voice. "We are prepared to prove our worth."

The examiner hesitated, his brash confidence breached at last. He turned and peered upward as though seeking guidance, and I followed his gaze to one of the balconies high above. Two angels stood there. I did not recognize them, but I could tell from the elaborate décor of their uniforms that they were part of the legion's command element. The taller of the two gave a slight nod of his head, and the examiner turned back to us.

"Very well," he said. "We shall test your worth." Standing, he walked around the desk, and shouted, "Clear a space!"

Everyone scattered at this command. Hosts backed away from the center of the room, leaving a vast ring of open space where the examiner, Agiel, and I stood. Looking about, the examiner selected a hulking warrior of the Flaming Sword legion from the crowd and pointed to him.

"You! What is your name?"

The angel blinked in surprise at being singled out, but recovered his wits enough to reply, "Nakir, sir."

"You wish to join the Morning Star?"

"Yes, sir!" he snapped.

"Then here is your chance." The examiner pointed at Agiel. "All you have to do is beat this one in wrestling."

Without hesitation, the big angel stepped forward and shouted, "Yes, sir!"

I stole a glance at Agiel, who did not seem concerned. I would have been. Nakir was huge, easily two heads taller than me and at least one taller than Agiel.

I looked sidelong at my friend and asked, "What is your plan?"

Agiel grinned at me. "I was thinking about challenging him to a battle of wits."

"Let us hope your hands are as quick as your tongue."

Agiel stripped off his robe, revealing his barreled chest and bulging arms, not quite as large as Nakir's, to my dismay.

"Listen," The examiner said, stepping into the middle of the circle between the two angels. "Here are the rules. If you submit, you lose. If you leave the circle, you lose. If you cannot continue, you lose. Any questions?"

There were none. I stepped back to the edge of the circle. As I did, I heard the roar and felt the energy of the crowd's mounting anticipation.

"In that case," the examiner said, "begin!"

As he stepped back, the two angels crouched slightly and brought their hands up, ready to grapple. The crowd roared. Agiel and Nakir circled each other, both looking for an opening to exploit. Nakir made a mock lunge, but Agiel sidestepped, and his opponent moved back.

They sized each other up, attempting to ascertain each other's speed, strength, and skill. This continued for some time; one making a move, countered by the other. Some were faints, intended to trick the other into overcommitting. Others were serious attempts to take hold, but in each case, the opponent slipped the move, and the adversaries stepped back to reassess each other anew.

Finally, as though by mutual consent, the pair crashed together, hands flying about, seeking a hold. Nakir was fast, but Agiel was faster. He dove low and wrapped his arms around Nakir's waist. As his hands clenched behind Nakir's back, Agiel lifted the huge angel and pivoted, slinging him to the ground. If Nakir was stunned by being slammed onto his back, he showed no sign.

My friend bent over his adversary and attempted to execute a front chokehold, but Nakir defended this by thrusting his legs up and wrapping them around Agiel's waist. At the same time, he brought his forearms around in front of his face and, rocking from side to side, used them to bat away Agiel's grasping hands.

Both angels sought for holds amid the fray, and in the flurry of blows and counter-blows, Nakir's hands found Agiel's head. One hand gripped him behind the neck while the other pressed hard against his forehead, forcing my friend's head back while his body was still held fast by Nakir's leg guard. Agiel struggled against the pressure and sought to grasp Nakir's wrist to pull it away, but his opponent used the legs wrapped around his waist to rock back and forth which kept Agiel off balance.

They continued to struggle this way for a time, and the crowd began to grow restless at the apparent stalemate. Some of the onlookers began yelling out suggestions to the contenders. To my irritation, most of the advice was offered to Nakir rather than to my friend. I was about to add my own voice to the shouts when Agiel fell forward onto Nakir's chest.

Capitalizing on Agiel's attempt to resist his head being pushed backward, Nakir had suddenly reversed the hold, releasing the hand that pressed on Agiel's forehead. All the latter's strength had been applied to resisting that pressure, and this abrupt change caused his head to snap forward in the opposite direction.

As Agiel's upper body fell forward, Nakir wrapped both of his massive arms around my friend's neck. Then he released his right arm and used it to push off from the ground, twisting his core. I watched with horror as Nakir succeeded in rolling sideways. Agiel was now on his back with Nakir sitting atop him, and I winced as he began pummeling my brother's head with his huge fists.

Agiel performed the same defensive move that Nakir had, pulling his forearms in front of his face and wiggling from side to side to avoid the heavy blows. But with the whole weight of the hulking host atop him, Agiel had no room to maneuver and could not hope to get free.

I admit I began to despair of my friend's imminent defeat when he surprised me. As one of Nakir's crashing blows descended toward his head, Agiel twisted hard to the side. Nakir's hand struck the ground with a crack. If he yelled in pain, I never heard it, for just as quickly, Agiel torqued his body back the other way and delivered a devastating elbow strike that took Nakir full on the side of his head. He fell, freeing Agiel, who leapt to his feet. As Nakir tried to stand, Agiel jumped behind him and wrapped his left arm around Nakir's neck. Then he did something unexpected.

Agiel hooked his other arm around the base of his opponent's right wing. Bending his knees to lower his center of gravity and take his opponent off balance, Agiel tightened his left arm about Nakir's neck while simultaneously pulling up with his right. His hands met and grasped each other to complete the hold. Then his arms bulged as he squeezed.

This created a massive amount of force on both Nakir's neck and the base of his right wing. For the first time since the match began, Nakir let out a yelp. The mighty warrior of the Flaming Sword flailed wildly, desperately seeking any sort of contact that might allow him to free himself, but Agiel held on doggedly. The crowd fell silent, shock registering on the faces of the gathered host.

"Do you yield?" Agiel asked.

Nakir did not answer but continued to struggle. Agiel wrenched up on the wing again, and Nakir's eyes went wide.

"Do... you... yield?" Agiel repeated for the benefit of all present.

With a gasp, a single word escaped Nakir's lips. "Yes!"

Agiel released his adversary without hesitation. Nakir fell to his knees, holding a hand to his throat while my friend stood over him in triumph. The silence in the room persisted for only a moment longer. Then almost as one, the host began cheering. I was taken aback by this sudden reversal. Agiel had gained acceptance by this group of hardened warriors, who only a short time before had mocked us and the legion we represented. Smiling broadly, I stepped forward into the center of the ring and addressed the examiner.

"We have passed your test, sir," I said respectfully, yet with expectancy. "Will you now accept our applications?"

The examiner appeared irritated. I suspected he was embarrassed at having underestimated us. That or his contempt for the Trumpet Legion was so great that he did not wish to accept the outcome of the contest. As he turned to glare at me, the sly smile returned to his face, and I shuddered. Something about the examiner made me extremely uncomfortable.

"Your friend has certainly proven his worth," he said icily, "but you have still to prove yours."

The energy in the room surged anew as the crowd realized they would be treated to a second spectacle. My elation at Agiel's victory faded, for I still had a challenge of my own to surmount if I was to join him. Then a wave of calm determination settled over me. My destiny was in my own hands, and I trusted my hands.

"Very well," I said. "I am ready. Who shall my opponent be?"

The sly smile grew wider on the face of the examiner as he said, "Me."

I shuddered again. This angel was determined to dash my dreams and deny me entry into the Morning Star. His previous scheme with Nakir had failed, and he would not leave this challenge to anyone else. He would face me himself.

So be it.

Chapter 7

The Duel

"So, what shall my test be?" I asked.

"You claim to be adept with a sword," the examiner said, his eyes narrowing. "Let us find out."

His hand moved to the hilt at his waist, and the blade sang out as it left the scabbard. He slashed the blade through the air in a series of loops and smooth strokes, ending with a brisk cut that brought the gleaming blade up into the salute. This angel knew his swordcraft. I reminded myself he was a legionary of the elite guard and would be a formidable opponent. With his flourish at an end, he brought the sword down crisply, and the crowd cheered afresh.

"Do you need the loan of a sword?" he asked me. "You Trumpet legionnaires don't carry blades under your choir robes, do you?"

It was my turn to smile, and to my satisfaction I noticed the unexpected reaction caused the examiner's own grin to falter. Doubt clouded his face, and my smile grew in response.

"Most do not," I agreed, "but as I told you, we are not like most angels of our legion."

As the last word left my lips, I tore away my robe in one smooth motion, letting it fall to the floor. A collective gasp escaped the mouths of those gathered about as surprised realization dawned on the encircling crowd. There I stood, clad in full armor, the shimmering white lamellar plates glittering in the light of so many gathered auras. My own sword, which was indeed strapped to my side, sang out as it left its scabbard, and I performed a flourish of my own to match the one executed by the examiner. The crowd roared in approval.

The expression on the examiner's face set into fierce determination. He may have underestimated me, but that did not mean he would flinch from the challenge. For honor's sake, he could not. But he also still relished the thought of denying me my goal.

We both settled into our ready stances and began circling one another, much like Agiel and Nakir a few minutes earlier. But this was no wrestling match. We held swords, and it occurred to me that the examiner, who had so painstakingly laid out the rules for Agiel's match, had not done so with our own. We had not established how a winner would be determined, nor how far the match would go.

The examiner stared me down as he sidestepped around the circle. He flicked his blade left and right, its glittering edge sending rays of reflected light in all directions. He wanted me to look at it, but I knew better. I kept my gaze on my opponent's eyes. Those eyes narrowed a split second before he lunged, and I was ready for him.

Sidestepping, I parried his thrust, and the song of swords striking each other filled the space, ringing out as the two blades met. With my opponent's sword brushed aside, I thrust my own blade forward, but it stabbed empty air, for my adversary was no longer there. He had used his momentum to spin away before I could attack his exposed side.

We both stepped back, reassessing the other. He was quick, this angel of the Morning Star. We circled one another again, looking for an opening or weakness in the other's position. Without warning, the examiner leapt forward with a lunge that he arrested at the last moment, and as my own sword came up to parry, he pulled back and changed his angle of attack. At the same time, he sidestepped, and I was still in the act of parrying when his blade caught my arm just below the shoulder.

I winced as I pulled away, and my opponent stepped back to a roar of approval from the crowd. I took advantage of the lull to examine the wound. He had struck me in an unprotected area, high up on my arm just below the sleeve of my tunic. The cut was not deep, but a shaft of light lanced forth from where the examiner's blade had found its mark. As I watched, the wound closed, and the light winked out, my aura contained once more. I glanced back to the examiner who eyed me with a satisfied smirk. The crowd cheered, and it was not my name they shouted.

"Va-ssa-go!" the angels chanted, "Va-ssa-go!"

I recognized that name. Vassago was a high-ranking lieutenant in the Morning Star Legion and famous for his swordcraft. Feeling my anxiety rise, I wondered if I had perhaps taken on more of a challenge than I was equal to. But honor dictated I must carry this through to the end. I adjusted my grip on the sword hilt and resumed my stance.

Vassago's next attack came in a flurry of slashes and thrusts, designed to test my reflexes and expose an opening. I backed as he advanced on me, our swords a blur of movement. I parried the rapid attacks with blinding speed, and my confidence recovered as I realized my skill was not deficient after all. Still, I found myself entirely on the defensive with no opportunity for a counter attack.

Then Vassago overextended himself with a particularly aggressive lunge, and I recognized my opportunity. Parrying his sword aside, I thrust with my own blade and felt the tip strike home upon his chest armor. Vassago stumbled back, stunned and confused.

The crowd fell silent, all except for Agiel who shouted with triumphant glee as he ran forward to congratulate me. He was met by a furious glare from Vassago who leveled his sword at my friend.

"Get back to the edge!" he shouted. "This match is not over!"

Vassago turned back to me, rage in his eyes, and the sword blade flashed as he whipped it about in a fresh flourish. But Agiel did not budge.

"The match is over," he said. "Malachi scored a hit on your breastplate. By match rules, he wins."

"Who said we were playing match rules?" Vassago shot back.

"If you had been playing to first cut, you would have stopped the match after you scored the hit on his arm," Agiel argued, "but you did not."

"We will continue until one of us cannot!" Vassago spat. "Now get back!"

"That is enough," a new voice interjected. At the sound, Vassago hesitated, glancing about in apprehension. Then he froze, no longer looking at me, but past me. His sword arm dropped, and I recognized something on his face I had not seen at any point during our fight. Fear.

The angels in the crowd behind Vassago also stared past me as though in shock. Puzzled, I turned my head to find that the crowd had parted, and at the edge of the circle, stood Lucifer.

This was the first time I had ever seen the Morning Star close up, and I was stunned into near paralysis. He was clearly the tallest angel in the room, towering over those gathered about. Lucifer's aura, so bright and far-reaching, washed out the angels closest to him.

The way he held himself, his poise and posture, left no doubt he was the premier angel in heaven. He held his head high, his chin lifted so that I could see the long neck underneath. This gave him the appearance of being even taller, and it caused him to look down at everyone he might speak to, an inescapable reminder that he was above them in every way.

Lucifer stepped forward into the circle, his face stern, but not threatening. I remember having the impression that he appeared so relaxed and calm, in complete command of his emotions. Later, I would contrast that against what I had experienced in front of the city gates. But for now, I stood mesmerized along with everyone else in the hall.

"Stand down, Vassago," he said, though not unkindly. "This host has proven his worth."

Vassago nodded his head, and without hesitation, sheathed his sword. Turning, Lucifer addressed the entire assembly and seemed to make eye contact with every angel present.

"These two angels of the Mighty Trumpet Legion bring great credit upon themselves and the Morning Star. They demonstrated initiative by learning the skills of a warrior when it was neither expected nor required by their superiors."

He stepped toward Agiel and me, placing a hand on each of our shoulders. "It honors our legion for members of the Worship Corps to strive to join its ranks, to rise above their station. What greater testament could there be to the glory of the Morning Star than to have its membership so greatly sought?"

The assembled hosts began to applaud and cheer. Lucifer beamed, his overpowering aura washing over the gathering to embrace every angel present. I recall thinking I would do anything for this titan of heavenly virtue, obey any order, surmount any challenge. It makes me shudder now to think of it, but I was completely enamored with him, as was Agiel. Lucifer's charisma was undeniable.

He turned back to us and, smiling, said, "Come with me."

Then he spread his wings, and I felt a strong wind as he lifted himself into the air. We followed both his order and example, rising to join him. He led us up toward the high balconies, and we landed on the topmost. As I tucked my wings behind me, I realized this balcony opened to the outside. Following Lucifer's lead, we stepped forward to the edge of the exterior facing balcony and looked out upon the cityscape of Heaven.

The breath caught in my throat as I gazed out at the view. From here we could see it all, the city gates, the sprawling mansions, all the way to the Holy Mountain and the Palace of the Almighty. I noticed, almost as an afterthought, the pinprick of light, still showing far out in the void.

"Magnificent, is it not?" Lucifer smiled warmly.

"Yes, sir!" both Agiel and I responded in unison. It seemed like the only thing to say.

Lucifer's smile broadened as he said, "At ease."

We obeyed, relaxing a degree while Lucifer turned back to the view.

"I remember when there was no city," he said in a small voice, "only the mountain and the palace, the Holy of Holies, and the Lord God... and me."

Agiel and I glanced at each other. We did not know what to say. Lucifer seemed to be mulling over his own thoughts and allowing us to join in his reverie. But he did not appear to expect any response from us, so we stayed silent and listened.

"Things change. Oh, they take millennia, and they alter so gradually that you might not notice, but they do change. I remember when the Lord and I would sit in the Holy of Holies and talk for ages, just He and I. Those were simpler times."

Lucifer stood transfixed for a long moment, saying nothing. Then, as though waking from a dream, he turned to look at us and changed the subject.

"You both wish to join the Morning Star?"

"Yes, sir," we said, again in unison.

Lucifer smiled. "Good. I think we can use dedication such as yours. So, you will pledge yourselves to me?"

That struck me as odd. I did not understand why any pledge was necessary. We had expressed our interest, undergone a grueling test, and passed. Surely, our desire was apparent. Then there was the strange way in which he posed the question. Lucifer did not ask if we pledged ourselves to the legion, but to him personally. I shrugged off my discomfort, though, for Agiel replied without hesitation that he would. I did not wish to seem hesitant, so I echoed agreement almost instantly. Lucifer's smile broadened again.

"Good," he said. "In that case, you should go and inform your unit commander that your transfer request has been granted. Report to the training division of the Morning Star Legion tomorrow at the proclamation assembly. Your training will begin immediately after dismissal."

"Yes, sir!" There was no hesitation in my voice this time.

Agiel and I were both grinning now, for our dreams had come true. Or so we thought.

Chapter 8

The Training Unit

"So, you have requested a transfer."

Agiel and I stood rigidly at attention in the command office of the Mighty Trumpet Legion headquarters. Gabriel paced before us, his delicate chin resting on his chest as he pondered the significance of our decision. If we had given the matter any thought, we would have known that Gabriel would not be pleased. But the truth was we had not considered it, elated as we were to be accepted into the Morning Star. I felt a sudden and unexpected pang of guilt for my selfishness. It was not sufficient to dim my excitement, and certainly not enough to make me second guess my decision, but it was there. The Mighty Trumpet Legion had been my home since creation, and I was abandoning my family to join another.

"I cannot say I am surprised," Gabriel continued as he paced. "It is no secret you both have wished to be Guardsmen for some time now. Still, I hate to lose you."

I felt I needed to say something, to assuage my guilt if for no other reason, so I spoke up. "We are proud to have served in the Trumpet Legion and will sorely miss our brothers."

Gabriel paused in his pacing and raised his head to look at me. Then he pursed his lips. He is the only angel I have ever known to do that, a very human facial expression. He appeared to be weighing the truth of my words but must have concluded that if not entirely genuine, my statement was at least offered in the right spirit. He turned and began walking again.

"This new offer of Lucifer's is curious," he mused. "For countless millennia, the Morning Star Legion has been kept small as a mark of its honor. But now it seems Lucifer wishes to grow the legion's ranks to rival those of the Flaming Sword. Indeed, most of those applying to join Lucifer's legion come from Michael's unit. You two are the only ones who have approached me about a transfer."

As he spoke, Gabriel's eyes glazed in introspection. His head sank, the chin slowly drawing back down toward his chest as he continued his analysis of the situation.

"The fact that you were accepted is also curious." Perhaps realizing how his words might be interpreted, his head jerked up, and he added quickly, "I do not mean to impugn your martial skills. They are evident, but it is interesting he is accepting hosts of such wide-ranging abilities, to say nothing of the timing."

Gabriel's voice trailed off, and he turned to gaze up at an enormous wall map of the Holy City as though answers might be found there. After a long moment of staring at his back, we heard him speak again.

"You should remember that the Morning Star is another legion of the Army of the Lord, nothing more. I caution you not to get carried away. Angels of that unit tend to put on airs, to confuse the glory of God with their own. You would do well to avoid that temptation."

"I understand," I said, and Agiel voiced his agreement as well.

Gabriel's body did not move. His back remained squared to us, but his head turned sideways and his eyes locked on us as he said, "I am not certain you do."

He meant no offense. Nor was he being condescending, for it was not in his nature. He was simply stating the facts as he saw them. Gabriel was nothing if not pragmatic. Turning to face us, he said, "However, you will soon experience the differences for yourselves, and I hope you will bear my advice in mind."

"We will, sir," Agiel said, a little too quickly.

Gabriel pursed his lips again and stared at Agiel for a long moment. My friend wilted under his gaze. I knew he wished for the interview to be over, and I guessed Gabriel suspected as much for himself. Still, he did not press the matter.

"Very well. You are dismissed."

I let out a sigh of relief as we left the Trumpet Legion headquarters for the training ground. We sped up a pace, for the proclamation assembly would begin shortly, and we did not wish to be late for our first formation with our new unit.

As we walked across the field, past the formation of our now former unit, I pondered on Gabriel's words. He had verbalized my own thoughts and concerns considering the peculiarities I had noticed with the Morning Star. Various loose threads of thought began to coalesce in my mind; the mural in the Morning Star headquarters, the attitude and behavior of Vassago, Lucifer's mesmerizing hold over the other angels of the legion, and finally, that odd insistence on a pledge. It was Gabriel's advice, a warning really, that the Morning Star was given to self-glorification that started the pulling together of those loose threads. I had not yet reached any conclusions, but the concerns were there, hovering in the back of my mind, and they stubbornly refused to fade.

I shook my head violently to clear it of these unwelcome thoughts. What was I doing? I had at last achieved my dream, and now, in the moment of triumph, I was second guessing everything. I wanted to be elated, to be wholeheartedly enthusiastic about joining the Morning Star, just as Agiel was. He did not seem to hold any of these doubts. When I shared my thoughts with him, he dismissed them with a laugh.

"That is the difference between an elite unit of warriors and the worship corps of the Trumpet Legion," he said easily. "The Morning Star legionaries regard discipline, martial virtue, and loyalty to the unit much more highly. Of course they carry themselves differently. You cannot have an elite unit if the members of that unit are not considered special. That is what makes it elite!"

His logic was sound, but those stubborn threads still hung in the back of my mind. My concerns faded, though, as we passed the hosts of the Flaming Sword and I saw the Morning Star Legion formed up in all its glory. For countless ages, I had stood on this hallowed ground, eying that perfectly ordered and disciplined formation from across the field and longed to be a part of it. Now I was, and all my doubts vanished as we approached our place in the formation, the training unit.

The formation was much larger than I expected it to be. Tens of thousands of recruits formed up on the left wing of the unit, more angels even than those of the adjacent veteran company, the legion's original compliment. The Morning Star had always been a small unit compared to the other legions. That was one of the things that made its membership so desirable, its exclusivity. Now it swelled to over three times its original size. Glancing over at the Flaming Sword, formerly the most numerous of the three, I was startled to see how reduced it had become. Lucifer's legion must now comprise well near a full third the complement of the heavenly host.

Disappointment washed over me, my excitement diminished by the fact that my achievement was shared by so many. Still, I was here, and that was enough. The unit might not be as exclusive as it once was, but it was still an honor, especially considering the obstacles Agiel and I had overcome to be here. Then my elation gave way to despair when I recognized the lead instructor of the training division. Vassago. When he saw us, a smirk appeared on his hawk-like face, and the familiar shudder returned. He sneered as we took our places.

"I see our musicians have arrived. Care to play us a tune?"

Agiel did not reply, so I responded. "No, sir!"

"Do you hear that?" Vassago said to the rest of the training unit. "Malachi does not wish to play us a tune. Well, I suppose it is a good thing Malachi is a recruit, which means he does not get to do what he wants. He gets to do what I want!"

I groaned as I realized my mistake. Vassago had tricked me into giving the answer he wanted, one which would provide him with the excuse he needed to torment me.

"Recruits Malachi and Agiel," Vassago shouted, "front and center!"

We had no choice, so we marched out of formation and snapped to attention in front of our new commander. Vassago eyed us triumphantly, knowing he held us in his power.

"Play us a mighty tune, trumpeteers," he said.

"But," Agiel objected, "we have no instruments, sir."

I knew it was a mistake as soon as he uttered the words. A gleam came into Vassago's eyes, and he grinned with malice.

"Oh," the Instructor said as though surprised, "you do not have any instruments? Well, then I suppose you will just have to improvise!"

The vicious smile widened, and his voice grew harsh. "Play us a tune with imaginary instruments."

Agiel and I glanced at each other, which was also a mistake. Vassago was upon us in a flash, thrusting his face close to mine, his nose almost touching my own.

"You do not look at each other!" he barked in an odd sing-song manner, placing emphasis on certain words. "You lock your bodies and stare straight ahead. You do not move, you do not speak, you do not think independently unless I give you an order to do so. Do you hear me?"

He drew out the last four words, accenting each one with punchy emphasis.

"Yes, sir!" we both responded as one.

"Outstanding!" he said in mock pleasure. "Now, play us a tune."

With hesitation, I brought my hands up to my mouth and began making the motions of playing the flute while approximating the sound with my mouth. Agiel did the same, and a few short bursts of laughter erupted from the assembled group of recruits. Vassago's head snapped around and he scowled before disappearing from my view as he launched himself into the formation. I heard him berating those who he could identify as having broken their discipline, and when he returned, it was with the unfortunate offenders in tow.

One of them was Nakir, the angel who had wrestled with Agiel. He looked sullen and resentful as he was told, since he thought it was funny, to join us in our music making. One might have thought Vassago was being fair and evenhanded in his abuse of the recruits, but I knew better. He was tormenting Nakir because he had failed to defeat Agiel for him. Nakir appeared sullen as he reluctantly joined our mock chorus. Now he would have even more reason to hate us.

As we were still playing our music, the sound of three deep thuds drifted across the crowd toward us. It was the staff of the cherubic guard striking the floor of the proclamation platform; the signal the assembly was being called to order and Zadkiel would appear momentarily.

"Recruits," Vassago snapped, "halt your merriment!"

That was one order I was happy to obey. At a further order, we faced about and marched to retake our places in formation. I barely made it to my station before the trumpet blast sounded. For the second day in a row, Zadkiel walked out onto the high balcony, rod in hand, followed by Lucifer, Michael, and Gabriel.

"Hark, angels of the heavenly host!" he recited the familiar line. "Hear the word of the Lord!"

Every mouth was silent in anticipation of his pronouncement.

"The Lord God Almighty, Maker of the universe, has continued His new creation in the void. He has created a planet and called it Earth. He has commanded the waters of this planet to separate and has created a firmament to separate the waters below from the waters above. He has called the firmament heaven. As it is the will of the Lord..."

"Let it be so," all the angelic voices of Heaven thundered out.

The rod struck the ground again, and Zadkiel said, "That is all. You are dismissed."

To the accompanying blast of the trumpet, Zadkiel disappeared back into the building, the three archangels turning to follow.

I was nonplussed. I did not understand what water was, much less why it needed to be separated from itself. Then there was this mention of heaven. It could not have meant the Heaven we populated, could it? Was God creating a new heaven? What would that mean for this Heaven? Things were growing stranger by the day, but these thoughts did not dominate my concentration for long. The other legions dispersed from the field, as did the veterans of the Morning Star, but we recruits were left in our places, standing stock still. After what seemed like an eternity, Vassago addressed the formation.

"Recruits, prepare for inspection!"

We were already standing at attention, so there was really nothing to prepare for. All I could do was stay still and wait for my turn to be inspected. An unfamiliar voice drifted toward me from further down the line asking questions and making comments to someone, I assumed to Vassago. He must be the inspecting officer. I did not recognize the voice, so I doubted it was Lucifer. Some other officer of the legion then?

The voice grew closer to me by degrees, moving angel by angel down the line until the officer paused just to my right, addressing Agiel. I dared not look, but instead remained still, eyes pointed straight ahead as I relied on my hearing to take in what transpired.

"What is your name?" The voice had a syrupy smoothness to it that exuded a smug, arrogant authority.

"Agiel, sir!"

"And why did you join the Morning Star?"

"To serve the Lord God Almighty, sir!" Agiel said briskly. His response was a good one, but apparently not good enough for the inspecting officer.

"Is that all?" I could visualize the patronizing smile spreading across the officer's face as he spoke. "You could do that in any legion, could you not? So why join the Morning Star?"

Agiel did not respond right away. He stammered, confused and unsure as to what the officer was looking for. Mercifully, the officer cut him off and asked a different question.

"Who was the first angel?"

"Lucifer!" Agiel said, relieved to be asked a question to which he knew the answer.

"And how long did Lucifer exist, alone with God, before the creation of the Holy City and the angelic host of Heaven?"

Again, Agiel hesitated. "I... I do not know, sir."

My friend must have expected a rebuke, but one did not come. Instead, the inspecting officer appeared to be educating us because he spoke loudly enough for the entire unit to hear.

"No one does, not even me," he said. "Our great captain existed alongside the Lord God for an untold space of time before any of the rest of us were created. To stand in his presence is the nearest any of us will ever get to understanding what it must be like to stand in the direct presence of God."

My eyes narrowed at that statement. I admit, having stood in the presence of the Morning Star, he was an imposing figure, awe-inspiring and intimidating, but he was still just an angel. Surely, this host was not suggesting Lucifer was anywhere near on par with the Almighty? I did not have time to think about it further, though, for the officer continued his speech.

"That is why we joined the Morning Star Legion, to be part of that great legacy, to be closer to the glory of God." As he spoke, he moved into my path of vision and addressed me next. "What is your name?"

"Malachi, sir!"

I realized I knew this angel, or rather I knew of him. He was the second in command of the Morning Star Legion, Lucifer's right hand. In retrospect, I also now realized he was the angel on the high balcony who Vassago had looked to in the hall when we challenged him to test us. This was Malphas, the first lieutenant of the Morning Star.

He was an impressive figure, tall, imposing, and carried himself with an aristocratic air. He held his strong chin high, and his deep voice evoked confidence and authority. Unlike many angels, whose hair is golden, Malphas' hair was black as the void and shown with a luster like jet. The distinction gave him a harder, more serious appearance. But the most unsettling features were his eyes. They were nothing but narrow slits. The auratic light scarcely escaped them, giving off an eerie faint glow about his face. Those eyes gave nothing away, as though closed off to prevent anyone from gaining insight into Malphas' thoughts.

"And why did you join the Morning Star, Malachi?" he asked.

I now understood the answer he wanted, but I could not bring myself to say I had joined in order to bask in the glory of the Morning Star. I revered Lucifer. We all did. Standing in his presence was an awesome, overpowering experience, but I would never go so far as to say it was akin to standing in the presence of God. The thought was ridiculous. Still, I did not wish to make my position in the legion any more difficult than it already was. I racked my mind to think of a response that would satisfy Malphas without betraying my conscience. The answer I came to was trite, yet it served the purpose.

"To be the best of the best, sir!"

Malphas said nothing. He just stared at me for a long moment. I sensed the weight of his gaze, the examination of those unsettling eyes which narrowed even further. I felt completely exposed, as though he must see right through me. I even wondered if he might be able to read my mind. My conviction was on the brink of collapse, and I teetered on the verge of blurting out some other statement that might be more to his liking. But before I could, Malphas turned and stepped away.

Vassago walked past me to stay with his superior, but his eyes were locked on mine, stabbing at me with a glare of pure derision. I was sure my interaction with Malphas had been an embarrassment for him. Now he would have renewed cause to resent me.

Malphas addressed the next angel in my row, but I heard none of it. My mind raced as I attempted to process everything I had experienced over the last two days. Gabriel's words kept ringing in my mind with the relentlessness of a drumbeat. I was growing more and more aware that things were much different in the Morning Star Legion.

The angels of this unit seemed to hold an unhealthy reverence toward their captain that went beyond mere respect. Still, I was not yet concerned enough to second guess my decision to join the legion. I told myself it was possible the sense I got from Malphas was not indicative of every angel in the unit. He was at the very top of the hierarchy after all. Being so close to Lucifer himself, it made sense for him to display the greatest degree of loyalty, overzealous as it may be. I hoped I would find the legion overall to be much more moderate, yet I remained wary.

I told myself I must stay grounded in the truth of what Lucifer was and was not. I made a mental note to discuss it with Agiel and to share my concerns with him. I had to make sure he was aware of these idiosyncrasies so he could guard himself against them as well.

Chapter 9

The Harrowing

Unfortunately, I had no opportunity to share my concerns with Agiel that day. We were kept busy, racing by foot or by wing, lifting, wrestling, practicing our swordcraft, or drilling our formations and marches on the training ground. My arms were sore, my wings ached, and my legs trembled as though they might give way at any moment.

Vassago drove us all relentlessly. Yet, he never missed an opportunity to torment Agiel or me. If one of us made the slightest mistake, he would be on us in a flash. There were tens of thousands of recruits, so Vassago had split us into units of one hundred and assigned an instructor to each. He took our group for himself, and I was sure that was no coincidence.

The other recruits gave us a wide berth. None of them wished to draw Vassago's attention by associating with us. They benefited from his obsession with Agiel and me, as it spared them much of his otherwise equally applied persecutions. In our rare breaks, Agiel and I sat alone, unaccompanied by any of our fellows.

While most of the recruits were content to merely keep us at wing's length, a few demonstrated outright hostility. This small yet vocal group contended that we had somehow tainted the quality of the Morning Star Legion; that the leadership relaxed their standards to allow us entry, which in turn diminished the significance of the achievement for themselves.

Chief among these was Nakir. In consequence of his losing the wrestling match to Agiel, Vassago had initially rejected his application to join the legion. He was forced to reapply, which involved a grueling test of speed and skill. He succeeded in securing a place in the training unit, but he still bore a significant grudge against both Agiel and me. I was sure his assignment to our training group was also no coincidence, as it gave Vassago an opportunity to stoke the enmity between us.

Nakir made a point of challenging me in every contest. If there was a one on one match, he managed to become my opponent. He appeared to have focused in on me, avoiding any direct conflicts with Agiel. I assumed he did not wish to be further embarrassed by losing to him again and considered me an easier target. Still, in any group contest, such as races, he did his best to interfere with the both of us. He would jostle us, trip us, or if the race was by wing, fly ahead and attempt to tangle our wings with his feet.

When this behavior first began, I thought about issuing a complaint but did not do so out of fear of appearing weak. I later realized it would have been futile anyway. Vassago became aware of Nakir's antics, and far from punishing him, he applauded his efforts.

In a long speech, for which I was perversely grateful because it served as a respite from the grueling training, Vassago said that a Morning Star legionnaire does not complain about things being unfair but finds a way to improvise and overcome his circumstances. He lauded Nakir for doing what was necessary to win, for it was better to win by any means than to allow the glory of the Morning Star to be tarnished by failure.

I could not tell from his choice of words if he referred to the legion or to Lucifer himself, the actual Morning Star. In time, I came to understand that was the point. To his mind, there was no distinction between Lucifer and the legion. They were one and the same, integrally linked.

In those times of introspection, Gabriel's cautionary words came flooding back to my mind, and the disconcerting thoughts returned. But I was never given the luxury of time to contemplate those threads. They would be whisked away again by the flurry of activity required to complete the next challenge. When we did rest, I was too tired to ponder anything beyond my gratitude for the brief spell of inactivity.

The following day brought much of the same, more running, flying, wrestling, and sword practice, the routine of physically exhaustive exercises broken only by the monotonous tedium of formation drill. We were given no rest that day except for the proclamation assembly, and during that, I was only half conscious with fatigue.

All I could remember was something Zadkiel said about God gathering the waters of the earth into one place and letting dry land appear. I still did not understand what water was, though now I at least had some sense it was not land. The waters He gathered were to be called seas. Then God had said the earth should bring forth grass, herbs, and fruit trees. I had no idea what that meant either, and I was too exhausted to care. At the end of the day, I remember collapsing in a heap along with the other angels of my unit. I lay there, exhausted and undignified, grateful for the opportunity to simply not move.

The third day of our training, the fourth of the Lord's new creation, promised to be much of the same. We had already run two races that morning, one by foot and the other by wing, and were now practicing our drill on the parade ground prior to the proclamation assembly. Vassago marched us up and down in front of the headquarters building. Column left, column right, by the left flank, by the right flank, to the rear, we marched endlessly, it seemed. Vassago moved up and down the line as we went, inspecting our intervals and making corrections.

We were marching forward when I winced at a sudden impact on my right arm. The sting of it was familiar to me now, but the frequency of the experience did nothing to diminish the anger it caused in me every time. Vassago had hit me with the flat of his sword blade. I felt his hot breath on my face as he got as close as possible to yell into my ear.

"Keep your elbows in and your arms straight, Musician!"

That is what he called me; never my name, but rather some mocking reference to my tenure in the Trumpet Legion. I was Musician, Trumpeteer, Minstrel, or some variant thereof, always as he shouted inches from my face that I was too slow, too weak, too undisciplined to be part of the Morning Star. I longed to lash out, take the sword from him, and turn it on its master. But then I would regain control of my emotions and remind myself that my revenge would be to pass his tests and take my place in the ranks of the legion.

Those thoughts were racing through my mind when, inexplicably, I crashed into the angel in front of me. At first, I thought I had not heard the command to halt, and I braced myself for Vassago's fury. He would dress me down for being clumsy, slow, or just plain incompetent. But no assault came. Then the angel in the rank behind stumbled into me as well, and the weight of the entire column pressed against my back as this happened all the way to the rear. The same baffling event was occurring to my left in the other ranks as well. Angels stumbled past me, the formation crumpling in upon itself. After a moment, the pressure relented as the angels behind me regained their footing.

Still, no command came, nor any admonishment for this terrible breach of discipline. Confused, I looked for Vassago. This was a risky thing to do. Even when he stood directly in front of a recruit, we were not allowed to make eye contact with our instructor. Instead, we were to lock our eyes forward and look through the instructor. To do otherwise would result in punitive exercises.

But this was such an unprecedented event, I had to know what was going on. Why had Vassago not addressed the collapse of our drill order? It took me a moment to locate the instructor, and when I did, I realized this was no mere training mishap. Vassago stood stock still, the sword hanging from his limp arm, mouth agape and staring wide-eyed in shock. I peered past him to see what was so remarkable that it caused him to lose his composure. Then I saw it, and I gaped as well.

The void was exploding.

Bright flashes of light erupted in the blackness beyond Heaven's borders. Just as with the single flash of light that Agiel and I had seen from the walls near the city gates, these bursts of light would flash out, then retract to settle as tiny pinpricks in the distance. But this time it was happening everywhere. Just as one flash of light would begin to recede, another would leap into existence. The void was alive with them, like bubbles erupting on the surface of boiling liquid.

Entire swaths of these lights formed in the void, covering vast areas of space. Some grouped together to form belts, blurring into giant glowing spirals that rotated in upon themselves. Others melded more loosely together into gigantic blobs or clouds. The brilliant explosions continued, although more sporadically until they subsided entirely. What remained afterward was a spectacle of beauty at least as impressive as the forming of it had been exhilarating. In every direction, the sky was filled with these myriad pinpricks of light. They permeated the void, which was no longer void. It had become a universe of light.

In the aftermath of this incident, not a single angelic host moved or spoke, and it must have been that way throughout the Holy City, for never had I experienced such overwhelming silence. Then, with a rush, everyone began talking at once, asking questions of one another that no one could answer.

Discipline had utterly broken down. Training for the Morning Star Legion meant nothing in the wake of this incredible event. Everyone wanted to know what had happened and why. Other angels flocked to the training ground in anticipation of a pronouncement from Zadkiel.

Sure enough, the commanders of the various units began arriving and forming up their angels in preparation for the proclamation assembly. When Malphas arrived with the veteran corps of the Morning Star, Vassago reported to him that all recruits were present and accounted for. After an agonizing wait, the trumpet sounded, and Zadkiel stepped out on the balcony to address the Army of the Lord, the archangels flanking him as usual.

"Hark, angels of the heavenly host. Hear the word of the Lord!"

No one spoke. Every host listened with rapt anticipation.

"The Lord God Almighty, Maker of the universe, has expanded His new creation. He has created stars to light the void, and to serve to divide the day from the night. They shall be for signs and seasons, for days and years, and they shall be to give light on the earth."

I did not comprehend all Zadkiel meant, particularly this talk of signs and seasons, but I grasped these stars were for lighting the Lord's new creation. It struck me that the word star had been used at all. Up until this point, the word star had been exclusively reserved as a descriptor for Lucifer, the Morning Star, the bright one. The term seemed appropriate, though, for what better word to describe the awesome beauty and power of these brilliant lights in the sky?

"The Lord God has also created two great lights," Zadkiel continued, "a greater light to rule the day, and a lesser one to rule the night, to give light on earth, and to divide the light from the darkness. As it is the will of the Lord..."

"Let it be so," every angelic mouth proclaimed.

Not every mouth though. I noticed Lucifer did not say the required words. His face tensed with barely contained anger, his brows furrowed and his mouth tight. He stared straight ahead as though it required every bit of his discipline to prevent an outburst. I found it curious at the time, though I realized much later that this was the moment Lucifer's pride began to burn him from the inside.

By creating these fabulous points of brilliant light that rivaled his own, and by calling them stars, Lucifer believed God had denigrated him in the eyes of the other hosts. He believed God intended to diminish his prestige, and his pride could not abide the perceived insult.

The rod moved to the other hand, and Zadkiel continued. "Only the Lord God knows His full plan. We must trust in Him and have patience. Think not of what is to come, for it is beyond our control. Trust in the Lord and have peace."

The rod struck the ground, and he concluded, saying, "That is all. You are dismissed."

The trumpet sounded, but no one moved. The entire angelic host was stunned into paralysis. We now understood that this new creation of the Lord's was not a limited event, no minor amusement or distraction. It encompassed the entirety of the universe and would forever alter the course of Heaven. But what was our place in that new universe? We were mere bystanders, observing pivotal events that would have significant ramifications for our order, but we had no concept of, much less control over, what those would be.

For the first time in my life, I experienced tremendous anxiety. With the introduction of such change, the future was no longer predictable by angelic beings. We now had to come to terms with the fact that we must trust in God for tomorrow. Never before had it occurred to us to do anything else, for never had angels experienced this kind of uncertainty. But now it was necessary for us to embrace a new concept.

Faith.

It was a moment of awakening, a coming of age. A line of demarcation was forming in how the various hosts would react to this new dynamic. Some, like Grigori, wholeheartedly embraced the notion, taking comfort in the knowledge that they were in God's hands. They let go of their uncertainty, trusting in the Lord. They had faith. But others allowed doubt to cause them to question not only what God was doing, but why.

I was shocked to observe this delineation forming before my own eyes with the recruits of my unit. Whatever training agenda Vassago had planned for the remainder of the day was set aside after the chaos of the *void incident*, as we began to refer to it. He was summoned to a council of the command element of the Morning Star. Lucifer, Malphas, and the other leading officers of the legion would confer to discuss the recent events. While they conferenced, we gratefully took the opportunity to rest. After a time, many of the recruits became restless and began to converse amongst themselves, holding their own impromptu conference to discuss the unfolding drama.

"I would like to be a guard in the council chamber at headquarters right now," one recruit named Belial said. "Do you think they are trying to figure out what is going on?"

Another recruit, a tall angel named Valac, who had assumed something of a leadership role within the unit, responded, "I am sure they know what is going on, at least Lucifer does. The lesser commanders like Vassago may not have been informed, but Lucifer is second in command only to the Lord God Himself. Surely, the Father shared His entire plan with him."

Several other recruits made sounds of assent, indicating they felt this must be true. Valac pressed his argument. "In fact, I would not be surprised if it were Lucifer who was giving Zadkiel the updates to announce at the proclamation assemblies. It makes much more sense for God to tell Lucifer, rather than Zadkiel, a mere cherub. Lucifer is probably briefing the other unit commanders on the plan this very moment."

"Not that Vassago will tell us anything when he returns," Belial said in grudging agreement. "It will be right on to the next exercise!"

"Of course," added another recruit named Anamalech. "It will be 'hurry up and wait' as usual!"

The conversation turned to Vassago, the training, and the normal gripes of recruits constantly harried by their instructors. Agiel and I stayed out of the conversation. We sensed our opinions would not be welcomed, and to speak up would serve only to remind the others we still existed, something we were happy to allow them to forget. We kept our silence while the recruits grumbled, rubbing our sore feet and enjoying the rare luxury of uninterrupted inactivity.

"What I do not understand," Belial said, "is why God is doing all this in the first place. Why does He need to make a new creation at all? Is Heaven not enough?"

"Right!" said Anamalech. "Where does that leave us? Are we going to be allowed to go into this new creation, or are we to be excluded?"

"Look at how much the Lord has created," said another, an angel named Marut. "We have become small in the grand scheme."

"This is still the Holy City," Valac reminded them. "There may be a greater universe now, but this is still Heaven, where the Holy of Holies resides."

"How do you know?" Marut said, growing agitated. "How do you know the Lord has not created a new Holy of Holies and plans to reside there from now on? You heard Zadkiel. God has created a new heaven. What if we are being replaced?"

"That is nonsense," Valac said, although he did not seem wholly convinced. "Zadkiel said God would return after His creation is complete."

"What if He changes His mind?" Anamalech interjected. "What if we are abandoned?"

"Someone should talk to Him about it," Belial said, "to ask what His intentions are."

"You do not question the Lord God!" I heard myself saying, surprised to find I could hold my tongue no longer. Agiel placed a cautioning hand on my arm, but I would not be silenced.

"What is wrong with all of you?" I scolded them. "We are angels of the Lord. We serve at His pleasure and exist to glorify His name. Our needs, our wants, our fears matter not. All we must do is trust in the Lord God and obey His commands."

Every eye was on me now, and the looks they gave were not kind. The faces turned toward me held a mixture of surprise, resentment, and hostility. My opinion was no more welcome here than was my presence, and I had rebuked the group harshly. I had just set back my cause in gaining acceptance, but I could not sit by silently while angels of the Lord questioned His plan.

"Is that why you left the Trumpet Legion and joined the Morning Star," Nakir asked, my involvement bringing him into the conversation for the first time, "because your needs and wants do not matter? You were not content to remain in the Trumpet Legion where you had been assigned. You applied to join the Morning Star because it was what you wanted, and now you dare to criticize us? You are a hypocrite!"

His words stung because they held truth. I did join the Morning Star out of a desire for personal glory. I was dissatisfied with my station in the Trumpet Legion and wanted more, not for God's sake, but for my own. I felt ashamed of my pride, my selfishness, and my lack of faith in God.

"You are right, Nakir." I saw the statement surprised him, so much so that he sat back. "I did place my wants and needs ahead of my faith in the Lord, and for that I am repentant. But I will not question God's decisions or His plan. We must have faith."

No one spoke for a long moment. Nobody wanted to openly dispute that point, to blatantly challenge the sovereign authority of the Almighty. They may have been disgruntled, but they were not foolish enough to speak blasphemy aloud.

"All I said," Belial grumbled, "is someone should speak to the Lord to find out what He wants from us. We just need to know how to proceed, that is all. I did not mean any disrespect."

"Of course not," Valac said. "We are all loyal angels here. Anyone who says otherwise is imprudent and judgmental."

He stared at me as he said these words, and everyone understood them to be an admonishment of my temerity. The group lapsed into sullen silence, with angels cutting accusatory glances at me from time to time. The uncomfortable situation seemed to drag on indefinitely until, finally, Vassago returned. I never thought I would be grateful to see his sour face, but at that moment, I was.

Valac's prediction proved true. Vassago did not offer any insight into what had been discussed in the meeting at headquarters. Without any preamble, he snapped an order and curtly announced the next drill. To a chorus of groans and sighs, we all sluggishly rose to our feet.

Chapter 10

The Crucible

The fourth day of our training was also the last. As I walked out of the legion barracks that morning with Agiel, we were tired, sore, and a bit dazed. But we were also enthusiastic because the following day we would graduate and take our places in the ranks of the veteran legion of the Morning Star. First, though, we must make it through this day, and this day promised to be the most challenging of any thus far.

We normally began our days on the training ground, but not this day. Instead, we had been instructed to meet at the front gate of the city. Once we had formed up and been inspected, Vassago stepped to the front of the formation and addressed the unit.

"Today, you will face your final and most difficult test. We will begin with a race by wing along the walls of the city. This will be followed by a series of contests; you will participate in both wrestling and sword tournaments. This will be followed by a final race by foot. Points will be awarded based on how you finish each segment. The host who finishes with the highest overall score shall be named the unit leader at graduation and will command the new unit."

Agiel and I discreetly cut our eyes at each other in mutual understanding. If one of us won the contest, we would be in charge of the unit. The other angels would have no choice but to respect us then. But if Nakir won, our lives as veteran angels of the legion might well resemble our lives as recruits. Neither of us relished the prospect of being in their power.

Another thought occurred to me as well. If one of us led the unit, we would be in a position to influence the views of those under our command. This might be an opportunity to correct the thinking of those who had begun to adopt the ideas of Malphas.

More and more, I saw my fellow recruits being influenced by those with a propensity to over-glorify Lucifer. I heard the rumors whispered amongst the other recruits, that Lucifer was not being shown the respect he deserved. With one of us in charge, we could work from the inside to bring the Morning Star Legion back to the center of the path. But first, we must win.

The first contest would be a race by wing, flying three laps around the circumference of the city. Agiel and I lined up next to each other on the wall-top near the front gate. Our starting positions were determined by our average times in prior races, and Agiel and I always raced together. We found ourselves in the top tier of the first racing group with Nakir ahead of us and Valac just to our rear. My eyes met Agiel's, and he nodded in understanding of the situation. We would have to contend with them both.

"On the line!" Vassago yelled. "Ready... Begin!"

The entire host of angels launched themselves into the air as one. I beat my wings, doing my best to gain altitude and speed at the same time. If I managed to get ahead of Nakir, the sheer mass of crowded bodies would make it difficult for him to regain position.

The rules forbade us to leave the vicinity of the wall. We could move up or down in space, but we must stay within the horizontal limits of the wall which was just wide enough for six angels to stand shoulder to shoulder. However, with wings spread in flight, there was only enough room for two angels to fly abreast. This forced the racers into a compacted space and limited opportunities for passing.

After the first few frantic seconds of jockeying for position, the racers settled into their places, and I found that nothing had really changed from our starting positions. Nakir was still ahead of me with Agiel to my right, while Valac stayed just behind us. For now, we focused on pure speed, using powerful strokes of our wings to gain ground and create space between us and the angels behind.

Agiel and I had learned from our experience in previous races. While the other angels pursued their own advancement, we developed a cooperative strategy. We remained abreast of each other, effectively filling the space between the ramparts and preventing any angel from passing us. We also varied our vertical position, randomly rising and dipping in elevation, to prevent anyone from passing us above or below.

By the time we completed the first lap, I sensed we had gained ground on Valac. He was far enough behind us now, at least three angel lengths back, that he no longer presented an immediate threat of passing. I turned my attention to Nakir, himself two lengths ahead. We pressed forward but did not gain on him. Something would have to change for one of us to win this race.

I had a difficult decision to make. I was faster than Agiel. Where he excelled at wrestling and contests of strength, I was the fleeter of foot and wing. I could leap ahead at any moment and leave Agiel behind, but I hesitated to do so. My reticence was not due to any reluctance on my part to beat my friend in the race. Neither of us held any illusions about that. We had discussed it, and both agreed we should not hold back for the sake of the other. What mattered was that one of us win.

What caused me to hesitate was strategy. If I left Agiel's side, we would both become vulnerable to passing. I was sure Valac, maintaining his pace behind us, was faster than he was currently flying, and I suspected he was conserving his strength for an opportune moment. For now, it was more important to maintain our position. I decided to conserve my own strength and make my move on the final lap.

When the final lap eventually came, positions were very much as they had been up to that point. Still, I hesitated. I did not wish to commit myself until we were closer to the finish line. I hoped Nakir was growing overconfident. Alerting him now would only serve to sacrifice the element of surprise.

I waited until we were halfway through the final lap to make my move. Reaching over, I tapped Agiel on the shoulder twice, tilting to ensure our wings did not become entangled. That was the agreed-upon signal, and Agiel nodded his head in acknowledgment. I set my jaw, and with concentrated effort, pounded my wings, launching myself forward. Behind me, Agiel would be moving to the center and doing his best to fill the space, preventing anyone else from making a similar move.

I closed rapidly on Nakir, and soon I found myself fighting the backdraft created by the motion of his wings. He did not seem to have noticed me yet, so I took a moment to assess the situation. He was flying in the center of the wall. I might possibly get past him on either side, although it would be risky.

It seemed to me the best tactic would be to fly over him. Although it would require much energy to gain altitude and speed at the same time, I was confident I had sufficient stamina to manage it. That maneuver also had the added benefit of making it less likely that Nakir would detect me. By closing from above, I would remain outside his peripheral vision until the last second. But just as I steeled myself for the maneuver, something gripped my left ankle. Shocked, I felt myself losing speed. I glanced back in panic to see what had taken hold of me.

Valac. He must have shot past Agiel and caught up with me. The fact that he did not attempt to pass me, but merely focused on slowing me down, meant his goal was to help Nakir win.

"Let go!" I shouted at him, but he only grinned at me.

I thrashed about but could not shake Valac's iron grip. I kicked with my other foot, but to no avail. Then, looking back past my antagonist, I spotted Agiel catching up fast. Valac was slowing me down, but by doing so, he slowed himself as well. Agiel surged forward like the relentless force of an oncoming wave. Without any hesitation, he flew up beside Valac, and with a slight rocking motion to the outside, came swinging back to crash into him.

I felt the grip on my ankle loosen. Tilting the angle of my wings, I twisted left. My body rolled, spinning my legs up and away from Valac. The fingers holding me slipped away and released. I was free.

"Go!" Agiel urged me.

I righted myself and applied all my remaining energy to gaining speed. Nakir was fast approaching the finish line. I was not certain I had enough time to catch him, but I had to try. As I surged forward, I stole a glance back at Agiel who still grappled with Valac. The latter attempted to get past my friend once more, but Agiel used his massive arms to grasp the slimmer Valac and throw him bodily backward where he collided with the racers behind. Agiel threw me a quick grin, and I turned back to Nakir with a grin of my own.

I put all my strength into that last desperate sprint. My wings burned in agony as I forged ahead, gaining steadily on my opponent. Nakir glanced back to see me gaining on him. He surged forward, also applying his last reserves of energy. The finish line rushed toward us as I closed the gap, but with despair, I realized there was not enough time to catch him.

Nakir crossed the finish line with me right on his heels. Another few yards and I would have passed him, but it was not to be. He had won the race. Wheeling about, I saw Agiel come across the finish line behind me, securing a third-place finish. Valac finished right behind him, a strange mix of annoyance and satisfaction on his thin face. Although we had beaten him, he had accomplished his primary goal, to deny either of us the victory and secure it instead for Nakir.

Agiel walked up to me and bent over at the waist, his hands resting on his knees. I laid a hand on his shoulder and leaned on him. We were both exhausted, but there was little time to rest. The next test would soon be upon us. As we stood there relishing our break, I turned to see Valac and Nakir standing next to each other, talking in low voices while they peered in our direction.

Agiel followed my gaze and gave voice to my own thoughts by saying, "We will have to contend with them as a pair for the remainder of this tournament."

I nodded my agreement. But for all Valac and Nakir's conspiring, they would be unable to aid each other in the next two contests. The wrestling and sword tournaments would be tests of individual ability. Agiel was the best wrestler in the unit, and I was sure I was a match for any of the other trainees with a blade. Between the two of us, I was certain we would dominate those two contests.

The wrestling tournament went exactly as I expected it would. Agiel easily vanquished all those pitted against him. His size and quickness were unmatched, and he defeated most of his opponents straight away. I was not as tall or strong as Agiel and Nakir, and wrestling has never been my best skill, but I was wiry and determined. I defeated most of my opponents, though not as quickly or effortlessly as Agiel, and made it nearly to the semi-final match before being defeated by a hulking angel named Agaliarept.

After I picked my sore body up off the ground, having been viciously slammed there by Agaliarept, I went to see how Agiel fared. I limped over to one of the other circles and learned he had just won his latest match against a smaller, but quick recruit named Chemosh. Only four contenders remained, Agiel, Nakir, Agaliarept, and another huge angel named Sargatanas.

Agiel was pitted against Agaliarept, who had defeated me, while Nakir faced Sargatanas. I watched both matches with marked interest. Assuming Agiel won his match, I attempted to gauge who I would rather see him face, Nakir, whom he had defeated once before, or Sargatanas, who I had not previously observed. It was, of course, a ridiculous notion. I could no more affect the outcome of that match than I could ensure Agiel won his own.

Fortunately, my friend did win his match, and it was with mixed feelings of dismay and hope that I found Nakir won his as well. Nakir was probably the most challenging opponent Agiel could face, and although he had already defeated him once before, it had been close. I also suspected that Nakir had underestimated Agiel in that first match. He would not make the same mistake twice.

When Agiel removed his tunic, however, I was encouraged. My friend had always been large and well-muscled, but the training regimen of these last few days had caused him to absolutely swell in size. Although we trained on our own during our time with the Mighty Trumpet Legion, our regimen was nothing compared to what the other two legions submitted themselves to on a regular basis. As a member of the Flaming Sword Legion, a fellow warrior-based unit,

Nakir was used to this type of physical conditioning, but it also meant his body had not responded to the last few days in the same way that Agiel's had. I saw with no small share of satisfaction that Nakir recognized the change as well, his face unable to conceal his surprise.

To Nakir's credit, though, he did not hold back once the match commenced. He launched himself at Agiel and immediately sought to gain a hold. Agiel responded by sidestepping left and ducking underneath Nakir's right arm as it passed over his head. He rose with lightning speed and brought his shoulder up, driving it into Nakir's armpit. Agiel wrapped that arm around the front of his opponent's neck. With this move, he pinned Nakir's arm in an upward vertical position, held there against his own neck by Agiel's hold. My friend then pivoted on his right foot to bring his body in close behind Nakir. Raising his left arm, he hooked it around the back of Nakir's head, and the two arms locked around his neck. Then he squeezed.

Nakir's eyes bulged in sudden surprise and panic. He tried to squirm out of the hold, but Agiel held him securely. All my friend had to do was flex his arm muscles to apply pressure to his opponent's neck. When he did, Nakir bucked wildly, flailing about in a futile attempt to free himself from the chokehold. Agiel expected the reaction, though, and bent his knees to lower his center of gravity, creating a stable platform that Nakir, despite his desperate contortions, could not shake.

Agiel began moving backward, slowly and deliberately, toward the edge of the circle. With small controlled steps, my friend maneuvered his opponent closer and closer to the edge of the boundary. Then he pivoted, and with something akin to contempt, calmly tossed Nakir out of the circle.

Chapter 11

Duplicity

The match was over, and Agiel had won a dominant victory. I was pleased but also a bit shocked, and I was not alone. Silence fell over the unit. Even Vassago did not speak for a long moment. Agiel had stunned everyone with his dominant strength and explosive speed. I looked at the faces of angels who had, up to now, dismissed us as pretenders and saw that judgment replaced by one of grudging respect, at least for Agiel. I sensed I had not yet earned that acceptance for myself, but I would soon have my opportunity. The next event, the sword tournament, was one in which I excelled.

That event would have to wait, though, because it was time for the daily proclamation. Vassago formed us up and ordered us to face right. As we marched toward the training ground to await the announcement from Zadkiel, I stole a glance out past the walls of the city at the expanse of the former void, now filled with bright stars, and wondered what new development would be announced today.

"Hark, angels of the heavenly host," The voice of Zadkiel thundered across the training ground. "Hear the word of the Lord!"

"The Lord God has created living creatures in the earth," he announced. "He has created birds to fly above the earth across the face of the firmament of the heavens. He has created great sea creatures to populate the waters of the earth. He has commanded these creatures to be fruitful and multiply, and to fill the waters in the seas, and for the birds to multiply on the earth. As it is the will of the Lord..."

"Let it be so," every mouth said, including Lucifer's. There must not have been anything about this announcement that offered him offense.

The rod moved to the other hand, and Zadkiel continued, "The Lord's new creation is almost complete. Tomorrow shall mark the final proclamation regarding the earth. That announcement shall immediately follow the graduation ceremony of those who successfully complete the training requirements to be accepted into the Morning Star Legion."

The rod struck the ground, and he concluded, saying, "That is all. You are dismissed."

Vassago ordered us to face left. As we began marching back to the training ground for the sword tournament, my mind wandered, mulling over Zadkiel's words. The Lord had commanded these creatures to "be fruitful and multiply". What did that mean, and how would it be accomplished? Of course, I had no notion of how earthly creatures procreate. But that minor curiosity was completely overshadowed by a more pressing question.

What were these things called birds? The only descriptor we had been given was that they flew. Did that mean they were some new sort of angel? Was Marut right after all? Had the Lord created a new heaven and new angels to displace us?

I chided myself for my doubt and lack of faith. We must trust in God's wisdom. Besides, if He did decide to build a new heaven and create new angels for that Kingdom, what right did I have to question His decision? If that was His will, then that was His will. The Lord God Almighty did as He pleased. He owed us nothing, and if He desired to wipe out the angels of Heaven and start over, that was His prerogative. Selfish, paranoid thoughts on my part would affect nothing, nor should it.

"As it is the will of the Lord," I mumbled to myself as I marched, "let it be so." If I could not affect the future, it was pointless to agonize over it. A peaceful calm settled over me as I surrendered myself to the will of God.

Vassago called a halt, then began spreading us out and pairing us up for the sword tournament. As with the wrestling contest, an angel would be eliminated in each match until only one remained. But this was my best event. With a confident grin, I pulled my sword from its scabbard and inspected the bright, gleaming blade. I was ready.

My first few opponents did not present much of a challenge, and I defeated them without much effort, scoring hits on their breastplates to end the match quickly. The competition became steeper as the subsequent rounds pitted victorious angels against each other. After seven such rounds, I was tired but confident. Only three other angels remained, Agiel, Valac, and Nakir. It seemed we were destined to face each other.

I was wondering whom I would be pitted against first when Vassago stepped forward to address the unit. There was a sly smile on his pointed face that made me uneasy. I had the distinct impression he was up to something.

"For the semi-final round of this tournament," he said, "you will be paired with a fellow angel, and each pair will face off against the other."

I glanced at Agiel and he at me. It was apparent to me what Vassago was doing. He would pit us against Valac and Nakir and allow the pair to team up against us. Vassago, it appeared, was concerned we were still enough in contention for one of us to potentially win the command of the unit. He was determined to prevent that from occurring. However, when he next spoke, I was shocked to learn I had gotten it wrong.

"Malachi and Valac shall face off against Agiel and Nakir."

The angels who had been eliminated in earlier rounds, and now served as the audience, roared in approval. Vassago allowed the breach in discipline to pass. His grin grew wide and unguarded as he reveled in what he must have considered a brilliant move. I grimaced as I realized he was right. This way, one of us, Agiel or I, was sure to be eliminated and would not make it into the top two.

The standings currently had Nakir in the lead, as he had won first and second place in two matches. Agiel was in second since he had taken third in the race and first in wrestling. I was third, having taken second in the race by wing and fifth in the wrestling match. Valac held a distant fourth place because although he had taken fourth in the flight race, he had not even placed in the top five of the wrestling tournament.

Vassago's plan became clear to me then, and I had to admit it was genius. If Valac and I won, we would face each other in the final. I was confident I would win, but even with a first-place finish added to my total, Nakir would maintain his lead. Meanwhile, Agiel would fall further behind.

On the other hand, if Agiel and Nakir won, I would be all but eliminated from contention. It would come down to the last race, the foot race, in which Nakir had the advantage over my friend. My mind raced to consider all the potential outcomes and compute each scenarios' impact on the scores. I was still calculating the best possible result when I sensed someone step close to me.

"You have to win this match," Agiel said. He spoke in low tones without looking at me. I opened my mouth to object, but he raised a hand to silence me. "I have done the math. If Nakir and I win, we will both be far ahead in the standings. You will not be able to catch up."

"I do not need to catch up," I said, following Agiel's example by keeping my head pointed straight ahead. "All that matters is that one of us wins."

"That is my point. I cannot beat him in the upcoming foot race. He is faster than me. The only chance we have is for you to win here. That will bring us into a virtual three-way tie going into the last contest. I cannot win that race, but you can."

As my friend spoke, I completed my own calculations and realized he was right. Nodding discreetly, I said, "I appreciate the vote of confidence, but I would still feel better if we had a chance to take both first and second. Vassago certainly knows what he is doing here by pitting us against each other."

I heard the bitterness in my own voice as I spoke. Our situation was anything but fair. We had been undermined at every turn. If one of us were to win the overall contest and thereby command of the unit, it would be despite all Vassago's efforts to deny us.

"I agree," my friend said, "but this is the only way. When we begin, make sure you and I face off against one another. I will allow you to eliminate me quickly. With me out of the match, you and Valac should have no trouble eliminating Nakir for the win."

I nodded, though with resignation. I did not like it, but I recognized this was our only hope of victory. We took our places, I facing Agiel while Nakir and Valac stood across from each other. I glanced at Valac. He was standing too close to me, within arm's reach, so I suggested to him we should spread out to give us both more room to work.

"No," he said, shaking his head. "We need to work together. Those two are larger than either of us and will overpower us individually. Our best chance is to stand shoulder to shoulder and lend each other support."

While I was pleasantly surprised and touched by Valac's seemingly genuine desire to stand with me, I disagreed with his assessment of our situation. We were both quicker and agiler than our opponents. In a swordfight, speed counts for more than size, and we would be better served to spread out and separate our competition. Still, for the purposes of my plan with Agiel, it did not matter, so I saw no point in disputing Valac's flawed tactics. I let the matter drop, and we both drew our swords. Across from us, standing shoulder to shoulder as well, Agiel and Nakir did the same. Vassago stepped to the center of the circle, between us, and raised his hands.

"Stand ready!" he said. Then, dropping his arms, he stepped aside and commanded, "Begin!"

At the signal, I bent slightly at the knees to balance my body weight and take on a less rigid stance. Transferring my weight to the balls of my feet, I leaned forward and bobbed from side to side, beginning the footwork that would allow me to move fluidly. My reflexes were sharp, my body nimble, and my sword grip firm.

I fixed my eyes on Agiel and was about to step forward when, inexplicably, I felt something sharp punch itself into my chest. I reeled from the impact and peered down to see a sword blade protruding from my breastplate armor. The tip only penetrated a finger's width, and there was no pain, but it dawned on me that something disastrous had just occurred. I turned to my right to see a viciously smiling Valac looking at me with an expression of triumph and perverse glee. He had reversed his hold of his sword, and at the very onset of the match, used it to eliminate his own teammate.

In shock, I looked up and across at Agiel. To my horror, I realized Nakir had simultaneously affected the same coups on his side, striking my friend in the breastplate just as Valac had done to me. We had been set up and betrayed. The enormity of it crashed down on me as I realized Vassago's plan had been even more deviously ingenious than we previously thought. Now it would not be just one of us who fell in the standings, but both. Nakir would secure a first or second-place finish, which would give him an insurmountable lead going into the final event.

Anger boiled up within me, and as it overflowed, I thrust Valac's sword aside. I advanced on him, all rage and indignation. He backed away, the look of triumph replaced by one of surprised fear. He held up his sword to guard against attack, but with a flick of my wrist, I sent it flying. Disarmed and helpless, Valac cowered before me, raising his hands over his head in a pitiful defense. An angry roar, like that of a wounded beast, filled my ears, and I realized as I raised my sword that the incensed bellow came from me.

"Stand down!" I faintly heard Vassago shout angrily, but the order did not sway me. Valac trembled, terror in his eyes, and pleaded with me for mercy, but I was unmoved. My muscles tensed, and I sneered as I drew back my arm to strike.

Chapter 12

Conviction and Uncertainty

"Malachi!"

Agiel shouted my name, and only the voice of my friend managed to penetrate the fog of rage that engulfed me. I hesitated for only a moment, but it was enough. Strong arms grabbed me from behind, and then Vassago appeared between the cowering Valac and me.

"I ordered you to stand down!" he spat. "You dishonor the legion with your actions!"

I turned on him, my anger, at last, finding the appropriate target, the source of all my frustrations. Shaking off those who held me, I tossed my sword to the ground with contempt.

"My actions dishonorable?" I challenged him. "When you have done everything in your power to interfere and block both Agiel and me at every turn! You encourage the others to conspire and work against us. You even changed the rules of the contest to allow them to execute this treachery, and you dare to accuse me of being dishonorable?"

Vassago took a threatening step toward me. His eyes narrowed and he bared his teeth in seething anger. But his lips also curled up in a smirk of grim satisfaction. It dawned on me I had blundered badly. By verbally attacking the instructor of my training unit, I had committed insubordination. Nothing could have pleased Vassago more. He now had reason to eject me from the training unit and disqualify me from joining the legion altogether.

He had opened his mouth to rebuke me when someone yelled, "Unit! Attention!"

Everyone present, including Vassago, stopped in their tracks and stood to attention, locking their bodies in rigid obedience. I was no different. From my right side, a melodious voice said, "Vassago, what is going on here?"

It was Lucifer. I did not look at him, for I would not break my discipline, but as I stood directly in front of Vassago, it was not long before Lucifer appeared in the corner of my eye. He was accompanied by Malphas and several other high-ranking angels, although I could not tell who.

"Sir, this recruit was insubordinate toward his instructor," Vassago accused me.

"Is that true, Malachi?" Lucifer asked in a soothing tone.

I remember thinking at that moment only how honored I was that he remembered my name. Without moving my eyes, I responded to his question in a loud, yet respectful tone.

"Yes, sir!"

"An unhesitatingly honest answer," Lucifer said, with what seemed like surprised respect. "Look at me."

I obeyed, and as I turned my head, I saw that no less than ten high-order angels made up his entourage. As ordered, I looked the Morning Star in the eye as he asked for an explanation.

"I did speak to Instructor Vassago in an insubordinate and disrespectful manner, sir, and I regret that. But I stand by the truth of my words."

"Which were?"

"Instructor Vassago has harassed me and obstructed my training from the beginning. He does not want me in the legion, much less as the unit leader. He intentionally altered the rules of this competition to prevent me from having a fair opportunity to win."

"I see." Lucifer's eyes narrowed. Turning to Vassago, he asked, "And what do you have to say about that Instructor?"

"He is a liar, sir," Vassago spat. "He is soft and weak. A true warrior does not complain about fairness. A true warrior overcomes any obstacles placed in his path. He does not ask for them to be removed for him."

Lucifer considered his subordinate's opinion. He peered at me as though examining my worth, and time ground to a halt under his implacable gaze.

"I seem to recall this warrior of the Trumpet besting you in a sword contest, Vassago," Lucifer said, smiling. "Perhaps you are selling him a bit short?"

Anger flashed across Vassago's face at the reminder of that embarrassment, but Lucifer did not give him an opportunity to respond.

"Where does Malachi stand in the rankings?"

"He is currently in third position, sir," Vassago answered, although not gladly.

"Third! And you would dismiss a host whose abilities are so obviously apparent?"

"His insubordination!" the instructor began, but Lucifer cut him off.

"Is not acceptable, but I think Malachi will apologize, won't you Malachi?"

I did not want to apologize. I had been wronged, and apologizing would legitimize Vassago's behavior. But I was a soldier, a host of the Army of the Lord, and I had committed a breach of discipline. Regardless of my reason, I should have held my composure and my tongue.

"Yes, sir," I said. With only the slightest hesitation, I turned to Vassago and uttered the distasteful words. "I apologize for my insubordination, sir."

"But!" Vassago started to object to this leniency, but a sharp look from Lucifer caused the objection to die in his throat. Vassago clamped his mouth shut and stood silent.

"Well," Lucifer said with a disarming smile, "I think I have disturbed your training long enough. I will take my leave of you. Please, carry on."

As Lucifer departed, his entourage in tow, I glanced at Vassago. His eyes bored into me with an intensity of pure hatred I was not aware could exist. I stared back at him, determined to display no weakness. After a long moment, Vassago broke the stalemate by turning to address Nakir and Valac.

"You two will now face off to determine first and second place."

As the pair prepared for the final bout, I kept my eyes on Vassago, mentally daring him to turn back my way. I felt a hand grasp my arm. It was Agiel. I turned a fierce glare on him, but my friend was undeterred. Pulling gently on my arm, he led me aside.

"Just walk away," he said. "You do not need to make this any worse."

It was a gentle rebuke, but a rebuke nonetheless. I was not used to being chastised by my friend, and I especially did not appreciate it in this instance. I was the aggrieved party here, yet he spoke to me as though I was the one at fault. Was he so eager for acceptance that he was asking me to overlook Vassago's dishonorable conduct?

"We are so close, Malachi," he continued. "Our dreams are about to come true, but you are allowing your pride to endanger it all."

"My pride?" I stammered.

"Yes. You need to let go of this feud with Vassago. You are not only placing your own future in peril, but mine as well."

I stopped in my tracks. Agiel took a couple more steps forward before he realized it and paused to turn back. His words stunned me. He thought I was the one in the wrong?

"If there is a feud between Vassago and me, it is of his making, not mine," I insisted. "He has resented me ever since I defeated him in the sword challenge. All I have done is try to overcome his obstructionism, but I could no longer keep my silence, not after he engineered that treachery."

"Vassago did not plan what Nakir and Valac did," Agiel said. My mouth fell open, and it took a moment for me to find my voice.

"He did not... what? How do you...?" I could not complete the thought. My head spun in confusion.

"Oh, he planned the pairing to advantage Nakir," he explained, "but it was Nakir and Valac who came up with the idea to eliminate their own partners. Valac admitted it to me after we pulled you away from him. You truly terrified him, and he kept going on about how it had all been Nakir's idea."

I was struck dumb. Had I wrongfully accused Vassago? Surely, he was still guilty of skewing the contest in favor of Nakir and Valac, but was that the same as collusion?

Agiel pressed his argument. "We can be angry at Vassago for making the contest more difficult for us, but that is his job, to challenge us and evaluate how we overcome obstacles. We can be angry with Nakir and Valac, but they were really doing no more than we were when we decided to allow you to eliminate me. We all pursued our own strategy to gain the points we needed to win. Their strategy happened to win out over ours. I, for one, cannot fault them for that."

He was right. We had conspired to manipulate the contest. I justified our plan because, in my mind, we were only seeking to level the field against Vassago's attempt to skew it. Nakir and Valac used that to their advantage, but if they had not conspired with Vassago as I assumed...

My confidence crumbled at the realization I had misread the situation and accused Vassago of more than he was guilty of. That meant my insubordination was completely unmerited. If it had not been for the timely intervention of Lucifer, I might have been expelled from the unit, and I would have had no one to blame but myself.

I stood stunned as my reality came crashing down around me. I no longer possessed any certainty about who was right and who was wrong. What else had my temerity led me to misperceive? Was I incorrect about my impressions of Malphas and others in the Morning Star?

My head spun with the myriad implications of my flawed perceptions and conclusions. Recognizing my distress and self-admonishment, my friend reached out and laid a sympathetic hand on my shoulder.

"Malachi, you are my friend, and I will always stand beside you, but we are part of something greater now. The other angels and I need you to settle this enmity between you and Vassago. It is not good for the unit."

"The other angels and I," I repeated those words in a confused mumble.

I began to understand that the dynamic between Agiel and me had changed. We came into the legion as outsiders fighting for acceptance. He had won that respect while I continued to fight, no longer for acceptance, but out of resentment for Vassago. We were no longer partners in this struggle. While I kept myself apart, he had become one of them, and more than that, he was growing into a leader.

"I understand," I said, "and I am sorry if I have created difficulties for you."

Agiel laughed, the old personality of my friend breaking through the severe façade. He squeezed my shoulder affectionately.

"Our difficulties are nearly at an end," he said, all sternness fading from his voice. "One more race and we complete our training. We will be full legionaries of the Morning Star at last."

"But we cannot win now," I pointed out with sorrow. "Nakir is far ahead going into the final race. I am too far back in the standings now to have any chance of winning. You are the next closest, but even if you take first place, all he has to do is secure third, and he will still win."

"True, and I am nowhere near as fast as he is. You could beat him, but as you said, you are too far back now for it to matter."

"It looks like Nakir is going to be our unit leader." The enormity of the unwelcome realization settled upon me.

"Then you had better make your peace with him." He slapped my back. "Come on. One more race. Then we take our places in the elite guard."

I was numb as we walked back to the front gate. It occurred to me I had been operating out of fear. I was no longer competing to prove my worthiness to be in the legion, but had instead become obsessed with winning the contest and becoming the unit commander.

When this journey began, all I wanted was to be part of the Morning Star, to have a place in the ranks. Somewhere along the way, I began to feel that if Agiel or I was not in command of our unit, we could not be happy. How had it come to that? When had joining the legion become not enough?

Shaking my head, I scolded myself for my foolishness. Agiel had gained acceptance by this group of warrior angels. He no longer needed to be the leader to be happy in the legion, and as such, he no longer hung his hopes on winning the tournament. I resolved I must do something to undo a portion of the damage I had caused, so I too could attain the contentment Agiel had achieved.

We reached the main gate and stretched our wings to join the other angels on the city wall preparing for the foot race. Vassago hovered near the starting line, his wings flapping slowly as he bobbed up and down in space. I too rose into the air, but rather than heading to the starting line, I made my way over to Vassago. When he saw me, his expression changed, and the hatred on his face almost made me lose my resolve. Bracing myself, I flew up to him.

"Sir," I said, "I would like to apologize."

"You already did that," he snapped.

"I realize that sir, but I want you to know I mean it sincerely."

He eyed me with suspicion. He said nothing, but his expression seemed to say, "Go on."

"I realize you think I have no business in the Morning Star, that I am not worthy, and perhaps my recent conduct has proven you correct. For that, I apologize. All I ask is a fair chance to prove myself to you and earn a place in the ranks."

After a moment of hesitation, his jaw set and his eyes locked on mine.

"Then do so," he said matter-of-factly. "Do not tell me. Show me."

"I will, sir."

"In that case, stop wasting my time," he ordered, pointing to the starting line, "and get up there!"

"Yes, sir!" Banking my wings, I swung away.

Chapter 13

Finishing the Race

As with the race by wing, our starting positions for the foot race were determined by our average performance in past runs. I had typically done well in this contest, so I found myself in the front rank beside Valac with Belial and Marut to the left and right of us. Nakir was behind me with Agiel next to him.

The main difference between this and the race by wing was apparent since each rank was comprised of four angels standing shoulder to shoulder, twice that of the flight race. Without our wings spread, the track would be that much more congested. In fact, we were prohibited from using our wings at all. We were not allowed to fly for any reason, which meant our success or failure would be determined solely by the speed of our legs. It also meant there would be more room for passing.

As we took our places, I was determined to make a good showing in this contest, but not because of any hope I might win the leadership position. That was now out of my reach. No, I needed to do well here to gain the respect of the other recruits, just as Agiel had done. This was my last opportunity to prove I deserved to stand with them in the Morning Star Legion.

"What did you say to Vassago?" Agiel asked me as I took my place.

"I apologized for my conduct and assured him I just wanted to prove myself worthy."

"And what did he say?" I was shocked to realize it was Nakir who asked.

"He told me to stop blubbering and do it."

Valac laughed at that, surprising me. With a broad smile on his face, he said, "Vassago acts tough, but he almost dropped his feathers when you turned on him."

Nakir scoffed, "You mean you could see that from your spot cowering on the ground?"

Valac cut a petulant look at him. "I would not have been on the ground if you had not talked me into that ridiculous plan. I thought Malachi was going to skewer me!"

"He was," Agiel retorted, "and you would have deserved it, too. You picked a fight with the best swordsman in the unit who was supposed to be your partner. Absolutely brilliant!"

Valac cut his eyes at Agiel, but then looked back at me and smiled. "I admit it was not the best idea, but it was worth it to see you put Vassago in his place. That took real courage."

I stared at Valac, stunned by his sudden change in demeanor, and struggled to reconcile this genial interaction against our previous encounters.

"Either that or he really is as addle-minded as I have said all along!" Nakir put in. "You Trumpet angels really are something. You feel you have to take on the whole host of Heaven to prove you aren't just a harp-stringer, and you draw so much attention to yourselves in the process that you make life miserable for the rest of us!"

Nakir sounded harsh, but I now realized it was with affected gruffness rather than genuine hostility. I was completely dumbfounded by this sudden development. Something had happened to alter the relationship between me and these angels, and I did not understand it. Perhaps my confrontation with Vassago had earned me their grudging respect. They held no more love for the instructor than I did. He had made all of us miserable. That was his job. Still, by standing up to him, I had done what every member of the unit wished they could do but dared not.

There was another possibility though. Perhaps I had misjudged Nakir and overestimated his hostility. If so, it meant I was the one who had placed the wedge between us and prevented this comradery from developing. I shook my head vigorously, overcome with self-doubt and confusion.

"Perhaps," Agiel responded to Nakir, "but these harp-stringers are going to leave you behind. Prepare to be humiliated."

"We will see," Nakir said with a sneer.

Before anyone could say anything more, Vassago shouted for us to take our places and be ready. We tensed all along the line. Then he gave the signal, and we were off, the mass of angelic bodies springing forward. Valac jumped out ahead early. He was built for running, tall and thin, and it was not long before I was staring squarely at his back as he outstripped me.

I might not be as fast as Valac, but I sensed I had created distance between myself and the other runners. Belial and Marut disappeared behind me, and soon I left them far behind. Then out of the corner of my eye, a streaking form appeared on my left. I turned my head and was shocked to see Nakir. He may not have been built for running, but he was immensely strong and was using his massive leg muscles to power his way to the front of the pack.

I leaned forward and increased my stride. Glancing behind me again, I was gratified to see him fall back. I lessened my pace a touch and settled into a comfortable rhythm. I had to be careful not to wear myself out. In a race such as this, it was best to reserve some energy for the final stretch. I only wanted to cause Nakir to give up hope of passing.

The first half of the race was uneventful, and I spent most of it watching Valac pull steadily away from me, unable to match his lightning speed. As we rounded the first turn, I glanced left. The rest of the unit was strung out behind. I banked through the sharpest part of the turn and spotted Belial and Marut, several places back. Agiel was behind them. This was not his best event, and it was possible he might not even place in the top five. The race would come down to Valac, Nakir, and me.

In the straightaway, I sensed Nakir's presence as he closed on me. He was making his move. If I allowed him to get ahead of me, he would block me with his large size, so I needed to protect my position. Another turn just ahead marked the halfway point of the race. I sensed Nakir edge left, which meant he planned to pass me on the inside as we came through the turn. I drifted that direction to cut him off and barely managed to close the gap as we banked into the turn. With the inside track cut off, Nakir swung to the outside and attempted to pass me there, but I held the advantage. As he swung out, I gained distance on him.

In the next stretch of the wall, I decided I needed to take Nakir out of the race then and there. I tapped into my reserves and furiously pumped my legs. Clear space stretched ahead of me now. Valac was nowhere to be seen. I assumed he was on the fourth straightaway approaching the finish line, but it did not matter. I was not racing for first place, but second. All I wanted was to beat Nakir.

We approached the final turn, and I sensed him close behind me. I risked a glance back and saw he was right on my heels, charging forward like a rampaging bull. I drifted left to cut off the inside lane again. This time, though, he stubbornly refused to give way. As I cut the corner, he wedged himself between me and the wall. He could not generate enough speed to pass me on the outside, so he was using his superior size and strength to push his way past.

I pushed back, determined not to give way. A shoving match ensued that continued into the straightaway. We were in the home stretch now, and if I had retained my senses, I would have pressed forward and used my superior speed to leave him behind. But this had become a contest of wills, and neither of us would disengage. We drifted right as we continued what must have looked like a wrestling match on the move, and soon we were close to the outer rampart of the wall.

Nakir grinned as he shoved me, and I nearly collided with the wall as a result. If I allowed him to push me into the ramparts, I would be sent sprawling. He would shoot past, and I would have no time to recover. I refused to let that happen. I shoved back at Nakir, but he relentlessly pressed his newfound advantage. Time slowed as I sensed him lean to his left as a prelude to the shove that would send me into the wall and end my hopes of victory.

So, I sidestepped.

As he veered mere inches away from slamming into me, I planted my right foot and cut left. Nakir was fully committed to his angle with no way to adjust in time. He passed in front of me, disappearing off to my right. I smiled as I spotted the finish line straight ahead. I had turned the tables on Nakir and would take the race. He might still be the unit commander, but he would have to respect my achievement.

Then I heard the crash behind me.

I turned back to see that he had hit the wall at full speed. The wall-top was crenelated, creating a saw-toothed pattern where the tops of the wall alternated between sections at shoulder height and those that were lower. It was one of the lower sections Nakir hit, and because of his great height, the top of the wall came up only to his hip. Careening into the ramparts there created a pivot point that pitched his upper body over while his feet flew out from beneath him. To my horror, I watched him flip over the battlement and disappear into the void beyond.

I reacted without hesitation. It never even occurred to me to leave Nakir behind and finish the race. I could not do that considering I was the one who had sent him over the wall. I skidded to a halt and spun around. Running back to where he had fallen, I leaned out and over to discover him hanging from a section of gold brick that protruded from the otherwise smooth surface of the wall. He peered up at me; panic in his eyes.

"Fly up!" I shouted. All he had to do was spread his wings and flutter up to the top of the wall, but he shook his head emphatically.

"I will be disqualified if I use my wings."

"You would rather drop into the Void?"

"I have to finish," he said, and I recognized the despair in his eyes.

I came to understand Nakir at that moment. What I had mistaken for contempt of Agiel and me was, in fact, a reaction to his own insecurity, a need to prove he belonged in the unit. He had been embarrassed by his loss to Agiel in the grand hall of the Morning Star Legion headquarters. He had been forced to reapply and fight his way back to earn a place in the training unit. He must have faced self-doubt every day. He had pushed himself to not only pass recruit training, but to be the best, not out of scorn for Agiel or me, but for his own personal validation.

I saw myself in his face, my own insecurities, my own self-doubt, and realized he and I were more alike than different. I could imagine the torment that would consume him if he were disqualified. He would still make it into the legion. He had performed well enough to this point to ensure that, but he would feel the sting of failure and the dishonor that would follow from having dropped out of this final test. He would allow himself to fall into the void before he would concede defeat in that manner.

I could not allow Nakir to suffer that fate, not alone. So, before I could think better of it, I grabbed onto the top of the wall with my left hand and pitched myself over after him. I hung there, suspended by one hand and reached down with the other.

"Grab on!"

For what seemed a long time, he stared up at me dumbfounded. I repeated my order, and with effort, Nakir brought his right hand up to grasp mine. I pulled with all my strength. Nakir's other hand grasped my tunic, and he hauled himself up. With immense effort, we managed together to get him high enough to grab onto the top of the wall. His feet rose past my face, and I raised my head in time to watch him disappear over the rampart.

As I waited for him to return and help me back over, I glanced down, peering into the void below. I was amused to see stars here as well, these new pinpricks of light that had only recently popped into existence across the universe. I had never thought about the likelihood of there being stars below Heaven as well as above and around it, but of course, there were, and they were beautiful.

I looked back up and wondered where Nakir was. Had he abused my kindness, leaving me to continue the race? Then to my relief, his head appeared, and he leaned over, reaching down with an outstretched hand.

"Come on!"

I lunged up with my free hand to take his. Grasping it, he hauled me up over the wall-top. We both sat with our backs against the ramparts, panting with exhaustion as angels raced past us into the final stretch. We would be the last to cross the finish line, but I did not care. All I wanted to do at that moment was sit and rest.

A figure descended to land in the space in front of us. I looked up to see Vassago looming over us. His arms were crossed, and he glared at us with a disapproving scowl.

"Did I tell either of you to take a break?" he snarled.

"No, sir!" we both managed to answer.

"Then get your pathetic selves up and across that finish line!"

"Yes, sir!" we acknowledged, and with effort, stood to do just that.

As we stood, Nakir sunk back down abruptly. He winced, favoring his right hip, the one that had hit the wall when he fell over. Moving to that side of him, I grabbed his right arm and draped it over my shoulder.

"What are you doing?" he asked me.

"We are both finishing this race," I said. "Now come on."

"I do not need your help," Nakir said, but he did not attempt to remove my arm.

Neither of us spoke any further as we walked the remainder of the track. Our fellow recruits stood grouped together, just on the other side of the finish line, silently watching our approach. As we crossed it, they all began to cheer. Agiel stood in front, grinning from ear to ear. I gave him a sardonic look and said, "What are you smiling at?"

Gently, I removed Nakir's arm from my shoulder and eased him to a sitting position on the ground. Angels flocked to us and patted both Nakir and me on the back, congratulating us on completing the race. Agiel stepped up to us.

"You are looking at the new unit leader," he proclaimed.

"You won?" I was incredulous. "How?"

"After you and Nakir took each other out on the wall, I was able to take third place behind Valac and Belial. With you two finishing last, that left me as the overall points leader."

Nakir rose to his feet. I could tell as he stood that his hip had healed. He stepped up to Agiel and held out a hand. "Congratulations," he said.

"Thank you, Nakir." Agiel took the offered hand. "If it had not been for your accident, it would have been impossible for me to catch up. You are a strong and worthy contender."

Nakir nodded. I was impressed at his acceptance of the situation. He did not seem to hold any resentment toward Agiel for having taken the prize he coveted, nor did he appear overly disappointed at having lost the command of the unit. He had retained his honor and proven himself worthy to be a legionary of the Morning Star. That was apparently enough for him, and I supposed it should be enough for me as well.

Vassago ordered us to form up. Once we had, he addressed the unit.

"Alright, you pathetic excuses for angelic hosts," he began in his typical mocking tone, but then his voice changed to one that perhaps more resembled magnanimity. "You have completed the final challenge. As unlikely as this outcome was, you have all made it into the Morning Star Legion. Congratulations."

Somebody let out a whoop, and the cheering began anew. For once, Vassago did not call for order or silence. He stood with his arms crossed over his chest, and for the first time since I met him, he smiled.

Agiel and I embraced. We had proven ourselves worthy to be counted among the ranks of the Elite Guard. Not only that, but we had formed a bond with these angels who had once dismissed us as upstarts. Nakir and Valac walked up to us, and we exchanged congratulations. More than anything, the fact that we had earned their respect proved we had accomplished something significant.

We were still offering our mutual felicitations when Agiel, Valac, and Nakir all stopped speaking and peered past me. Puzzled, I turned around to find Vassago standing before me. The hum of voices faded away, and I understood without looking that the rest of the unit was watching with rapt anticipation. Vassago's expression gave nothing away. We both stared at each other for a long moment. Then, without a word, the former instructor held out a hand to me. I took it, and the angels of the unit erupted into cheers once more.

"I knew you could do it," Vassago said to me. "All you needed was the right push."

"Thank you, sir," I said and meant it.

He sneered in mock derision and replied, "Don't get sentimental on me now, Musician."

I laughed. "I won't, sir."

As Vassago turned away, Agiel grasped me by the shoulders and laughed triumphantly. My friend and I beamed at each other. We were legionaries of the Morning Star, members of the elite guard. The dream had become a reality, and our lives would never be the same. It was one of those moments when you knew everything was about to change.

If only I had understood how right I was, and at the same time, how very wrong.

Part Two

The War In Heaven

"Now war arose in heaven, Michael and his angels fighting against the dragon. And the dragon and his angels fought back, but he was defeated, and there was no longer any place for them in heaven. And the great dragon was thrown down, that ancient serpent, who is called the devil and Satan, the deceiver of the whole world—he was thrown down to the earth, and his angels were thrown down with him." (Revelation 12:7-9)

Chapter 14

The Interruption

"If only I had understood how right I was," the angel said, "and at the same time, how very wrong."

Malachi paused in his oration, an odd look coming over his face. Paul was puzzled by it until he heard the latch of the door squeal as it was dragged across the metal of the locking bar. The door swung open, and two guards entered the small cell. Paul saw them clearly and distinctly in the light provided by Malachi's aura, and he wondered what they would do when they spotted the angel. But then he watched them make their way across the cell, carefully and slowly. One of the guards carried an oil lamp, but he still strained to see. Paul knew then they could not perceive the angel, nor the light he exuded.

The guards placed small ceramic bowls next to the sleeping bodies of the prisoners. They did not bother to wake their charges, but simply left the bowls within reach for when the prisoners would eventually rouse themselves. One of the guards, the one who held the oil lamp, placed a bowl on the ground beside Paul, and noticing that he alone was awake, said to him, "Time to eat, prisoner."

Paul nodded in acknowledgment and watched as the other guard stepped over to the prone figure of Silas, placing a bowl there as well. That guard hesitated over the unconscious missionary.

"Is he dead?" the guard closer to Paul asked.

"No," his companion said, "I don't think so."

"You'd better be sure. If he dies, it will be both our skins."

The guard near Silas knelt beside him and held a hand in front of his face. After a couple of heartbeats, he dropped the hand and sighed with relief.

"He's breathing."

"Thank the gods," the guard next to Paul whispered.

"I didn't mean to hit him in the head. The rod got away from me."

"You enjoy giving beatings too much. One of these days you're going to kill someone, and then it'll be you strapped to the pillar."

The other guard waved a dismissive hand at his companion and stood up. He walked past the first guard, who still stood close to Paul, and left the cell muttering. Malachi watched all of this in silence.

The first guard turned back to Paul. "How are you feeling?"

It took Paul a moment to realize the jailer was speaking to him. Uncertain whether he was expressing genuine concern or mocking him, Paul gave a curt reply. "I will survive."

"I'm sorry for your friend," the jailer offered with what appeared to Paul to be sincere regret. "Sometimes Minos forgets himself."

"I appreciate your concern," Paul said, more graciously this time.

"Do you really believe in just one god?"

The question caught Paul off guard. He had expected the jailer to leave as abruptly as he had come in. Now it seemed he might genuinely be interested in learning more about him. The instincts of a missionary took over, and Paul sat up straight.

"We do."

"So, you don't worship Zeus or the other gods?"

"No," Paul said. "There is only one true God, and He is the creator of all things. He sent His Son to die for our sins so all mankind might be saved and have eternal life."

"Your god died?"

Paul smiled patiently. "God is three-fold, meaning He manifests himself in three persons, the Father, the Son, and the Holy Spirit. All three are God, but they are also distinct. The Son, Jesus Christ, took human form and walked among us. He was crucified by the Romans, and His death served as a sacrifice for all mankind. But He rose from the dead on the third day, and later ascended into heaven to sit at the right hand of the Father."

"So, he's alive?" the jailer asked.

"He is."

"But why would he do that? If he's a god, why would he sacrifice himself?"

"Because we are His creation and God loves us as His children."

"Our gods don't love us," the guard said. "The most we can hope for by worshiping our gods is to stave off their wrath."

"They are false gods," Paul retorted. "The one true God knows you and loves you. He died to save you from your sin."

"What is sin?" asked the jailer, and to Paul's surprise, he squatted down beside him on the cold stone floor.

Paul glanced over at the angel, who sat motionless and silent. Malachi smiled at Paul and nodded to him encouragingly. The missionary turned back and continued.

"Anything that is evil, immoral, or contrary to God's law is sinful and serves to separate us from God. If we are to be pardoned, something innocent must be sacrificed in our place."

"I sacrifice to my gods."

Paul nodded in understanding. Many peoples of the earth made animal sacrifices. These votive offerings were intended to please their false gods and win their favor. In return, they would expect help from their idols, a good harvest, safe childbirth, or health and long life. The Jewish people also offered sacrifices to God, but for a wholly different reason. It was important for Paul to help the jailer understand the distinction between the two practices.

"My people, the Jews, sacrifice to the Lord in atonement of our sins, for only through the shedding of blood can sin be washed away. But, those sacrifices are temporary and imperfect. No matter how pure and blameless the lamb, it is still of this world and thus an imperfect sacrifice. Therefore, God the Father sent His Son Jesus to die in our place."

The guard shook his head. "You have strange ways. It's no wonder the magistrates consider you dangerous men. Your beliefs are odd, which is none of our concern, but teaching those beliefs to the citizens of this province is not wise. We try hard to be good Romans. Talk of our gods not being real offends the established order."

"I know," Paul said. "I realize it won't be easy to get the people of Philippi to listen, but I must try. It is my mission and purpose."

"I would advise you to go somewhere else where your teaching would be more welcome. You've already been punished once for your mission. The magistrates will meet tomorrow to decide what to do with you. If you can reassure them you will move on from here and not return, they'll likely be happy to let you go in peace. But, if you antagonize them further, you may never leave here alive."

"I appreciate your concern," Paul said, truly touched by the humanity of the jailer.

"I'm not like Minos. I don't enjoy hurting people, but if you keep up this teaching, I may not be able to save you."

Paul smiled and laid a hand on the jailer's shoulder. "I am already saved. All your magistrates can do to me is end my mortal life, and by doing so, release me from my earthly bonds. If it's God's will for me to join Him in Heaven, so be it. If not, He will provide. Either way, I am content."

The jailer shook his head in amazement at the faith and resolution of this prisoner. He had never met anyone so confident in his beliefs. He wished he had as much conviction in his own gods, and he wished his gods cared about him as much as the prisoner believed his did. Still, he had done his best to advise him. If he chose not to heed his advice, his conscience would be clear. Standing, he made his way to the door but paused to look back before exiting.

"I hope for your sake you're right in your beliefs. Your God sounds like one worth worshiping. I just hope He's worth dying for."

Then he was gone, the door shut and bolted behind him. Paul looked back to Malachi, who sat waiting.

"I think you may have gotten through to him," the angel said, smiling.

"We'll see." Paul sighed.

"It's interesting to hear you speak of sin. What you said about its effect is very true. It does create separation from God. What I sometimes think you humans forget, though, is that sin did not originate on earth. Your scholars and teachers like to talk about the concept of the original sin, that which the first man and woman committed."

"Adam and Eve," Paul acknowledged.

Malachi nodded. "The belief that sin originated with Adam and Eve in the Garden of Eden is only partially true. While sin originated in humanity at that point, that was not the first sin. No, the original sin was committed by angels in Heaven. I have explained how angels are singularly susceptible to the sin of pride. It was Lucifer's pride that led to his fall and expulsion from Heaven, but it wasn't a sin he committed alone."

"You refer to the other angels who rebelled with him."

Malachi hesitated before answering. "Yes. A full third of the hosts of Heaven rebelled against God, many of them my friends."

Malachi stared into empty space for a long while. There was sadness in his eyes, those intensely powerful orbs that glowed bluish white. It seemed to Paul he would weep if he were able, but apparently, he was not. Paul gave him the time he needed and waited patiently for him to continue.

The angel shook himself out of his reverie. "I apologize. Even now, it's difficult for me to speak of this."

"I understand. If you would rather not continue, I will respect that. You have shared so much with me already."

"No. I made you a promise, and in a way, I find it comforting to talk about it with someone."

Paul nodded. "I do have a question if you don't mind."

"Of course."

"It's clear to me Lucifer was nostalgic about the time before Heaven grew, and I can see how the new creation made things worse for him. But what pushed him over the edge and led him to attempt to overthrow God? Moreover, what made him think he could do so? Surely, he must have known he could not assail the power of God. What made him think his rebellion could possibly succeed?"

Malachi smiled. "There you hit upon the crux of the matter. To answer the last part of your question first, I refer back to pride. High order angels, like Malphas, fully believed Lucifer was somehow akin to God, and his skewed doctrine had infected the ranks of the Morning Star Legion. Because Lucifer had been extant alongside God before any of the rest of the angels, some of the host mistook that to mean his power was comparable to that of the Almighty.

"I was exposed to this propaganda shortly after the events I just described. Following the foot race, Vassago brought us together with the other units of the training division. We had experienced little interaction with these other recruit units during our training, but now that it was concluded, we began to mingle and compare stories. I was shocked to learn how completely many of them had immersed themselves in the ideology of the legion.

"Many of them spoke of rumors of a hidden 'truth' regarding the early days of heaven. This alternative history was based on the belief that God had poured so much of His power into Lucifer at the time of his creation, that Lucifer had become like God. They reasoned that was why the angels created after Lucifer possessed dimmer auras. God could no longer afford to put so much of Himself into His creations.

"It is nonsense, of course, but it seems that over time, Lucifer came to believe the idea himself. He lived in a bubble surrounded by angels who revered him and constantly proclaimed his power and glory. In time, he convinced himself they were right, that he was akin to God. He began to look at the Almighty as, if not quite an equal, at the very least, barely superior."

Paul nodded in understanding. "So, at some point, Lucifer became discontented with the order of things in Heaven, and not only did he wish to confront and displace God, but by then he had come to believe he might actually be capable?"

"Exactly."

"But what about the first part of my question?" Paul pressed. "What caused him to reach his breaking point, to decide to actively rebel against the Lord?"

"Again, pride. He felt insulted by the Lord's new creation. Every new wonder God brought into existence detracted, in his view, from his own personal glory."

"Was he already planning rebellion then, when you joined his legion?"

"I don't think so, at least not at first. I think he was preparing without a clear objective when the new creation first began. He grew more resentful as the days passed, but I don't think he finally decided to revolt against God until the day the Lord made what Lucifer viewed as the most outrageous and demeaning creation of all."

"Which was—" Paul prompted, knowing the answer.

"You."

Chapter 15

The Announcement

Of course, when I say you, I do not mean you personally, but mankind. God was about to complete the scope of His creation, and that final product would prove to be the catalyst for the crisis to come.

Everything God had created up to that point was a curiosity which, although spectacular and interesting, remained on the periphery of our awareness. None of the host had yet been permitted to venture beyond the borders of the Holy City. We could see the stars, but we had not visited them. We knew of the earth, but we had not beheld it. All this was happening as though seen from afar, like looking down from a mountaintop at a bustling town below. It was there, perceptible and observable, but we were not a part of it. In a way, it had not yet become real to us.

All that changed on the sixth day of the Lord's creation. The entire populace of Heaven formed up on the training ground for the proclamation ceremony. But first, the hosts of Heaven would witness the graduation of the Morning Star recruits.

A whole array of dignitaries took turns stepping out onto the high balcony to address the assembled hosts in commemoration of the occasion. After several other instructors had spoken, Vassago stepped to the dais. He outlined the rigors and trials we had overcome and spoke of his pride in this group who had achieved such a monumental honor. Then he shocked me by referencing Agiel and me.

"We even had two members of the Mighty Trumpet legion who stepped forward to join the ranks of this august body. They were at a significant disadvantage, not being warriors, yet they persevered. They worked harder than any angels I have ever had the pleasure to train, and they earned the right to stand next to us as brothers. This, more than anything, demonstrates the honor and prestige of the Morning Star. For members of the worship corps to train on their own time and on their own initiative for the hope of one day being allowed to prove their worth, shows the dream of being counted among the ranks of the elite guard is held in the heart of every host of Heaven."

I could hardly believe what I was hearing. It had been a pleasure to train us? Perhaps I had misread Vassago after all. Maybe he had just been testing and pushing us. Still, it was difficult to accept that he was simply performing his duties as an instructor and had never held any real animosity for me. Part of me thought he was rewriting history considering our success. After all, if he could not stop us from graduating, he might as well take credit for it.

Next, Malphas stepped to the dais. No creature has ever unnerved me like Malphas. He did not gesture with his hands the way Vassago did or sweep his gaze to take in the entire audience as Lucifer would. He stared straight ahead and spoke matter-of-factly with the coldness of a leopard stalking its prey. Perhaps I was merely in the direct path of his unwavering line of sight, but those cold, narrow eyes seemed to be fixed on me the entire time. He spoke of dedication and loyalty to the legion, and to one another.

"The Morning Star Legionnaire is part of something much greater than himself. He does not pine after renown for his own sake, but for the greater glory of the unit. He does not think of his own wellbeing, but that of his brethren. He subjugates his will and sacrifices his desires for the greater good of the legion, for he is the legion, and the legion is he."

This speech was met with roaring applause from the members of the Morning Star, veterans and recruits alike. I could not help but notice that not once did Malphas reference God or His glory. The disconcerting thoughts returned, and I was no longer able to dismiss them so easily. I tried to remind myself of how Agiel had explained away my misgivings, but the rationalizations eluded me.

Lucifer was the last to speak. As he stepped to the podium, it seemed the entire host of Heaven erupted into raucous cheers. He beamed as he took in the adulation of the crowd. His smile was broad, his face warm, and he reached out his arms as though he would embrace us all at once. This only caused the roar to increase, and it was a long time before the cheers died down enough for him to continue. I noticed he did not attempt to quiet the crowd or cut short their adoration. Finally, the roar died away, and Lucifer lowered his hands to speak.

"Angels of the heavenly host," he said in a grand, measured tempo. "I am honored by your warmth and sincerity. Please join me in congratulating these who have overcome so much to prove themselves worthy to stand with the hosts of the elite guard."

The crowd erupted into a fresh series of cheers, and again, Lucifer did nothing to curtail the collective show of adoration. When the assembly did, at last, come to order, he focused in and spoke to us, the graduating class, directly.

"You have come a long way. I remember when Heaven was a fraction of the size it is now before any of you were created. I was there when each one of you came into existence, and I have watched your progress with the care and attentiveness of a loving father."

I gasped aloud, instantly hoping no one noticed. Did Lucifer just compare himself to the father of the angels? The Almighty was our father, God the Father.

I cut my eyes left and right, attempting to gauge the reaction of those around me. I saw nothing to indicate that anyone in my own unit was disconcerted by these words. If anything, they beamed with pride, and a few grinned unabashedly. Shifting my gaze over to my old unit, I saw that some faces appeared to show discomfort with Lucifer's words, but not the shock and outrage I expected. Apparently, the hosts of the Mighty Trumpet and Flaming Sword legions did not comprehend the true meaning of his words. Perhaps a few of them found his choice of phrase a bit inappropriate, but no one appeared to grasp the full implications.

Perhaps I was misreading the situation, but I did not think so. I was beginning to appreciate just how well the leaders of the Morning Star had insulated the legion from the rest of the Army of Heaven. Unless you were a part of the legion, unless you experienced the culture first hand, it was impossible to grasp the extent of the indoctrination we were exposed to. Seen through the lens of the legion's belief system, I knew it to be more than just a poor choice of words. It was a manifesto.

Still, none of my concerns were actionable. All I had was a feeling that things were not quite right with Lucifer and his legion. I had heard rumors, yes, but those were only rumors. In any case, what could I do about it? Should I go and tell Gabriel or Michael my concerns? They were well acquainted with Lucifer's propensity for self-glorification. Gabriel told me as much and warned me about it before I left the Trumpet legion.

Furthermore, I had no reason to suspect a crisis was imminent. I would like to be able to tell you I foresaw what would happen next, that I fully recognized the danger we were all in, but I did not. I had concerns, yes, but no conception of how deep this rot went or how close we were to an irreparable breach. Besides, who was I to challenge the foremost angel in Heaven? Who was I to question the Morning Star?

I pushed these thoughts to the back of my mind as Lucifer concluded his speech and we were proclaimed full members of the Morning Star Legion. We were each dressed in the formal attire of the elite guard, a gleaming set of lamellar armor trimmed with gold, and given a mark of our station, a bursting star, to wear on our chest plates.

When the graduation ceremony concluded, Lucifer moved aside and allowed Zadkiel to step forward. The trumpet sounded and, as he had done for the last five days, Zadkiel proclaimed the words of the Lord. However, this time it was with an announcement that would shake the foundations of Heaven.

"The Lord God Almighty has completed His new creation. He has said, 'Let the land produce living creatures according to their kinds: the livestock, the creatures that move along the ground, and the wild animals, each according to its kind.' He has made wild animals, all sorts of creatures that move along the ground, and he has said, 'Let Us make mankind in Our image, in Our likeness, so that they may rule over the fish in the sea and the birds in the sky, over the livestock and all the wild animals, and over all the creatures that move along the ground.'"

A profound silence lingered as Zadkiel finished speaking. The announcement that God had created something called man in His own image, sent shockwaves through the assembled masses. What did it mean for mankind to be created in the image of God? Did that place man higher than the angels? The Lord had given man dominion over all the earth, so it followed that he would have a highly prominent place in the Lord's new order. The old question reasserted itself. Where did that leave us?

The next announcement Zadkiel made, however, overrode our questions and concerns. For the time being, elation would overcome apprehension.

"The Lord God has proclaimed that the angels of Heaven may depart the gates of the Holy City and visit the new earth the Almighty has created."

There was a sudden eruption of excited murmuring until the staff came down sharply, the echoing crack silencing the assembled crowd. Once order had been restored, Zadkiel continued, "You may observe and interact with the terrain, plants, and animals which God has created, with one exception. You may not interact with or make yourselves known to the man. You are beyond the normal perception of this creature, and it is the will of God for him to remain ignorant of your presence."

This statement brought a measure of peace to my mind. If the man could not perceive us, then he could not be intended to rule over us. Perhaps we did not have anything to be concerned about after all. But those thoughts were secondary to the excitement of being allowed to leave the gates of Heaven and venture into the new universe.

Lucifer did not seem to share this excitement. Indeed, he appeared annoyed. Perhaps he was displeased that this news had overshadowed the graduation ceremony. Perhaps he did not like that all the hosts of Heaven would be allowed to leave and visit the new creation, rather than him receiving an exclusive first look. It might have been both. I never found out for sure, but neither possibility would surprise me. I had begun to develop an understanding of Lucifer. His arrogance predisposed him to be offended by anything that he interpreted as an affront to his prestige or dignity.

"You may spend the remainder of this day on the earth," Zadkiel said. "Afterward, you must return to Heaven, for the Almighty has declared tomorrow a day of rest. The day after that, the Triumphant Processional shall take place, and we shall glorify the Lord for His power and majesty.

"As it is the will of the Lord," he concluded.

"Let it be so!" all the voices of Heaven boomed.

"Dismissed."

For a few moments, we all looked around at each other, not certain whether we were really permitted to depart. Should we immediately go to the City gates? Everyone appeared to be waiting for someone else to decide. Then Lucifer launched himself into the air, and the other archangels did the same. That was enough for most of the rest of us, and we likewise took flight, heading for the boundary of Heaven. As we arrived, a large crowd formed in the open space in front of the gates, which were still shut. Lucifer was there, speaking with the cherubic gate guard while the rest of the host waited, somewhat less than patiently. I landed off to the left of the main body, and others of my unit landed nearby. Agiel walked up to me, flanked by Nakir and Valac.

"What is the delay?" he asked as though I had not landed only a few seconds before him.

"I have no idea," I replied, craning my neck to better see what was happening ahead of us.

"The gates are still shut," Valac pointed out unhelpfully.

We heard a shout and the roar of cheers. Then Nakir said, "Look! They are opening!"

Indeed, the gates were opening, but no one made a move to go through them. We understood why a moment later when the melodious voice of Lucifer drifted over the crowd to reach us.

"Hosts of Heaven, we are about to depart. I urge you to be cautious and remember the instructions given to you by Zadkiel. Do not allow the mortal creations of this earth to perceive your presence. They are lower creatures and would likely be terrified to behold the power of an angelic form."

I got the sense Lucifer was attempting to assert his authority by giving this speech. It was not necessary to remind us of Zadkiel's directive but doing so allowed him to take control and create the illusion that he was the one giving us permission to visit the earth.

"Now, are you ready?" Lucifer asked.

"Yes!" a chorus of affirmative responses erupted from the anxious throng.

"In that case," he said grandly, as though it were all his doing, "let us go!"

He was the first one through the gates, and none of the hosts behind hesitated to follow his example. We launched ourselves into space, beginning our journey to visit the new creation. In my glee, I looked back to locate my brothers, Agiel, Valac, and Nakir, only to realize they were not behind me as I thought. There were so many pairs of wings flying through space that it was difficult to see, but I eventually located them, still standing before the open gates of the City. I did not understand why they lingered in Heaven when we were, at long last, going to explore the new universe before us.

Then I saw someone else standing there, conversing with them. At first, I could not tell who it was. Then I spotted the black hair and recognized the unmistakable form of Malphas. I wondered, why had he held those three back? I briefly considered returning to join them, but curiosity and the excitement of viewing the Lord's creation overrode that idea. Agiel and the others would just have to catch up to us. I was not waiting. I was going to visit the earth.

Chapter 16

The Garden

We arrived at the new earth as the sixth day was waning. The star closest to the planet, what you call the sun, lay behind me and bathed the earth in a light that was warm against my back in the otherwise stark coldness of space. As a body, the hosts of Heaven descended upon the earth like a swarm of locusts.

My first view of your world was from high above, and I was struck by how vast it is. There were great blue bodies of water, that enigmatic substance of which we had been told. And there was so much of it! Indeed, the world appeared to be made up mostly of water with a few giant slabs of land here and there. As I drew closer, I managed to discern more detail in the land below, which at first appeared only as alternating smudges of green and tan.

I flew over dense forests and vast grassy plains where herds of animals roamed to and fro. I soared over enormous stretches of sandy desert that appeared lifeless until I got much closer, and then I realized life was everywhere. I gazed at high mountains topped with snow and low valleys carpeted in rich grasslands. Everywhere across the landscape roamed the animals the Lord God had created to populate the earth. They ran, they swam, and they flew.

Looking back up into the sky, I spotted something far off in the distance. At first glance, I thought it might be a fellow host, but as I approached, I could tell the creature flying high above the earth was no angel. This creature had no aura and was much too small to be one of the host, although it did have wings like ours. I decided to take a closer look and banked left to come up with it.

The creature's feathers fluttered as it glided through the air, very like angelic feathers, but varying in color. The flying animal did not have arms, but it did have legs, and those were pulled back and up against the underside of its tail feathers. Those limbs ended in formidable looking claws with sharp talons. At the other end, its head was narrow and streamlined with intelligent, forward-looking eyes and a sharp downward curving beak that seemed to slice through the air like the tip of a spear.

I followed this majestic creature from the mountains, past a deep valley, to a plain that stretched out for hundreds of miles toward the sea. A mighty river wound across the land far below us, and it occurred to me the creature was following the course of that flowing body of water. I looked up ahead to see that, far in the distance, this great river diverged and split into four smaller rivers, each winding its own way out into the expansive land.

The creature began to descend toward a patch of green foliage, and I followed. A tall hill overlooked the river amongst the trees, and this appeared to be the creature's intended destination. Peering forward, I spotted a lone figure standing atop the hill, peering up at the flying creature. I came to a stop in mid-air a few yards from the standing figure. It did not seem to perceive my presence, so I took a moment to look it over.

The figure was unknown to me, yet oddly familiar. It had the same basic form and shape of a heavenly being but without wings. Its head, arms, and legs were like those of the host, although its skin was not flawless or luminescent like an angel's. The most obvious difference was the lack of any aura, for it exuded no light at all, despite the fact it was naked. This being was mortal, but even so, the creature evoked in me an automatic response of respect, for there was one being in Heaven whom this creature did resemble, right down to the lack of wings; God the Son.

This must be the man we had been told of. He had been made in the image of God and given dominion over the earth, the plants, and all the animals. My friend, the flying creature, completed its descent toward the man, and as it closed on him, he reached out his arm to receive it. The winged animal lighted on the proffered arm and settled contentedly. It peered into the man's eyes as though they communicated without words. After a moment, it relaxed and began preening itself, dropping its beak to scratch at the feathers on its chest. The man stroked its head and back with affection. Then, for the first time, I heard the man speak.

"You are a majestic creature indeed," he said in admiration, his voice soft and soothing, "and you deserve a truly majestic name to match." He pondered for a few moments before saying, "I shall name you Eagle, for you are surely the noblest of all birds."

A bird! This was a bird! Finally, I understood. As noble as this creature was, it could not be intended to replace the angels. The eagle's beak opened, and it let out a loud cry as though in appreciation of its newly given name. Then it flapped its wings to take flight once more and left the man where he stood. The eagle rose high into the air, riding the air currents back to the mountains from whence it came.

The man stood still and watched the eagle for a long time until it disappeared into the distance. Then he turned and walked down a path that wound down the hill toward a lush valley below. This must be the place where he came to receive and name all the birds God sent to him from all over the world. He had worn a path in the delicate grass with his coming and going, fulfilling the work the Lord had given him.

I decided I would follow the man on foot and descended to walk behind him. As we strolled down the path, I with him, but he oblivious of me, I took in the complexity and diverse beauty of this earth. There were all kinds of species of plant, each entirely unique in minute ways.

And so many animals! From the birds in the sky to the rodents of the field and the fish in the waters, life was everywhere. There were even millions of tiny insects living in and on the ground. I was astounded by the attention to detail the Lord had given this world-scape.

This was no mere façade, meant only for examination at the surface. This was a deep and well-designed world where everything connected. The bees pollinated the flowers which enabled the plants to reproduce. The animals ate the plants, and then their waste fertilized the ground to feed the plants in turn. This world recycled dead and decaying plant and animal matter to clear it of the surface, but also to reuse it to feed and energize the next generation of flora and fauna.

Only the mind of God could conceive of all the intricacies necessary to develop such a complex machine that would sustain itself perpetually and in such harmony of function. Only the incredible foresight of the Almighty could plan a system that would grow, adapt, and change as circumstances dictated to maintain itself indefinitely. I was overawed.

So deep had I been in my reverie, the giant cat took me by surprise. We were rounding a corner on the winding path down the hill to the valley floor when the man suddenly stopped in his tracks. He peered at the massive animal standing in his path, a huge feline creature, tan in color, with a bushy collection of fur around a head that was as high as the man's chest. Its jaws were filled with sharp teeth, dominated by four massive fangs, each the size of one of the man's larger fingers. Muscles rippled beneath its furry skin. I had the sense this noble animal was also highly dangerous to any other mortal creature it might encounter.

It made a low, deep sound with its throat that I felt as well as heard, as though it reverberated through the air and into my body. The creature crouched slightly, its eyes locking on the man, and I half prepared to intervene, but it did not pounce. Instead, it calmly strolled forward and lowered its head, offering it to the man who reached down and stroked the mane of the majestic feline.

"I shall name you Lion," he said in the same voice he had used with the eagle, "for you are surely the king of the beasts."

The lion turned its head and purred as the man scratched one of its ears. I noticed a dark brown patch of fur around one eye, its right eye. I marveled that even within creatures of the same species, the Lord introduced variety and uniqueness to each.

The lion lay down and rolled over, offering its belly to the man, who knelt to rub and scratch it. The lion continued to purr, and its head settled onto the ground in relaxation. After a while, the man stood, and the lion flipped back over onto its haunches. It remained sitting as the man walked away, continuing down the path, and I followed behind, amazed as ever.

The man continued his journey until he came to a tree that stood out from the others. This tree was large and stout, with a plethora of ripe fruit hanging from its branches. The man picked one of these and ate it. As he did, my eyes beheld a sight that struck me with awe and confusion. At the first bite of the fruit, I witnessed an intense white light wash over the man, traveling from his head down his whole body until it faded and disappeared at his feet.

This was auratic light, the same we hosts emit. It appeared for only a moment and was gone just as quickly, but there was no denying it. The power of heaven had been absorbed by the man, which confused me, for was not this creature mortal?

"Amazing, is it not?" a voice behind me said, and I turned to see an angelic presence. When I realized who it was, my face lit up with undisguised pleasure.

"Grigori!" I exclaimed, for it was indeed my old friend from the Trumpet legion, jovial and kind as ever.

"Good afternoon, little brother." We embraced, and he patted me heavily on the shoulder.

"Afternoon?" I asked, confused. He pointed to where the sun hung high in the sky like an orange ball suspended by a string.

"That is the sun, and it is at its zenith. The Lord has called this part of the day afternoon. Later, the sun will begin its descent back toward the ground over there, and it will be called evening. At the end of the day, when the sun has dipped below the horizon, and darkness creeps over the earth, that is night. At that moment, the stars and the moon will be visible in the heavens, and most of the creatures of this world will sleep."

I was amazed, but Grigori was not finished. "Tomorrow, the sun will reappear on that side of the horizon." He indicated the opposite direction. "It will rise again, and that will be called morning. Then the cycle will repeat."

This explanation made it seem as though the sun was circling around the earth. Later, I came to understand that other forces were at work. However, I should avoid too much commentary on that. There are some things mankind will just have to discover on its own.

"You have been busy to learn so much in so short a time," I said to him, impressed.

He shrugged. "Not really. Gabriel learned these things from the Lord, and he told me."

As I nodded in acknowledgement, my attention was drawn back to the man finishing his meal. He tossed the unused portion of the fruit to the ground and rubbed his hands in some of the grass that grew thick and green about the base of the tree. Then he turned and walked right between the two of us, oblivious of our presence. He headed down a path toward a nearby stream, and we turned to follow. As we strolled after the man, I looked back to Grigori, my curiosity apparent.

"You saw the light flash in him," he said, anticipating my question.

"Yes."

"The man is mortal, and without the fruit of the Tree of Life, he would eventually die. God placed this tree here to sustain the man. So long as he eats of it, he is granted a measure of immortality. The effect is fleeting, so he must return daily. What you observed was the briefest flashes of heavenly power being infused into the man. The light is imperceptible to him, of course, but not to us."

"I do not understand," I said. "Why did God make him mortal if He intended to give him the means to maintain immortality? Why make man dependent on the tree?"

Grigori let out a booming laugh and slapped me on the back so hard I stumbled forward a few steps.

"You are asking the wrong person that question! I can tell you what I have learned thus far about what is, but I cannot tell you why. Only one person can do that if He is so inclined."

"Right," I concurred, "and thus far He has not been inclined to explain much of anything."

Grigori cut me a sideways glance, and disapproval flashed across his otherwise genial face. "Take care, little brother," he warned. "The Lord God does not owe us an explanation."

"I know," I responded, abashed. "I did not mean to question the Lord. It is just all so new and overwhelming."

The smile returned to my friend's face. He grasped me by the shoulder as we continued to walk after the man.

"You have a pure heart, Malachi, but I am concerned about some of our other brothers. More than a few have begun to question what the Lord is doing and why. Such doubts are dangerous."

"I have heard it as well, and I have found myself asking questions on occasion," I admitted. "Although, I usually realize what I am doing and admonish myself for my lack of faith."

Grigori nodded. "That is good. We are not perfect like the Lord God, but we should strive to remain pure of thought. That is something I fear everyone in your new legion does not always remember."

I recognized the caution in his words, and I sensed he was probing to determine if I would be receptive to a deeper discussion about the Morning Star. Of course, he had no way of knowing if I had given myself over to the philosophies of Lucifer's legion. It occurred to me there must be many who shared my concerns and Grigori might be one of these. He was ever so gently broaching the subject to see how I would react.

This might be an opportunity to discuss my concerns with someone unaffiliated with the Morning Star. Here was someone with whom I could share my thoughts and fears, who would not explain them away or chastise me for my lack of loyalty to the legion. But as much as the thought of being able to openly express my concerns intrigued and excited me, it also terrified me. What if my legion brothers found out about the conversation? They would ostracize me or possibly even dismiss me from the legion. Could I trust Grigori?

Of course, I could. Grigori was a faithful host of the Trumpet Legion. He lived to worship and glorify the name of the Lord. I had to take advantage of the opportunity to have an open and honest conversation about my fears with someone who would understand.

I had opened my mouth to speak my thoughts aloud when, abruptly, the man stopped in his tracks and knelt. It took me a few heartbeats to realize why, and when I did, I instantly dropped to my knees as well. Grigori did the same, for standing there, just beyond the man and facing him, was God.

Chapter 17

Flesh of My Flesh

It was God the Son, here in the Garden He had created. I realize you met the Lord that fateful day on the road to Damascus, but you were blinded in the encounter and did not see Him. Few mortals have. There are those who met Him during His time on earth, but that was as a human when He became flesh. I am speaking of Christ in His pre-incarnate form.

Whereas the Father is the manifestation of God's Power, the Son is the manifestation of God's Love. He is the physical representation of God in a form with whom we angelic beings can interact and fellowship. He looked like a man, or rather man was made to look like Him, but there was no mistaking Him for anything less than God. His aura shined brighter than ten thousand angels and had no equal in all of Heaven, for that powerful glow was not a reflection of heavenly power as was the aura of the angels. It was the source.

He wore a simple white robe, spotless and pure that shown with the brilliance of a thousand suns. I noted on this occasion that the Lord had subdued His aura, so as not to overwhelm the man. As I knelt before the Son, He gestured with his hands, palms up, in a rising motion. Then gently, He said, "Stand."

I was not sure if he spoke to the man or us. Yet, as the man began standing, so did we. We kept our heads bowed in reverence, but I peered beneath my brow to take in the scene. The Lord stepped up to the man and smiled.

"How are you finding this place?" He asked. "Do you have everything you require?"

"I have food in plenty, Lord," the man replied. "But I am alone."

The Lord nodded in understanding. "I have sent to you all the creatures of this earth for you to examine and name. Have you not found among any of them a helper comparable to you?"

"There is not, Lord. All these creatures are amazing and wonderful, but none are suitable to be my companion."

I was amazed by how casually the man spoke with the Lord. We angels always assumed a very formal demeanor when conversing with God in any of His forms. I began to understand that the man held a different, special kind of relationship with the Almighty. It was apparent to me how important this creation was to the Lord for Him to allow this degree of familiarity. There was more here than the normal bond between creator and creation. It was more akin to how a parent interacts with a small child; nurturing, encouraging, kind. There was love here.

The Lord nodded to the man and turned to indicate a nearby patch of grass. "Rest," He commanded.

The man lay down on the grass, closed his eyes, and instantly fell into a deep sleep. We watched as the Lord knelt over the unconscious form. God reached out with His hand and passed it into the body of the man, pulling out one of his bones, a rib. As His hand withdrew from the man's body, the flesh closed, and there was no indication anything had happened. There was no wound and no scar. The bone itself was clean, white, and dry as though it had not just been pulled from a living body.

The Lord stood and turned to look at Grigori and me, and I reflexively bowed my head further. "Grigori, Malachi, what do you think of My garden?"

"Amazing, Lord!" Grigori exclaimed. "Wonderful!"

He turned to me. "And what about you Malachi? What are your thoughts?"

"I am astounded, Lord. The amount of detail and complexity, the way everything works together, it is fantastic!"

"And yet," He said knowingly, "you have questions you would ask." It was a statement rather than a question.

My jaw dropped, and I found I could not speak. I was not surprised the Lord knew of my questions. He knew everything. But there is a difference between abstract knowledge and being confronted with the reality of that truth. The Lord God had just asked me about my questions. Would it offend the Almighty to voice my concerns aloud? It would do no good to deny I had them, and to refuse to answer would be unthinkable. Therefore, I did the only thing I could. I answered truthfully.

"Many of us do, Lord, but we have faith."

"It is true," He said, but then added, "that many of you do." The unspoken implication of His words, that some also did not, hung thickly in the air. My eyes dropped to stare at the ground in response.

I have always felt more nervous during interactions with the Son than with the other forms of the Trinity, which is counterintuitive. God the Father is the most intimidating, for He is the manifestation of the Almighty's power. But the only time most angels will commune with the Father is during the Triumphant Processional, and since I am kneeling alongside my brothers with my head bowed, I do not find the experience uncomfortable. Then there is the Spirit which fills the Holy City, but that presence is ethereal.

With God the Son, you can look upon His face and know you are in the direct presence of God. That realization is extremely intimidating, at least for me. Also, the Son enjoys communicating with His creations, and although He is kind, gentle, and generous, He is still God. Moreover, He expects us to communicate back, which has always terrified me.

I was terrified at that moment, but I could not depart without being dismissed. After what seemed an eternity, the Lord glanced down at the bone He held in His hand and changed the topic of conversation.

"It is not good that man should be alone. I will make a helper comparable to him."

He lifted the hand that held the rib, palm up, and opened His fingers. The Lord pulled His hand away, and the rib floated there, suspended in midair. As the Lord stepped back, dust began to stir on the ground beneath the bone. A small vortex of air and dust rose and grew, enveloping the floating rib. An intense wind whipped about us as more and more dust was sucked into the whirlwind, obscuring the rib completely now. The wind roared and intensified as the cloud became denser, tightening in upon itself. Then the wind subsided, and the swirling cloud of dust fattened as it slowed, beginning to disperse. Dust settled to the ground, and the vortex faded.

As the last grains of dust settled or were carried off by the wind, I was amazed to see a new figure standing there. This creature was similar to the man, yet different. It had less hair on its body, and its form was slenderer, lither, the features softer and less bulky. There were anatomical differences as well. Of course, you are familiar with the differences in body shape and form between men and women, but at the time, I possessed no basis for understanding why this was the case.

The creature stood still, its eyes closed and unbreathing, for it was not yet alive. Then the Lord stepped forward and opened His mouth. He breathed the breath of life into the still creature, and her chest heaved as she took her first breath. Her eyes flew open, and she moved, arms and legs flexing, discovering their function for the first time. She glanced about and blinked rapidly. Then her gaze settled on the Son, and she bowed her head.

"My Lord God," she spoke for the first time.

The man stirred then. The Lord turned to him and said, "Adam, come here."

Waking, Adam got up and walked over to where the Lord stood with His newest creation. Awe and confusion were apparent on his face.

"What is it, Lord?" he asked as he examined her.

"She," the Son corrected him, "is your helper. I have formed her from a rib I removed from your body. You are of one flesh. Therefore, she will be a suitable companion for you."

Adam examined her, then peering into her eyes said, "This is bone of my bones and flesh of my flesh. She shall be called woman, for she was taken out of man."

The Lord nodded in approval. "You should show her the garden. As with you, she is free to eat from any tree in the garden, including the Tree of Life. However, neither of you are to eat from the Tree of the Knowledge of Good and Evil, which is at the center of the garden, or you shall die."

"We understand, Lord," Adam said. Then he led the woman away to show her the pleasures of the garden.

God turned back to us. "Now he will not be alone."

"Lord," Grigori asked, "do they have no concept of the fact they are naked?"

"They do not," He answered. "They are innocent and possess no knowledge of sin. As such, they will not die so long as they partake of the Tree of Life."

"Amazing," Grigori said.

"I will leave you to explore the garden," the Lord said. Then He vanished. To where God had moved His presence, we could not know, but He was gone from our midst.

I shook my head in amazement. "This is incredible."

"Malachi," I heard a voice behind me say. I turned to see Agiel. Nakir and Valac stood with him a few yards away, and he gestured for me to join them.

"Agiel!" I said with pleasure. "Is this not wonderful?"

"Yes," he agreed, but then he stared at me, his brows furrowing in irritation. I was confused. Seeking to relieve the awkward tension, I gestured to my companion. "You remember Grigori."

"Agiel," Grigori greeted him warmly, "I hope you are well."

Agiel returned his warmth with a cool response. "Grigori." Turning back to me, he said, "Come, Malachi. We must go."

I looked back at Grigori in embarrassment, not knowing what to say. He recognized my distress and relieved it for me by saying, "Go. It was good to see you, little brother."

"It was good to see you as well, my friend," I said, taking him by the hand. "We shall see each other again soon. Farewell."

Nodding, he released my hand and turned to walk away to a different area of the garden.

I stepped toward the trio and threw up my hands in exasperation. "Now, what was that about?"

Nakir appeared irritated while Valac just looked uncomfortable. Agiel wore an expression somewhere in between. He laid a hand on my shoulder and led me in a different direction than the one Grigori had taken.

"I realize you and Grigori were friends in the Trumpet legion, but we are Morning Star now. We need to keep to our own."

I stared at him in confusion. "What?"

"Malachi, the reason we wanted to join the Morning Star legion in the first place was that we wanted to be part of something elite. To be elite, a unit must be separate, held apart from the more common elements of the other legions. Otherwise, we risk losing what makes us special."

I was taken aback. Was he saying I should not socialize with Grigori and the other angels of the Trumpet legion? Was he implying we should segregate ourselves from the rest of the Army of the Lord?

"Agiel, it is Grigori. He is my friend, our friend!"

"I know it is hard, but you need to let go of previous attachments. We do not need outsiders sowing doubt or causing us to question our convictions."

"What are you talking about?" I asked, shaking my head.

"My friend," he said with affected patience, as one would speak to a small child, "you have been slow to understand, but surely you comprehend that we in the Morning Star possess truths the other angels do not."

"What truths?" I demanded, incredulous.

"We know the true history of Heaven because we have the firsthand account of the oldest and most powerful of all hosts."

"Which is?" I prompted, fearing to hear the answer, but unable to simply let it go.

"Lucifer is the prince of angels, but he is more than that. He is the first-born of the Almighty, and as such, he shares a likeness with God. The other angels are too afraid to acknowledge that fact, but we know the truth. That is why we were attracted to the legion because we were attracted to the power of the prince."

I stopped walking and stared at each of the three in turn. I had heard the rumors and knew some angels in the legion held unhealthy notions about the nature of Lucifer, but never had I heard it spoken aloud, much less so blatantly. It took me a long moment before I could find my voice. When I finally did, I was unable to disguise my disgust.

"Think of what you are saying, Agiel. This is blasphemy!"

Nakir spoke up. "That is a term used by those who would deny and suppress the truth. It is the watchword of the ignorant and the tyrannical."

I stared open-mouthed at them while Valac took up the argument. "We should never be afraid to ask questions. Anyone who would tell us to be silent is not interested in the truth."

"What truth?" I laughed in my exasperation. "That Lucifer is somehow like God? Is that what you really believe, that he is in some way comparable to the Almighty?"

"He is," Nakir insisted. "You have witnessed his power for yourself. His aura is blinding in its brilliance, and none of the host compares to him. When the Father created Lucifer, He poured more of His power into him than He intended, and the result was a creature nearly as powerful as Himself."

"Lies!" I accused them. "The Lord God does not make mistakes! He may have made Lucifer more powerful than any of us, but he still pales in comparison to the power of the Almighty!"

Valac shook his head. "That is what they teach us in the other legions. That is what we learn in our histories, but Malphas has told us the older, more accurate truth that has been suppressed and withheld from our brethren." He shook his head slowly, as though in pity. "It is not their fault. They are victims, sad pawns who have been misled to perpetuate a fictional reality, to maintain the status quo."

Agiel spoke up once more. "We have a responsibility to liberate them, to expose the truth so the proper order of things can be restored."

Nakir finished the thought. "So that Lucifer, the Prince of Heaven can take his rightful place at the right hand of his Father, as it was in the beginning."

I threw up my hands in disgust, my patience exhausted. I flicked my eyes from one to the other of them and could not believe what I saw in their faces. They actually believed this lie. They believed Lucifer was a son of God. I stepped backward abruptly, consumed by an overpowering need to separate myself from their company.

"I cannot believe you are saying this," I stammered, "and I will not listen to it any longer." Turning to Agiel, my voice changed to one of despair, and I pleaded with him. "Agiel, we are brothers, the closest of friends. Please, do not do this. Do not place this wedge between us. Recant before there is no hope of redemption."

Agiel shook his head sadly. "This is why Malphas did not speak to you along with us. He felt you were too weak to see the light of truth, that you would reject it. I told him we would speak to you, that we could help you see."

"All I see," I shot back, "are three blasphemous traitors who shall receive judgment when your treachery is laid bare."

"You will see," my former friend said with intense sadness on his face. "In the end, you will understand, all of Heaven will."

I stared at him in dumfounded exasperation. I was repulsed by them and could not abide to be in their presence, so I turned and ran.

I just ran. I tore through the trees and bushes of the garden, throwing myself blindly through any obstacles I found in my path. My head spun as I attempted to come to grips with the shattering truth of Agiel's betrayal, not just of the Lord, but of me as well. He had destroyed our friendship. If I could have wept, I would have flooded the oceans with my tears.

I finally stopped running from fatigue, not physical, but emotional. I walked now with no destination or purpose in mind except to just keep moving forward. My feet seemed to continue of their own accord as though I had no control over them. I was numb.

I stopped when I heard voices ahead of me. Coming back to myself, I found my despair momentarily displaced by curiosity. Remaining quiet so as not to disturb the figures ahead, I moved cautiously through the tall, thick grass until I reached a small clearing. Remaining hidden behind a curtain of plant life, I peeked through a gap in the foliage to see who was conversing in the clearing beyond. The breath caught in my throat as I realized who stood there. It was Lucifer with God the Son, and they were arguing.

Chapter 18

The Accuser

I say they were arguing, but in reality, it was Lucifer who was arguing with the Lord. He gesticulated wildly with his hands as he stomped about, pacing this way and that, all the while, railing against the injustices he saw as having been done to him. The Son stood still, evincing no discernable emotion. This appeared to frustrate Lucifer even further, and he wheeled about to face the Lord as he continued his diatribe.

"I do not understand why You thought You needed to create all this in the first place! Was Heaven not enough for You? Were we not enough for You?"

The Lord said nothing, seemingly willing to allow Lucifer to vent all his frustrations before responding.

"And You did it all without even a mention to me!" he pressed, waving his hands. "I am not saying You needed my approval, but I would have thought You would at least give me the courtesy of foreknowledge. You left me out of Your plans and forced me to find out what happened as it unfolded as though I was one of the common angels!"

I was struck by this different Lucifer. This was not the calm, confident leader of the Morning Star Legion. This was not the smooth, haughty speaker who addressed the masses of heaven from the lectern and evinced such authority. This Lucifer was a petulant child throwing the angelic version of a tantrum. It reminded me of the first time I had seen him without his public demeanor.

I thought back to that day in front of the City gates when he confronted the cherub about wanting to leave Heaven. It seemed a long time ago, although it had only been a few days. I had seen this side of him then as well, the private side, the one the congregation of Heaven was not permitted to see. It made me wonder, which was the real Lucifer? Was the Morning Star we were all treated to in public just a façade, a carefully constructed ideal meant to reinforce his prestige? If so, he was an accomplished liar.

Lucifer continued his rant. "I have been extraordinarily patient and understanding! I did not object when You expanded Heaven and created all the other angels. I did not complain when You stopped spending as much time with me in the Holy of Holies.

"All that was well and good. You are God, and that is Your prerogative. But then You go and do all this!" He spread his arms and turned about to indicate the earth. "You create an entire universe of amusements for Yourself and leave me out of the planning. You did not even tell me You were going into the void! You left me to find out at the same time as everyone else, and from a cherub!"

He infused the last word with the derision one might when referring to an unclean animal. The aura burned white hot in him, and his voice shook the ground around him in his fury. It occurred to me he had been holding onto this rage, burying it deep in anticipation of this interview with the Lord. His anger had not been allowed release for the entire week in heaven as God proceeded with His creation. Lucifer had been confined there without the opportunity to give vent to his frustrations.

He could not discuss them with the other angels in Heaven. That would have breached the veneer he created for himself. Except for that first lapse in front of the palace at the end of the Triumphant Processional, he had purported to know everything the Lord was doing.

That had been the first crack in the armor. His surprise and embarrassment at not having possessed foreknowledge of the Lord's departure had been evident. After that, he managed to reconstruct the image of his position, to restore the illusion that he was privy to the mind and actions of God. He could not admit his ignorance to any in the Holy City without shattering that illusion. He had held onto this anger and frustration for days, and now it was achieving release, like a dam that had been breached, unleashing a torrent of emotion.

"And worst of all," he pressed, his fury unabated, "You go and create this mortal creature, this man, and You give him a soul! You make him mortal, yet You provide a means for him to attain eternal life. It is unnatural, an abomination!"

Lucifer brought his hands up and peered into the palms as though an explanation to the Lord's actions might be found there. He stared at them as he concluded his argument.

"You give this man dominion over the earth and treat him as though he possessed some sort of majesty. He is weak and frail and unworthy of Your affection. It is an affront to me and the other hosts of Heaven. It is insulting, and I will not stand for it!"

The hands came down sharply as Lucifer finished this last statement, and he glared at the Lord intensely, the light of his aura lancing forth. With Lucifer's tirade exhausted, the Lord God spoke for the first time, and although His voice was quiet and calm, it rumbled with barely restrained power. Chills ran up my body as the Lord said, "Listen to Me, Satan."

Lucifer took an involuntary step back. He looked like he would object to this name being applied to him, but he must have found himself unable to speak, for the Lord continued in the same calm, quiet, resonating voice.

"I call you Satan, for you are the accuser of your God. You dare to question My plan and My will. You speak of your dignity and your pride. You speak of an affront to you as though you were entitled to foreknowledge of the plans of God. You speak of insults while insulting the Almighty to His face. You complain that I treat you like a common angel. I tell you, that is what you are and have always been."

The dam broke entirely then. I witnessed Lucifer lose all hold on restraint and reason. His hands formed into fists, and he glowered at the Lord in his fury. His wings shot out to full spread, an impressive sight since Lucifer's wingspan was the greatest of all in heaven.

"I am not a common angel!" Lucifer's aura burned brightly in his anger. "I am the first-born of God, and I will have the respect I deserve!"

The Son shook his head, a mixture of anger and sadness on His perfect face as He said, "Lucifer, I have loved you as I love all my heavenly creations, but that you happened to be created first does not make you any more akin to Me than any of My other angels."

Lucifer leaned forward threateningly. "Lies!"

Then the Lord shouted, and the shockwave of his anger was violent enough to throw Lucifer bodily backward.

"God does not lie."

It was a calm statement but delivered with such power that Lucifer was pinned to the ground for a matter of moments. When he finally regained his feet, he glared at the Lord with such malice, I was certain God would destroy him then and there.

Instead, He said, "I will bring you low, Satan. You have become inflated with arrogance and have caused many of the faithful of Heaven to waiver in their allegiance. You have led them astray, and for that, you must be punished." Lucifer's eyes bulged with shock and horror at the Lord's next words. "I shall remove you from the captaincy of the Army of the Lord and your title of Archangel shall be revoked. You shall be humbled for your pride."

Lucifer's face contorted and twisted into a mask of pure rage as he shouted, "No!" He balled up his fists and advanced upon the Lord, stopping only a few feet from Him.

"I will tell you what I will do, Lord," he said, infusing the word with scorn. "I will claim my birthright. I will ascend into heaven. I will exalt my throne above the stars of God and sit on the mount of the congregation. I will ascend to the heights of the clouds. I will be like the Most High."

"No, Satan," the Lord said, and I shivered as He spoke the words of condemnation. "You shall be brought down to hell, to the sides of the pit."

Lucifer's eyes went wide, and he let out a deafening roar, his face trembling in his rage. He launched himself into the air, soaring high above the trees, and looped about over the clearing where the Lord still stood. Then he let out a shout that caused the air to reverberate and the plants around me to flutter. As he hovered there, a shadow fell across the ground.

The air grew colder, and a roaring sound grew above my head. I looked up to find the sky filled with winged creatures, blocking out the sun in their masses. Tens of thousands of angels flew overhead. They circled the clearing, gathering into a compact cloud of wings that grew ever denser as more and more hosts joined it. Then Lucifer exited the center of the cloud and flew away. His legion, my legion, followed his example, and I watched as they flew off into the distance, following Satan, their leader.

In shock, I brought my head back down to look at the Lord, still standing in the clearing, and I jumped involuntarily when I realized he was facing and looking directly at me.

"Come out of there, Malachi," He said. I trembled in fear, but there was no trace of the anger I had heard in the Lord's voice a moment earlier.

I obeyed, stepping from the foliage and crossing the clearing to stand before the Lord. As I reached Him, the shadow returned. Once again, I heard the sound and felt the wind of thousands of wings beating the air. I looked up, half expecting to see Lucifer returning with his traitorous horde to attack the Lord. I was relieved to see it was the opposite. All around me, angels of the Flaming Sword Legion began landing in the clearing, shaking the ground with the heavy impacts of their descent. They took up defensive positions facing out, forming a wall of warriors that ringed the Lord and me. High overhead, a contingent of hosts remained in the air, circling about in looping patrol patterns.

A massive form descended to land near the Lord. Michael, archangel and commander of the Flaming Sword Legion, strode toward us. I had never been so close to him before, and I was stunned by how formidable he appeared. Although not quite as tall as Lucifer, he was broader and more muscled, a warrior in every way.

His armor glinted reddish in the light of the setting sun, making him look like he was wreathed in flame, an appropriate illusion considering the name of the legion he led.

"Lord God," Michael addressed the Son, bowing, "the enemy has fled. It appears they have taken shelter on a large island far west of here, an island of fire and ice."

"I know," the Lord said. He was reminding Michael that He was aware of all things. This was not meant as a rebuke, but to reassure the hosts gathered around Him.

"What about this one, Lord?" Michael asked. To my shock, I realized he was referring to me!

"Malachi is a loyal host of Heaven," the Lord said. "He stood by Me when the others of his legion gave way to the delusions of Lucifer."

Michael nodded and turned to address me. "What can you tell me about their plan?"

"Nothing, sir," I replied in despair. "They kept me out of their plans until the very last moment. All I know is they seem to believe Lucifer is somehow akin to God and that the 'truth' of that has been suppressed. They wish to see Lucifer raised up to the throne of Heaven to sit alongside the Father as though he were part of the Godhead. That is all I know. As far as their plan of action, I have no knowledge of strategy or tactics, only intent."

Michael gave a curt nod in acknowledgment of my report. His eyes narrowed as he considered the implications. Then he addressed me once more.

"You have proven yourself a capable and loyal host, Malachi. I hereby order your transfer to the legion of the Flaming Sword of the Spirit. You will stand alongside your brother angels against this threat."

In truth, I had not given any thought to my place in the ranks until that moment. It dawned on me I had become a host without a legion, and I was suddenly overcome with the enormity of it all. Lucifer was a traitor, and that meant all the hosts of my former legion were traitors as well, including Agiel. Despair threatened to overcome me, but I could not afford to waste time on my own feelings. This was a moment of crisis, and I needed to stay focused.

Nodding my head in acknowledgment of Michael's orders, I reached up and tore the badge of the Morning Star from my tunic, flinging it to the ground. I was part of the Flaming Sword now. I was still a warrior, but unlike the Morning Star, I had no doubts about the rightness of this legion's viewpoints. They were loyal hosts of Heaven, and I would stand with them against the forces of Satan. Relief flooded over me as, for the first time in a long time, I felt the conviction of knowing I was in the right place.

Michael turned back to the Son and said, "Lord God, I would suggest we return to Heaven immediately. We must assume Lucifer and his legion are planning to attack the Holy City."

The Lord shook His head. "I have designated tomorrow a day of rest. I shall remain here and honor the Sabbath day. You and your legion should return to Heaven and await Me there."

"But my Lord," Michael said, hesitating, "what if Lucifer attacks You here?"

"Are you concerned for My safety, Michael?"

Michael flinched at the Lord's words. One could admire his desire to stand by the Son and protect Him, but was it necessary? Did God need protection? It would be unthinkable to say He did, yet Michael hesitated to leave His side. The archangel's discomfort was apparent, but the Lord relieved him of the obligation to respond to His question.

"Fear not, Michael," He said gently. "Lucifer will not attack tomorrow, here or otherwise. Return to Heaven and await Me there. I shall return after My day of rest, and at that time, We shall have the Triumphant Processional. Then We shall address all the host of Heaven."

Michael nodded. "As it is the will of the Lord, let it be so."

He ordered his angels to depart, and one by one they launched themselves into the air. When it was only the Lord, Michael, and me standing in the clearing, Michael turned to me. I assumed he would order me to join the others, but the Lord interrupted him.

"I would like Malachi to stay a moment. He shall join you shortly."

"As you wish, my Lord," Michael said. A moment later, he too rose into the sky.

As the host departed, I expected the light of the sun to return, but it had dipped below the far horizon. God the Son and I were left in darkness, our auras lighting the clearing. I could not guess why the Lord wanted me to stay, but I bowed my head and waited for His words.

"Thank you, Malachi," He said. I was taken aback. What did the Lord God have to be grateful to me for? I was about to say as much when He continued. "You alone of all the Morning Star legionaries stayed loyal. You were forced to choose between loyalty and your dream, between your friends and Me."

"There was no choice, Lord God," I said without hesitation. "The Morning Star was never Lucifer's legion, it was Yours. That is a fact he forgot. It is true I am deeply saddened by my loss of Agiel's friendship, but I did not abandon him. He abandoned me when he asked me to choose between him and loyalty to You. As I said, there was no choice."

The Lord nodded. I thought He would dismiss me, but he did not. It seemed He wished to talk further.

"You wonder why I did not stop Lucifer." Again, it was a statement rather than a question.

"Yes, Lord," I answered. "You must have known, yet You allowed him to gather his forces."

"I did. I have known since the day I created Heaven that Lucifer would betray Me. I knew he would grow increasingly prideful and resentful as I expanded Heaven, and I knew this new creation would serve as the catalyst for his final betrayal."

"Then why—" the unutterable phrase died on my lips.

"Did I continue?" the Lord finished for me. "Because I have a plan, and the knowledge that Lucifer would not approve did not factor into My decision."

I nodded my head in acknowledgment.

"I knew he would disappoint Me, just as I know that one day, man will disappoint Me. Yet, that does not deter Me from My plan. Indeed, knowing what will occur in advance should demonstrate just how important this plan is to Me. I am willing to incur all the disappointments and betrayals, knowing full well they will occur because I also know that in the end, the full scope of My plan shall come to fruition. Even the disappointments are critical to the development of the overall design. If I were not prepared to accept all that would occur along the way, I would not have proceeded. However, *I Am*."

"But why not restrain Lucifer?" I asked, emboldened by the Lord's openness and willingness to answer questions. "Why not prevent his treachery and change his heart?"

The Lord did not answer right away. His face took on a stern look, and I wondered if I had pushed things too far. Then the look softened, and the Lord's voice took on a more introspective tone.

"You must understand, Malachi. It is important to Me for all my creations to possess free will. The ability to choose is critical to the relationship. If My creations have no choice but to worship Me, then that worship has no value. I may know what will happen, but that does not mean I necessarily direct what will happen. I can, and I do upon occasion. But for the most part, I choose to allow each creation to determine their own choices. In this way, I ensure those choices are genuine and meaningful.

"This is why I have given the angels, otherwise perfect in every way, the capacity for sin. You are immune to most forms of sin, but pride is your weakness. You honor Me by mastering your pride and holding it in check, by not allowing it to tempt you to sin. But to have that opportunity, you must also have the opportunity to do the opposite. Without the potential for sin, there is no victory in overcoming it.

"Lucifer and his angels have chosen the pathway of sin, but the other two-thirds of the heavenly host have chosen to reject sin and remain loyal. That brings glory to My name. If I forced every angel to remain obedient, or if you did not have the capacity for sin through pride, such honorable actions on your part would be hollow and without meaning."

"I believe I understand, Lord." I was beginning to, at least.

"You should go now. Return to Heaven and await Me there. I shall join you once I have concluded My day of rest. Then We shall deal with Lucifer and his legion."

"As it is the will of the Lord," I said, bowing my head, "let it be so."

Without further delay, I shook out my wings and rose into the air. Flying high above the earth, I was struck by how dark everything had become. Without the light of the sun, the features of this world were mere outlines and shadows without definition or color. Even the light of the moon did little to clarify the image.

I realized this was a perfect corollary to how I felt at that moment. I was still the same angel, but I was dull and colorless. I had lost the light that made me recognizable. I had lost my friend. I had lost my dream of being part of the Morning Star. I was like a shadow of my former self.

But as I rose high above the clouds and into the space surrounding the earth, the light of the sun lanced forth from behind the planet, and I felt my spirits rise. I reflected on what certainties I did have. I was on the side of right. I was still a warrior, and I had a purpose, to protect the Kingdom of Heaven from the treachery of Lucifer and his minions.

As I made my way toward heaven, I was full of determination. I had no time for doubts or regrets. I must prepare myself for the coming confrontation. I must prepare myself to face Lucifer, Agiel, and all my former legion-mates.

I must prepare for war.

Chapter 19

The Calm Before the Storm

I returned to Heaven as the day of rest, the Sabbath, began on earth. Things were very different in the Holy City from when I left it. The gates were shut, and angels of the Flaming Sword, dressed in full combat armor, lined the walls. In one hand, they held long spears at the ready while with the other, they grasped large round shields that they held across their chests. The power of their auras stabbed out like beams of light through the eye holes of their helmets as banners flew high above the gates.

There was Gabriel's banner of the Mighty Trumpet Legion, a golden horn on a field of white trimmed with gold. Michael's banner of a literal flaming sword against a field of light blue hung next to it. Unsurprisingly, there was no sign of Lucifer's Morning Star banner, a bursting white star against a field of black.

Then I spotted another banner I had never seen before. The field was white with some sort of creature emblazoned upon it. As I drew closer to the gates, I recognized the animal. This was the same creature I had witnessed the man name in the garden, that most majestic of beasts, the lion. There was also another animal represented beside and overlapping the lion, although I did not recognize this creature. This animal was pure white, and although it did not appear as majestic or formidable as the lion, it did exude an undeniable quality of purity. I did not know whose banner this was, and before I could contemplate further, I was challenged by a voice from the gate.

"Halt! Who goes there?"

I stopped in my tracks and peered up at the parapet atop the gate to see two figures. They held spears and shields, but they were not soldiers of the Flaming Sword. I could tell, even through their helmets, that these were cherubs. As ordered, I identified myself to the gate guards.

"Malachi, of the Morn—" I quickly corrected myself, "of the Flaming Sword!"

The two cherubic gate guards glanced at each other, and one of them said, "This is the loyal Morning Star host we were told to expect."

The other cherub nodded and turned back to me. "Report to headquarters immediately."

"Of course," I responded, but my head was swimming. What could they want with me at headquarters?

As I stepped through the gates, I wondered if I would be questioned and perhaps held accountable for failing to report my suspicions about the Morning Star before the break. Would I be punished for keeping my fears to myself? I decided if that was the case, then that is what I deserved. I should have reported my concerns right away. Instead, I had hesitated and rationalized my silence. If I had come forward, perhaps all this could have been prevented.

Or could it? What of the Lord's words to me in the garden? He said He had known Lucifer would betray Him, and He did not stop him because of free will. In that case, did it matter if I raised the alarm or not? Yet, just because the Lord knew what would happen, did that absolve me of responsibility for doing the right thing?

No, it did not. Just because God knows all things and foresees all things, does not mean our actions do not matter. I had a responsibility to act, and I had failed in that duty. If punishment were due me, I would accept my fate with honor.

I arrived at the headquarters building and made my way to the Archangels' chambers on the top floor. I had never been here before, and the sight of the expansive hall took my breath away. The room was enormous, with massive rectangular banners hanging down at regular intervals. Benches lined the walls where angels in attendance would sit, and a huge circular table dominated the center of the room. The archangels themselves would sit in ornate chairs set around this table. Four such chairs were visible, but one had been removed and set against the wall.

Three figures stood leaning over the table, their palms outstretched and resting on it as they peered at the center. I recognized Michael, Gabriel, and the cherubic captain, Zadkiel. As I came closer, I saw the table displayed a massive map of the universe. At its center, I recognized the system that held the earth, the sun, and the other planets. That was when I realized this map was not static, but a real-time image of the new universe. The planets moved and rotated on their axes while comets and meteors streaked through space. The sheer scope of the Lord's creation was awe-inspiring.

The stars at the edges of the map disappeared as the picture zoomed in upon the earth. The planet filled the table, and we seemed to fly through clouds and descend toward the surface. The image stabilized over a vast blue sea and in the center, an oblong island. The entire landscape was white as though made of ice, but a huge gash ran down the length of the land mass like a vicious scar. A thick liquid, red and orange, erupted from the scar like a belching monster. Something very hot and bright poured forth from this giant rent in the earth.

"What is it?" I heard myself say, and I instantly regretted my temerity, as I had not yet been announced to these commanders of the heavenly host.

All three of the commanders turned to look at me, and I felt I would rather be thrust into that chasm of fire than stand under the intensity of those gazes. However, they seemed to accept my presence, and it was Gabriel, my former captain, who answered my impertinent question.

"It is lava," he said matter-of-factly, "liquid rock. The earth is pulling apart at this place, and hot molten rock from deep within the earth is surging up to spill out onto the surface. As it cools, new rock will form, and the breach will expand. Over time, this process will push the giant land masses further apart. This is an ingenious, dynamic system God has created. Everything about this earth is designed to renew itself. The Lord has thought of everything, of course."

The image zoomed in further until I saw forms moving on the surface of the island, which I now realized was not made of ice after all but stark gray rock blanketed by snow. This landscape was bleak in contrast to the lushness of the garden, but I felt it was appropriate, for I recognized the forms that moved across its surface. They were the fallen angels.

I spotted him then, Lucifer, sitting on a gray and white boulder with several high-ranking Morning Star angels gathered around him. Malphas was there, as were Vassago and Agiel. I felt the anguish return at the sight of my friend. He looked so starkly different. His expression held an intensity I had never seen. Anger had etched itself onto the features of his face. I involuntarily took a step back, but Gabriel reached out a hand and pulled me forward again.

"Watch," he instructed me, "and listen."

I heard it then; voices. They talked over one another, and I could not make out what any particular angel said, but we were definitely hearing as well as seeing. Lucifer held up a hand, and those gathered around him gradually fell silent.

"Friends," he said in a voice that was oddly pitched and distant. "The long-awaited day of our deliverance is at hand!"

The fallen host cheered, and my body shuddered at the sound. Tens of thousands of angelic voices were raised in celebration of their treachery.

Lucifer continued, "The time has come to take back our birthright!"

As the angels cheered yet again, I noted Lucifer had reverted to his public persona, the confident, smooth, and magnanimous visionary leader. He was motivating his troops with a rousing speech designed to make it appear as though everything he did was for their benefit, while in reality, they were mere pawns in his play for power.

Malphas came forward and stepped up onto the rock, his jet-black hair stark against the icy white landscape. He addressed the crowd.

"Brothers, for too long our captain has been forced to deny his true heritage. For too long he has been compelled to subordinate his birthright to a God who increasingly seeks to marginalize him and create the illusion he is merely a common angel. This outrage has gone on long enough!"

The cheers erupted yet again, and many moments passed before Malphas continued speaking. When he did, it was in a low ominous voice that sent chills up my body.

"Tomorrow, we shall march on the Holy City. We shall confront the forces that have conspired to subvert the truth. We shall compel them to accept the true lineage of our captain and acknowledge him as the true prince of Heaven!"

The roars of the cheering crowd were deafening now as the rebellious angels thrust swords and spears high into the air. Lucifer raised his hands in acknowledgment of his followers, his gaze sweeping over the crowd in a slow, deliberate arc. Then he stopped, and after a brief pause, his head tilted up. His eyes lifted to the sky until I realized, with shock, that he was staring directly at me.

I started backward. Lucifer smiled as though he saw and took satisfaction from my reaction. The picture winked out of existence, and I was left looking at a plain table top in the cavernous room along with the commanders of the heavenly host. If I possessed a heart, it would have been pounding. Gabriel turned to look at me, his expression even more grave than usual.

"So, tomorrow then," he said.

Michael spoke next. "The Lord did say Lucifer would not attack today."

"But how will that attack come?" It was Zadkiel who asked the question.

"Malachi?" Gabriel prompted me.

I had no idea how he would attack and said as much. "I was kept out of everything. They did not trust me."

"But you do know them," Gabriel said. "You understand their personalities, their temperaments, their tendencies."

Michael picked up the thought. "You know their tactics, their organizational structure, and their operational methodology. Based on your experience and training, tell us what you think we can expect."

I thought for a moment, then gave the best assessment I could. "The Morning Star Legion is organized into three companies. The Vanguard unit is led by Lucifer's second in command, Malphas. They are equipped with heavy armor, spears, and shields, and are typically arrayed in phalanx formation. They serve as the forward element, and, as such, will seek to establish a fixed position from which to control the battlefield and the operational tempo of the engagement.

"The second unit is commanded by Abaddon. They are equipped with light armor and short swords only. They will be airborne and have a dual mission. First, they will attempt to establish air superiority and prevent enemy hosts from circumventing the battle lines established by the Vanguard. Secondarily, they will harass and probe the enemy line for weaknesses. As a tertiary objective, if an opportunity presents itself, they will use their speed and maneuverability to outflank the opposing line."

I paused in my oration, but the archangels gazed at me intently, and Gabriel nodded for me to continue.

"The third company was mine, commanded by Vassago. They will be used as auxiliaries and will be employed to shore up any weaknesses as well as to secure the flanks. They will be equipped with lamellar armor as well as swords and spears, but no shields. They are expected to be flexible and move fluidly about the battlefield as needed."

Michael nodded in silent acknowledgment of my assessment while Gabriel pursed his lips. Zadkiel was the only one who spoke.

"Thank you, Malachi. That is most helpful. Now, if you will excuse us, we have plans and preparations to make."

I nodded and turned on my heel to exit the room. I hoped what little I knew about the Morning Star Legion's organization was enough to help Command formulate an effective strategy for the upcoming conflict.

We outnumbered the Morning Star two to one, but half the loyal forces were Trumpet legionaries, untrained for the most part in close combat. In theory, every angel was a warrior of the Army of Heaven, but the reality was that most of them had little practical skill in martial matters. The Morning Star, on the other hand, was the elite guard. Lucifer's troops were better trained, better conditioned, and better organized than either the Mighty Trumpet or the Flaming Sword legions. They were highly motivated and competently led.

And the angels of the Morning Star had one other thing the loyal hosts of Heaven did not.

They had nothing to lose.

Chapter 20

The Battle

When Lucifer and his angels came, it was not as we expected. He did not storm the gates or assault the walls of the Holy City. When he came, it was peaceably and in good order. His legion was formed up in column and marched toward Heaven in the same orientation as it would to lead the Triumphant Processional.

I was standing on the ramparts of the gate next to Michael. He had kept me close ever since my return to Heaven. Whether that was because he valued my advice or because he did not trust me, I could not tell. On the other side of Michael, God the Son stood motionless, staring out at the scene with silent intensity as the angels of Lucifer's legion approached.

The landscape outside the gates of the Holy City does not fall off sharply into the void as it does outside the city walls. There is a large field that spans the area past the gates, and it was across this plane that the Morning Star Legion marched on its approach to the Kingdom of Heaven, the sound of their footfalls creating a kind of thunder that presaged the confrontation to come.

All along the walls, the stolid figures of Flaming Sword hosts stood implacably with their spears and shields at the ready as the angels of Lucifer marched relentlessly toward the inevitable clash. The Lord broke the tension of the moment by turning to Michael and giving an order that drew gasps from the surrounding angels, despite our discipline.

"Open the gates," He said.

Michael turned to Him, and although I could not see his face, I could imagine the shock and horror it held.

"Open the gates?" he asked in puzzlement.

The gate guards must have realized it had been posed as a question rather than a command, but they had all heard the Lord and decided to act on Michael's utterance as an order. They leaned into the heavy gates, the sound of their opening reverberating clear across the Holy City.

"Lord," Michael cautioned, regaining his composure, "with the gates open, I cannot guarantee the security of the perimeter."

The Son turned to Michael, and His expression made it clear that He would not be willing to debate the issue. Michael straightened and assumed the position of attention at this expression of Divine authority. The Lord did not look upon him unkindly, however, and made His meaning clear a moment later.

"As I told you in the garden, on this day We shall have the Triumphant Processional and I shall address all the hosts of Heaven. I am going now to be with the Father. I shall await you at the Palace."

"As it is the will of the Lord," Michael said, "let it be so."

We bowed our heads to the Son as Michael spoke these words. When I once again raised my gaze, the Lord had gone. I turned back to the approaching legion. The thunder of their footfalls was growing louder, and I could recognize distinct faces now. As expected, the legion was formed up by companies, each led by their commander who marched alongside to the right of the column. First came Malphas, followed by Abbadon and Vassago. Lucifer marched in the front of the column, flanked by two standard bearers, each carrying the banner of the Morning Star.

Earlier in the day, before Michael had come to the gates, I asked one of the Flaming Sword legionaries, a host named Jophiel, about the strange new banner that had appeared atop the walls the previous day.

"It is the banner of the Lord," he said. "He has taken on the badge of the lion and the lamb."

I would not understand the full significance of the symbolism inherent in this iconography for some time. However, I sensed a certain poignancy in the selection as it exemplified both the power and purity of the Lord.

The oncoming legion was very close to the gates now. They showed no indication of slowing or stopping, and I recognized the consternation on Michael's face. It went against everything he knew of good strategy and tactics to open a breach for the enemy to simply walk through. He obviously did not like it, but the Lord had made it clear we would have the Triumphant Processional, and it was beginning to look like that would include the legion of the Morning Star. With Lucifer mere feet from the open gate, Michael turned and bellowed an order to his legion that placed us on a collision course with a now unavoidable culmination of events.

"Flaming Sword, form up!"

I joined my fellow hosts in the open space just inside the gate and formed up in line. I was in the front rank, which gave me a close-up view of my former legion-mates as they marched past. Malphas entered my field of view, and he turned his head to lock those menacing narrow eyes onto mine. I fought a powerful urge to recoil from his icy gaze.

Malphas shouted, "Company, eyes right!"

At that order, the entire mass of marching angels crisply turned their heads to the right in choreographed unison. Every angel glowered directly at me as they passed, and those faces contained nothing but hatred and loathing. I was determined not to show any emotion in response. Any reaction on my part would lend credence to the implied accusation of disloyalty. I stared back as the first two companies paraded before us.

When the Auxiliary Company came into view, I found myself staring back against Valac and Nakir in the front rank. Next, came Belial, Marut, and Anamalech followed by the hulking forms of Sargatanas and Agaliarept. Rank after rank of my former friends and brothers marched past me, and the eyes of each locked onto mine in silent condemnation. I have never felt so small.

When Agiel came into view, I feared I might break at last. He alone wore an expression other than pure rage and hate. Worse, he gazed at me with hurt and disappointment, and it took all my power of will to not break my discipline and look away.

After my unit came the remainder of my old company, former angels of the Flaming Sword who now marched on behalf of Lucifer. Halfway through the ranks of the company, Vassago appeared, and when he saw me, his jaw set and his eyes narrowed. His expression seemed to say, "I knew I was right about you."

Then he disappeared from my view. The rest of the legion filed past until, finally, the last rank marched by. As it did, Vassago gave the order, "Eyes front!"

The fact that this order was given as the last rank passed me only, rather than the Flaming Sword Legion as a whole, confirmed that the entire maneuver had been for my benefit alone. The Morning Star had made their opinion of me clear. I was a traitor.

Except that I was not. I was not the one who had turned his back on God. I was not the one who held illusions of divine power and glory. I was a loyal host of the Army of the Lord. They were the traitors.

As the last of the Morning Star legionnaires passed the front rank of the Flaming Sword's formation, Michael gave the order to right face, and I obeyed. By turning, we were now in column formation, and as the order was given to forward march, we fell into place behind the Morning Star Legion on our way to the Mount of the Lord. Beginning the ascent up the winding road, I heard the horns and singing of the Mighty Trumpet Legion behind me and knew they had formed up behind us as well. The Triumphant Processional was proceeding like it always had as though nothing had changed.

I have already described the course and maneuvers of the parade of hosts that is the Processional of the Lord, so I will not do so again. However, when at last we reached the courtyard of the Palace and formed into line once more, I found myself looking at the scene from a wholly different perspective. I had always formed up on the right with the Mighty Trumpet legion. Now, being part of the Flaming Sword, I stood in the center of the overall formation, just behind where the Archangels marched forward to present themselves before the Lord. Indeed, I found myself staring at Lucifer's back as the maneuvers were completed. Michael stood to his left and Gabriel to his right, each of them one step behind.

As one, all the hosts of Heaven, including Lucifer, dropped to one knee and bowed our heads. An ominous silence descended upon the scene as we waited. My body tensed, the stress and energy of the moment mounting within me. Then the heavy golden doors of the Holy Palace swung outward, and we waited in excruciating silence before, at last, I heard the booming voice of the Father.

"Lucifer, son of the morning, stand and come forth."

Although it was technically against protocol, I raised my eyes slightly and peered underneath my brows at the scene before me. Lucifer stood and stepped forward. His head was still bowed, and I assumed his eyes were on the ground as he approached the Throne of God. His body obscured my view of the Father, which was why I dared to look at all. The ultimate power of the Lord shown out and around the silhouette of Lucifer's body. Indeed, the captain of hosts appeared dark and in shadow beneath the brilliance of the Father, as though he possessed no aura at all in comparison.

When Lucifer stopped and stood to attention, his head still bowed, the Father spoke once more. "Lucifer, first of My creations, why have you betrayed Me?"

"You are the one who has betrayed me, Lord," he said, his voice thin and cold as though he were far away. "You have denied me my rightful place at Your side. You denigrate me before the lesser hosts of Heaven and treat me as one of the common angels when You know I am much more. I am Your firstborn, and I deserve to be worshiped as such. I demand You recognize my claim and acknowledge me as Your son!"

I now understood the reason Lucifer had not assaulted the walls of the city and instead approached peacefully. He still hoped he could attain his goals without outright rebellion. He thought the threat of violence might allow him to gain the acknowledgment he so desired without having to resort to actual warfare. He would be disappointed in that ambition.

"I will not acknowledge what is not true," the Father replied. "You have forgotten yourself and become deluded in your pride. Did you create any of what you see before you? Did you stretch forth your hand and bring the host into being? Did you construct the universe and the earth with a word? Did you breathe the breath of life into man and give him a soul?

"You have done none of these things, for you have no power to create, only to destroy. You have brought yourself low, and not only yourself, but also those who stand with you."

The rage bubbled up in Lucifer as he spoke again. "I am the Morning Star, the prince and true heir of Heaven, and I will have my inheritance!"

"I tell you now, Satan," the Lord proclaimed in a terrible voice, "the only kingdom you shall rule is the kingdom of hell."

With that, I witnessed the aura of the Lord shift, and something unprecedented occurred. God the Father turned his back on Lucifer. Then Satan made a move of his own, just as unprecedented, but much more unthinkable. He raised his head and drew his sword.

Both Michael and Gabriel stood, drawing their blades in response. I stood as well, and hosts rose around me as the entire Army of the Lord readied itself. The Morning Star legionaries followed suit, but no one moved yet. We all stood still and waited, the tension of the moment mounting. It reached critical mass a moment later when Satan let out a defiant shout, and I witnessed the power of his aura erupt in a white-hot explosion of rage.

A searing hot wind slapped me in the face, and I was thrown backward a step before regaining my footing. Michael and Gabriel, who were much closer to the source of the blast, were thrown bodily away from Satan. They rolled across the ground like debris caught in the wind of a storm. Gabriel made it to his feet close to his own legion, but Michael was closer to Satan's troops than his own. As he stood, I recognized the danger of his proximity to the enemy.

That danger manifested itself a moment later when Satan shouted, "Morning Star! Take your birthright!"

That must have been the signal for my former brothers to attack, for the traitorous legion surged forward. In response, I stepped forward with my sword held high and yelled, "Flaming Sword, protect Michael!"

My true brothers ran with me as we launched ourselves to our left to assault the right flank of the Morning Star Legion. Ahead of me, the first of Satan's angels reached Michael. He had barely made it to his feet before they were on him, swords slashing in all directions.

Michael moved at lightning speed, deflecting blows and parrying thrusts. His form appeared to have two legs but a multitude of blurred trunks, arms, and heads as he defended against the assaults of multiple foes. Indeed, the angels who attacked him seemed to move in slow motion, as though they were outside of time and space compared to the archangel.

Michael defended himself mightily, but he could not ward off all his many adversaries much longer. He needed assistance and quickly. I reached him just as I was sure he would be overwhelmed. Lowering my shoulder, I slammed into a small group of Morning Star angels, forcing them back. My momentum carried me forward, and I fell as I broke through the line of assaulting enemies. Loyal angels ran past me as I picked myself back up. I spun around to see that Michael was still on his feet and much less harried now. Two loyal angels stood with him, and there were fewer enemy hosts around to assault him now that the Flaming Sword had engaged the enemy.

The fighting had broken down into small pockets of conflict. My careful description of the enemy's battle plan, how I expected this fray to unfold, had not materialized at all. This was a brawl, rather than a well-ordered and directed battle. This was every angel for himself.

I glanced down and saw one of the enemy hosts I had toppled attempting to stand. I kicked him viciously, my thigh impacting his jaw, and sent him flying backward again. He landed on the ground, and for the moment at least, he did not move. I spun around to assess threats behind me and was just in time to see a spear coming for my throat. Desperately, I brought my sword up and batted at the shaft of the incoming weapon. At the same time, I twisted away and spun, allowing the adversary to rush past me.

A spear is a very effective weapon for maintaining distance and dealing damage while staying outside your enemy's reach, but once you make it past the point, the spear becomes much less of a threat and is difficult to counter with. As I spun back around, I slashed my sword down on the arm of the fully committed spearman. He yelled in pain as my blade bit deep. I continued to spin, coming around again, but this time, instead of attacking with the blade, I struck with the pommel and landed a crushing blow on the spearman's helmet that sent him reeling.

As he fell, I recognized the attacker. You have met him. It was Tannin, the same who you cast out of the young fortune-teller girl. As I told you, he was always taking on more than he could manage.

Turning away from the prone figure of Tannin, I found myself standing alone in an area of the battlefield that was now relatively free of conflict. I paused as I heard something strange coming from my right. It took me a moment to realize what the sound was and why it seemed out of place. Someone was singing.

Turning to locate the source, I could not help but grin as I realized it was Grigori, my old friend, fighting off three Morning Star angels. He did not possess a sword or spear but was using one of the banner shafts like a staff, wheeling it about with blurring speed. He sang a hymn of praise as he engaged the enemy warriors. Bringing the long pole around, he struck a mighty blow on the head of one traitorous host.

"In the name of the Father!" Grigori sang as the enemy angel flew backward, spinning in the air.

"And of the Son!" the words accompanied a backswing of the pole that caught another of the legionaries on the back of his legs, sweeping them out from under him. His helmet smacked against the ground with an audible crack, after which he lay still.

"And of the Holy Spirit!" Grigori finished as he spun and brought the butt of the staff into the gut of the one remaining enemy host. It landed with a deep thud, and the defeated angel doubled over. As his head came down, Grigori brought the shaft of the pole back up, and it met the face of the Morning Star angel with a sickening crack that sent the host flying backward.

As Grigori stood back up, he noticed me and his eyes met mine. "Amen," he said, a broad smile spreading across his face.

Grigori was still smiling as he was abruptly shoved forward from behind by some unseen force. I was confused as the smile melted from his jovial face. Then I spotted it, the point of a spear protruding through his chest plate. I gasped and took a halting step forward as my friend dropped to his knees. I could do nothing but watch helplessly in horror as, with a groan, he keeled over to one side.

"No!" I shouted. I looked up from where Grigori had fallen to identify the angel who had impaled my friend.

It was Nakir. He had been cut in at least a dozen places, small shafts of auratic light lancing out in all directions from multiple wounds. His golden hair was a disheveled mess, and one wing had lost several feathers. He stood with his legs far apart and his arms spread wide as though he invited all the hosts of heaven to attack him, but he was glaring at me.

Nakir pointed his sword at me and yelled, "Traitor!"

I did not say a word but lowered my head, locking my eyes onto my target. Flipping the sword in my hand, I whipped it about in a brief flourish as I stepped forward. The rage took me then, just as it had when I attacked Valac during our training, but this time there would be no check upon my fury. Like the angel of vengeance that I was, I strode toward my once and current adversary.

A vicious calm descended upon me as we closed on each other. Time seemed to slow, but not me. So great was my focus that Nakir's ponderous motions appeared sluggish. He was so slow, and I was so very fast. He rushed forward and brought his sword down in a mighty two-handed chop that threatened to split me in two, but I was not there. I had ducked and sidestepped, and the powerful blow wasted itself against the vacant ground.

I heard the crack of the blade strike the golden bricks of the plaza, but I did not see it, for I was moving and was now to the side of Nakir. I saw his face turning back to me, the minute movement of his head so excruciatingly slow, and as it came around, I recognized the horror in his eyes. He knew he had overextended himself, that he was totally exposed.

Lowering my right shoulder, I cocked my hips. My balance was perfect, my form like flowing water. The sword moved in my hand like an extension of my arm, and my blade swept out in a slashing arc that caught Nakir in the side. My arm swung out wide to my right, and I held that pose as I turned my head back to examine the effectiveness of my strike. I heard it before I saw it.

Nakir was screaming.

My blade had struck well and deep. The light that poured out from the wound temporarily blinded me, forcing me to turn my head aside. I waited to see what Nakir would do. He let out a feral growl and brought his sword back around at me in a mighty, one-handed swing.

This clumsy blow was avoided as easily as the last, and as I parried it, I brought my blade down onto his sword arm. The edge sliced deep, and the sword fell useless from Nakir's now powerless grip. His left hand came up to grasp the wound while he glared at me with a mixture of rage, hate, and surprise. But there was no fear in his eyes, only defiance.

"Damn you, traitor!" he growled in hateful spite.

"No," I answered calmly, "you are the one who is damned."

Then I struck.

My sword punched into Nakir's chest, and his eyes went wide. Twisting the blade, I pulled back and felt the heat of his aura as it shot out at me. Nakir, my former adversary, then perhaps-friend, then enemy, fell to his knees. There was no expression on his countenance, just a blank stare as he fell over onto his face.

I stood there gazing down at my fallen enemy, but the fury did not abate. I was unsatisfied. Glancing about, I searched for another enemy to attack, to spend my anger upon. A short distance away, Gabriel and Malphas were engaged in a sword battle. Gabriel is an archangel and a powerful host, but he is no warrior. Malphas moved like nothing I have ever seen, and I could hardly follow the movements of his sword. He was pressing Gabriel hard, and I worried my former commander would soon be overcome by the fearsome lieutenant of the Morning Star.

Before I could move to assist, someone from behind me shouted my name, and it sounded like an accusation. I spun on my heel and found myself peering into the intense eyes of my former friend and brother, Agiel. His bottom lip quivered and his whole head vibrated with the energy of his mounting wrath. Yet his eyes were softer, full of hurt and betrayal. It was as though his face could not decide which emotion he felt more, sadness or rage.

"What have you done?" He was looking at the fallen form of Nakir as he spat the words at me.

"What have I done?" I shot back at him. "Look what he did to Grigori! He was our brother!"

"Nakir was our brother, not Grigori!" he said. "Look around you Malachi, we are winning. Lucifer will be raised up to sit upon the throne of God, and we will be his cherubim! Join us before it is too late. I will speak to Lucifer on your behalf. We do not have to tell him what you did to Nakir."

"If Lucifer was capable of replacing God," I pointed out, "he would not have to be told what I have done. You will soon see the futility of this rebellion and this battle. The Lord God cannot and shall not be overcome."

"This is your last chance brother," he said, not hearing my words. "Join us or share in Grigori's fate."

"I am an Angel of the Lord," I said defiantly, raising my sword.

Agiel strode toward me, sword in hand, and there was no hint of our past friendship in his fierce expression as he replied to my final declaration of loyalty.

"Very well."

Chapter 21

The Fall

Agiel attacked with much greater speed than I would have thought him capable. I parried his thrusts and slashes without too much difficulty. Still, I found myself pressed backward by the weight of his assault. I was the more skillful with a sword, and Agiel knew this. He did not attempt to match me for finesse. Instead, he intended to use his great size and strength to overpower me by brute force.

I let him drive me backward, allowing him to think he had me on the defensive. I began parrying his attacks more raggedly and with feigned difficulty. As I intended, he grew overconfident and reckless in his assault, his movements more exaggerated and his recoveries less disciplined. He must have thought he was winning, but in fact, I had him right where I wanted him.

Then I stumbled.

I had not sensed the body lying behind me until my heels were touching it. I suddenly found myself without foot room while still being forced backward by Agiel's pressing assault. I was off balance when my former friend hit me with a massive swipe of his sword that I just managed to block with my own blade. The blow sent me reeling, and I fell backward over the obstruction at my feet.

I knew I had to keep moving if I was to avoid being skewered, so as I fell, I spread my wings. I hit my back, but as I did so, I brought my knees up to my chin and pushed off with my wings. Of course, this is not the function of angelic wings, and the lift generated by this maneuver was slight. But it was enough, along with the momentum of my fall, to allow me to continue rolling backward and get my knees past my head. Inertia handled the rest, and I was able to complete the roll, ending up on my feet once more. I tucked my wings back behind me as I stood, facing Agiel who was still on the other side of the obstructing fallen host. He nodded appreciably of my maneuver before stepping over the body to renew the engagement.

That was when I struck. With one foot on either side of the obstruction, he was now off balance, and I launched myself at him in a flurry of slashes and thrusts. He parried well at first, but the sheer speed of my attack overwhelmed his reflexes, and he was unable to maintain his defense for more than a few seconds. My blade struck his forward leg above the knee, and he sank down with the sudden loss of strength in that limb. As he fell, I sidestepped and back swung my sword in an arc that caught him in the abdomen. This caused him to double over at the waist, and I finished my attack with a vertical chop that was intended to catch him on the helmet.

Despite his treachery, I did not wish to critically wound Agiel, only stun him. However, I misjudged the rate of his fall. As he pitched forward, instead of hitting him on the crown of the helmet as I intended, I found my blade slicing deep into his left wing. Agiel gave a yelp of pain as he twisted away and the outboard half of his severed wing fell to the ground.

He turned and glowered at me, grimacing through the pain, and I recognized the complete loss of control on his face as rage overtook him. I backed away as he charged at me. He did not slash or stab. He just ran at me, intending to tackle me. Knowing that if I allowed this, I would be at his mercy, I backed away, attempting to gain distance and room to maneuver.

Agiel rushed me with the relentlessness of a raging bull. I allowed him to come within arm's reach of me before I reacted. Then, dropping abruptly into a crouching position, I rolled toward him. The impact took his legs out from under him, and he flew forward as I rolled underneath and past. Standing, I turned back, readying myself for his counterattack.

It never came.

I froze with horror to see my friend had fallen onto a spear that had been left at an upright angle, wedged between the bodies of two fallen hosts. He had impaled himself on it and now stood with his chest halfway down the shaft. He dropped his sword and grasped the spear with both hands as though holding it there in place. Dropping my sword, I rushed to my brother and assessed the damage. I attempted to pull the shaft free, but he yelled in pain and pushed me away with one hand.

Agiel looked at me then, the fury gone from his eyes, and I saw the old spirit of my friend in his face. I recognized the childlike innocence and honest curiosity I had so appreciated in former days. I remembered his careless laugh and quick wit. I thought back to our long talks sitting atop the walls of the city when we used to dream of joining the Morning Star Legion. That dream had turned into a nightmare, and it had stolen my friend from me. I wept. Not with tears, for angels are not capable, but I sobbed as I held my friend and mourned the loss of everything that had been taken from us.

"Malachi," he croaked, gazing up at me sadly. Then his head sank upon his chest, and he went still.

My entire world went silent. Angels still fought, but it was as though all sound had fallen away. My head spun. I was dizzy with the overwhelming assault of conflicting emotions that buffeted me. I had lost my friend. He had been stolen from me by this ridiculous rebellion perpetuated by a self-serving egotist who cared nothing for the angels who followed him. My anger boiled as it coalesced into focus around the true target of my rage. There was one person responsible for the evils that had befallen us all. He had taken my friends away from me; Agiel, Grigori, and untold others. This was Lucifer's doing. He alone was deserving of my wrath.

And he would feel it.

I turned in place, searching the battlefield for Satan. To my dismay, I realized that Agiel had not been wrong. Lucifer's angels did appear to be winning this battle. The loyal hosts were being pressed hard, and many had fallen. There were not as many pockets of conflict as there had been when the battle first began, which made the fray even more disjointed. Gabriel and Malphas were nowhere to be seen. I assumed they still fought somewhere amongst this chaotic scene, but I could not be certain. I hoped Gabriel still stood.

That was when I spotted the target I sought. Lucifer. He was engaged in a duel with Michael. It seemed the leaders of the two sides had found each other at last. Michael was holding his own, but barely. The captain of the Flaming Sword was physically superior to Lucifer; broader and stronger, but Lucifer was the more powerful. His sword movements blurred as they clashed with Michael's blade, and I could tell my new captain's motions were just a touch slower and less reactive than those of the Morning Star. Michael might be holding his own for now, but that could not last long.

I scanned the ground around me and located my dropped sword. Retrieving it, I slid the blade into my scabbard then bent over again to pick up a spear that lay abandoned on the ground. Hefting the spear, I twirled it around me in a series of loops, familiarizing myself with its weight and balance. Satisfied, I couched the spear in the crook of my arm and stretched out my wings. With a couple of strong strokes, I rose into the air, gaining altitude. There were a few hosts up here, fighting airborne, but most were below me on the ground.

I located my target, still battling with Michael, who was now being pressed backward at a steady clip. I had only a matter of seconds if I were to be of assistance, so I banked my wings and transitioned into a fast dive. As I did, Michael stumbled, and with a flick of his wrist, I witnessed Lucifer disarm my captain. Michael's sword flew from his hand, and he fell back onto the steps of the Holy Palace.

I hurtled toward my adversary, increasing speed as I dove. I was intent on reaching him before he could administer the finishing blow to my captain. As I dove, Lucifer placed the tip of his blade at Michael's throat, and although I did not hear what he said, I could imagine his arrogant, triumphant gloating.

I swept in fast from behind Lucifer, his back to me. With his attention on Michael, I was certain I could take him by surprise. I pulled back my arm, cocking it to deliver a devastating strike with the spear. Then, at the last moment, I was shocked to see Lucifer spin around and bat my spear away with his sword. His other hand shot up and grasped me by the throat, arresting my descent instantly and stunning me with the shock of the impact.

I hung there, unable to move. Lucifer's grip was like iron, and it tightened as he snarled at me. I glanced past him to see Michael attempting to stand. Hope surged in me until I saw Lucifer move his left leg and, without so much as a glance in his direction, plant a foot on Michael's chest. My captain struggled to dislodge the obstruction but to no avail. The power of Lucifer was such that he was capable of holding down the foremost warrior of heaven with a single foot.

"You!" Lucifer sneered as my identity dawned on him. "You are the traitor."

I tried to respond, to assert that he was the traitor here, but I found I could not speak. The grip on my throat was too tight. All I managed was a gasp that Lucifer apparently took as an admission of guilt. I felt myself spinning through the air as Lucifer pivoted to slam me down next to Michael. I hit the ground with enough force to break the bricks of the plaza. They cracked beneath me, and the stars above me spun as my vision clouded. Lucifer held me down by my throat while with his other hand, he raised the sword high above my head.

"You are a fool!" he shouted at me, grinning like a madman. "I have won! If you had stayed loyal, you would be celebrating with me in victory!" The grin disappeared and Lucifer's lips curled back in a threatening snarl. "Now you shall suffer the fate of traitors." He raised the weapon even higher to strike, and the shadow from it fell across Lucifer's face like a dark mark.

I do not know why, but at that moment when I should have been focused on my impending doom, I was instead overcome by an intense curiosity. A very bright light glinted off Lucifer's blade, and it cast a shadow across his face. That made no sense.

I have told you that in Heaven all light is evenly distributed by the presence of God, and because of that, there are no shadows. Likewise, there is little distinction between other sources of light. That is not to say there is no distinction. Some auras are brighter than others, and I had seen light glint against sword blades before, such as during my bout with Vassago, but I had never before seen a shadow in heaven. For a shadow to be cast by the sword in Lucifer's hand, a light source more powerful than any angel must be shining on the other side.

Light glinted again as the sword flashed down to sever the head from my body. It seemed to happen in slow motion. I was aware I was about to be ended, but all I could focus on was the shadow that grew larger across Lucifer's face as the sword fell. Then I gasped as I realized the only Being in the Kingdom of Heaven who possessed an aura bright enough to cast a shadow in the overall brilliance of the Holy City was...

"Enough!" I heard the booming voice of God the Father proclaim. "Be still."

The blade of Lucifer's sword had stopped mere inches from my face. It hovered there, and I recognized the confusion in Satan's eyes. He grunted as he attempted to pull the sword back up for another strike, but he found he could not move. He tried again, but with the same result. Finally, he realized he could not overcome the power that held him in its invisible grip.

That was when Lucifer, son of the morning, the firstborn of the angelic host, realized the utter futility of his attempt to overthrow the Almighty. With a single word, the Lord had put an end to his rebellion. God had spoken, and all of creation had obeyed. I witnessed the growing comprehension on the face of Satan, the dawning of this undeniable reality. He now knew he was wrong. He was not the son of God. The Lord had not erred when He created him. He possessed no portion of God's power. He was unable to resist the direct command of the Father, which meant there had never been any hope of displacing Him.

God did not need angels to fight this battle for Him. He did not rely upon the Flaming Sword vanquishing the forces of the Morning

Star. All this violence had been a futile attempt to defeat a Supreme Power who could not be defeated. Lucifer had beaten the Angels of the Lord. He had devastated the entire Army of Heaven, but he could not defeat the Lord God Himself. He had won the battle and then lost it because he never stood a chance in the first place. I watched that final realization wash over Lucifer's face. I recognized the utter despair as he came to grips with his ultimate failure.

"No!" he shouted in frustration.

As he shouted, he was snatched backward, and my throat was released from his grip. I attempted to stand but found that I too was incapable of movement. God had commanded all to be still, and that included me as well. I felt a warmth surge all around me. The light of heaven grew, intensified, and became overwhelming. The palace above me blurred into overlapping shafts of white light, and its features became softer as detail faded. Then my entire vision was overcome by the light. I could see nothing but pure white. I no longer felt the ground beneath me. I could not tell if I were still lying flat or if I was tumbling through void space. All was light. All was nothingness.

Then the light began to fade. I saw detail return to the universe around me. I felt something solid beneath my feet. I was standing, and others stood around me. Glancing about, I realized I stood in formation with my brothers of the Flaming Sword, and that the scene had utterly changed. No bodies lay on the ground. There were no swords or spears strewn about. It was as though the battle had never happened.

I noticed to my right that the legion of the Mighty Trumpet had been formed up as well. I spotted Gabriel at the head of his unit and behind him, Grigori. I smiled to see that my friend was well. It dawned on me that if Grigori had been restored, so might have Agiel. Or would he? Did God restore the fallen angels also or just we loyal hosts?

I peered left to where the Morning Star Legion should have been but saw only empty space. They were not there. My vision was still clearing, though, and I could now see further than just a few yards. Looking back toward the palace in front of me, I now saw angels standing there as well. I recognized the armor of those hosts and knew it to be the Morning Star. They had been placed between the palace and where the two loyal legions congregated. The Father sat upon His throne, looking down at the defeated traitorous legion.

That is the only time I have ever looked directly at the Father. He had placed a provision upon the hosts of Heaven to allow us to look at Him, but not just Him. The Son sat at His right hand, and the Spirit was there as well, the ethereal presence coalescing about the figures of the Father and the Son like a fog.

With a jolt of clarity, I realized I had observed this scene before. It was just as it was depicted on the mural of the Morning Star headquarters. Lucifer stood before the Trinity of God, and his angels stood behind him, just like on the mural. This scene, I realized, had been foretold, yet misinterpreted by the angels of the Morning Star. It was not the scene of Lucifer's apotheosis, but rather of his judgment.

"Lucifer, son of the morning," the reverberating voice of Zadkiel said, "you and your legion have brought war upon the Kingdom of Heaven. You have defied the will of God and raised arms against your fellow hosts. You have sought to unseat the Lord and overthrow His throne. Instead, you shall be brought low."

As Zadkiel spoke these words, an agonized scream filled the air. It took me a few moments to realize that it emanated from Lucifer. He flailed about in painful spasms. Then the rest of his legion was struck by the same mysterious ailment, and they too began to writhe and shriek.

I was dumbfounded at first, but after a few seconds, I began to comprehend what was happening. Inexorably, the light of their auras was being extracted. It rushed from their eyes, their ears, and their screaming mouths. Swirling wisps of light flowed out and up, escaping from thousands of hosts to coalesce in the space above the formation. This continued for a long while. When it was finally over, the collected light of the confiscated auras dissipated into the overall heavenly light of the Holy City. Below, the mass of fallen angels was left heaped together like refuse.

They had been utterly changed in the process. Their skin was no longer perfect and glowing. Instead, it had an unhealthy gray pallor to it. Their eyes no longer shined with white light, but now glowed bright red. The wings of many of the fallen hosts showed dark, bare patches where the feathers had fallen out during their contortions. A blanket of white feathers carpeted the ground beneath them, and more feathers were dropping all the while, further exposing the leathery bat-like wings beneath.

They wailed and sobbed in their grief and torment. I was not certain whether the process of transformation was painful in and of itself, but I did understand the primary reason for their distress and despair. I have told you that our auras are the light of the Lord within us. It is the loving embrace of the Father, ever present. Through it, we are connected to Him and infused with His power. The Lord God had just removed that gift from these fallen ones. They were now separated from His presence and disconnected from His power. The loss of that connection must have been excruciating. I can only imagine the utter emptiness that each must have felt at that moment.

"Former hosts of the legion of the Morning Star," Zadkiel proclaimed, "you are hereby banished from the Kingdom of Heaven. Henceforth, you shall no longer carry the title of angels of the Army of the Lord. From this moment forth, you shall be known as demons, the fallen of the heavenly host."

The sobbing continued. The demonic horde was coming to terms with the consequences of betrayal and failure. They dropped low to the ground, crouching and holding their arms in front of their faces, shielding their eyes. The light of heaven was intense and overwhelming to them now, its brilliance painful to their demonic eyes.

Zadkiel continued, "You shall be expelled from the Kingdom of Heaven, never again to enter the gates of the Holy City. You shall wander the void and bear witness to the power of God throughout His vast creation. As it is the will of the Lord."

"Let it be so!" I intoned automatically, and my brothers with me. I could not tell if the former angels echoed the time-honored reply, but I doubted it.

The demons were escorted from the Holy City, a train of vanquished and humiliated enemies. They hung their heads as they shuffled down the road from the mountain to the gates of the City, flanked by warriors of the Flaming Sword. Lucifer marched in the lead, and he alone carried himself with some form of dignity. I could tell it hurt him to hold his head high and look straight ahead, braving the intensity of the painful light assaulting him. He squinted tightly, his eyes a couple of thin red lines on his face. I could just discern the tremors he fought to keep in check, determined to leave Heaven as defiantly as he had entered it. I shook my head. Lucifer's pride had not been suppressed by his fall, but his resentment had increased.

Once the last of the defeated former angels departed the City, the gates were shut behind them. I had flown to the top of the ramparts and now peered down upon a defeated army of demons. They milled about aimlessly, unsure of what to do next. Then Lucifer shoved his way through the crowd and stood before the gates. He looked up to where Michael and Gabriel gazed down at him, his red eyes burning brightly. He raised a clenched fist to the archangels, his former peers, and I noticed the nails of his hand were now black and shiny, like the claws of an animal.

"This is not over!" he said in a broken voice, as though that too was undergoing a change. "I will have my revenge!"

With that, he turned and flung his wings wide. Feathers dislodged and floated to the ground, revealing even more leathery patches. The remaining feathers fell as he flapped his now bat-like wings. His fellow demons followed his example, and as a body, they rose into space. As their forms receded into the distant vastness of the former void, I felt a hand rest on my shoulder. I turned to see Grigori standing beside me.

"I have a feeling we will be seeing them again soon," he said.

"What makes you say that?" I asked.

"Because I recognize their course. They are heading to earth."

Chapter 22

A New Mission

It felt like years had passed since the last of the departing demons faded from view, but it must have been mere moments. I was contemplating the implications of Grigori's words, his belief that the demons were heading to earth, when a cherub landed on the wall and addressed us formally.

"Grigori and Malachi, your presence is required at Headquarters at your earliest convenience."

I glanced around to see that Michael and Gabriel were both gone from the wall. Perhaps more time had passed than I first imagined. In any case, we had been summoned by the archangels, and regardless of the polite phrasing of the order, I had a feeling it should be convenient to report without delay.

"We shall come at once," I said. The cherub gave a curt nod and flew away without another word.

"I wonder what that is all about," Grigori said. I just stared at him.

"What?" he asked.

"How do you feel?"

"What do you mean?"

"I saw you fall on the field of battle," I explained. "You were impaled through the chest, but the Lord restored you, and now it is as though nothing happened."

"It was a very interesting experience," he admitted. "I am not quite sure how to explain it. All I know is I lay there helpless for a long time."

"So, you were still aware? You were not," I searched for the right word, "gone?"

"Gone?" He smiled and stretched out his arms to indicate Heaven. "Where would I go?"

"I do not know! I am just trying to understand."

Grigori laid a meaty hand on my shoulder and squeezed. "No, I was not gone. I am not even sure that is possible for angels, but I was definitely helpless."

Shaking my head, I said. "We had better go."

Grigori nodded. "Come on, little brother."

When we arrived in the hall, we found Michael and Gabriel standing at the conference table. A tall mountain with long, sloping sides filled the viewable area. Unlike the previous image I had seen here, this place was not erupting with lava, although smoke and gas seeped from various fissures in the mountainside. This must be one of the volcanos I had heard of, and although the smoldering mountain was not currently erupting, it was far from inactive.

Michael noticed our approach and waved us over. "Malachi, Grigori, come and see."

The image zoomed in on one side of the mountain where green patches of grass spread out between rocky outcrops. The demons were there, dark gray specks against the lighter green of the surrounding grassy landscape. The image continued to grow until it settled on Lucifer, sitting on a large rock that resembled a roughly hewn throne. He was speaking with three other demons, Malphas, Abaddon, and Vassago.

"What are we to do now, Master?" A disembodied voice said. It was Vassago, but he sounded different, his voice deeper and strained, like humans sound when they inhale too much smoke.

"I will tell you what we do," Malphas responded for Satan. With a shudder, I saw that his eyes, those eerie narrow slits, now glowed bright red. The smoldering incandescence of that scarlet glow lit up his dark gray face like a bonfire on a moonless evening. The evil red glow intensified as he continued.

"We will target the Father's proud new creation. We will destroy man and show God the folly of His plan."

"Can we attack the man and woman?" Vassago asked, sounding dubious.

"Not directly," Lucifer answered. His voice had lost the melodious quality that had always mesmerized me. Instead, it sounded deep and raspy. "The Father will not allow us to harm them physically, but we do have other, more subtle options."

"Like what?" Abaddon asked in his gruff tone.

"Look here," Satan said. He extended his arm, indicating an area just below them on the gentle slope of the mountain. The demons turned to follow his gesture. Further down the slope, an animal approached the lush grasses near the demon congregation. It was a graceful, four-legged creature, its hooves testing the soft ground with tentative steps. The most distinctive features of this animal were the antlers that grew out of its head and split off into branches, reaching up to frame the space above its head. It sniffed at the grass and moved forward slowly.

"What is it?" Vassago inquired.

Satan answered, "It is called a deer, and it is about to die."

The deer continued forward, oblivious to the demons gathered about. When it reached a particularly dense patch of grass, it stopped and began chomping at the bright green sprouts.

"Do you not find it interesting," Satan quizzed his lieutenants, "that the vegetation grows thick and green at the base of this mountain when the surrounding area is so bare?"

Abaddon, never one for deep thought or contemplation, replied, "To be honest, I had not."

Lucifer ignored the belligerent response. "The gasses that seep from this mountain are heavier than the surrounding air. They settle and form a blanket that hovers close to the ground. The gas is highly nutritive to the plant life, but acts as a deadly poison to the animals which feed upon the vegetation."

As he spoke, the deer stumbled, its knees buckling under its weight. It steadied itself, raised its head, and recovered momentarily. Then it lowered its head again and resumed grazing.

Lucifer continued his narrative. "The gas is thick and stays low to the ground. So long as the deer keeps its head above the fog, it will survive. But to feed upon the rich grasses, it must lower its head to the level of the deadly gas which is odorless and tasteless. The deer is completely oblivious to the danger. All it is focused on is what it desires, the food at its feet. The more it is drawn to it, the more it is drawn into the trap."

Indeed, the deer faltered again, and this time, it did not reach its head back up to breathe the clean air above. Instead, it sank to its knees and lay down on the soft grass. It still attempted to feed on the green vegetation, but it was growing increasingly weak and disoriented.

"Desire is a deadly temptation," Lucifer continued as the deer settled its heavy head onto the grassy blanket, "and those things which are forbidden are the most desirous of all. All creatures want most those things they cannot have, and the more they reach for that forbidden fruit, the further they slip into the trap. Then, just as they have their desires seemingly within their grasp, they succumb to the gentle embrace of the sleep from which there is no waking."

As he finished speaking, the deer let out a last long gasp and lay still among the green stalks fluttering in the wind. Satan smiled, and his eyes narrowed menacingly.

"I will offer the man and woman something they desire. I will tempt them to disobey the Father, and thereby lose His protection. Once they sin, God will have no choice but to separate Himself from them, just as He has us. Without His favor and protection, we will be free to destroy them. Then, perhaps the Lord will realize His folly and restore the old order."

As Malphas nodded his agreement, the image faded from the surface of the table. Michael turned to Grigori and me. "You two will return to earth and visit the garden. There you will monitor the situation and watch over the man and woman."

"What do you think Satan meant?" Grigori asked. "Is it true the Lord will not allow him to harm the humans?"

"That is why you are going," Michael said, "to ensure no demon attempts to harm the man and woman in a direct or physical way. You are to observe all that takes place. Above all else, however, you are to preserve their free will."

Gabriel explained further. "Under no circumstances are you to infringe upon the choices of the humans or their right to make their own decisions. At the same time, you are to prevent any demonic interference which might also infringe upon that free will. Remember though, the absence of choice is not the same as free will. You should not seek to shield them from any outside factors that may tempt them. They must make their own decisions."

I admit I was thoroughly confused. I did not understand how the choices of the man and woman might factor in, but if I had learned anything over the last few days, it was that God knew what He was doing. I must have faith and obey.

"Yes, sir," I said at the same time as Grigori. Then I added, "We shall depart immediately."

We turned to leave, but after I had taken only a few steps, I heard Gabriel call my name. I turned back to him. "Sir?"

"Do you wonder why the Lord allowed the battle to take place?"

I was astonished to realize the question had not occurred to me. I said so, and Gabriel grunted as though he expected as much. "The Lord was not dependent upon the outcome of the fray. He stopped the battle, Himself, with a word. So, why do you think He allowed it to go on for as long as He did?

I stammered, "I do not know."

"He did it for you."

"For me?"

He nodded. "You and the other hosts. You all had a choice to make. The other angels of the Morning Star could have chosen to stand by God, but they did not. Likewise, you could have decided to go over to them, but you chose to remain loyal.

"It was not until you were confronted by Agiel that you made your final declaration of loyalty, rejecting Satan and overcoming the trap of his temptation. Up until that moment, you could have chosen at any time to change your allegiance and join your friends against the loyal forces of the Lord."

I became aware my mouth was hanging open slightly as my mind raced to process what Gabriel was saying.

"Of course, God knew you would make that choice. Still, if He had not allowed the battle to continue, you would not have had the opportunity to do so. For God to know something will happen is not the same as Him allowing it to happen. You needed to make that choice, and you made it. You decided to stay true when all those around you made other choices. That is what makes your loyalty so valuable. You exercised your free will and made the right decision. Make sure they," he meant the man and woman, "have the same opportunity."

I nodded in acknowledgment, but more from habit than understanding. With my mind swimming in a fog, we took our leave of the archangels and headed for earth.

Chapter 23

The Snake in The Garden

As we arrived on earth, I remember commenting that if the entire demonic horde decided to attack and kill the man and woman, Grigori and I would be a wholly inadequate defense. My friend reminded me, though, that we had been told God would not allow such a direct attack.

"If they were to attempt such a thing, I am certain the Lord would provide us with the means to defeat them. He would not place us in a situation we could not overcome."

I smiled as I noted the difference between my conversations with Grigori and those I had experienced with Agiel while in training. Whereas Agiel continually justified and rationalized the questionable behavior of the Morning Star, Grigori spoke of faith and confidence in God. The change was refreshing, and it brought me peace.

We found Adam and his wife in good health. They were lying upon a patch of soft grass beside a small stream, an outlet of the great river that bisected the garden. The burbling sound of the water as it ran past was quite soothing, and perhaps because of this, the pair had fallen asleep. Grigori and I landed on the side of the stream opposite the humans.

"Why do you think they sleep?" I asked. "The thought of losing consciousness and being completely helpless is terrifying!"

"I agree," my friend replied gravely. "It reminds me of how I felt after I was struck down during the battle. I would prefer not to relive that moment."

The woman's eyes fluttered open, and she sat up, stretching her arms. She gazed at the face of her husband, who still slept, and bent over to caress the dark hair of his head. She stared at him for a long moment, then kissed his cheek and stood. After one last look at Adam, she turned to stroll down the side of the stream.

I glanced at Grigori. "What should we do?"

"Go with the woman. I shall stay here and watch over the man."

Nodding, I followed the woman, staying parallel to her on the opposite side of the stream that ran toward the center of the garden. She strolled down a grassy track that ran alongside the water, tiptoeing around muddy patches that were interspersed in the lush carpet of grass.

She was in no hurry and appeared to be playing a game as she went. At one point, she stretched out her arms like the limbs on a tree and placed one foot directly in front of the other as though balancing on a log. She giggled to herself as she teetered left and right, trying to maintain a straight path. After a few steps in this manner, she jumped a short distance and laughed as though she had just made it to the other side of a wide chasm. The woman smiled to herself and resumed walking normally.

After a while, the grassy track began to widen until the trail opened into a small clearing. There, in the center of the clearing, the stream split and flowed around a mound of earth, coming back together on the other side to continue its journey. At the top of that mound stood a lone tree. In the open space of the clearing, the rays of the sun shined down upon the tree as though it were on display. Shafts of sunlight lanced through gaps between the leaves and lit the ripe fruits hanging from every branch, causing them to glisten in the noon-day sun. The woman stopped and stared at the tree but did not approach.

"She is curious," a voice behind me said. Startled, I whirled around to identify the speaker.

It was Lucifer, leaning carelessly against a nearby tree at the edge of the clearing. His arms were crossed, and he lounged there as though innocently enjoying a relaxing day in the garden. My hand instinctively moved to my sword, and it was halfway out of its scabbard when Satan laughed at me.

"There is no need for that, Malachi," he said in that newly deep and disturbingly raspy voice. "I will not violate the peace."

I shivered at the sight of him. His skin was a pale gray, mottled and sickly. The wings that arched behind his stooped back were now bare and leathery. His eyes glowed a fierce red, and his long blonde hair had turned black like Malphas'. His high forehead, once so proud and aristocratic, was now deformed. Two large bumps, like buds, had begun to grow there. Even his teeth had changed, the canines becoming longer and more pointed. I decided to myself that this ugliness was not new. Rather, stripped of his angelic veneer, the evil he had become was laid bare for all to see.

"Your very presence here threatens the peace," I shot back.

"True," he acknowledged softly. Then with a sneer, he added, "but unless I make some overt move to physically harm the Lord's little pet, you cannot act against me, can you?"

"No," I admitted, sliding the sword back into place, "I cannot, but I will be watching you, Satan, so mind yourself."

"Do not call me that!" the demon prince snapped. He pushed off from the tree trunk and took a threatening step toward me. The red eyes flashed with anger as he snarled, "Listen, pup. You act very smug, but you are still a minor angel. You will show me respect!"

"I will show you no such thing, deceiver."

I let my aura grow hot as I took a step toward him. He shrank back, crouched down, and brought his hands up to cover his face.

"You have no power anymore, Satan," I scorned him. "Do not dare to threaten me."

To my surprise, I heard him laugh from beneath his shielding arms. There was something eerie and disturbing in that maniacal laughter, and I shivered despite myself. He continued to cackle as he backed away. I allowed my aura to recede, and as I did, Lucifer lowered his arms. He glared at me beneath bony gray brows and smiled sinisterly, the sharp canine teeth shining like fangs in his long mouth.

"You understand so little, child," Satan said, in full control of himself again. His erratic behavior was confusing and disturbing. I could not decide if he had lost his mind when he was changed, or if this was who he had always been, an unstable personality.

"I may have lost my angelic aura," he continued, "but I still have plenty of power. In fact, I have discovered new talents."

He glanced up at a branch of the tree he had been leaning against. There was something suspended from it that had escaped my notice before, a creature of some kind, long and slender. The animal was almost all tail, with a flat head and large eyes with slits for pupils. It did have legs, but they were short and seemed designed only to help it climb better. Its feet terminated in five articulated digits, each equipped with long black talons. The animal was wrapped around the branch with each of its four sets of claws clinging to the wood for extra support.

The creature lowered its head to hang in mid-air, and to my astonishment, it turned to look directly at Lucifer. Satan grinned and laughed aloud while reaching up to stroke the animal under its chin.

"Clever, clever creature," he said, clearly impressed with its ability to perceive his presence. The animal apparently perceived me as well, for it turned its head and stared in my direction. A forked tongue flicked in and out of its mouth. Then it hissed at me.

Lucifer chuckled. "I don't think it likes you, Malachi," he said, gazing at the serpent. "It must have good taste."

I set my jaw and narrowed my eyes, determined not to allow Satan to goad me. But then he did something unexpected. Before I understood what was happening, he evaporated into a cloud of black smoke, and that smoke wafted up to be drawn into the nostrils of the serpent. The reptile breathed the devil into its lungs, and its eyes flashed bright red momentarily as the possession was completed. The snake smiled, and I knew it was Satan who grinned at me.

The sword left the scabbard then. I strode forward, whipping the blade about in circles as I closed on the creature. I stopped short, though, when it did something I did not expect. The serpent spoke.

"Go ahead, Malachi, break the peace," it said, drawing out the end of the word in a hiss. "Then I will be free to do the same and destroy these puny creatures with my own hands. That will be much more satisfying than what I originally had in mind, although so much cruder."

"What are you doing, Satan?" I challenged him. I felt only slightly ridiculous speaking to this possessed animal.

"Watch, and you will see."

The serpent slithered down the tree, winding about the trunk until it reached the ground. Using its feet, it walked to the side of the stream where it glided smoothly into the water. The snake pulled its legs and feet back against its streamlined body and moved in quick sidewinding motions until it reached the other side. Then it climbed back onto its feet and walked up the island to the base of the tree trunk. The woman had turned away from the tree and begun walking back toward where Adam lay sleeping when Satan spoke to her.

"Where are you going, woman?" he asked with a hiss.

The woman stopped and turned around, but she could not at first identify the source of the sound. The snake had climbed up into the tree and now hung from one of its branches. It moved out toward the end of the branch, and that was when she noticed it.

She took a step back toward the tree. "What did you say?"

The snake moved even closer to the edge of the branch. "Has God indeed said, 'You shall not eat of every tree of the garden'?"

The woman stepped toward to the edge of the stream, just below where the snake hung from the branch. A single piece of fruit dangled from this branch, and it glistened invitingly in the mid-day sun.

"We may eat the fruit of the trees of the garden," she said to the serpent, "but of the fruit of the tree which is in the midst of the garden, God has said, 'You shall not eat it, nor shall you touch it, lest you die.'"

Satan chuckled and chided the woman. "I am touching it, am I not? I am not dead."

"True," she conceded, "but you are not of man."

"You are right," Lucifer, within the serpent said soothingly. "I am a much lower creature than you. Has God not placed all of creation under your care and dominion?"

"Yes," she agreed, "He has."

"Then surely if a lowly serpent can touch and eat of the fruit, so can you, being superior."

I took a step forward, understanding Lucifer's plan at last. This is what Satan meant when he said he would tempt the man and woman with desire to their deaths. If they ate the fruit, they would no longer be innocent. By disobeying God and committing sin, they would know the difference between good and evil. They would no longer be pure and could no longer stand in God's presence. Lucifer was counting on God's perfect purity to force Him to separate Himself from the man and woman. He hoped God would remove His protection from the humans and allow Lucifer to destroy them.

At that moment, Adam approached. He had awoken from his slumber and walked up to where the woman stood. Grigori followed a few steps behind. Flapping my wings, I hopped over the stream to join him. I opened my mouth to tell him what was happening but stopped when Adam spoke to his wife.

"What are you doing? Remember, the Lord has said we are not to eat of this tree, or we will die."

I was encouraged. Surely, he would not allow her to commit this sin. But Satan was not about to concede so easily. He spoke to them both saying, "You will not surely die. For God knows that in the day you eat of it your eyes will be opened, and you will be like God, knowing good and evil."

The man and woman glanced at each other, and I could tell the serpent's words had them questioning God's command. They had existed for all of three days. Everything was new to them. They did not know of the struggle between God and Satan. They knew God had created both them and the earth, but they were still so ignorant and curious about the world. They yearned for a fuller understanding, for wisdom, and the serpent was offering them that.

The woman peered back up at the fruit hanging from the near branch, and her hand lifted to come within reach of it. I stepped forward but stopped as Grigori placed a cautioning hand on my arm.

"What are you doing?" I said. "We have to stop them!"

"We cannot. They must make their own choices."

"But Satan is manipulating them!" Grigori did not know that Lucifer had possessed the snake. Only I appreciated the true danger of the situation.

"It does not matter," he replied, perhaps understanding after all. "He is not forcing them, only tempting them. Remember, we must preserve their free will."

"But he is lying to them!"

Grigori cut me off with a wave of his hand. "Stand down, little brother. We must respect their right to choose, even if they use that freedom to make the wrong choice. Remember Gabriel's words to you."

I did remember. Still, it was agonizing to witness Lucifer tempt the humans to sin, knowing I could stop him, yet being forbidden to do so. At the time, I felt that doing what I saw as the right thing was more important than allowing the man and woman to choose. Shouldn't those of superior knowledge and experience protect them against the decisions they were ill-equipped to make on their own?

I realize now, of course, that was a flawed idea. More than that, it was dangerous. I was heading down a chain of thought used by tyrants throughout time to justify their repression and domination of others. Despite my lack of confidence in their wisdom, I must let them make their own decision. Otherwise, doing the right thing would be meaningless.

At the time, though, I was in agony. I was barely able to restrain myself from reaching out and knocking the fruit from the woman's reach. I could do nothing but watch helplessly as her hand moved ever closer to the forbidden fruit.

I hoped Adam would say something to arrest this evil. I waited for him to tell her to retract her hand and obey the command of God. But he did not. He simply looked on with unfeigned curiosity, flicking his eyes back and forth between the woman and the serpent.

He appeared to be just as tempted as she was, but content to allow her to be the one to act. The woman moved her hand to bring it underneath the fruit, her fingers closing around it from every side. She came within a hair's breadth of touching it, hesitated, and glanced back at her husband. This was his opportunity to stop this sacrilege, to speak up and advise against sin.

He did not. He must have thought that by staying silent and non-committal, he was somehow not culpable in the woman's actions. The woman looked back to the fruit, and her fingers rotated around it as though appraising its value. She hesitated momentarily, but then the snake cooed seductively. With the lightning quickness of final decision, her hand snapped shut, snatching the fruit from the branch.

Satan grinned in triumph. "See, you have touched the fruit, and you have not died. Now, go ahead. Eat, and have your eyes opened."

Again, she looked at Adam and waited for him to either endorse or denounce her action, but he did neither. He just stared as before, waiting to see what she did and the consequences thereof. Turning back to the fruit, she closed her eyes and did as the serpent suggested. As her lips closed on the flesh of the fruit, I saw light flash behind the lids of her eyes. They opened, and I perceived that her mortal mind had been opened as well. She smiled at her newfound wisdom, her newfound understanding. Then she turned to her husband and held out the fruit to him. He took it without hesitation.

I gasped, "No."

My own eyes closed as he bit into the fruit, knowing I had failed. I opened them again a moment later to see him pull the fruit from his mouth. As the sweet juices ran down his chin and dripped to the ground, light flashed in his eyes as well. He gazed about in new understanding. But then his expression changed, and he stared at the woman with concern.

"Woman," he said, "you are naked."

She glanced down at her bare breasts and, understanding, reached up to cover them with her hands. Then she recognized Adam's nakedness as well and pointed it out to him in turn. The pair were suddenly embarrassed by their nudity. They ran to the edges of the clearing and began grasping at leaves and vines to cover their bare bodies. Then they both stopped abruptly and glanced around them, their eyes wide in apprehension. They had heard something.

I heard it too, footsteps, rustling in the foliage further down the path. When a voice called out for Adam, the two humans ran and hid in the nearby bushes. Grigori and I glanced at each other nervously, for we had failed in our mission, and we knew who approached.

-

Chapter 24

The Judgement

We heard Him before we saw Him. The sound of vegetation crunching beneath His feet carried through the trees, as did the soft echo of His voice, calling out the name of the man.

"Adam," the Lord called again, but He received no response. Then the Son came into view, walking down the path that ran alongside the brook and stepped into the clearing which contained the Tree of the Knowledge of Good and Evil. When he reached the spot where we stood, I attempted to explain.

"Lord God, I tried to stop the serpent," I began, but He held up a hand to silence me.

"I know," the Lord said and walked past us. He continued to the edge of the clearing where the couple cowered in the bushes.

"Adam," He called, "where are you?"

Of course, He knew exactly where they were, but as a parent wishes to let their child expose their own disobedience, so did the Lord on that day with the man and woman.

"I am here," the man finally responded, standing and stepping out of the bushes with the woman in tow. "I heard Your voice in the garden, and I was afraid because I was naked, and I hid myself."

"Who told you that you were naked?" God asked. "Have you eaten from the tree of which I commanded you that you should not eat?"

Adam stared at the ground, more from shame than reverence. I saw in his eyes the frantic workings of his mortal mind as he sought some explanation that would absolve him of responsibility. When he spoke, it was with a feeble and wholly inadequate excuse.

"The woman whom You gave to be with me, she gave me of the tree, and I ate."

I was astonished. Did Adam really think that he could deflect blame onto the woman, that he could somehow avoid responsibility by casting it upon her? Then there was the more brazen implication that perhaps God Himself was partially at fault by creating the woman and giving her to him, as though, by doing so, God was culpable in some way.

The woman stared up at Adam with an expression of shocked betrayal, but the Lord did not give her time to speak.

"What is this you have done?" He asked her.

The woman lowered her head in shame. She too sought some reply that would mitigate her guilt. After a moment's hesitation, she said, "The serpent deceived me, and I ate."

That was when I noticed the serpent had made its way out of the tree and was at that moment swimming back across the stream. I could tell that Satan no longer possessed the loathsome creature. As it reached the bank and crawled out onto dry land near where we stood, the Lord turned to the serpent and caused it to stop. Then He addressed the creature directly.

"Because you have done this, you are cursed more than all cattle and more than every beast of the field." As the Lord spoke, the legs of the creature began to shrink and become absorbed into its body. "On your belly, you shall go, and you shall eat dust all the days of your life. And I will put enmity between you and the woman, and between your seed and her seed. He shall bruise your head, and you shall bruise his heel."

The snake flipped up and over repeatedly from its back to its belly as though it found itself on a hot surface. It hissed in pain as the legs were absorbed the rest of the way into its body. Now, truly nothing more than a head and tail, it slithered away into the brush. Of course, God knew that the creature had not acted alone, but it had willingly allowed Satan to possess it, so it deserved its fate. Next, the Lord turned to the woman.

"I will greatly multiply your sorrow and your conception. In pain, you shall bring forth children. Your desire shall be for your husband, and he shall rule over you."

The woman buried her head in the man's chest and sobbed. He stood stiffly, holding her. He was clearly unhappy, for he sensed that his punishment would be proclaimed next. In that, he was correct.

"Because you have heeded the voice of your wife," the Lord said to him, "and have eaten from the tree of which I commanded you, saying, 'You shall not eat of it': Cursed is the ground for your sake; in toil you shall eat of it all the days of your life. Both thorns and thistles it shall bring forth for you, and you shall eat the herb of the field. In the sweat of your face you shall eat bread till you return to the ground, for out of it you were taken; for dust you are and to dust, you shall return."

A tear rolled down the man's face and disappeared beneath his chin into the hair of his mate. They had brought this judgment upon themselves by their disobedience. They had attempted to blame their sin on others, but they could not escape responsibility for their decisions, nor could they offer a compelling defense of their actions. Now they would suffer the consequences. Because the man and woman were naked, and now aware of their nakedness, the Lord caused tunics of furs to be made for the couple, and He clothed them in these garments.

Turning to Grigori and me, He said, "Behold, the man has become like us to know good and evil. And now, lest he put out his hand and take also of the tree of life, and eat, and live forever—"

The Lord let the words hang as he stretched out a hand. In a flash, two cherubim descended from Heaven like streaks of lightning. The ground shook as they landed and knelt before the Lord. I recognized one of them as Ophaniel, the cherub who had first rebuked Lucifer on the first day of the Lord's creation. He held a long sword that glowed, wreathed in blue flame. The pair bowed their heads before God.

"You shall post yourselves at the East end of the garden and guard it," the Lord commanded. "The man and woman shall no longer have access to this place, nor their descendants. It is closed to them forever after."

"As it is the will of the Lord," Ophaniel proclaimed.

"Let it be so," his companion finished for him.

The cherubim left to carry out their mandate. This whole time, the man and woman, oblivious to the presence of the angelic host in their midst, huddled together and spoke encouragingly to one another. It was during this exchange that Adam gave his wife her name. He called her Eve, for she would be the mother of all humanity. The Lord turned again to Grigori and me.

"You two shall take the man and woman from here and place them safely in a land far away. There they shall make a life for themselves, the man tilling the soil and the woman raising their offspring."

Following the example of the cherubim, Grigori said, "As it is the will of the Lord."

"Let it be so," I completed the phrase.

We each took hold of a startled human. They perceived us then, and their terror was palpable. I shook out my wings and prepared to ascend, but the Lord spoke again, causing us to hesitate.

"See that no harm comes to them. They are to be untouched by Satan or any of his followers."

We nodded in acknowledgment of the divine command and, holding tight to the humans, rose into the air. As the sun reached its zenith in the sky above, we departed the Garden of Eden for the last time. I have never again seen that pristine paradise.

We deposited Adam and Eve in an area between two of the rivers that ran out of Eden, the Tigris and the Euphrates. Whereas the garden had given up its fruit easily, this land would struggle against the man. Adam would find rocks and roots in the soil, and his labor would be significantly greater than it had been.

When we first set them down, the man and woman just stood there looking around and at each other, unsure of what to do. Then Eve told her husband she was hungry, and I saw true fear on his face.

For the first time since they had been created, food was not readily available. At that moment, the full consequences of their disobedience became clear to them, and they both began to weep.

Eventually, they ceased their sobbing and decided they must find food. They looked around on the ground but found nothing suitable. Then they located some nearby trees and separated to search them more efficiently. After much foraging, Adam found some bitter tasting nuts. He ate a mouthful and carried the rest to his wife. She had located some tiny berries, and she offered him those that she had not already eaten.

"I am still hungry," Eve said, at once sad and confused. They had never experienced true hunger.

"Me too," Adam agreed, holding his hand to his belly. The hunger pangs must have taken hold already. That added a new feeling to his short experience; pain. By eating the fruit, their eyes had certainly been opened to new knowledge, and now they were paying the price for that understanding.

With their meager meal at an end, the couple began to survey the land into which they had been delivered. It was dry and rocky compared to the garden, with a few sparse trees and bushes dotting the dusty landscape. Life here would be hard but manageable, assuming they survived long enough to build shelter and cultivate crops.

That survival was threatened immediately. I heard the danger before I saw it, and it was Grigori who pointed to the approaching horde, a black cloud of demonic wings in the distant sky. They came on like a swarm and landed all around us in a ring of dark evil figures. Lucifer landed within the circle along with his three lieutenants, Malphas, Abaddon, and Vassago. Grigori and I drew our swords and positioned ourselves between them and the humans who huddled in the shade of a sycamore tree, oblivious to the tension around them.

"I win, Malachi," Lucifer said, his mouth spread wide in an evil grin. "Step aside."

"Never!" I shouted defiantly. "The man and woman are under the protection of the Lord God Almighty!"

"Nonsense," Satan scoffed. "They have committed sin against the Lord and have been banished from His garden. They have forfeited the protection of Heaven. Now stand aside. Let me end this so we can go back to the way things were, the way things are meant to be."

"There is no going back, Satan," Grigori interjected.

Lucifer snarled at him before turning back to me. "Once the man and woman are destroyed, God will see reason and restore the old order. We can go back to the way things were. You can return to the Morning Star Legion, where you belong."

He held out a hand, and Agiel stepped from behind Lucifer. I experienced a surge of conflicting emotions at the sight of my friend; relief, despair, hope, anger. He was so changed. His posture was stooped, and his gray head hung as though it were too heavy for him to raise. He too appeared deformed, the buds prominent atop his forehead.

Lucifer indicated Agiel. "Do you not wish to redeem your friend, to restore him to his rightful place?"

Agiel looked at me with sadness in his eyes, and I felt the pang of grief at the loss of our friendship. Those eyes, like Lucifer's, were fiery red orbs, and they bobbed up and down as though he were on the verge of tears at what he had become. Agiel stepped forward and beseeched me.

"Please, brother. Help us," he said in a voice that reminded me of days long ago, sitting atop the walls of Heaven. "Help us regain what we have lost. Help us to become angels again."

I admit, his words touched me. When Agiel had been banished from Heaven, it was as though a piece of me had gone with him into the void. I longed for a return to the way things were, to undo all the damage and pain caused by Lucifer's betrayal. But I knew there could be no return to happier times.

"I am sorry Agiel," I said sadly, "but this act will not gain you the redemption you seek. You cannot undo one sin by committing another."

I turned to Lucifer and put steel back into my voice. "I have been charged with the safety of these creatures, Satan, and you shall not touch them."

Lucifer's expression changed, no longer the sad, pleading supplicant. It morphed into the angry, petulant, and vengeful expression I had come to expect from him. He growled at me and stood up straight, no longer seeking to appear meek and unthreatening.

"Very well, child," he snarled. "I have tried to do this the amicable way, but you leave me no choice. If you will not stand aside and allow me to do what must be done, I shall go through you and do it just the same."

I crouched into my fighting stance, sword at the ready. I felt pressure against my back and knew Grigori was there, back to back with me, ready to fight off threats from either direction. Still, it would not matter. We could not prevail against so many enemies. Moreover, we would be unable to defend the humans. We were only two and could not hope to stay between them and the demonic horde for more than a few seconds. We would fail.

Suddenly, my gaze was drawn heavenward by a long, lone trumpet blast that cut through the sound of the clamoring demons like thunder through fog. Those of the horde glanced up and about, wondering what the bold sound presaged. Then they understood, and their confidence faltered as all around us, angels of the Lord began to appear.

They came like streaks of light from above, crashing down to earth in a flash and causing minor tremors in the ground as they struck. One after another, they landed upon one knee, only to rise a moment later and draw their weapons. They were warriors of the Flaming Sword all, clad head to toe in the full Armor of God. They formed a ring of protection around the humans as well as Grigori and me. The demons squealed and shrank back at the sight of them.

Lucifer, his three lieutenants, and Agiel crouched defensively and glanced around like cornered animals. They had been surrounded by the glowing ring of hosts and were cut off from their own troops on the outside. Satan glanced at the pair of humans a few feet away beneath the tree, and he must have thought he could still get to them before any of us could interfere, for he made a move to step their way. But then Michael came crashing down out of Heaven and planted himself between Satan and the pair of huddling mortals.

That was when Lucifer snapped. He began wailing and stomping about while pulling at his hair, tearing it out in clumps as he railed against those who had denied him once more. The red of his eyes intensified, and smoke rose from the sockets as he stood there trembling in his rage. Then he stopped and seemed to regain his sanity for a moment.

He turned on Michael and shouted, "I swear to you, Michael, I will have my revenge." He held out one claw-like hand and pointed a black talon-tipped finger at the man and woman. "You cannot protect them forever. I will bide my time and wait for my opportunity. Then I shall destroy them."

"No," a booming voice proclaimed from the heavens, "you shall not."

With a flash of light, the Lord appeared within the ring of hosts. He was dressed in a simple, pure white robe. Behind him stood two cherubim, each holding a staff with the new banner of the Lord, the lion and the lamb, hanging from it.

The Son stepped toward Lucifer, and Satan stumbled backward, his lieutenants backing away as well. The intensity of the Lord's aura burned them as they back peddled toward the edge of the ring. When they reached the perimeter, the hosts there parted, allowing them to pass. The Son continued walking forward until he reached the perimeter while Lucifer and his lieutenants shrank back to join the rest of the fallen legion. There, he and his cohorts cowered before the power of God.

"Listen to Me, Satan," the Lord said. "You and your ilk shall not harm the man and woman. You are forbidden to attack them or their descendants. I shall allow you to tempt them, but you may not harm them physically. Likewise, you may not possess any who are unwilling."

Satan protested, "But they have sinned! They have disobeyed You and forfeited Your protection. By Your own words, they must die!"

"And they will," the Lord said. "By committing sin, they have forfeited the right to eat from the Tree of Life. They will die, but it shall not be you who kills them."

"Why not destroy them now?" Lucifer pressed, sounding like a prosecutor making a case. "Why prolong their suffering? A merciful God would end their existence quickly. Their lives have no meaning now. They will languish in their sin and bring You only sorrow and disappointment. Let us end this and restore the old order. Let my angels and me return to Heaven. Restore our angelic forms, and we shall worship You forever more."

"Do not presume to tempt the Lord your God, accuser," the Son replied. "You and your demons have rebelled against God and have been punished for your sin. Likewise, the humans have been punished for their disobedience. They will die. However, I shall make a provision for them, and through My grace, they may find redemption."

"What?" Satan was livid now. "You would redeem them but not us? You would save these loathsome mortal creatures instead of your own immortal kin?"

The Lord shook His head sadly. "You still do not understand. We are not kin. I am God. You were made to serve Me. You were infused with the power of the Spirit of God, but you squandered that gift in pursuit of your own ambitions."

The light of the Lord increased, washing over all present and causing the demons to cower in fear. He rose into the air, and the heavens opened to shine upon Him. Then He spoke to the fallen angels in judgment of them.

"There will be no redemption for you, Satan, for you have learned nothing. There is no true repentance in your heart. You regret only your failure and the consequences of it, not your actions or your motives. Your heart is evil and cannot be redeemed. You shall walk the face of the earth until the time I have appointed when you shall be thrown into the pit for all eternity."

Satan stood then in defiance of the Lord. It must have hurt him, but he was determined to preserve his dignity. As the Lord said, he had learned nothing.

"If I am to be damned," he hissed, shaking a fist at the Lord, "I will not be damned alone! I know You, Lord God. I know You cannot abide the presence of sin, and that any who die in sin must be condemned.

"I will be a scourge to man across future generations. I shall tempt them to sin and bring them into iniquity. I shall cause them to curse the name of the Lord and turn their backs on You. My revenge will be the pain I cause You every time You are forced to send one of them to hell. Mark my words, Lord God, You will regret having made man, and You will resolve to wipe them from the face of the earth. That is my vow!"

With that final statement of defiance, Satan and his demons launched themselves into the air. They flew off in all directions, screeching as they went. Once they had disappeared into the distance, the Lord descended again to stand beside Grigori and me. He addressed us as a pair.

"I would like for you to stay with the man and woman and watch over them."

"Yes, Lord," Grigori said, but God was not finished.

"You are not to spare them any hardship or danger that is inherent to the earth, but you will protect them from any direct physical threats by Satan or his followers. They will tempt them and try to persuade them to sin. You may not interfere in this, for you are to preserve and protect the humans' right to free will. But you may encourage them and give them strength. Between these two influences, temptation and encouragement, they must make their own choices, be they righteous or sinful."

I nodded my understanding, and we both bowed before the Lord. When we stood again, He and the angels of the hedge had gone. We stood alone with the man and woman who still huddled beneath the tree. The woman trembled in her fear and anxiety. The man held her, speaking reassuringly to her, but he too must have been terrified. I sheathed my sword and walked over to where they sat. Kneeling, I placed a hand over each of their heads and spoke encouraging words to them.

"Trust in the Lord, and He will protect you. Honor the name of the Lord in your hearts and minds and seek to give Him glory for His deliverance of you."

As I spoke, I sensed them relax. Although they could not hear my words, they felt the influence of angelic encouragement within their spirit. Their breathing became more regular. They ceased their sobbing and gazed into one another's eyes with renewed hope and optimism.

I continued, "Go now and make a home for yourselves. Till the soil and make it yield its fruits to you. Worship the Lord and have faith in Him all the days of your life."

"Amen," Grigori intoned.

Part Three

The War On Earth

"Now Adam knew Eve his wife, and she conceived and bore Cain, saying, 'I have gotten a man with the help of the Lord.' And again, she bore his brother Abel. Now Abel was a keeper of sheep, and Cain a worker of the ground." (Genesis 4:1-2)

Chapter 25

Old Friends and New Enemies

"Amen," the angel intoned, indicating it had been Grigori who uttered the word so long ago. Paul noticed a change come over Malachi's face as he recounted these events. The intensity of his expression and the wistfulness of his gaze offered witness to the singularly transformative nature of the moment he described. Paul could tell this had been a pivotal event, a moment in which Malachi matured as an angel and found his true purpose at last.

Malachi's eyes closed, evidenced by the winking out of the auratic light that typically shown so brightly from them. He sat there for a long time in silence as Paul waited patiently. Finally, the angel opened his eyes again.

"My apologies," Malachi said at last. "Even now the memories of these events drudge up emotions that threaten to overwhelm me."

"I understand," Paul responded. "So, you not only witnessed Adam and Eve expelled from the Garden of Eden, but you were the one who evicted them?"

Malachi nodded. "Grigori and I."

"Amazing. Of course, all Jews from childhood are taught the story of the creation and the fall of man, but I had no idea the fall of Lucifer and his angels was so wrapped up in that story. You have truly opened my eyes to a hidden truth. I thank you."

The angel nodded in acknowledgment as Paul continued. "So, were you left to watch over Adam and Eve throughout the remainder of their lives, or was that merely a short-term assignment?"

"I remained with them until they died, which was a very long time. Although the man and woman no longer ate of the Tree of Life, its influence was still strong within them, and hundreds of years passed before its lingering effects began to dwindle. In fact, even their descendants, right up to Noah, experienced extremely long life thanks to the residual power of the auratic fruit. Adam himself lived to be nine hundred and thirty years old and Eve lived almost as long."

Paul stared in wonder. "You must have witnessed so much pivotal history."

The angel laughed. "It wasn't as glorious as you might suppose."

"What do you mean?"

"Those first few years were a struggle for survival. The first humans had to learn quickly if they were to stay ahead of hunger, exposure, and the dangers of the new world into which they had been thrust. They managed to cultivate crops in their third year, but before that, they were reduced to scavenging for anything they could find. Nuts, berries, dates, and olives were their main diet.

"They did learn to make bread from the wild wheat that grew nearby, but until they managed to grow a stable crop, there wasn't enough grain to maintain a steady diet. To ensure a surplus, they first had to learn how to fire clay pots and jars to store grain for replanting from year to year. And remember, at that time the Lord had not yet blessed man with the right to eat meat. They were limited in their food resources and often hungry those first few years."

"I hadn't thought of that," Paul conceded.

"They had to learn how to do everything. I like to refer to Adam and Eve as the Great Inventors, for they had to innovate constantly to survive.

"Fire was an interesting discovery. Rain had not yet fallen upon the ground, but the firmament above was highly charged, and lightning was a frequent occurrence. During one such thunderstorm, lightning struck a tree near the cave in which they were sheltering and started a small blaze. After examining the fire for a while, Adam gathered a flaming branch and brought it back to the cave. They cultivated the fire and learned how to keep it going. Later, they discovered they could make fire themselves by creating friction with sticks, but that it was much easier to tend the fire and keep it alive.

"They made wool from the coats of sheep and dried animal hides to make leather. They eventually learned how to make larger sections of cloth, and from that, they were able to build tents to live in. Afterward, they no longer had to shelter in caves."

Paul shook his head, astounded.

"And then there were the wild beasts," Malachi continued. "We were forbidden to protect them physically from the natural dangers of the world, and of those there were many.

"I remember one especially poignant example. The day began much like any other. Adam was walking down to the nearby stream to gather water for his crops. Grigori had stayed with the woman while I accompanied the man. It was a beautiful day, and I spied my old friend, the eagle, soaring high overhead. So focused had I been on following its progress, the giant cat took me by surprise. We had just come over an embankment near the stream when I sensed Adam stop abruptly. Looking back to him, I saw a large lion standing in his path, growling.

"Adam carried a long wooden spear with him everywhere he went. It was not a true spear, for he had not yet worked out how to attach stone or metal to the end, but it did have a fire hardened tip which had proven useful for defense in the past. Adam leveled this spear at the lion that now crouched in front of him, the corners of its mouth pulled back in a threatening snarl.

"I have extraordinarily fast reflexes, but even so, I was surprised at the speed at which the lion struck. It leaped from its crouch as though released by a taut rope. Adam had no time to react. All he could manage was to fall onto his back as the giant feline pounced. As luck would have it, the lion impaled itself upon the shaft of the spear, the butt of which had become firmly wedged between some small rocks on the ground.

"The lion writhed in pain and anger upon the shaft of the spear and lashed out at Adam who lay flat on his back, frantically scuttling away from the feral beast. He was just about clear when a swipe of one of its massive paws caught him on the thigh. He screamed as the claws dug into his flesh and blood poured forth in a gush. That was the first time I ever saw blood. I was intrigued by how bright it was. And the smell. A very distinctive metallic odor.

"Adam managed to scramble backward out of reach of the lion, and I watched as he examined his wounded leg. The claws had bit deep into his flesh. He tore a strip off the woolen garment his wife had made for him and wrapped it around his leg to staunch the bleeding. Then he stood and limped over to where the lion now lay, still alive, but fading rapidly. It no longer thrashed about and instead lay there heaving in deep breaths.

"As it expired, a strange look came over Adam's face, as though he suddenly realized something of significance. He knelt next to the deceased lion and lifted its head to peer at the face, a face with a brown patch over one eye.

"This was the same lion that Adam had first encountered in the garden years ago, the one he named. They had encountered each other once again but with a starkly different result. Adam began to sob. It was not just the pain of the injury that caused his tears. The death of this noble beast was a stark reminder of the consequences of his sin. Where once he and the lion had lived in harmony, now they were enemies. It was a powerful illustration of the unpredictable ramifications of sin, how it destroys not only the lives of those who commit the sin but also those others affected by our choices. Adam sat for a long while weeping over the body of the slain beast." Malachi sighed. "And I have never forgotten that moment."

Paul and the angel sat in silence for a long while, each reflecting on the memory shared by Malachi. The angel stared at the cell floor as though lost in thought, and Paul did not wish to press him. He waited until Malachi stirred and looked back up. Then he asked the question he had been pondering.

"You were with Adam and Eve for the entirety of their lives? So, you witnessed the birth of all their children?"

"I did."

"So, you must have witnessed the sin of Cain against his brother Abel?"

"Indeed."

"Perhaps then, you could answer a question that has vexed me since my earliest studies. The scriptures state that after Cain was banished, he went up to the land of Nod. There he and his wife had a child, Enoch, and that he founded a city of the same name."

"Yes," Malachi confirmed.

"Then, if Cain and Abel were the first children of Adam and Eve, the first people, how was Cain able to find a wife in Nod?"

Malachi threw back his head and laughed heartily. Paul's face reddened until the angel looked back at him and smiled with genuine pleasure.

"Where in the scriptures," the angel asked, "does it say that Cain and Abel were the first children of Adam and Eve?"

"Well," Paul said, thinking as he did so, "I don't know that they do. I just always assumed."

"And that would be your first mistake," Malachi chided him gently. "You must keep in mind that the scriptures are not intended to provide a complete history of the earth from creation until today. They recount significant events the Lord wants His children to be aware of. To assume that nothing other than these events occurred simply because these are the only ones mentioned would be a foolish error."

"That is understandable. So, Adam and Eve had other children besides Cain and Abel?"

"Oh, many more! Remember, Adam lived to be nine-hundred and thirty years old. He and Eve had many sons and daughters along the way. In fact, they had Cain and Abel when they were over one hundred years old. Adam and Eve had begotten children who had their own children and so on, long before Cain and Abel came along.

The brothers were born into an extended family community. It was a grandniece who Cain took as a wife. He did not find her in the land of Nod, for no one lived in the area at that time. No, he took her with him when he left. In fact, that was the first time anyone had ever left the original settlement."

"I admit," Paul said, "I have always been perplexed by the paradox of how the species grew without Adam and Eve giving birth to any daughters. I suppose it makes sense that they did, but why do the scriptures not mention these other children?"

"The scriptures may not explicitly mention these others, but they are implied. After all, the reason God put the mark of protection upon Cain was that Cain worried that 'anyone who found him would kill him.' If there were no other peoples upon the earth, who would he have been speaking of?"

"Fair point," Paul agreed.

"As I have said, the scriptures do not recount every historical event, only those the Lord considers significant. There were four generations born before Cain and Abel, but none of them were significant in any way. In fact, the only contribution they made was that it would be their descendants who caused the Lord to send the Great Flood, for their wickedness spread along with the growth of their numbers. That event is the closest Satan ever came to accomplishing his overall goal."

"The destruction of humanity," Paul noted.

Malachi nodded. "Satan may have lost the battle in heaven, but that only moved the war to a new theatre. This phase of the conflict had different rules. Lucifer could not attack the Lord's children directly, so he opted for a different strategy. As he had vowed, he sought to corrupt all of mankind and drive a wedge between them and the Lord. The first battle in this new phase of the war was fought over the community of Adam and Eve."

"But surely, he was defeated as before," Paul said.

The angel looked at him gravely and replied, "No. That event tore the community of Adam and Eve apart. It was Satan's first significant victory."

Chapter 26

Awan

I vividly remember the day it began because Awan was crying.

You would not have noticed her tears right away, for she did not pause in her work. I have always been fascinated by women's ability to complete mundane tasks while their minds focus on other things. Their hands seem to have minds of their own, continuing the repetitive mechanical motions necessary to complete whatever task they are engaged in, seemingly of their own accord.

Awan sat at her loom, weaving cloth as she did every day. I perched in the corner of the tent, observing the routine of the women. Of course, they were oblivious to me, for none of the community had ever been allowed to perceive the angels in their midst. I had watched this growing family for over one hundred and twenty years now, and this day promised to be much like any other.

The tent was small, only spacious enough to house the loom and a couple of roughly hewn wooden tables. Short tallow candles sat on one of these tables, giving off just enough sputtering light to allow the women to see their work. The melting animal fat pooled on the surface of the tabletop, forming tiny rivers that followed the grain of the wood until it reached the edge and dripped to the dusty ground below.

Awan sat at the loom, passing a shuttle back and forth through the weave. Occasionally, she would tap the newly run cross-thread with a paddle a few times to ensure the weave was as densely packed as possible. Then she would repeat the process in reverse, her thin, delicate fingers running the shuttle back through from the other side. This was the monotonous routine Awan mindlessly maintained as she quietly sobbed to herself, tears running down her delicate cheeks and dropping with irregularity onto the bright red cloth below.

A few feet away, her mother sat absentmindedly performing her own task. Lasha spun the yarn that Awan would use to weave her cloth. In the crook of an elbow, she held the shaft of a distaff, around which had been wrapped a mass of combed wool. A line of unfinished wool ran from the bulbous end of the distaff to the hand of Lasha's other arm where she held a spindle, a smaller wooden object that she spun in her hand to wind the wool into yarn. Once the spool was full, Lasha would dye the yarn and wind it around a shuttle for Awan to use in her weaving.

Lasha continued this way for some time before she realized that her daughter was upset. Her mind had wandered, as it often did while spinning, and the quiet sobs had not registered until that moment. When the sounds of Awan's distress finally penetrated the fog of monotony, Lasha paused her work and glanced up at her daughter, whose shoulders bobbed minutely as she sniffed, her lower lip quivering.

"Awan, dear, what's the matter?"

Awan started in surprise at the sound of her mother's voice and dropped the shuttle. She knelt and picked it up, then raised her eyes to return her mother's gaze, but found she could not meet it. She glanced around the tent as though seeking a suitable explanation for her behavior, but the empty space provided no answers. Her mother's expectant gaze beckoned a reply, and the sudden realization that this conversation could not be avoided caused Awan to burst into a fresh bout of tears.

Lasha instantly stopped her work and laid down her tools. Crossing the room, she knelt and wrapped her arms around the small shoulders of her diminutive daughter. Awan buried her face in her mother's breast and sobbed uncontrollably. Lasha waited patiently until the sobs abated.

"What is it, dear?" she asked.

Awan just gazed at her for a long moment, her large blue eyes glistening. Her mother loved those eyes. Everyone else in the village had dark brown eyes, but Lasha's daughter was different. Her eyes were blue like the sky and seemed to glow with brilliant intensity. They were made even brighter in contrast to the olive tone of her skin and the jet-black hair that hung loosely about her shoulders. Awan was a lovely young girl, and the uniqueness of her features only accentuated that beauty.

Lasha smiled with affection as she gently stroked her hair. Leaning forward, she kissed her daughter lightly on the forehead before resting her own forehead against hers. She stayed that way for a long while, waiting until she heard her daughter slow her breathing and cease her sobbing. Once Awan had calmed herself, Lasha pulled her head back and gazed reassuringly into those deep blue eyes.

"Dear child, I understand how you feel. I wept before my wedding day as well."

Awan's bottom lip drew back and again began to quiver, her eyes welling up once more. Lasha reacted by quickly resuming her embrace. After a brief squeeze, she pulled back and smiled at her daughter.

"It'll be alright. Cain is a fine man, tall and strong, and he's shown himself to be quite resourceful. He will give you a good life."

Awan closed her eyes and nodded, in surrender more than agreement. Then her eyes shot open, and she pulled back from her mother with a jerk. So focused had she been on her daughter's distress, Lasha had not noticed the sound of the tent flap opening.

"Good afternoon, ladies," a cheerful voice said. "I've brought you a present."

Awan frantically wiped at her eyes and cheeks, erasing the evidence of her emotional episode. Lasha smiled at her before turning to greet the newcomer. He carried a sizable basket overloaded with wool that partially obscured his face, but the soft masculine voice was unmistakable.

"Good afternoon, Abel," Lasha greeted him.

Abel moved to where a pile of fluffy wool lay upon the floor. This was the raw material Lasha would need to clean and comb before it could be attached to her distaff and spun into yarn. He stooped to deposit the basket then stood and smiled at the two women.

Abel was a young man, a mere twenty years old, but his youthful features made him appear even younger than he was. He stood bare-chested, having just come from sheering his flocks, and wore only a red ankle-length skirt. His chest was smooth, the sun-browned skin glistening in the flickering light of the nearby candles. The high cheekbones of his face and the smoothness of his bare cheeks enhanced his youthful appearance, as did his eyes. They were a deep dark brown that twinkled in the candlelight. That boyish face was framed by dark hair that was made short by natural curls which caused it to draw back in upon itself.

"That's the last batch," he said.

Lasha peered critically at the basket of wool. "It will have to do."

The flock Abel had managed to gather and nurture was still relatively small, and it scarcely provided enough wool each year to clothe the people of the village. They also depended upon the wool to make blankets and fabric for their tents. It would be enough, but just barely.

"That's a pretty design you're working on, Awan," Abel said, indicating the pattern of red cloth the young girl held in her hand.

Lasha glanced over at her daughter just in time to spot something of surprising interest. Awan was blushing. She smiled sheepishly at Abel, her eyes darting down and away. Lasha smiled to herself.

"Well, I must go," Abel said, not noticing the girl's reaction. "I need to take the flocks back out to the fields before it gets dark, and I'd like to see Mother first."

"Of course," Lasha replied. "It was good to see you, Abel. You should come to the village more often."

Abel smiled, but without any real feeling. He explained his thoughts on the matter, saying, "I feel hemmed in when I come here. It's like the air is thicker somehow. I prefer the open fields, the wide skies, and the gentle breeze that comes off the cool waters of the river. I sleep under the stars and awake to the rising sun. I feel closer to God there, and I am free."

Lasha nodded in understanding, but said, "You can't raise a family in the fields, Abel. One day you will have to set up a tent and put down roots."

"Perhaps," he said, "but not today. Farewell Lasha. Farewell Awan." He gave them both a boyish smile, the dimples of his cheeks puckering.

"Farewell!" Awan said, a little too loudly. She blushed and glanced away again.

As Abel stepped out of the tent, the flap falling back into place behind him, Lasha turned to peer at her daughter, but Awan would not meet her gaze. Laying a hand on her knee, Lasha said, "You're more than just apprehensive about your wedding. There's another reason for your distress."

Awan did not look at her mother but nodded her head slightly. Fresh tears rolled down her cheeks.

Awan had been betrothed to Cain, Abel's older brother, when she was only nine years old. It was an arrangement made between Adam and Awan's father, Asher the Younger, who was himself the grandson of Adam. There had been some discussion about whether Awan should perhaps be promised to Abel instead, but Lasha's husband had quashed that. Asher did not approve of Abel's lifestyle and did not want his daughter supported by a shepherd.

Cain worked the fields and provided the bulk of the community's food resources. Asher also saw Cain as the natural successor to Adam, a man who would one day take his father's place as leader of the community. He wanted his daughter to be part of that legacy. Lasha had not been consulted in the decision, and no one had thought to ask Awan her feelings on the matter. That was the way of things.

In the past, it had not been an issue. The first two children of Adam and Eve, Asher the Elder, and Nava, had married out of necessity. There had been no other option, for they were the only two. But then Adam and Eve conceived again and begot another son named Enoch. There were no other women, and therefore no one for him to marry. Years passed, and no more children were born to Adam and Eve. It began to look like Enoch would not have a wife. Then Asher the Elder was gored to death by a wild boar. After his death, Enoch took Nava to be his wife.

Before Asher's death, Nava had born him two children, a son, Asher the Younger, and a daughter named Rachel. Afterward, she bore three children to Enoch, two sons, Tamir and Jared, and recently, a daughter, named Sara. Lasha was the daughter of Tamir and Rachel, who died giving birth to her. When she came of age, she had been married to her own uncle, Asher the Younger, and it was from him she had begotten her daughter Awan.

The twisted and stunted features of this first family tree spoke to the tenuous nature of mankind's initial hold on survival. There were hardly enough marriageable people to keep the species going. If too many children of the same gender had been born, or if more of them had died before procreating, mankind might have died out before it could gain a foothold. It was not until Lasha's daughter had been born that a wife could be offered to either Cain or Abel, the newest of Adam and Eve's children. If not for Awan, the family tree might have stopped.

In fact, there were already dead ends on the branches of that family tree. Jared had no wife. His sister Sara was only five years old, and there had already been talk of promising her to Abel when she came of age. There was no one for Jared, who remained a bachelor.

Lasha stroked the hair of her daughter. "You have feelings for Abel, don't you?"

Awan did not deny it, nor would it have done any good. Lasha knew her daughter too well for that. She also understood the pain of unrequited affection.

"I too did not marry the man I preferred," she told her, uttering this scandalous truth aloud for the first time in her life. Awan peered up at her mother, her expression a mixture of surprise and confusion.

"You didn't want to marry Father?"

"Your father is a fine, strong man," Lasha said, understanding the delicate nature of this conversation, "but, no, Asher wasn't the one who I had hoped to marry."

Confusion clouded Awan's face until realization dawned. Her eyebrows rose, and her eyes widened. She peered back at her mother and said, "Uncle Jared!"

Lasha smiled and nodded. "Your father is thirty-seven summers my elder, but Jared and I are of an age. We grew up together and would disappear for hours at a time, exploring the nearby caves and walking along the riverbanks."

"Like Abel and me!" Awan said, recalling how, growing up, she and Abel would spend most of their time together. They had been so close back then.

Lasha nodded in understanding and agreement. "We were the best of friends and would've been more, but it was not to be. Your father was the elder, and it was to him I was promised."

"Did you tell grandfather how you felt?" Awan asked. Tamir was a kind man who loved his only child. Surely, he would have listened to Lasha's pleas.

Lasha eyed her knowingly. "Have you told your father how you feel?"

Awan's eyes fell to gaze at her lap. The answer did not need to be spoken. Awan embraced her mother. They were very close, but now they also shared an experience, more than that, a disappointment, which gave them even more in common. They both knew heartache.

After a while, Lasha moved away from her daughter and picked up the distaff and spindle once more. Awan went back to her weaving, and the two women began their work again without a word. It was as though the recent conversation had not even occurred. The women did not possess the luxury of dwelling on their own desires or pining after what might have been. This was the way things were, and it would do no good to think too much about what they could not change. Resigned, they lapsed back into their mindless work, their delicate fingers moving about the woolen threads, seemingly of their own accord.

Chapter 27

The Community

I did not expect to see much more of interest in the ladies' tent that day, so I left to survey the rest of the community. Of course, I did not leave through the tent flap as a human would. Rather, I passed through the roof and rose into the air above. From here, I could survey the entire village.

The settlement was nestled in the bend of a river that flowed through a broad valley on its way to join with the Tigris to the southwest. Tall mountains framed the eastern horizon, the hazy gray peaks just visible in the distance. A dozen tents like the one in which Awan and her mother worked peppered the area. Most were dwellings where the various families slept. Few were used for work.

Tent cloth was a scarce and precious material, and most work was better accomplished outside in any case. The few candles the villagers possessed were too valuable to be wasted on lighting a tent when the sun provided all the light they needed. Only the women worked indoors, and then only if they were weaving. Fires and ovens, which were too dangerous to be housed in a woolen tent, were kept outside.

As I rose higher through the air, I scanned the surrounding area, pinpointing the people who worked outside in the spaces between the tents. I spotted Tamir, Lasha's father and Awan's grandfather, standing in his workshop beneath an awning of tent fabric that shaded him from the sun as he toiled. He was the carpenter of the village and had built the loom as well as the rough tables and chairs at which Lasha and Awan sat to perform their work.

I saw Jared, the bachelor Lasha had spoken of, sweating before his large clay forge. He had fathomed out that a certain type of greenish rock could be broken down and heated to yield a metal he called copper. Jared formed the metal into many shapes to meet several different applications. The copper could be sharpened to take an edge, which was very useful for cutting, although the soft metal dulled quickly and had to be re-sharpened often.

With the help of Tamir, who fashioned the wood, Jared made axes, knives, and all kinds of other tools that made work easier. He forged shovels and hoes that Adam and Cain used to furrow the soil, preparing it to take seed. Jared relished his work, hard and hot as it was, and he could be found at his forge most of the time.

Turning, I looked in another direction to see Asher the Younger, the husband of Lasha and father of Awan, toiling at his labors as well. He grunted as he rolled a massive round stone back and forth across a great flat slab of granite rock. The two stones crushed wheat and barley grains between them, separating the grain and grinding it into flour. Asher was the village's miller and baker. His job was to take the grain grown by Adam and Cain and turn it into bread. I smiled as I caught the smell of his baking and watched the heat of the clay oven rise, distorting the air above.

I did not see Enoch, Lasha's grandfather and the father of both Tamir and Jared. He was most likely off in the fields, tending the grapes he would later mash and turn into wine.

With my survey of the immediate area complete, I turned back to Abel. He was strolling toward a tent, the largest one in the village, and was a few feet away from it when something suddenly collided with him. He stumbled backward a step and bent over at the waist, wrapping his arms around the projectile. Then he laughed.

Sara, five years old and full of energy, had run around the tent at full speed and straight into Abel. Her head jerked up and, for a second, there was fear in her eyes, but that evaporated when she recognized him. Her face lit up, and she laughed aloud.

"Abel!" Sara threw herself at him once more, wrapping her stubby arms around his legs. Her long brown hair flew in all directions, a bird's nest of knotted strands. Dirt colored her face and knees, which were skinned from play. She smiled up at him, the gap of a missing tooth prominent in the front of her mouth.

Abel knelt, pulling a small purple flower from the sack that hung from his shoulder and handed it to her. "For you, little one."

Sara squealed as she took the present. That was when her mother came hurrying around the tent, panting. Nava was not a young woman. She had seen her own children grow and have children of their own. Now her great-granddaughter, Awan, was about to marry. Nava and her husband Enoch had not planned on having another child, so when Sara was conceived, it had been a surprise. She had forgotten how exhausting raising a young child could be. Nava came to a stop when she saw her daughter with Abel and sighed, grateful someone had managed to slow the girl down.

"Sara," she said, bending over at the waist and breathing heavily. "What have I told you about running off?"

Sara ignored the admonishment. "Look, Mother, Abel is back!"

"I see that. Good day, Abel."

Abel smiled. "Good day, Nava."

"He gave me a flower!" Sara beamed, showing it to her mother.

"That's very nice. Now, come. Your father needs our help to press the grapes."

Sara squealed with delight, clapping her hands while jumping up and down. Stepping on the grapes to render the juice was her favorite chore.

"Can Abel come?" she asked her mother.

"I'm afraid not," Abel said. "I have to get back to the fields."

Sara frowned, her lower lip poking out. Abel mussed her hair. "But I'll see you in a couple of days at the wedding feast," he said.

Sara's face brightened at that, and she threw her arms around him again. After a firm squeeze, she let go and turned to leave with her mother. Then she turned back and eyed him seriously.

"Two days," she said sternly. Those eyes threatened grave consequences should he not fulfill his promise.

Abel laughed. "Two days," he confirmed with a smile.

"Farewell, Abel," Nava said as she led her daughter away.

"Farewell."

Abel paused at the door of the large tent to remove the sandals from his feet before disappearing into the interior. The flap was held open to allow sunlight to enter, but it was still rather dark in the enclosed space. Of course, my angelic eyes do not need light to see, so I had no trouble observing the occupants.

Eve was there. She was over one hundred years old, but appeared to be only middle-aged. The auratic power of the Tree of Life was still strong within her, and it would be centuries before she would begin to truly grow old. She sat at a table, arranging a collection of fruits and vegetables into a variety of ceramic bowls. When she saw Abel, she clasped her hands in excitement and rose from her work. They met in the middle of the tent and embraced. Pulling back, Eve gazed intently at the face of her son as though inspecting it for wounds or other damage. Seemingly satisfied with what she saw, she pulled him close again and kissed his forehead.

"Abel, my dear son, you've been in the fields too long. I've worried about you!"

Abel smiled, the dimples of his cheeks showing. "I've missed you too, mother."

Eve indicated a nearby stool. "Sit," she ordered.

Her son obeyed. Eve began setting food in front of him, and Abel ate almost as fast as his mother could serve him. There was bread, stewed cabbages, dates, and pomegranates. Abel ate all of it. His favorite was the mashed chickpeas that she made into a paste. This he scooped up with pieces of bread and ate along with olives.

Eve poured him a draft of wine from a skin into a clay cup, and he drank with relish. He ate with both hands, alternating between the two as one fed his mouth while the other sought the next morsel. One might have thought he had not eaten in days. He had, but certainly not this well. Out in the fields, Abel lived off his provisions and supplemented those with whatever he could gather in the wild. His mother gazed at him as he ate, a look of bemused satisfaction on her weathered face.

After a while, Abel slowed his feasting. Still chewing, he bent over to retrieve the cloth sack, and setting it on the table, began filling it with food. He still ate, but slower now, and divided his efforts between eating and storing away the food he would take back into the fields.

His mother frowned. "Are you leaving again so soon? Why not stay the night and head back out tomorrow?"

Abel smiled at her, but it was as a parent smiles at a small child. "I can't, Mother. My flock must return to the fields so they can graze and water."

Eve's disappointment was apparent, but she did not wish to quarrel with her beloved son, so kept her feelings to herself.

"Besides," he said as he closed the bag, "I don't think Father would appreciate them being in the village any longer than necessary. Aside from the smell, they would get into all kinds of trouble."

Eve knew her son was right, and she also knew she would not be able to persuade him otherwise. Suddenly remembering something, she stood and said, "I'll be right back," then hustled out of the tent.

Abel shrugged and poured himself some more wine. He tipped the cup up and was drinking from it when a gruff voice issued from the tent door.

"So," it barked, "you have finally decided to come back to civilization."

Abel turned, his cheeks pushed out from the gulp of wine he had just taken. He swallowed the sweet liquid and laughed aloud.

"Hello, brother!" Abel said to the hulking man standing framed in the doorway, his face in shadow against the outside light.

Cain strolled into the tent, then stopped and stood frowning at his younger brother. Abel just chuckled.

"Are you going to greet me," he asked the larger man, "or just stand there as though appraising my value?"

"It wouldn't take me long," Cain scoffed. "I doubt I could get a bushel of weeds for you."

Abel laughed again, carelessly and without concern. His older brother had always been overbearing and domineering, but it did not bother Abel. He spent most of his time in the fields and only had to put up with this treatment during his short visits to the village.

Abel's brother stood a head taller than he and was built like a bull. He smelled like one too, having just come from toiling in the fields. He was broad shouldered and hairy, very hairy. Where Abel's smooth hairless features made him appear more youthful, Cain's long hair, beard, and hairy chest made him appear much older. Like Abel, his skin had been darkened by time in the sun, but unlike his brother, the sun had caused Cain's skin to toughen and take on the consistency of leather. There were wrinkles at the corners of his eyes, which were narrowed, giving the impression he was perpetually squinting. It gave him an intense, frustrated appearance, which often matched his mood.

Cain walked over to the table, sat down, and poured himself some wine. Then he noticed the sack and frowned, his eyes narrowing further. Before his brother could react, Cain snatched it away from him. Abel objected, but Cain pulled the sack close to him and opened it to inspect the contents.

"Oh, I see," he growled. "So, you only come into the village to help yourself to our food and take it with you. Do you have any idea how long it took me to grow these fruits, or to cultivate the grain from which this bread was made?"

Abel retorted, "Do you know how long it took me to raise and tend the sheep whose wool you wear? Without my toils, you would be naked, brother!"

"Toils! You've never toiled in your life!"

Without warning, Cain's arm shot out and grasped Abel by the wrist. The younger brother tried to pull away, but Cain's grip was too strong. He turned Abel's hand palm up and inspected it. Then he grasped that hand with his other and squeezed firmly. Abel winced.

"Do you feel the callouses on my hands, brother?" he said in a low, gravely voice. "Yours are like those of a child, smooth and soft. You sit about all day while your sheep gorge themselves on grass, turning the air fetid with their flatulating. You're as lazy and pampered as they."

Cain let go of his brother's hand at a moment when Abel had made a fresh effort to pull away. The sudden release caused Abel to fly backward, and his stool pitched back with him in it. He hit the ground with a thud. Cain laughed.

Abel jumped back to his feet, his eyes burning with anger. Cain stood as well, his towering frame dwarfing that of his smaller sibling. His eyes flashed with intensity, daring Abel to give him an excuse to turn the argument into a brawl. Abel was no coward, but he knew his brother was physically superior. It would be folly to allow his pride and anger to goad him into a confrontation he could not win.

Abel's dignity was saved by Eve's return to the tent. She walked through the door with a bundle in her hands and a broad smile on her face. Her mouth was open as though she meant to say something, but then she saw her two sons standing there with fists clenched. She stopped short in her tracks, the smile frozen on her face.

"What's going on?" she demanded.

Abel was the first to react. Smiling as though nothing was amiss, he turned to her. "Nothing mother. Cain was simply helping me pack."

Cain made a noise, somewhere between a growl and a scoffing laugh. Sitting back down, he contented himself with partaking of the meal laid out before him. Reassured, Eve stepped forward, remembering her original purpose. She handed the bundle to Abel and grinned as he took it.

"It's a cloak," she explained. "I had Awan weave it for you."

Cain glanced up at the mention of his betrothed, his brows furrowing as he scrutinized the woolen garment in his brother's hands. With a sneer, he turned back to his meal. Raising the cup, he gulped wine, though his mouth was full of food. Thin rivulets of purple liquid ran down his beard to stain his tunic, but Cain did not seem to notice or care.

"It'll keep you warm during cold nights in the open," Eve said.

Abel smiled and embraced his mother, thanking her for the kind gift. As he pulled back, a shadow fell across the doorway of the tent. When he recognized who had entered, Abel grinned widely. "Father!"

"Abel!" Adam exclaimed, his tired eyes brightening, "Welcome!"

Adam made his way from the doorway to where his wife and son stood together, limping as he moved. He often said that God gave him the limp as a reminder of the lion and the consequences of sin. Reaching the pair, he kissed his wife and embraced Abel. Then noticing Cain for the first time, he laid a meaty hand on his shoulder and squeezed. Cain nodded to his father but did not otherwise interrupt his meal.

"It's good to see you, Father," Abel said, "but I must go. I need to get the sheep back out to the fields before dark."

Adam sat down but looked up and nodded to his youngest son. "I understand, but we'll see you back here in two days for your brother's wedding feast, correct?"

"Of course," Abel replied, eyeing his brother. Cain did not acknowledge the reference to his upcoming nuptials, preferring instead to maintain his focus on the meal before him.

"And don't forget," Adam continued, "the following day will be the time for the annual sacrifice."

"I remember, Father," Abel assured him. "I have selected the firstborn of my sheep as well as the youngest and fattest to offer the Lord."

Adam nodded in approval. Turning to Cain, he said, "And you?"

"I am prepared as well, Father," he said. But then, frowning, he added, "The timing isn't ideal, though. I must provide my first fruits to the Lord in the sacrifice, but at the same time, I must provide for my own wedding feast. There's barely enough to do both."

Adam paused, one hand hovering in midair above a bowl of dates. His eyes narrowed and his brows curled together, nearly touching in the middle of his forehead. He turned slowly to his eldest son and said, "It's called a sacrifice, my son, because it isn't intended to be convenient. We give up what is precious to us so that we may demonstrate to the Lord we put nothing before Him. If there isn't enough to do both, then you know which should take precedence."

"I know that," Cain snapped. "That's what I meant. It just… it came out wrong."

"Words spoken without thought are usually the most faithful reflections of our true feelings," Adam chided him further. "Take care of what's in your heart. Then you will never have to explain what you say."

Cain's face reddened, and he glowered at the table, refusing to meet his father's eyes. No one spoke for a long while. This was not the first time Cain had rankled under his father's admonishments. The tension in the tent grew thick until Abel broke the silence.

"Well, I must go," he said, gathering his bag and the bundle. "I'll see you all in two days."

Eve took the cloak from him and wrapped it around his shoulders. "Be safe." She kissed his cheek, and they embraced.

Next, Abel turned to his father, who stood, and they embraced as well. As they pulled back from one another, Abel looked at Cain. "Farewell, brother."

Cain did not look up as he shoved more food into his mouth. The only acknowledgment he gave his brother was a grunt that could have been him clearing his throat. Abel shrugged and turned to leave.

Hovering in the corner of the tent, I shook my head in disappointment. Cain had always been gruff and brooding, even as a child. He resented his younger brother, whom his mother doted upon, and felt the pressure of his father's high expectations. He had grown up fast, but had not matured emotionally. He was perpetually suspicious and jealous of those around him, contriving slights and insults from the smallest of interactions. My thoughts went to Awan, that sweet young girl who was terrified of marrying this rough, irritable man. I felt sorry for her.

I decided I would go with Abel and spend the night watching over him. Before leaving, I took one last glance at the three remaining figures in the tent. Eve sat and poured herself some wine while Adam and Cain ate without speaking. All joy seemed to have left the tent with Abel, replaced by sullen silence. The awkwardness reinforced my decision, and I accompanied Abel into the fields with his flock.

Chapter 28

Abel

Abel frowned, then counted the sheep again. For the third time, the count came out the same. One of the sheep was missing, one of the lambs. That was when Abel realized which lamb was missing, and his search became frantic. He ran to each corner of the pasture and peered out into the distance. It was nowhere to be seen. Undeterred, Abel picked up his staff from the ground, and slinging the sack over his shoulder, set off in search.

The flock was grazing next to the winding river, which was a blessing, as it limited the directions the lamb might have gone. Cain's fields sat to the east, and sometimes the sheep would wander off that way, drawn by the fruits and vegetables grown there. Abel turned and peered into the sky behind him, bringing his hand up to shield his eyes. The sun was about halfway toward the further horizon. It would not be long until the great orb dipped below that far boundary and disappeared, plunging the world into darkness.

I walked alongside Abel as he searched. The lamb must have made it quite some ways by now. I began to worry that some misfortune might have befallen the creature. There were rocky foothills nearby that contained caves as well as deep crevices and crags in the earth. It was possible the lamb might have fallen into one of these gorges, or it may have been preyed upon by a lion or another such wild beast. Abel would not know for sure until he found the lost lamb, and he would not rest until he had.

The evening air was cool as we walked across the valley floor, the short grasses waving in the wind amongst our feet. I could hear the bleating of the sheep to our rear, growing more faint and distant. Glancing over at Abel, I recognized the consternation upon his face. He was concerned about the lamb, but also about the upcoming sacrifice. This was one of the lambs he planned to offer to the Lord. It was the youngest and most valuable of his flock. Abel was concerned because if the lamb were dead, or even injured, he would no longer be able to offer it. The sacrifice must be pure and without blemish. If the lamb were damaged, it would be unfit.

The sacrifice was a ritual that had begun one year after Adam and Eve were expelled from the garden. Every year since, on the anniversary of that day, they and their descendants made an offering to the Lord. This sacrifice was a penance for their sin, but it also showed their thankfulness for God's goodness, His faithfulness, and His grace. This was to be Abel's first sacrifice. It was the year of his coming of age, and as such, he would make his first offering to the Lord. Now he worried it might not go as he had planned.

I heard him begin to pray. He spoke aloud to the Lord, asking that he be allowed to find the lost lamb, not for his own sake, but so that he may offer it to Him. He prayed the lamb would be unhurt, unblemished, and still worthy of sacrifice. At the same time, he acknowledged the Lord's wisdom and surrendered himself to His will. If the lamb was injured, or worse, he told the Lord he would still give Him the best of his flock.

I smiled to myself. Abel's faith was strong. His time in the fields, alone with his sheep beneath the stars, had served to strengthen that faith even further. I was confident the Lord would honor his prayer. At least, I hoped He would.

We reached Cain's fields as the sun dipped low over the far horizon, threatening night. First, we encountered a row of high fruit trees, those Adam had planted a century before. Some were towering monoliths while others stood short and squat. There were shrubs as well. A myriad of different fruits hung from the various plants;

apricots, figs, dates, and pomegranates, to name a few. These fruits represented the bulk of the food that was eaten by the community of Adam and Eve.

Stopping in the grove, Abel called for the lamb, a peculiar, sing-song type of call. He stood still and listened intently. Nothing but the sound of the wind came back to his ears. The musical whine of grasshoppers could be heard in the distance, but nothing that would indicate the location of the lost lamb. I could have scouted ahead to locate the lamb and had considered doing so, but even if I found the creature, I could not have alerted Abel to its location. That would be in violation of standing orders. I was not allowed to help him directly without the express permission of the Almighty. Events must progress naturally and without my interference.

After standing still and listening for a long while, Abel began walking again and soon exited the grove. Stepping out of the long shadow of an olive tree, he strolled into the rows of vegetables Cain had so painstakingly cultivated. At that time, no plow had yet been invented. Cain was forced to dig furrows into the soil with nothing more than the copper-tipped tools that Jared fashioned for him. It took days to prepare the field to take seed, and the work was backbreaking. He had only managed to dig five rows, each for a different type of plant. There were cabbages, lentils, cucumbers, and root vegetables. Kneeling, Abel stooped beside a plant in the far row. He rose holding a large cucumber.

He especially liked the cool refreshing vegetable and was happy to have found a ripe one. If Cain caught him helping himself to what he found in the fields, he would be furious, but the thought did not bother Abel. Everyone in the community contributed in their own way. Only Cain seemed to attach some sense of ownership to what he produced.

In fairness, Abel did not envy his brother. He acknowledged that Cain's labors were more physically demanding than his own. Still, that was the life he had chosen. It did not give him the right to lord over the others. Everything they grew, made, or cultivated was for the good of the community.

Smiling, Abel took a bite of the cucumber and began walking again. He entered the grain fields that grew beyond the vegetable garden, the waist-high stalks waving in the gentle breeze. Abel stretched out his arms, holding them over the tops of the wheat, and let the swaying grain tickle the palms of his hands. Then a puzzled look came over his face, and he stopped, cocking his head to one side. I had heard the sound as well, better in fact than Abel. He took a few tentative steps forward before stopping again.

Leaning in, I whispered into his ear, "Over there, listen."

The sound came again. It was carried by the breeze blowing down from the mountains and was just loud enough for Abel to determine the direction from whence it came. Dropping the half-eaten cucumber, he hurried off in that direction. The sound became louder and more distinct as Abel neared the source. He was closer to the foothills now. Rocky ground replaced the soft grasses that characterized the floodplain near the river. Here the ground was hard and dusty and the slope less gentle. Abel grunted as he lifted his knees and pumped his legs, pushing himself up the rocky hill. The sound was very close now, and it was almost certainly the lost sheep. I could tell from its bleating that it was scared and possibly in pain.

Another, more curious sound drifted toward us as well, a series of sharp barks and yelps overlaid by a cascading whining noise. Abel's face took on an intense look, and he increased his pace. He clamored over a boulder and was about to jump off the far side when he skidded to a stop and froze. Small rocks, disturbed by his frantic slide, skittered off ahead of him and disappeared over the boulder's edge into a wide chasm. I reached out and placed my hand on Abel's chest, steadying him. He could not feel my touch, but he could sense reassurance. I felt the pounding of his heart before pulling my hand away.

Abel squatted atop the boulder, heaving in deep breaths as though he had just completed a headlong sprint. Cautiously, he peered over the edge. The gorge was not exceptionally deep, perhaps only twice the height of a man. Still, if he had fallen that distance onto the rocks below, he would have been gravely injured. The upward slope of the terrain and the boulder had obscured the sudden drop, making it undetectable from below.

The bleating came again, and the sound brought Abel back to his senses. He squinted his eyes in the failing light, searching for the source. There it was, the small lamb, laying on a rocky outcropping about halfway down the crevice wall. A number of these stone shelves dotted the wall of the gorge, forming a path of sorts that wound its way down until it ended abruptly at a sudden drop where the lamb huddled in fear. It could not climb back up onto the path above, and there was no way to crawl down any further. With nothing else to do, the lamb had simply laid down upon the stony shelf and begun to cry.

The more panicked bleating must have started when the jackals arrived. Abel saw them now, three of them, milling about below the lamb and seeking a way to get at the terrified creature. They were in attack posture, their long triangular ears raised and their thick bushy tails tucked down against their hindquarters. One of them leapt at the lamb, but the outcropping was just out of range.

The lamb panicked, skittering around the small ledge on its wobbly legs. I was afraid if it got too close to the edge, it might topple over and fall into the waiting jaws of the pack. Abel yelled at the jackals, and that caused them to scamper backward, but they did not flee. He threw stones, and though he succeeded in making the jackals scurry away, they circled back a few moments later.

I recognized the desperation on Abel's face. Knowing he could not handle the situation alone, he closed his eyes and began to pray. I smiled to myself, pleased that he had decided to let go of control and trust in the Lord. I hoped God would answer his prayer, but there was no guarantee of that. Such a response on the part of the Almighty would depend upon three factors; the faith of the individual, the motive of the entreaty, and God's willingness to accede to the request.

I had no doubts as to the first two conditions. Abel's faith was rock solid, and his motives were pure. He sought to save the lamb so he could offer it to the Lord in sacrifice. Moreover, he was devoid of any selfish motivation. He did not ask so that he would not have to offer up a different lamb in addition to the loss of this one. He was perfectly prepared and willing to give the best of what remained to God. But he wanted to make the best sacrifice possible, one worthy of the Lord, and this was the lamb designated for that purpose.

It was the third condition that gave me pause. If it pleased the Lord to save this lamb, He might do so, but if its demise were part of God's broader plan, He would not. Abel might never know the reason why the Lord had not granted his request. He would just need to have faith that He had not done so for a reason.

But the Lord did answer. He did not speak to Abel, but rather to me. I bowed my head as I heard the voice of the Father say, "Malachi, make the jackals depart."

Without hesitation, I replied, "As it is the will of the Lord, let it be so."

I reached out a hand toward the whining, barking creatures and struck out with my aura. It was imperceptible to Abel or the lamb, but I made it so that the jackals would see. They yelped in terror and pain at the intensity of the light, then turned and fled. Abel mouthed a prayer of thanks.

With the jackals gone, the lamb lay down upon the rocky shelf and whined. Abel surveyed the path to where the lamb huddled, shaking in fear. Once he made certain of the landing below, Abel turned and lay flat upon the boulder. He edged backward until his legs dangled off into empty space. Carefully, he continued until his sandaled feet touched solid ground. Then he eased off the boulder and onto the rocky path below.

I followed him, although not in the way he did. I merely stepped off the edge of the gorge and walked out onto the empty air in front of me. From here I could survey the scene and observe as Abel gingerly made his way down the path, his back to the rocky wall. The path ended a few feet above the shelf where the lamb had fallen.

Abel lay down on his belly and stretched out to take hold of the creature, but it was at the extreme limit of his reach, and he could not quite grasp the animal. After a few failed attempts, Abel decided on a different course of action. He sat up and let his legs dangle over the edge of the path. From here, his feet could almost touch the rocky outcropping below. With care, Abel pushed off with his hands and dropped onto the shelf next to his lost lamb.

The lamb started up in fear and almost fell off the outcropping in its panic, but Abel quickly knelt and grasped the creature, holding it tightly. He spoke to it in a calm, soothing voice, reassuring the animal it was safe. After a while, the lamb calmed itself. Abel sat down and laid the creature in his lap. He looked it over, inspecting it for any injury or damage. Thankfully, he found none. The lamb was filthy but unhurt. Abel mouthed thanks to God for answering his prayer.

Abel nestled the lamb in his arms and scooted out to the edge of the shelf. Then he slid off and dropped to the crevice floor below, his knees bending as he landed. The lamb was startled by the jump and writhed in Abel's arms, but he pulled the frightened creature close and held it against his breast. Then he lifted the small sheep up over his head and rested it on his shoulders, the legs dangling down across his chest. These he grasped with one hand to secure the animal while, with the other, he stroked its head.

By the time Abel found a path up and out of the chasm, the sun had set and darkness blanketed the valley. Still, he knew the way back, and it did not take him long to find his flock again. They were still there beside the gurgling waters of the small river. Most of them had lain down and fallen asleep in the soft grass. Abel approached the flock and laid the lamb, which had also fallen asleep atop his shoulders, beside another of the younger sheep.

Once he was sure of his flock, Abel made his way up the gentle slope of a nearby hill and spread a blanket on the ground. From this vantage point, he could keep an eye on the entire flock. Sitting, he pulled the sack around in front of him and opened it. He ate his evening meal, a piece of bread and a pomegranate, under the light of the moon. When he had finished his supper, he laid back on the blanket and folded his arms beneath his head.

Staring up at the bright stars above, he began to sing. It was a light, high melody that echoed through the valley. I sat down beside him. Closing my eyes, I listened to his clean, clear voice as it rose into the air above. It was a song of praise, an offering of thanks to the Lord. Abel praised God and thanked him for allowing him to find the lost lamb and for keeping him safe during the journey. I smiled at the words that were as sweet as the notes issuing from his lips.

Then my eyes shot open, for I sensed something. A mist coalesced around us as Abel sang. Instinctively, I bowed my head, for the mist was not mist at all. The Spirit of God had descended upon this place. The Almighty was listening to the worship offered by Abel.

And He was pleased.

Chapter 29

The Return

Abel's eyes were closed, but I could see them moving underneath the lids. This always fascinated me, the movement of human eyes while people dream. Although unconscious, his mind was still active, busy sorting things out. I sat there beside him and watched as light gradually moved up his prone form, outlined beneath the cloak his mother had given him. The sun was rising above the far mountains, sending a wave of light down this side of the valley. The light continued up his sleeping body until it reached his mouth, his nose, and finally, the closed yet rapidly moving eyes.

That was when he stirred. The light triggered something in his unconscious mind, and Abel's eyelids fluttered open. He squinted and raised a hand to shield his eyes from the glare of the new morning sun. Opening his mouth wide, he gulped in air, then rubbed his eyes and slowly sat up. The flock was already awake and grazing, leisurely moving across the landscape in search of rich grasses. The songs of birds carried on the light breeze that blew across the gentle slope of the hill. The world was waking up.

The first thing Abel did was count his sheep. They were all there, including the youngest lamb he had rescued the night before. The lamb had found its mother and was feeding. Although it had begun grazing, an activity that led to its wandering off the day before, the baby sheep still derived at least half its sustenance from its mother's milk. Abel knelt beside the young lamb and stroked its head and neck while it suckled. He scratched at its ears, and the lamb tilted its head in response, enjoying the gesture. Abel smiled. He stood and walked through the flock, touching many of the sheep as he went. He patted their backs and spoke to them like they were people.

Once Abel was satisfied that all the sheep were present and safe, he returned to his blanket to have his breakfast, a small serving of bread and dates. He would not eat from the sack for the rest of the day, preserving his rations. Instead, he would gather wild edibles as he went, living off the land. Once his breakfast was ended, he rolled up the blanket and picked up his staff, then made his way down toward the sheep. He began calling out to get them to move, gently prodding them with the staff. At first, they were reluctant, but soon enough one of them set off in the direction Abel had indicated. In a flock of sheep, the leader was often the first to move, and the others followed instinctively.

Watching from atop the hill, I shook out my wings and held them out at full spread, allowing the warmth of the morning sun to wash over them. I basked there in the sunlight for a long while, enjoying the gentle embrace of the star's radiating heat. I did this, not out of necessity, for hosts are not affected by cold, but out of a desire to open myself up to the world the Lord had created, to reach out and embrace the wonder of it all.

The complexity and precision of this planetary machine continued to amaze me. I thanked God every day He allowed me to remain here. From the comings and goings of the people of the community to the fluttering movements of the simplest butterfly, I was in awe of His creation. I was still contemplating when I heard someone call my name, which was surprising. It was only Abel and me out here, and he could not perceive my presence, much less know my name. I turned to see Grigori approaching.

"Good morning!," he greeted me with a broad smile. He was flying. Grigori was never one to walk when he could fly. His wingspan was enormous, which was necessary to support his huge frame.

I remember visiting a remote corner of the earth when we had only been here a few weeks. We were curious about the rest of the planet, so one night while Adam and Eve slept, we stole off to the other side of the world where it was still day. I was amazed at how different the geography of that area was, not to mention the animals. I recall seeing a massive brown creature with a long snout, huge paws, and thick, muscled limbs. Adam had named this creature, as he had all the others in the world, and I remembered him calling it a bear. That is the animal I think of when I describe Grigori, a bear. Well, a bear with wings and no fur, of course.

My friend fluttered down and wrapped those huge arms around me, crushing me in a tight embrace. "How are you, little brother?" His eyes twinkled in the light of the morning sun.

"I am well," I replied, smiling.

Only a few days had passed since I had last seen him, but it seemed much longer. It never ceases to amaze me how the perception of time is altered here on earth. Perhaps it is the segmentation of the days, clearly defined beginnings and endings as dictated by the regular cycle of the sun and the moon. Since there is no night in the Holy City, the passage of time is less determinable. Here it is relentless and absolute.

"What are you doing out here?" I asked him.

"I thought I would relieve you," he answered, his face changing. The smile faded to be replaced by something else. Concern? "I think you should return to the village and assess the situation for yourself."

"What is it? What's happened?"

All sense of mirth left my friend's face as he said, "Valac is here."

"Valac? Are you sure?"

"I'm afraid so. I saw him this morning, speaking with Belial."

Belial was a constant presence in the village. The demon had been there for nearly forty years but had thus far caused little trouble. Every now and again he would tempt one of the children to lie to their parents or to take something without permission. But mostly he just sat around, taking in the warmth of Jared's forge. For some reason, the demon was attracted to the heat. He was a nuisance, but nothing more. Valac was another matter entirely and represented a serious threat.

I gazed at the mountains in the distance, thinking quickly. "Valac hasn't been seen since Asher the Elder died."

Grigori nodded. "I always wondered if he might have had something to do with that. Asher was brash and headstrong, constantly feeling the need to prove his manhood. He went after that boar to prove he was the strongest in the village, and his pride led to him being gored to death."

"Valac specializes in pride," I said.

"Exactly."

"And now he's back?"

"Indeed. When I left, he was following Cain."

"Then you're right. I'd better get back and see for myself." I shook out my wings and rose into the air. "Thank you, my friend."

Grigori smiled sardonically, an unusual look for him. "Of course. I will stay and watch over Abel. See you soon, little brother."

I nodded to him, then turned and flew away.

Chapter 30

Vile Influences

I arrived at the village to find nothing unusual or out of place. Scanning the area, I spotted Cain speaking to Jared at his forge, so I banked my wings and descended toward the pair. As I landed, I sensed another presence, a darker presence. The demon lay stretched out on a pile of wood beside the clay forge. It had positioned itself on its side, one elbow propped up on the woodpile with its head resting on the closed fist of that hand. The demon did not appear to be doing anything, just lying there. Approaching, I realized this was not Valac after all.

"Belial," I snapped at the lethargic figure. He jumped at the bark of my voice, but when he recognized who had shouted his name, a sneer appeared on his ashen gray face.

"Malachi," he scoffed, "you're back. Had enough of the fetid smell of sheep dung already?"

"I prefer it over the stench of your evil presence," I retorted.

This was very much how my interactions with Belial typically began. After a round of mild insults, we would usually leave each other be. Belial was no great threat. So long as he continued to loaf about the forge, so long as he did not disturb the order of the community, I was content to leave him to his indolent existence. He had been here so long that his name had, in some subconscious way, found its way into the vocabulary of the people.

Beli ya'al, meant "without worth", and it was an apt description. Belial was a lazy demon, not especially adept at temptation. He had always been weak and skittish, even when we were brothers in the Morning Star training unit. His form and appearance might have changed, but his weasel-like demeanor had not.

"Where is Valac?" I challenged him.

"Oh, you heard about that, did you?"

Rising to a sitting position, he stretched his arms over his head like a child waking from a nap. Behind him, his black leathery wings stretched as well. That was the most I had seen him exert himself in months. He swung his legs down and let them dangle over the edge of the woodpile, resting his hands in his lap as he slouched forward and grinned mischievously. I had to remind myself that as lazy and ineffectual as he was, he was still a demon of Satan, and not to be too much underestimated.

"Yes," I responded coolly, "I know he has returned. Where is he?"

"Right behind you."

I turned to glance over my shoulder but saw nothing. Then I heard the cackling laugh of Belial and turned back. He had fallen over onto his back and was rolling around on top of the woodpile. He apparently thought he had managed quite the prank and was enjoying himself thoroughly. His laugh was a high-pitched shriek that cracked like the voice of a pubescent boy.

I shook my head and turned away from him again. I would learn nothing more from Belial. He was too lazy to leave the forge long enough to discover anything of Valac's mission and too obstinate to tell me anything of it if he had. I dismissed him from my mind and focused instead on the pair of mortals nearby. Cain and Jared were speaking about the upcoming wedding feast.

"I have fired some clay bowls for food," Jared was saying to Cain, "and twenty clay amphoras to hold wine. That should be sufficient for your feast."

"What about the ring for Awan?"

Jared's eyes lit up. "Oh, I have something special for you there."

He turned and reached for a wooden box that sat on a nearby workbench. Opening it, he showed the contents to Cain, whose eyes widened. He took the box from Jared and examined the ring more closely.

"It shines so brightly," he said with wonder. "What is it?"

"A new metal I've discovered. It doesn't tarnish, and it doesn't rust. It's the purest metal I've ever seen, too soft for tool making, but unequaled in beauty and brilliance. I call it gold."

"Amazing," Cain breathed, "much more impressive than the rings that Nava and Lasha wear."

The practice of wearing rings to symbolize marriage had begun with Adam and Eve's children, although Nava's first rings, the ones given her by Asher the Elder, and later Enoch, had been made of simple woven reeds. Later, when Lasha married Asher the Younger, Jared made her a ring of copper. He also made one for his mother, Nava, when she and his father Enoch celebrated their fifty-year anniversary, but those copper rings tarnished and left a green residue on the fingers of the women who wore them. The ring Jared had made for Awan would not.

Cain closed the box and handed it back to Jared. The latter returned the box to the workbench before turning back to Cain. "I think your betrothed will be pleased," he said.

Cain's face screwed up in frustration. "I hope so. Every time I see her, she turns her head as though the sight of me might drive her to tears."

Jared laughed. "She's a young girl, all knotted up on the inside with female emotion. She'll come around."

Cain did not seem convinced. "Well, she had best do so soon. I've been planning this wedding feast for weeks, and if she embarrasses me, it'll go hard with her once she's my wife."

"I imagine it will go hard with her either way," Jared said, opening the forge door to inspect a ceramic bowl that was heating up within.

Cain's face reddened. "What does that mean?"

Jared turned back with an unworried smile. "I meant no offense, but you aren't exactly the most gregarious of men, Cain. Can you blame the girl for being wary of her future life with you?"

"Why should she be wary? I'll provide for her. She'll have all she needs, a home, food, and a household to maintain. She'll bear my children and raise them as a mother should."

"Romantic," Jared scoffed.

Cain's face flushed again. "Do not mock me, Jared. I'm not feeling especially patient today."

Jared stood up and turned to face Cain. He was not as tall as his great-uncle but was stout and strong. His work at the forge had developed his chest and arms until the muscles were like knotted cords.

"I would suggest," he said calmly, "that you develop patience. I'm not a quivering girl to be intimidated. Besides, if you want jars and pots for your feast, you'll treat me with more respect."

Cain's eyes went wide with anger, and he took a threatening step forward.

"Hit him!" I heard a voice from behind me squeal.

"Silence demon!" I commanded, but Belial did not heed. He had leapt to his feet atop the woodpile, his former laziness forgotten, and crouched like a wild beast ready to pounce. His red eyes, which were trained intently upon Cain, glowed brightly. Turning back, I realized the demon's influence was having an effect. Cain trembled with rage, and his hands formed into fists. He was on the verge of losing his temper.

"Be still," I said soothingly. "Breathe and calm your anger."

"No!" Belial shouted from behind me, "He insulted you. Hit him! Make him pay!"

Ignoring the demon, I focused on Cain. "Think of the consequences. It will not profit you to make an enemy of Jared."

I watched with concern as Cain struggled between the conflicting influences. The muscles of his face twitched, and his eyes shifted subconsciously, first toward Belial, then me, back to Belial, and back to me again. Cain would make his own choice as to which influence he would follow, and I could not tell which way it might go. I had lost this battle before. There were times when Belial or another demon would win out over my or Grigori's more positive entreaties, when the passions of men ran toward the advice of demons rather than angels. Thankfully, this was not one of those times. Cain realized he had pushed things too far. His fists released and he raised his open hands in a mollifying gesture.

"Forgive me, Jared. I'm apprehensive about the upcoming wedding feast, and I fear I may have taken my frustrations out on you."

Jared gave a curt nod in acceptance of the apology. Belial huffed with disgust and disappointment. He lay back down on the woodpile once more, seemingly having lost all interest in the confrontation. I gave him one last warning look and turned my attention back toward the two humans. They were speaking of the wedding feast again but stopped when Jared's attention was diverted by something behind Cain. The latter turned to see what had caught his gaze.

It was Awan and Lasha. They were carrying finished cloth from the tent to some unknown destination, and the path of their errand happened to take them past the forge. Both men stopped their discussion and greeted the two ladies. Cain's face reddened when Awan's eyes dropped toward the ground and she increased her pace.

Lasha had a different reaction, however. She was looking at Jared. Her chin was lowered, and her eyes seemed to dance as she sauntered by, her hips swaying back and forth. She smiled at Jared and he smiled back. Jared was bare-chested, as he often was while working the forge, and I noticed he lifted his chest and pulled back his shoulders ever so slightly. Raising a hand to her, he waved in a friendly, nonchalant fashion.

The cracking voice of Belial behind me said, "Lasha is looking well today."

"You are looking well today, Lasha," Jared said, mirroring Belial's statement.

"Thank you, Jared," She blushed, or at least she gave the impression of blushing.

As the two women disappeared around the corner of a nearby tent, Cain looked at Jared, a strange mixture of astonishment and judgment on his face.

"What was that?" Cain asked.

"I don't know what you mean," Jared replied, turning back to his forge.

"You had best take care. Lasha is a married woman."

"Oh, I'm acutely aware of that," Jared said, his voice loaded with resentment. "Lasha should have been my wife, but Asher claimed her for himself, he being the older brother. Be grateful, Cain, that you are the elder. Otherwise, you might have found yourself doomed to bachelorhood while Awan was promised to your brother Abel."

"I didn't realize you and Lasha had feelings for each other," Cain said.

"No one ever asked. Or cared."

This conversation was taking a turn I had not anticipated. Suspicious, I turned to glance back at Belial. He was whispering, mouthing the words that Jared was saying, or was it the other way around?

"He had better save his concern for himself," Belial whispered.

"But don't worry about me," Jared said. "Save your concern for yourself. I know why Awan weeps at the thought of marrying you."

"What are you doing?" I demanded of the demon, but he ignored me. His focus was trained entirely upon Jared. To my chagrin, I realized his influence over the metalsmith was greater than I had thought. I had mistakenly believed Belial hung about the forge because he was lazy and enjoyed the heat. But it was clear to me now he had been worming his way into Jared's mind for some time. He had obviously become entrenched enough to influence his very thoughts.

Cain's eyes narrowed. "What do you mean?"

"He is witless," Belial whispered.

"Are you really that witless," Jared mimicked, "or do you just choose not to grasp my meaning?"

Glancing at Cain, I saw the anger rise in him once more. I turned back to Belial. He had opened his mouth to speak again, and I had the distinct impression that whatever he planned to have Jared say might cause Cain's anger to boil over.

So, I acted.

I did it without thought. Sweeping out a foot, I kicked a large log at the base of the woodpile. Its sudden removal caused the logs above to cascade downward. A small avalanche of wood ensued and, in the process, Belial was pitched over the edge. He fell to the ground with a thud and cursed.

It was a small violation of the rules, but I gauged it was worth it. In addition to Belial falling and breaking his concentration, both Jared and Cain moved reflexively to steady the woodpile that had inexplicably collapsed. They stooped to pick up the fallen pieces and replace them atop the stack. As he stood back up with a log in his hands, Jared shook his head as though to clear it of a fog. Whatever Belial was going to say had left his mind like a wisp of smoke.

"Are you saying Awan prefers another man? Who?" Cain pressed, eyeing him suspiciously. There were only two unmarried men in the community other than Tamir who was a widower and Awan's own grandfather.

"I've said too much," Jared replied uncertainly.

"Is it Abel she has eyes for?"

"Just be watchful."

Cain appeared to accept that as a friendly warning rather than a provocation. Standing to set a log atop the pile, he nodded and said, "I will. Thank you for telling me. I must go. I still have to see Asher and Enoch about their preparations."

Jared was still a bit out of sorts, but he gathered himself enough to say, "Very well. I'll have the jars delivered later today."

"Thank you." Cain turned to leave.

"Damn you, Malachi!" Belial spat in anger as he scrambled to his feet. "You deliberately interfered with my right to influence!"

"What do you mean, Belial?" I asked, feigning misunderstanding. "Did something come loose from underneath you? I hope you aren't hurt."

Belial bared his teeth, pointed and crooked, and snarled at me like an animal. I just laughed and walked away, following Cain.

Chapter 31

Cain

When Cain found Asher the Younger, he was hard at work, crushing grain with his millstone. He was called the Younger to distinguish him from his father, who had died years earlier, but he was not a young man. His long dark beard was flecked with gray, and the skin around his eyes was wrinkled like that of a much older man. Indeed, Asher appeared as old, if not older, than his grandfather Adam. Neither he nor his father ever tasted the fruit of the Tree of Life. What benefit he derived from it was passed down to him, but being three generations removed from the source, the effect was highly diluted. Asher would die long before Adam, and each succeeding generation would find their longevity reduced by degrees. The line of Seth would be different, for the Spirit of God dwelt with them much longer, culminating in the nearly millennium-long life of Methuselah, the grandfather of Noah.

Asher was a large man of few words who rarely smiled. Seeing Cain's approach, he greeted him with a curt nod of his head and a gruff sound that managed to acknowledge his presence without communicating any welcoming sentiment. Asher did not pause his work until it became apparent that his soon to be son-in-law was not just passing by. Seemingly resigned to the encounter, he rested the stone on the slab and sighed loudly.

"Cain. What can I do for you?" he asked.

"Good morning, Asher," Cain replied in an effusively respectful tone unusual for him. "I'm making final preparations for the feast tomorrow. I thought I would come by to ensure everything was well with you."

"It is well," Asher said flatly. "You'll have your bread. I've milled the grain extra fine to make a whiter flour, and I had Lasha pick through it to remove the husks. It should make for a lighter and sweeter bread than usual."

Cain raised an eyebrow in surprise and genuine appreciation. "Thank you," he said.

Asher nodded and turned back to his millstone, apparently assuming the conversation was at an end. When he sensed, a few moments later, that Cain had not left, an annoyed expression swept over his face. His brows curled in upon themselves and his head jerked sideways ever so slightly, just enough to confirm the feeling. Indeed, there he was, in the corner of Asher's eye, still standing there as though he might have more to say. Asher did not speak. He just stared at Cain, and his eyebrows raised as though to ask, "Well?"

Cain hesitated, looking uncomfortable. When he did finally speak, he did so haltingly. "I would ask you a question," he said.

"Then by all means," Asher said, "do so."

Cain cleared his throat and shifted his feet. He could not seem to find a stance that suited him. Asher let out a sharp breath, expressing his rapidly vanishing patience.

"I've heard," Cain began tentatively, "that Awan doesn't wish to marry me, that she might prefer another man."

"What of it?" Asher asked offhandedly as though the statement meant nothing to him.

Cain's eyes found new intensity at the nonchalance of Asher's tone. They flicked up to meet his soon to be father-in-law's cold gaze.

"Is it true?"

"What does that matter?" Asher did not appear the least bit concerned about the feelings of his daughter on the subject.

"It matters because she is to be my wife," Cain pressed.

Asher laughed gruffly and set down the millstone. He turned to Cain, but the look he gave was not kind or reassuring. "You want her to love you, is that it?" he asked.

"Of course."

"Bah! Love!" he spat. "What does love have to do with anything? Do you think my wife holds any love for me? I have eyes. I've seen how she looks at my own brother, how she goes the long way to pass by his forge. I knew when I married her she did not love me."

"But surely, she has grown to," Cain suggested.

Asher scoffed. "The only thing that's grown between us is resentment and loathing. She hates me, and I can barely stand to be in the same tent with her. We haven't laid together in months, and the thought of doing so makes my stomach turn."

He turned back to his millstone and smashed it down upon the grain as he continued, "Oh, she's a fine woman, but there is no softness in her touch. She is hard as stone and twice as cold. Do not place any faith in the kindness of time to soften a woman's heart. The sooner you abandon that hope, the better."

Cain stared openmouthed, his eyes blinking in astonishment. He had not known there was so much animosity between his betrothed in-laws. Asher continued to mash his grain with an intensity that told Cain it would not be advisable to continue to press him. Without saying anything further, he turned and walked away.

Cain made his way to the fields, a little south of where his own crops grew. This was where Enoch grew the grapes from which he made wine. Enoch was Lasha's grandfather and the great-grandfather of Awan, but he was also the much older brother of Cain and Abel. Cain found him tending to one of his vines, trimming it back to encourage further growth. When Enoch saw Cain, he greeted him warmly.

"Good morning," Cain said, but without much warmth in return. He was still disturbed by his previous conversation with Asher.

"I assume you're here to check on the wine for your wedding feast?"

"You assume correctly," Cain said, a little too sharply. Enoch paused and stared at him for a long moment. Enoch was a kind man with an easy smile and a gentle face, but he was not one to allow rudeness to pass.

Cain must have realized he had spoken offensively because he quickly added, "Forgive me. It's been a difficult morning."

Enoch accepted that with a nod. "Nava is preparing the vats now. I'm waiting for Jared to bring me the amphoras so we can transfer the fermented wine for storage."

"I just spoke to him. He's made twenty amphoras for the feast."

"No," Enoch corrected him, "He's made twenty amphoras, but only ten of them are for the feast."

"Ten?" Cain asked. "Will that be enough?"

"It will have to be. I must present my best product to the Lord for the sacrifice."

"Your best? Then what am I getting?"

"It will be serviceable. I've set aside the first juice as my offering. Your wine is made from the second and third pressings."

Cain's eyes narrowed. Enoch made his wine by pressing ripe grapes in a vat. His wife Nava and daughter Sara would step on them to render the juice, but not all of it could be extracted this way. Enoch would draw off the first juice and press the grapes with stones to extract more. That would be drawn off as well, and a final pressing would render the remaining juice. The first pressing produced the lightest and sweetest juice while subsequent pressings rendered an earthier, less pleasant product that brought with it more of the acidic properties of the skin of the grapes.

"Why didn't you blend the pressings?" Cain inquired.

"Because then I would be offering the Lord the same quality of wine that I'm providing for you." Enoch said as though this should be obvious to Cain. "We are to offer our best to the Lord, our first fruits."

"So, my guests must drink swill?"

The frustration of the morning was building in Cain. He was marrying a woman who might have feelings for another. He had been insulted by Jared but had to humble himself out of fear he might not deliver on his promises. Asher had offered no reassurance, only cold pragmatism. Now Enoch was telling him he was to receive only the lesser wine for his guests at the wedding feast.

"I suppose you could have them drink river water," Enoch chided him.

Cain reddened. I could sense his growing aggravation. Still, he retained enough self-control to realize the situation called for diplomacy, not bullying. He raised his hands and softened his tone. "I didn't mean to insult you, Enoch."

"No, you meant to demand." Enoch was sixty years older than Cain and not accustomed to having demands made of him by someone he considered a child. Cain took a deep breath and tried again.

"My apologies," he said, but added, "Do you think you could give me two or three amphoras of the good wine to begin the feast with? Once everyone has drunk well, they won't notice if the wine served later is of lesser quality."

Enoch scoffed. "You would have me give the Lord some of the lesser wine, so you may have some of what I have set aside for Him?"

"Not necessarily," Cain countered, "but you don't have to sacrifice ten amphoras to the Lord. Seven or eight would still make for a worthy offering."

Enoch threw his hands up in the air and turned back to his vines. "Listen to what you are saying. Holding back a portion of what should be offered to the Lord for selfish reasons invalidates the entire sacrifice. The point is not to offer something to God, but to offer your best. I would suggest you examine your heart before offering your own sacrifice if you wish to find favor in the eyes of the Lord."

Cain spun on his heel in his mounting frustration, and I could read the thoughts on his face. He had not come here for a lecture. He was a man about to the wed, not a child to be scolded. Still, he needed the wine, and it would not do to have Enoch withhold it from him. He swallowed his pride once more, regaining control, and turned back to Enoch.

"Of course," he said with tension in his voice, "you're right. I'm grateful for the wine you are providing."

Enoch made eye contact with his much younger brother and held the gaze for an uncomfortably long period of time. Then nodding, he turned back to his work. Cain moved to leave, but then he hesitated. Turning back to Enoch, he said, "I almost forgot. I was going to ask for the loan of one of your carts. I need to bring my yield back to the village for both the feast and my own sacrifice. May I borrow one?"

A burst of air escaped Enoch's lips, and he shook his head ironically. His chest and shoulders bounded up and down as he laughed softly to himself. Offering Cain a wry smile, he said, "Now you wish to ask another favor of me after the way you have treated my last kindness?"

Cain's mouth tightened and his jaw muscles tensed. He rankled at the word, favor. Cain despised being in anyone else's power. Any other day, Enoch would have gladly given him the use of the cart without another word. He would have to if he wanted regular supplies of fruits, vegetables, and bread. True, Asher was the one who baked the bread, but Cain supplied the grain. Now, because he was asking for such a vast quantity of wine from Enoch, he found himself playing the role of a supplicant. The thought galled him.

Enoch did not press the issue though. He waved a hand dismissively and said, "Take it."

Cain did not hesitate, but neither did he thank Enoch. He turned and left without another word, and I turned to follow him. Then I froze.

I felt something. I had not noticed it before, but now I sensed a presence, a dark presence. Turning in place, I scanned the area around me. Nothing. But there was definitely the imprint of a demon here. The more I focused on the impression, the more I understood it was residual, like an odor left after an animal has passed by. The cause was gone, but the scent lingered. Gazing sidelong, I realized I had sensed it earlier as well, back in the village at Asher's ovens. I now understood that it had not registered with me before because it had been masked by the presence of Belial. But this spoor was different and distinct, the scent of another animal, so to speak.

I followed Cain as he pushed the cart toward his own fields, muttering to himself as he went. I did not hear everything he said, but I did catch the names of Asher, Jared, and Enoch. His expression took on added fierceness when his rant turned to Abel and his flock.

"Idiotic sheep," I heard him mutter. "Dirty, smelly, lazy creatures. Abel is the perfect one to watch over such slothful cravens. They suit each other. What could Awan possibly want with that?"

The wheel of the cart hit a rock, and the impact jolted up Cain's arms. He cursed and gritted his teeth as he angrily forced the cart forward. The wheel bounded up over the rock and came down hard on the ground beyond. The action seemed to sooth Cain's temper, at least momentarily. He increased his pace to burn off the excess energy of his wrath.

Cain was so focused on his anger that the sound did not register immediately. When it did, he paused and cocked his head. There it was again, a low roar, like a distant waterfall. But he was far from the river. As he stood listening, a shadow fell over the face of the earth. Cain glanced up. Then he ran.

Chapter 32

Wrath and Ruin

Locusts.

Normally, the insects were merely a nuisance. But occasionally, something would trigger a shift in their behavior. Even their appearance would be altered. Usually green and solitary, the new brood would become larger and darker with strongly contrasting yellow and black markings. The most dramatic change, though, was in their social behavior. These gregarious grasshoppers would band together to form swarms of thousands. Clouds of locusts would roam across the landscape, devouring every bit of vegetation in their path. They could strip a field in hours, then move on, leaving barren ground behind them.

Cain reached the fields just as the locusts descended on his crops. He swatted at the myriad insects, but to no avail. They buzzed all about him, their wings beating the air like a million tiny drums. Cain shouted at them, but he was ignored, powerless to stop the onslaught.

I stood in the middle of the swarm and watched helplessly as the locusts devoured the crops the village depended on for its survival. If these fields were destroyed, there would be famine and hunger for the small community. I was contemplating whether there was anything I could do when I realized something about these creatures seemed odd to me. While they looked and acted like any other common insect, I had felt something.

With the swarm swirling around me, my hand shot from my side with the quickness of lightning, and I caught one of the locusts in mid-flight. Careful not to injure the fragile creature, I brought the insect up to my face and examined it closely. It appeared to be a normal grasshopper, but there was something within, something dark, sinister, lurking, hidden.

I concentrated my aura upon the creature, forcing the hidden presence to reveal itself. The two tiny compound eyes flashed red, and everything became clear to me. I closed my hand, crushing the tiny insect in an instant. For a moment, nothing happened. Then a whiff of black smoke drifted up through my fingers and retreated away from me. The smoke coalesced a few feet away into the familiar form of a demon, but not just any demon, for I knew this particular fallen host well.

Valac.

He grinned with his chin dipped low and peered at me from beneath bony brows, the red orbs glowing menacingly. He had grown darker since the last time I saw him, his gray skin taught and leathery. The buds atop his head had erupted into two shiny black horns. They were small, not much more than points, but they must be growing, becoming longer as the evil which had consumed my former legion-mate grew within him.

"What is this, Valac?" I challenged him.

"This?" he said in a broken, raspy voice. "This is a swarm of locusts, an act of nature."

"There is nothing natural about this particular swarm. You've manipulated it to serve your own evil purposes. You have broken the peace by possessing mortal creatures to directly harm the humans, which means I may act."

I brought my whole body in tight, contracting my core, building energy. Then I stood, throwing my arms out wide and my aura along with it. I unleashed the full power of the heavenly light contained within my angelic frame, exploding it outward. The effect was potent and immediate. The thousands of demons contained within the swarm of locusts erupted from their insect shells. A multitude of tiny black wisps flew outward in all directions and dissipated into thin air. Where the demons went, I did not know or care. I was prepared for a fight, but they did not offer one. The only demon who remained was Valac, and he made no overtly aggressive move toward me. He had thrown his arms across his face when my aura assaulted his allies, but he dropped them now and stood there motionless, staring at me with that unsettling grin.

I felt the wind change direction. As it did, the swarm of newly freed locusts changed course. They moved on, leaving the crops and fruit trees behind. I surveyed the damage, which was extensive. The swarm had only attacked the field for a few minutes, but the destruction it inflicted in that short time was extraordinary. Cain rushed about, frantically assessing what remained of his once ample crop.

"No, no, no, no, no!" he was saying. He knelt beside a row of cabbages and picked up the remains of one of the heads. It crumbled in his hands, the pieces falling through his fingers. He wept, his sobs a mixture of sorrow and outrage.

I looked back to Valac. He stood frozen like a statue, the evil grin etched onto his bony face. I advanced on him, and he shrank back, unable to stand before the power of my aura. He cackled as he gave way before me.

"Nice to see you too, Malachi," he said in mocking tone.

"What have you done?" I demanded of Valac.

"Oh, not much, not yet."

Cain had stood back up and was cursing under his breath as he stomped about the field. Everywhere he turned, he surveyed damaged fruits and vegetables. Only rarely did he find a piece untouched by the swarm. A few heads of cabbage, some lentils, and a very few cucumbers had survived the attack. These had been sheltered by leaves, but most of the crops had been exposed and ruined. A few might still be edible, but they would not be pleasing to the eye, and they would certainly not be worthy of the sacrifice.

Cain turned in place, trying to ascertain how much worthy produce remained. Then he stopped and stared off toward the edge of the field. I followed his gaze until I saw what had caught his eye. When I did, my heart sank. Valac cackled in perverse glee.

It was the lamb, the same lamb that had wandered off from Abel's flock the day before. It must have wandered off again, drawn by the vegetables grown here. It stood munching on lentils at the far end of the field, oblivious to the dramatic scene that had just played out. When Cain saw it, he flew into a rage and ran at the lamb screaming.

The lamb squealed and turned to run, but not quickly enough. Cain lashed out at it with a leg that caught the lamb full on its underbelly. Cain had been running at a full sprint, and the force of his kick lifted the lamb bodily off the ground. It cried out as it flew to land on its side a few feet away.

The lamb struggled to rise, but Cain was on it again, kicking and stomping viciously in his roiling anger. The lamb bleated desperately, its cries falling on deaf ears as Cain continued to pummel it mercilessly. When a few moments later, it stopped struggling, Cain paused just long enough to locate a nearby rock. Raising it in his hands, he held the stone high for a moment as he stared hatefully at the stricken creature. There was no mercy in his eyes, only rage.

The lamb made one last desperate attempt to stand, to scuttle away from this terrible attacker, but that movement only triggered Cain into action once more. The rock came down hard, and I heard the sickening wet sound of ripping flesh and bruising muscle, followed by the cracking of bone and joints as Cain repeatedly pounded the baby sheep with the jagged rock. He dropped to his knees to hold the animal more securely with one hand while he wielded the rock with the other. It rose and fell more rapidly and with devastating force.

Horrified, I glanced back to Valac and saw him mimicking the motions of Cain, his right arm rising and falling as though he were the one striking the defenseless creature. Or was it Cain who mimicked his motions? Valac's red eyes burned bright, a sure sign that his vile influence was concentrated on the rampaging human. The demon's mouth was open with a broad smile that exposed his long fangs. He was in ecstasy of this carnage.

Turning back to Cain, I watched helplessly as he continued the slaughter of the innocent creature. The rock struck the weakened animal in the face, crushing an eye socket and reducing the eyeball to jelly. Blood flew up and speckled Cain's twisted face. Over and over he struck until finally, the blows slowed as his arm tired and became heavy. With his energy and rage spent, Cain sat exhausted, heaving in huge gulps of air as he hovered over the body of the unfortunate animal.

I stepped forward, appalled and disgusted by the scene I had just witnessed. Gently, I reached down and touched the top of Cain's hand. At my touch, unperceived by him except on a sub-conscious level, the rock fell from his fingers to land upon the ground with a dull thud, covered in innocent blood, torn pieces of flesh, and bloody clumps of wool.

The whole world went silent. Even the heaving of Cain's chest as he breathed heavily seemed to make no sound. In the stillness of that moment, all I heard was the last ragged breath of the baby lamb. It was a long, weak, and wet sound, the last bit of air escaping from the shattered lungs of the poor creature. Horrified, I looked away from the gruesome scene.

As sound returned to the world around me, I became aware that Valac was cackling with glee. My anger snapped, and I turned on him in a rage, closing the distance before he could react. My hand clamped around his throat, and I lifted the demon high into the air. The evil laughter was replaced by a guttural choking sound. I could tell that the contact of my hand on his throat burned him, and I was glad of it. Let my aura burn the evil away. The demon's claw-like hands attempted to break my grip, but the white-hot aura of my arm caused the gray fingers to burn wherever they touched me. Frantic, Valac tried swiping at me with his talons. They opened small wounds that caused my aura to lance out like sunbeams until they closed a moment later. These shafts of heavenly light seared the skin of the demon, increasing his panic. He kicked at me, but without effect. He was at my mercy, and I was not feeling merciful.

Someone called my name, "Malachi."

I turned my head to see that Grigori was standing close by. In the heat of the exchange, I had not noticed his arrival. He peered at me disapprovingly.

"Let the demon go," he said. I looked at him blankly, as though I did not understand. The screaming intensified, and I glanced back to see smoke rising from beneath my fingers where I held Valac by the throat. I did not want to let go. I wanted to make him pay.

"Malachi," Grigori said again, softly, as a mother speaks to her child.

I felt my anger settle and subside. With a sigh, I let go of Valac. He dropped to the ground with a thud and scrambled away from me.

"You will pay for that, traitor!" he hissed. He never seemed to tire of reminding me that I had turned my back on the Morning Star and was considered a traitor by the entire demonic horde. "You risk open war by attacking me."

I waved a dismissive hand in his direction, but I knew he was right. The delicate balance that governed this conflict was dependent on avoiding outright violence between angelic and demonic forces. We were not permitted to attack each other directly, only to influence.

I ignored Valac and instead made my case to Grigori. "He broke the peace by using those locusts to attack Cain's fields."

"True," my friend agreed, "and you dealt with that violation in an appropriate and proportional manner. Let's not escalate the situation further."

I reluctantly nodded my assent, but I was not quite finished with the demon. Turning back to him I said, "You've been busy, Valac. I sensed your presence in the village and at the vineyard. What game are you playing at?"

Valac glared up at me, one hand rubbing at the burns on his neck. Demonic wounds do not heal as easily as angelic ones, and it would be some time before he was fully restored. I drew a small measure of satisfaction from that knowledge.

He bared his teeth at me, then smiled and said, "The same old game, Malachi. And just in case you were not keeping score, I am winning."

He turned to look at Cain as he spoke the last words, and I followed his gaze. Cain had stood and picked up the broken body of the stricken animal. He carried the lamb some ways to a gorge, much like the one where Abel had found it before. Without any sign of emotion, he contemptuously tossed the corpse over the edge and into the chasm. When Cain returned, it was with a blank expression on his face. His anger was spent but not sated. It was like the smoldering embers of a fire that has died down, ready to spring back to life with the introduction of new fuel. He turned in place, again surveying the damage caused by the swarm.

Raising his face to the heavens, he shouted angrily, "Why would You do this? I am supposed to have a wedding feast tomorrow and sacrifice to You the next day! Why would You allow this to happen to me? I can't offer my best to You when I have nothing left!"

"He's blaming the Lord," the demon pointed out with a laugh. "He will justify his next actions based on the belief that God has placed him in this position. He will absolve himself of any responsibility, seeing himself as the victim. So human."

I could see the demon had it right. Cain was already weighing the options open to him. There was not enough of his crop left undamaged to allow him to present his best to the Lord in the sacrifice while also making a good showing at his wedding feast. He would have to curtail one or the other, and based on what I knew of Cain, I had little faith that he would make the correct choice.

I felt my anger rise again. Turning, I glared at the demon and said, "Leave, Valac. I want you gone from my presence."

The demon scoffed. "You can't order me, Malachi."

I took a step toward my adversary, and that step held the promise of more pain for the vile creature. He threw up his hands and said hurriedly, "Fortunately for you, I'm done here for now, but I'll see you again soon. Of that, you can be sure."

He shook out his black wings and flew off, back toward the village.

"I will follow him," Grigori said.

"No," I replied. "I'll go. You had better see about Abel. He will be looking for his lost lamb again, and this time the search will not have a happy outcome."

He nodded agreement, but cautioned me, saying, "Do not allow Valac to manipulate you. Your anger is your weakness, Malachi. Do not give the demon the justification he needs to act more boldly. Keep the peace."

"I will," I promised him.

As my friend rose into the air, his broad white wings outstretched, he said, "I'll see you at the feast tomorrow, little brother. I have a feeling we will have much work to do."

In that he was correct.

Chapter 33

A Wedding and a Feast

The aromas of various foods wafted up from the table and mingled, combining to create a sensational fragrance that tantalized the assembled guests. A multitude of dishes were arrayed, covering the surface of the table; baskets of fresh bread loaves with crisp brown crusts, sweet cakes drizzled with honey, and ceramic bowls overflowing with fruits and vegetables. There were high domes of olives, dates, pomegranates, boiled lentils, stewed cabbages, cucumbers, and figs. Eve had combined boiled dates and figs mixed with honey to form a sweet paste that could be spread over bread. She had also made more of the mashed chickpeas mixed with olives that everyone enjoyed so much.

I smiled and took in the pleasant odors. I have often wondered what it might be like to eat food. Because that is something angels cannot do, I contented myself with smelling the sweet scents as the newly married couple entertained their guests.

The wedding had gone well and without incident. Awan had not cried, and Cain had not lost his temper. It appeared the young girl had accepted her fate, and having done so, was more emotionally prepared to follow through with the ceremony. Still, she did not look any happier. The sadness of her expression made her blue eyes appear that much larger, which ironically accented her beauty.

She was dressed in a long flowing robe of the finest cloth Lasha could make, dyed the lightest shade of blue and purple I had ever seen. It was nearly translucent, no mean feat for a garment made of rough spun wool. There were flowers in her soft black hair which had been pulled up behind her head, with thin, delicate curls cascading down about her olive face. On her left hand, she wore the ring of gold Jared had fashioned for her.

Cain was dressed in his best robes, dyed with bold colors of red and brown. His dark hair and beard had been trimmed and brushed, which was good. It made him appear less intimidating and more civilized. The new look had gone a long way toward putting Awan's mind at ease. She was still scared and secretly heartbroken, but she did not weep and even smiled sweetly when she greeted Cain for the first time as his wife.

Cain and Awan now sat at a small table near the front of the gathering while the guests milled about, socializing, dancing, and partaking of the plentiful food and drink. Occasionally, members of the family would stop by the table to offer the newlyweds blessings on their future life together. Many of them complimented Cain on the lavishness of the feast. He thanked his guests effusively, encouraging them to eat and drink as much as they liked. To their credit, none of the guests commented on the wine, which unlike the food, was barely fit for consumption. Cain had wrinkled up his nose the first time he tasted the bitter vintage, flush with the earthy tannins of later pressings, but he did not complain. It would not do to appear ungrateful to Enoch for what he had provided.

The lack of quality had certainly not prevented Cain from drinking his fill. Indeed, his face was flushed, and he spoke much more loudly than usual. In the beginning, the warmth he felt from the wine had made him more magnanimous and convivial, but as the evening wore on and he drank more, he began to grow irascible, his irritation quick to manifest itself. Most of that irritation was directed at Awan, who could not seem to do anything to her new husband's satisfaction.

Cain shoved more food into his mouth. He had refilled his plate more than once and it was already nearly empty again. Awan, on the other hand, had hardly touched hers. She sat stiffly with her hands in her lap and stared blankly ahead.

"Eat, my dear," Cain said through a mouthful of food, "and drink. This is a wedding, not a funeral!"

Awan smiled sheepishly. "I'm not very hungry, and I'm tired. It's been a long day."

Irritation flashed in Cain's eyes, and he grabbed his new wife's arm under the table, squeezing it so hard that Awan cried out in pain. Leaning over, he whispered roughly into her ear, the stink of his drunken breath hot and wet upon her face.

"This is our night of celebration. You will smile and enjoy yourself, and I don't want to hear any complaints. Do you understand?"

Awan nodded briskly, tears growing in her eyes. She blinked them away and affected a warm smile. Cain released her arm, but I could see from the pain on the young bride's face that he had hurt her. Concerned, I walked up to the pair and stepped around behind them. That is where I found Valac, crouched behind Cain and whispering to him in a low voice.

"She is embarrassing you," he hissed menacingly. "You have planned this night for weeks, overcome challenges and obstacles, and now she is complaining she is tired."

The red eyes glowed as the demon whispered, his hands clawing at the air as though drawing his victim's will toward him. Cain's head was turned to glare down at his wife, the expression on his face one of suspicion and scorn. I stepped closer to better hear what poison the demon was pouring into his mind.

"You know what she is really doing. She is sowing the seeds of her later excuses now, hoping she will be able to convince you that she is too tired to lay with you tonight." Valac grinned as he pressed his case. "She is already defying you. You should teach her a lesson once you have gone into your tent. Better to put her in her place now than to have her test your will in the future."

"Stand aside, Valac," I commanded and was rewarded by a startled expression on the demon's face. He scampered back away from me, and I turned to Cain.

"Do not listen to the voice of evil," I said. "Your wife is young and innocent. She does not mean any offense. She is nervous, but that is to be expected. Be kind to her. She is your wife, and your duty is to protect her."

Cain's face twitched. He looked back up and away from Awan, but his expression did not change. My words had reached him, but they had not touched him. I had the unsettled feeling he was more attuned to the influences of Valac than to me. I turned a threatening look at the demon who cowered a few feet away. When my eyes met his, he hissed and scampered off. He was not done, I was sure, but at least Cain would be free of his temptations for the moment. Peering around the pair, I watched the demon slink off to where Asher stood speaking with Enoch. I walked that way, intending to keep a very close watch on Valac.

Cain was not the only one who had drunk well. Asher spoke loudly to Enoch with exaggerated emphasis on his words as though he was making some profound point he wanted to ensure was not missed. Jared had enjoyed his fill also. He stood by the table of food, picking at the assorted dishes in between gulps of wine from the clay cup in his hand. Lasha stood with him, reminiscing about their youth when they had spent so much time alone together. I frowned when I saw Lasha reach out and touch Jared's arm lightly. I decided I would need to keep an eye on them as well.

Tamir conversed quietly with Adam and Eve about some project the woodworker was endeavoring to master. He had an idea that by mixing mud with straw and allowing it to bake in the sun, he could fashion buildings from something other than tent fabric.

"Imagine," he said, "a structure that's not susceptible to wind, that would remain cool in the summer and warm in the winter. It would be safer to have fires inside to heat the home and to cook with."

Adam nodded in agreement. "It would allow us to build larger structures as well."

Tamir's head bounded up and down with enthusiasm. "Exactly!"

Moving away from the small group, I spotted Nava. She was tending to her daughter, Sara, who had managed to smear honey all over her face. Nava had wet a strip of fabric from her tunic and was rubbing at the sticky residue on Sara's cheeks.

The only person missing from the gathering was Abel. He had missed the wedding entirely, and it looked as though he might miss the feast as well. When he did not arrive in time for the ceremony, Eve had showed concern. Cain, on the other hand, did not seem disappointed. Then Jared had suggested Abel might not have wished to witness the union, contributing to the idea that perhaps Abel had feelings for Awan. That rankled Cain.

It was Belial who had planted the idea in Jared's mind. The imp had been scampering about from person to person, whispering small lies and temptations into the ears of those he thought susceptible. I kept a close watch on him, but for the most part, he stayed near Jared. He left Adam and Eve alone, along with Enoch, Tamir, and Nava. He knew his sway over them was limited. They were closer to the Lord than Jared, Asher, or Cain, and their faith preserved them against susceptibility to the demon's influence.

I was concerned about Lasha, though. Belial had focused on her recently, and he was with her now, encouraging Asher's wife to act more forward with Jared. He sat perched behind her, whispering while Jared talked about his newest discovery, the metal he called gold.

"It's amazing," he was saying. "I can create molds to shape it into a wide variety of forms. It's a magical metal, pure and beautiful, just like you, my dear."

He bowed to Lasha as he said these words, and she giggled like a young girl. I doubted Jared would have made such a comment if he had not been feeling his wine. I needed to encourage him to slow down. The effects of drink make men more susceptible to the influences of the enemy. It lowers their defenses along with their inhibitions, weakening their ability to resist demonic temptation.

I moved that way, but then I caught a glimpse of light from the corner of my eye and turned to see Grigori descending from above. He wore a vexed expression.

"What is it?" I asked, "Where's Abel?"

"He will be here shortly," Grigori answered as he landed. "He found his lost lamb."

I could imagine the heartache Abel must have felt when he saw the condition of the stricken creature.

"That's why he is late for the feast," Grigori explained. "He realized the lamb had wandered away again and set off in search of it. He found it just before the sun set."

I nodded. "How is he?"

"Sad," my friend replied. "He doesn't realize anything nefarious befell the creature. He thinks it fell into the gorge again on its own. The jackals had gotten to it, so by the time Abel found the lamb, there wasn't enough left to discern the cause of its demise."

"That may be for the best," I commented.

Grigori gave me a pained expression and continued, "He buried the remains, then thanked the Lord for all the blessings in his life and asked forgiveness for allowing the lamb to wander off again."

I pressed my lips together and nodded slowly, a wry smile forming on my face. The contrast between how Abel had chosen to deal with adversity compared to his brother was a stark comparison. It occurred to me Abel possessed a spiritual maturity that Cain lacked.

I opened my mouth to share my thoughts with Grigori but was interrupted by an angry shout from my right. Turning, I saw Asher standing in front of Jared with Lasha attempting to separate the two. Asher was red-faced, and only some of that flush was from the wine.

"Stay away from my wife!" Asher shouted at him, reaching over Lasha's shoulder to grab at the younger man. There was an expression of intense bitterness on Lasha's face as she held her husband back. Grigori and I moved that way, and that was when I spotted the two demons. Valac was next to Asher while Belial stood beside Jared. They were shouting at each other as though they were the ones having the argument.

"If she is your wife," Belial screeched at Valac, "perhaps you should treat her that way!"

No sooner had Belial begun to say this than Jared echoed the statement, each syllable uttered a second after Belial had spoken.

Valac shouted back at Belial, and Asher parroted him in the same manner.

"Do not tell me how to treat my own wife!" Valac/Asher responded heatedly.

"Someone has to take care of her," Belial/Jared shouted back. "If you aren't man enough, perhaps I should do it for you!"

Grigori and I were still a few steps away when Valac shouted and lunged at Belial. The movement was copied by Asher. He punched Jared in the face, and the latter fell, knocking Lasha to the ground in the confusion. Asher pounced on top of him and began punching at his face with alternating fists. The scene was copied a few feet away by Valac and Belial, although as Valac pounded Belial's face with his own fists, Belial laughed with maniacal pleasure.

"Stop this," I implored the two men, but they could not hear me. Anger creates a cloud that acts as a barrier against angelic influence, and my words could not penetrate. Demonic influence, on the other hand, is intensified by rage, and the demons currently had nearly complete control over the two men.

Realizing that any effort on my part to encourage the combatants to settle down would be futile, I instead turned my attention to the bystanders. Adam rushed forward, limping toward the entangled pair as quickly as his bad leg would allow. When he reached Asher, he wrapped his arms around his waist and pulled back with all his strength. With effort, he tore one grandson off the other.

Jared lurched to his feet and tried to take advantage of the situation by attacking the restrained Asher, but Tamir jumped in front of him at that moment and held him back. The two men fought against those who held them, attempting to rejoin the conflict. Adam spun and flung Asher backward, creating more space between the antagonists. Asher, flush with drink, stumbled and fell. He regained his feet, albeit unsteadily. That was when Lasha came flying in, launching herself against her husband in a blind rage. She pounded his chest with her fists and cursed him.

"You aren't a man!" she spat. "You are a pig!"

Belial had abandoned Jared and transferred his attention to Lasha. The bright red of his eyes was focused on her as she railed against her husband. Valac, who had returned to Asher's side, lashed out at the smaller demon. In his rage, incapable of rational thought and too much attuned to the vile influences of Valac, Asher imitated his motion and struck his wife full in the face. She fell spinning, and landed face down, sprawled across the grass. Tamir, seeing what had just happened to his daughter, released Jared and flew at Asher. He punched him squarely in the jaw, and the older half-brother went down hard. Adam grabbed Tamir, restraining him in turn.

Then Cain entered the fray. At first, he had been mildly entertained to see the two men go at each other, but he had grown annoyed as the argument escalated. This was his wedding feast, and this fight was ruining it. Anger flashed in his bright red face as he waded into the engagement.

"Stop it, all of you!" he shouted.

Brushing past her new husband, Awan rushed to her mother, who still lay on the ground, and helped her to sit up. The momentary lapse in activity seemed to leech the energy out of the moment. The eyes of the men cleared, the fog of rage dissipating from their faces. But Lasha's rage had not lessened. Her bruised face set into an intense hateful visage as she glared up at her husband with an expression of pure loathing.

"I think it would be best," Adam spoke up, "if we put an end to this night."

Cain nodded. "Come, Awan," he said, reaching out for her.

The girl looked up at him, at first confused. Then the meaning of his words clarified in her mind, and she understood that the moment she had been dreading had finally come. She began sobbing and shaking her head. She clung to her mother, no longer lending support, but desperate to claim it for herself. Cain stepped forward, his patience exhausted, and grabbed her by the arm. As he pulled her up to him, Lasha reached out and took hold of her other arm.

For a moment, Awan stood stretched between them. Then Cain wrenched her away from her mother and wrapped his arms around her, not lovingly, but as a captive. Awan cried aloud and her legs released beneath her. Cain bent slightly at the waist as he struggled to hold her dead weight aloft. Awan sobbed uncontrollably in his grasp.

"Silence, woman!" he snapped at her. Adjusting his grip, he stood and pulled her upright again.

"Is this what you want?" Lasha demanded of Cain. "Do you wish for your wife to hate you as I hate my husband?"

"Asher," Cain said, turning to his father-in-law, "control your wife."

Asher obeyed. Stepping forward, he pulled her up by her arm as well, almost in imitation of Cain, and turned to take her away. Jared stepped forward, but Adam and Tamir prevented his interfering.

Fighting against Asher, Lasha turned back to Cain and shouted, "History repeats itself, Cain. Just as I was forced to marry the brother of the man I loved, so do you now force that fate upon your own wife. Mark my words, she will grow to resent and hate you as well. She may be your wife, but you can't command her heart. That, she holds for another!"

The blood rushed to Cain's face as he comprehended the meaning of her words. He had suspected that Abel was the man implied in Jared's warning, but now Lasha had confirmed it. Embarrassment and anger filled Cain's countenance as the truth descended upon him.

"What's going on here?" someone asked from behind the group.

Cain's eyes widened at the sound of this new voice, and he turned to glare at the source of the question, rage etched on his face. The newcomer stood confused and alarmed, oblivious to what had just transpired and why Cain might be looking at him that way.

"You," Cain breathed through tight lips and nearly clenched teeth.

Abel had finally arrived at the feast.

Chapter 34

The Sacrifice

Cain groaned.

The sun was rising, peeking out from behind the mountains to the east and bathing the valley in the warmth of its morning light. The door flap of the tent stood wide open, and a shaft of light lanced through, stabbing at Cain's closed eyes. He squeezed his lids tightly and rolled over, pulling the sheepskin blanket across his aching head. Lying next to him, Awan still slept, wrapped in a woolen blanket. The bed, little more than a pile of straw with furs laid atop, was uncomfortable and she had slept little. She spent most of the night staring at the roof of the tent with tears streaming down her reddened cheeks.

The night before, when Abel arrived at the feast, Cain had flown into a rage and had to be restrained by Enoch and Tamir. Unable to get at his confused brother, he had diverted his anger toward Awan. He pointed at Abel, but his head turned to glare accusingly at his wife.

"You would rather be with him?" he asked her.

She had not been able to speak. Her whole body trembled uncontrollably, tears streaming down her face, and she could not seem to breathe. Her belly contracted in a series of shallow bursts, but her lungs would not open to let in air.

When she did not respond, Cain pressed, "Do you prefer the smell of sheep dung? Would you like to sleep in the open fields, cold and bruised from laying on rocks?"

Still, Awan did not speak. Sobbing, she lowered her gaze to the ground and stared at her feet, focused only on slowing the rhythm of her heartbeat and calming her panicked chest. Eve and Nava approached then. They stood with the young girl and lay a woolen blanket across her shoulders. They had seen enough of the abuse she had taken and were determined to protect her from more. Likewise, Adam walked up to Cain and spoke to him sternly.

"She is young, my son," he said, "and I think she has been through quite enough tonight already."

Cain scoffed and turned away from his father. Abel, still confused by his unintentional role in this family squabble, stepped forward and asked, "What are you talking about, brother?"

Cain stepped within arm's reach of his younger brother and glowered down at him. Enoch and Tamir stepped closer to the pair, prepared to intervene again if need be. Cain turned his head left and right, acknowledging their presence, but did not appear concerned by it.

Turning back to his brother, he said with exaggerated calmness, "It seems that my wife did not wish to marry me, but would have preferred you instead."

Abel's mouth fell open and his eyes widened. He peered past his brother to where Awan stood staring at the ground, her shoulders bobbing up and down to the rhythm of her sobs.

He looked back to his brother and said, "I didn't know."

Cain's eyes narrowed. It was unclear whether he found this pronouncement of innocence reassuring or if lack of collusion might be irrelevant to him. Complicity on Abel's part might be unnecessary for Cain to feel threatened.

Perhaps sensing this, Abel added, "I assure you brother, I have no feelings for your wife, aside from friendship and the love I hold for all members of our family. I wish you nothing but happiness in your marriage."

I heard Awan gasp, and Cain heard it as well. Turning, he glowered at his new wife. She wilted under his gaze, but it was clear to all present that she was devastated by Abel's statement. That was when Adam stepped forward. Grigori had been speaking to him, encouraging him to take control of the situation. The demons had enjoyed too much success this evening. We needed someone to take a stand.

"Listen to me, all of you," Adam began, "tomorrow is the day of sacrifice. You should be spending this time preparing your hearts and minds to make an offering to the Lord, not bickering with each other."

Enoch stepped up next to Adam and added his own voice in support.

"Some of you have drunk too much wine. We should all go back to our tents and examine our hearts before we present ourselves to the Lord tomorrow. We must approach the altar pure of spirit."

Tamir voiced his agreement. Jared was nowhere to be seen. He must have left at some point after Abel's arrival. Cain stared at his brother for a long time. Then, without a word, he took his wife by the hand and tugged her toward him. As she stumbled forward, the blanket fell from her shoulders to the ground. Eve knelt and picked up the blanket, clutching it to her breast.

Dazed and stricken, Awan allowed herself to be guided toward Cain's tent, but she kept her face pointed back at her mother. There was an intense sadness in her eyes, but she had ceased to weep. She seemed resigned to her fate, her last hope dashed by Abel's rejection. Awan's gaze remained locked on the face of her mother until she was pulled into the tent and out of sight by her new husband.

Later, Cain had lain with his wife. He had not been gentle, his anger fueling his passion. Valac had been in the tent, urging him to be rough with her, to teach her not to defy him. I did my best to counteract his vile suggestions, but Cain closed his heart to my influence. When he was finished, Awan lay there unmoving, her body rigid while she stared at the roof of the tent. Cain did not seem to notice, and he was snoring loudly within a few moments. Awan continued to lay still as a corpse, the woolen blanket pulled up high beneath her nose, staring off into the blackness. It was a long time until sleep finally, mercifully, came to her.

Now, Cain was awakening. I could tell from his expression that his head ached, as it should. He was paying the price for his overindulgence the night before. Gingerly, he opened his eyes. The soft, warm light of the morning sun must have appeared overly harsh and bright to him, for he closed them again just as quickly. It took him a long time to rouse himself. When at last he did, he stumbled out of the tent to a nearby basin and dunked his head in the cold water. He gasped as his head emerged into the morning air, water cascading down from his head and running from his hair and beard. He shook his head violently, sending spray in every direction.

The cart he had borrowed from Enoch sat nearby and was loaded with the produce he intended to offer the Lord. I followed as he set off with the cart. It was not a long way to the place of sacrifice, an altar that Adam had erected on a nearby hill. Abel was there already, kneeling beside Adam at the bottom of the hill. He had three small lambs with him, each held by a leather thong about their necks. Abel knelt next to them, brushing their bright white wool and picking out any specks of dirt he could find.

Abel stood when Cain arrived, but neither he nor his father spoke. Instead, Adam glanced down at Cain's feet and made a gesture that he should remove his sandals. He and Abel were barefooted, for they stood on holy ground. Cain did as he was instructed.

Grigori walked up to me as Cain began taking the baskets of fruit from the cart and laying them upon the ground in preparation for the sacrifice. I scanned the area but saw no sign of any demons. They would not dare to step foot on holy ground, but they might be lurking nearby.

"Good morning," I greeted my friend.

"Good morning, little brother."

"How go the sacrifices?"

Grigori nodded his head. "Well, thus far. Tamir brought the wood to start the fire. It was seasoned wood he had spent months drying. He could have made many things from that wood, but he sacrificed the best of it to the Lord."

I nodded in approval, but still, I was wary. The night before had been a catastrophe. Never had the demons managed to set the humans at each other that way. Violence was rare, but the number of people involved was the most alarming aspect of the confrontation. It seemed that rifts were opening in the community.

"We have much work to do," I told Grigori. "Valac and Belial have been busy, and they've accomplished much more than we realized."

My friend nodded somberly. "The real danger is Valac. Belial is a nuisance, nothing more. He has been here for decades, hanging about the forge with nothing to show for it but a few small lies from the children. Valac is different. He is focused and driven."

"You're right," I agreed. "Belial is lazy and inept, but he does have one advantage that Valac lacks."

Grigori glanced at me as though to say, "And that is?"

"He's been here for decades, and while he has accomplished little, some in the community have grown very comfortable with his presence. Over time, his many small temptations have allowed him to build a momentum of influence. His level of control over the thoughts of some in the community is alarming."

Grigori mulled on that, biting his lower lip as he nodded. I smiled to myself despite the grave nature of our conversation. In these little moments, I appreciated how much we had begun to emulate the humans in our gestures and facial expressions. My friend glanced back at me and sighed, another very human reaction.

"I had not considered that, but you're right. It may explain how Valac has been able to accomplish so much in so little time. He's using the network established by Belial. Still, I feel he is the real threat. Without him, Belial will go back to tempting children to steal honey cakes."

I peered up at the altar as Abel led his lambs up the hill.

"Perhaps," I said. "I only hope that today can be a new beginning. They are sacrificing to the Lord, which should remind them of their need to resist temptation and overcome sin. We must leverage this focus to restore their faith and urge them back to righteousness."

Abel reached the top of the hill with his lambs and stood before the altar, a tall pile of roughhewn stone with a shallow pit in the center. Smoke rose from the pit where Tamir's wood burned. The various offerings made by the people would be consumed upon the altar, taken by God.

Abel tied the leather thongs to a nearby post to secure the lambs. Then he took hold of the smallest lamb and removed the strap from its neck. These lambs were the firstborn of his flock. The lamb slain by Cain had been the youngest, and it was that lamb that should have been sacrificed first, but with its demise, this one became the most precious Abel had to offer. He took the knife from his belt while he stroked the head of the small creature and spoke to it in a calm, soothing voice.

"It will be alright. Thank you for your sacrifice."

Then, in a louder voice, he said, "Lord God, hear the prayer of your servant. Blessed are you, Lord, our God. Accept this humble offering. I give to you the best of what I have, holding nothing back for myself, for you are Lord."

He did it quickly and mercifully. The lamb did not even make a sound. Its eyes closed as though falling asleep, and Abel laid the small body upon the stones of the altar. He did the same with the two remaining lambs, each in turn. When all three had been sacrificed, he placed them in the shallow pit where the wood burned hot. The bodies of the lambs caught instantly, the wool flashing brightly as the fire grew in intensity and rose high to consume the animals.

Abel stepped away from the altar, a look of serene contentment on his face. He had just sacrificed the prime of his flock, the newest and youngest of his brood, but he held no sense of loss. When he reached the bottom of the hill, he looked at his father, who smiled proudly back at him. Cain, by contrast, appeared impatient and annoyed. He busied himself with lifting the first basket of fruits. His father and brother assisted him, each taking another basket, and the three walked up the hill together. When Abel and Adam had returned to the bottom of the hill, Cain turned his eyes to the altar and shock registered on his face.

The lambs were gone. The wood still burned, but nothing remained of Abel's sacrifice. It had been completely consumed, burned up entirely by the power of God. With some trepidation now, he stooped to lift the first basket. Facing the altar, he said the words aloud.

"Lord God, hear the prayer of your servant. Blessed are you, Lord, our God. Accept this humble offering. I give to you," Cain hesitated, but then finished, saying, "the best of what I have, holding nothing back for myself, for you are Lord."

He said the last words hurriedly. Then he placed the basket upon the fire of the altar and stepped back. He waited, but the wicker of the basket did not catch. Cain cocked his head to the side, his brows furrowing in confusion. Leaning over, he lifted the second basket and placed it next to the first. Neither burned. Nonplussed, he placed the third basket upon the altar. The flames licked at the dry material, but it did not catch. It did not smoke. It did not burn.

Cain glanced back down the hill at his father, who gazed up at him beneath furrowed brows. Then Adam walked up the hill and looked closely at the altar and the three baskets sitting within the flames of the roaring fire. Gingerly, he reached out a hand and touched the exterior of one of them. He pulled his hand back and peered at his son, amazed and apprehensive at the same time.

"The basket is cool to the touch," he said.

"How can that be?" Cain asked, his irritation showing. The flames continued to flicker about the frame of the basket, but there was no blackening, nor any other sign that it might burn. Cain turned and pointed at his brother at the base of the hill.

"His sacrifice burned!" he said angrily.

"It appears," Adam spoke in a small voice, "that the Lord has rejected your offering."

"Why?" Cain shouted. "It's not my fault my crop was destroyed!"

"What?" Adam said, surprised. Cain had not told him of the damage to his fields.

"A swarm of locusts attacked and I lost half my crop."

"When?"

"Two days ago," Cain answered.

Adam's brows drew together, and he said, "You had a feast to commemorate your wedding day. I partook of fine fruits of the field. If you had such good produce to offer us, why would the Lord reject what you offer Him?"

Adam did not appear to expect an answer. He reached out and took hold of a piece of fruit from the top of one of the baskets. As he lifted it, a gasp escaped his lips. Without a word, he turned and showed the fruit, a pomegranate, to his son, and the look on his face said more than any words he might have uttered.

Whereas the top of the fruit, the part that had been visible while it lay in the basket, was bright and perfect, the underside was anything but. A quarter of it had been eaten away, the edges brown and shrunken. The other fruit in the basket, which had been covered up until a moment before, showed similar signs of damage. Adam stared at his son, the disbelief and intense disappointment apparent.

"This isn't my fault," Cain objected. "God put me in this position. He allowed my fields to be attacked, knowing I had to provide for both a feast and the sacrifice. Why should I give my best to God when he doesn't protect me?"

Adam was stunned. Grigori let out a long breath and shook his head, incredulous. It was bad enough that Cain had attempted to pass off inferior goods in the sacrifice, but now he was justifying his actions, rationalizing his selfish choices by blaming God. And he had made another mistake.

He thought the sacrifice was intended to gain favor and protection from God. He had forgotten that sacrificing to God does not obligate Him to render aid or reward, nor should the motive of the offering be based on any expectation of reciprocation. It is a duty owed because of who God is, not because of what he has done or might do for the individual. All this registered on Adam's face, but he apparently could find no words to express his disapprobation.

Cain's face flushed red with anger and embarrassment. His hands curled into fists, and I became uneasy about what he might do. I took a step forward, intending to speak calming words of encouragement to him, but then I heard a booming sound and felt the earth shake. I knelt, my eyes instinctively going to the ground, for God had spoken.

"Why are you angry?" the Lord said to Cain. "And why has your countenance fallen? If you do well, will you not be accepted?"

Cain dropped to the ground, as did Adam and Abel. Indeed, Cain prostrated himself, lying flat on the rocky ground. He did not respond to God's questions, nor did the Lord expect an answer.

The Almighty continued, "And if you do not do well, sin lies at the door. And its desire is for you, but you should rule over it."

"Yes, Lord God," is all Cain could say.

The rumbling ceased, and the ground was still once more. The men lay there for a long time until they were sure the Lord had nothing further to say. When they arose, Cain was crestfallen. His offering lay still upon the altar, unburnt and rejected. Now that the fear had ebbed from him, the anger returned anew, his face reddening. Adam tried to reach out a hand to take his arm, but Cain brushed it aside.

"Son," Adam said, "reflect on what the Lord said. He has spoken to you. That is a rare occurrence, even for me. He would not do so if He didn't love you."

"If He loves me," Cain spat, "why did He allow my fields to be attacked? He made me choose between honoring Him and honoring my new wife. Then he rejects my offering and chastises me. And I should honor Him?"

"Yes," Adam said, one eyebrow raised.

"Why?" Cain demanded.

"Because," his father replied, "He is God."

Chapter 35

My Brother's Keeper

"Cain, wait," Abel called, running to catch up with him. Cain gave his brother a sideways glance as he came up beside him, but he did not stop or change his stride.

"What do you want?" Cain snapped.

"I want to understand. Why didn't you give the Lord the best you had to offer? Surely, you knew you could not deceive God."

Cain stopped and turned to glower at his brother.

"You have no idea how hard I work to provide food for the family. I toil until my hands bleed, and what is my reward? God sends a swarm of locusts to destroy my crop just as I'm about to celebrate my wedding feast. What was I supposed to do, serve damaged and tainted food to my guests so the best could be burned upon the altar?"

The words came out in a rush, all of Cain's pent-up bitterness bubbling to the surface. Abel blinked rapidly.

"That's exactly what you should have done. Don't you understand? The sacrifice is about giving our best even when we can't afford it. It's about having faith. When we hold back from God, it shows we don't trust Him."

"How can I trust Him when he allows disaster to befall me?"

"That's when we must trust him the most."

Cain huffed in response and began walking again, faster this time. His brother hurried to keep up.

"Where are you going?" Abel asked.

"To the fields. Perhaps you should come with me. You can see for yourself what trusting God gains you."

Following behind, I glanced at Grigori who walked beside me. His face showed the same disappointment I was sure mine displayed. How had Cain become so resentful of God? The Lord had not sent the locusts. That had been Satan's doing, but Cain blamed God for allowing it to occur. That weakened his resistance to demonic temptation even further. In this state of mind, there was no telling what sin Cain might be capable of.

When they reached the fields, Cain showed Abel the damaged crops. The leaves of the plants had turned brown and begun to wither. Some of them might be saved, but most were lost.

"You see," Cain said, pointing to the dying plants. "This is what faith has brought me."

"Perhaps this is meant to test your faith so the Lord can be glorified when He overcomes your hardships. I endured a loss as well. My youngest lamb wandered off and was killed by wild beasts. I had planned to sacrifice it to the Lord, but with its death, I offered one of my other lambs instead."

A strange look swept over Cain's face as his brother spoke. Of course, he was well aware of the reason Abel had to change his offering, but he allowed his brother to continue without enlightening him.

"Without the young to replace the old, the life of my flock is endangered. Yet, I trust the Lord will provide. Perhaps he will reward my faith, perhaps not. But either way, I will trust Him."

"Then you are a fool," Cain spat.

Abel shook his head slowly while Cain walked over to one of the fruit trees to inspect it. As I followed, I felt a chill come over me. Peering up, I spotted Valac perched high on a branch of the tree, peering down at Cain from his vantage point amongst the leaves.

"Haven't you done enough damage already?" I challenged the demon.

"Not nearly," he replied with a sly grin. Hopping down from the tree, he slunk over to where Cain stood. Normally, the demon walked hunched over, slinking from one shadow to the next, but now he stood up tall and leaned over to whisper into the older brother's ear. Cain's head tilted to the side, toward Valac.

I stepped toward them, and the demon pulled back. Returning to his hunched stance, he scampered around to the other side of Cain and huddled behind him, cackling as he did so. Cain looked over at his brother, who stooped a few feet away, inspecting a row of damaged cabbages. An intense expression had formed upon Cain's face. His eyes narrowed, and his jaw clenched as he stared intently at Abel. Then he began moving toward his brother.

"What did you say to him?" I demanded of Valac, who scampered further back.

"Not much," the demon retorted, giving me a toothy smile. "I just put things in perspective for him."

Abel had knelt to inspect one of the plants. Placing a hand underneath a leaf, he said to his brother, "This plant grows on a two-year cycle, is that right?"

"Yes, that's correct," Cain confirmed, drawing nearer.

"Is it in its first or second year?" Abel spoke without turning, keeping his eyes on the plant.

"The first," Cain spoke nonchalantly as he edged closer to his brother. He had an unhealthy look about him, his eyes locked on Abel's back as he moved toward him in a deliberate manner. I turned back to Valac.

"What perspective did you give him?" I felt my anger rise along with my trepidation.

Valac chuckled, a sickly, cracking laugh.

"It seems to me," he sneered, "that Abel is the source of all Cain's unhappiness."

My eyes narrowed. "What do you mean?"

"It's not Cain's fault. His mother dotes upon Abel, always has. Cain must work ten times as hard as his brother, just to do what everyone expects of him. All this, while his brother strolls along with his herd, and no one expects more from him. It isn't fair."

Valac was speaking in an exaggerated manner like an actor delivering his lines. I could not tell if he really believed what he was saying, or if he were merely feigning his conviction. Meanwhile, Cain continued to close on his brother, who stood and walked further down the row of cabbages with Cain following behind.

"Some of these are not so damaged," he said as he walked, oblivious to the drama unfolding behind him. "I think they could recover."

He glanced back at his brother as he said these words, but nothing about Cain's stance or stride seemed to cause him concern. From his perspective, Cain was simply keeping pace with him. But I knew better.

Fixing Valac with an intense glare, I said, "There must be more to it than that."

The demon shrugged. "Perhaps."

I shot forward, a streak of light against the backdrop of the grove. In the blink of an eye, Valac was slammed back against the trunk of a nearby olive tree, pinned there by my hand that gripped him by the throat. Steam seeped through my fingers accompanied by a hissing sound as the fiend writhed in my grasp.

"Do not be coy with me, demon. Tell me!"

Grigori appeared then, placing a cautioning hand on my shoulder, but I was not to be deterred. I squeezed Valac's throat and was rewarded by a desperate squeal.

"The truth," I demanded. "Now!"

The demon grinned through the pain as he growled, "He knows his wife will hate him, just as Lasha hates Asher. She will always have eyes for Abel, and although he says he does not want her, Cain can't trust that. Even if he means it now, who's to say that one day he won't change his mind?"

"So, what did you tempt him to do?"

As I interrogated the demon, I turned my head to keep an eye on the two brothers a few yards away. Then my hand closed around empty air. Snapping my head back, I saw black smoke where Valac had been. It slid through my grasp and wafted away from me, gliding over toward Cain. I turned in time to see the demon coalesce into his natural form, facing me and grinning. At the same time, Abel stopped, something on the ground having caught his attention.

"There's blood here," he said, alarmed.

"Oh?" his brother asked.

"Yes, here on the ground. It leads off in this direction." Abel began moving that way and Cain followed.

"Then there is the insult of God's rejection," the demon said, his eyes glowing red. I understood what that meant. Everything he had told me to this point is what he had whispered into Cain's ear. What he said now was meant to further influence his actions.

"Even God favors Abel over Cain," Valac said loudly and with force. "Everything Abel does is perfect while Cain is disparaged. It was not his fault, what happened to his crop. Either God sent the locusts to devour his fields, or at the least, he allowed it to happen. Either way, it shows that God doesn't love him, that he favors Abel, just like everyone else!"

Cain's face reddened as the demon spoke, his hands clenching into fists. His brother, oblivious, followed the trail of blood, the dirt stained red by what must have been a significant flow. Abruptly, he stopped and knelt to pick up a rock. It was dark red, covered in dried blood.

"Abel is the source of all Cain's misfortune," The demon said, his voice rising in volume and intensity.

I recognized the expression of hate on Cain's face, saw the hand go to his side where the knife hung from his belt.

"No!" I shouted at Cain. I took a step forward, but Grigori held me back.

"Malachi," he said, his voice sad, resigned, "we can't."

Desperate, I shouted again, my aura flashing out. I had to get through to him. I had to make him listen. I sensed the world around me grow dark as my own light increased, washing out everything around me. All I saw was Cain and Abel. All I heard was my own voice, imploring him to stop and listen.

He did not heed. Cain was closed to me now, my influence completely shut out. He had made himself deaf to my voice. He had chosen the path of sin, of anger, of hate, of pride.

The cackling voice of Valac behind me shouted triumphantly, "The only way to stop the injustice is to be rid of the threat!"

That was when Abel spotted the strands of wool caked to the rock by the blood that had dried there. He pulled at a clump of it with his fingers and held it up to his eyes. The wool was red where the blood had dyed it, but enough of it remained unstained to see that it had once been the purest white. His eyes grew wide with sudden understanding and disbelief. Standing, he turned to face his brother. His mouth was open to ask the question that he feared to hear answered, but the sound never came. Instead, shock registered on his face as fire lanced into his belly.

Cain stood close, his left hand on his brother's shoulder, the other holding the knife that was now buried in Abel's gut. Bright red blood poured over the greenish tint of the tarnished copper blade. In an instant, I was there, broadside to the two men, looking at them, yet not believing what I saw. Abel could not believe it either. No sound issued from his open mouth, but his eyes said all that was needed. They accused, they denounced, and they implored.

"Why?" they seemed to say.

Cain leaned in close and whispered an answer to the unspoken question.

"Because," he breathed into his brother's ear, "I hate you."

Chapter 36

The Curse

Abel fell to his knees, the knife hilt still protruding from his abdomen. I heard the maniacal laughter of Valac behind me and turned to see him dancing in grotesque leaping motions.

"I hate you! I hate you! I hate you!" he repeated in sing-song fashion, cackling.

I peered back down at Abel in horror. Grigori was there, his arms wrapped around the dying man, speaking soft words of comfort to him.

"Fear not," my friend said, "you're going home now."

There was no fear on Abel's face. Pain, yes, and intense sadness, but no fear. With a sigh, he pitched over onto his back. Cain knelt beside his brother, and for a moment I thought perhaps he felt remorse for what he had done. But then he rubbed his hands on his brother's tunic, the blood staining it as he wiped them clean. When he was done, he stood and walked away.

Abel still lived, but he was fading rapidly, his ragged breath shuddering in his throat. His hands clutched the leather wrapped handle of the copper knife as though he intended to pull it free but could not. Then his eyes glazed over and the ragged breathing stopped.

Abel emerged from his broken body, a wisp of light rising from the darkness of this earthly realm. He appeared as a translucent version of his mortal form. He was dressed, not as he had been in life, but instead, in a simple, pure white linen gown. And he glowed, the light of heaven having come upon him. Standing, Grigori released the body, the empty shell of the spirit that now stood before us. Abel perceived us at that moment and glanced back and forth between the two of us, the wonder apparent on his face. Grigori took him by the hand and smiled reassuringly.

"Come," he said, "I will take you home."

The two rose into the air, Grigori's wings spread wide and Abel's gown billowing from the updraft they created. Then they were gone, two streaks of light flashing upward toward heaven. I smiled, but it did not last. I could hear the cackling laughter again. It was as though all sound had been muted until that moment, but now it returned, and my rage returned with it. I glowered at the prancing demon.

Auratic light lanced out in a flash of brilliant white as my sword left its scabbard and I surged forward, closing on the target of my wrath. Valac noticed me, or rather he recognized the piercing power of my aura as I bore down upon him. With a squeal, he launched himself into the air, his black leathery wings flapping desperately. My own wings shot out in response, and I rose after the demon. He flew backward, pulling away from me as he held his hands out in front of him.

"Malachi, you can't!" he pleaded, his voice cracking in panic. "The peace!"

He spun to flee, but I appeared in front of him as he turned. My hand found his throat, and I held him there. The demon's eyes bulged with fear as I raised my sword high. In truth, I did not know if I could kill him, but then, neither did Valac. He must have thought it possible, for he whimpered pitifully. But I felt no pity, only pure anger, a righteous wrath.

Then I came back to myself. My wrath was righteous, but my actions must be also, for I was an angel of the Lord. It was not for me to judge Valac. I released the hapless demon who scuttled backward in the air, the relief apparent upon his face. But I was not done.

"Be gone, Valac," I commanded him. "I do not want to see you in the village ever again."

"You cannot bar me!" he objected. I made a move toward him, and his hands shot up in submission. "But fortunately for you," he added quickly, "my mission here is complete. I must report back to Lucifer. He will be pleased with me."

He grinned as he said the last words. Baring my teeth, I raised the sword, and that was enough to send the demon into headlong flight. As he disappeared into the distance, I turned and peered back down to where Cain walked on his way back to the village. After a pause to collect my composure, I descended after him. I had just landed when the earth began to shake. Cain did not know what was happening, and fear came upon him in an instant. He staggered as the booming voice of the Lord rumbled all around him.

"Where is Abel your brother?" the voice of God asked.

Once Cain understood that this was not an earthquake, the fear left him to be replaced by something else. Petulance. Cain did not kneel, did not avert his eyes. Instead, he stood there and defiantly replied, "I do not know. Am I my brother's keeper?"

The ground shook again, more strongly this time, and Cain nearly fell as his feet threatened to come from beneath him. The Lord spoke again, this time with anger.

"What have you done? The voice of your brother's blood cries out to Me from the ground. So now you are cursed from the ground, which has opened its mouth to receive your brother's blood from your hand. When you till the ground, it shall no longer yield its strength to you. You shall be a fugitive and a wanderer on the earth."

The cloud of anger lifted from Cain's face to be replaced by terror. He dropped to his knees and beseeched the Almighty, clasping his hands together in front of him.

"My punishment is greater than I can bear!" he pleaded with the Lord. "Behold, you have driven me today away from the ground, and from your face I shall be hidden. I shall be a fugitive and a wanderer on the earth, and whoever finds me will kill me!"

I shook my head. Even at this moment, the selfishness of Cain was paramount. He had no remorse for what he had done, only for the consequences to himself. He displayed no sign that he regretted slaying his brother. Still, the Lord was merciful.

"Not so!" God replied. "If anyone kills Cain, vengeance shall be taken on him sevenfold."

Cain suddenly doubled over, screaming in pain. His hands flew to his head, and he writhed, bending forward on his knees with his head in his hands upon the ground. He rocked back and forth, his screams fading to a whimpering moan. After a while, he stopped and stood carefully as though unsure of his balance.

That was when I saw the mark. It had been seared into the flesh of his forehead, seven ragged lines like lightning bolts, pale pink and embossed into his skin. Cain reached up and gingerly touched the mark with the tip of a finger. It must have hurt, for he winced and pulled his hand away.

Raising his face to heaven, he cried out, "Lord, what should I do now?"

No answer came.

"Lord God!" Cain implored once more, but the Lord did not answer. Cain was alone. Disoriented and afraid, he did the only thing he could. He started walking again.

When he finally stumbled into the village, he found the others gathered for the mid-day meal. Cain staggered into their midst, and many of them stood reflexively to assist him. Awan rushed to her husband, but he pushed her away from him roughly. She scuttled back to where her mother stood while the group erupted in a chorus of murmuring. When they saw the mark on his forehead, they drew back. They did not understand what had happened to him, but they had a sense of foreboding that caused them to react warily.

"Cain," Asher said, "what's happened to you?"

"The Lord placed this mark upon my forehead," Cain stammered, "to protect me."

"From what?" Tamir asked.

"From us." The voice came from behind Cain. The others looked up as Adam limped toward them. His expression mingled anger, sadness, and determination.

Enoch stepped forward. "What do you mean, father? Why would Cain need protection from us?"

"Because," Adam said emotionlessly, as though he was numb, "he has killed his brother Abel."

There was a shriek as Eve fell to her knees. Nava rushed to her mother's side and wrapped her arms around her while the others gasped in disbelief.

"What?" Enoch asked. "How do you know?"

"The Lord told me. He has cursed Cain. No longer shall the ground yield its strength to him."

Asher shook his head. "If he is cursed, if the ground will no longer yield to him, he has no more usefulness to this community."

Cain gaped at his father-in-law, ever his staunchest supporter, in appalled astonishment. His eyes seemed to plead with Asher not to turn his back on him. All he received in return was a look of callous disinterest.

Adam continued, "He is to be cast out of our community to wander the wilderness. That is the judgment of the Lord."

"What of my daughter," Lasha asked, wrapping her arms around Awan. "Surely she is not to go with him? The marriage must be canceled!"

"The marriage is consummated," Adam said. "It shall not be undone. Awan must go with Cain. They will wander together and try to make a life elsewhere."

"No!" Lasha objected. "I won't allow my daughter to become a wanderer for the sake of this murderer. He should be punished, an eye for an eye."

Adam shook his head. "The Lord has placed a mark on Cain's forehead to protect him. If anyone kills Cain, he shall be punished seven times over."

Lasha gripped her daughter even more tightly and made to object again, but Asher gave her a sideways glance and said, "Silence, woman!"

Lasha's mouth opened and closed as though she meant to say more, but no sound issued. Perhaps thinking better of whatever she would have said, she shut her mouth and stood still. With no further objections by Asher or Lasha, Adam turned to address Cain, a single tear rolling down his cheek.

"My son, many years ago, your mother and I committed a grave sin against the Lord and were cast out of paradise. Consequently, our lives became a struggle to survive, but survive we did, by trusting in the Lord and seeking to honor Him. Now you have sinned against God and man. You too will struggle to survive. I urge you to turn to the Lord for your deliverance. You can't take back what you have done, but you can choose now to honor the Lord with the remainder of your life."

Cain stood frozen in shock and disbelief. He started to ask for mercy, to be allowed to stay, but Adam simply shook his head.

"Go," he said.

And Cain went.

He took Awan with him. They were allowed to break down their tent and pack it up along with some clothing, tools, and provisions. All of this was loaded onto a cart and harnessed to a mule. As the couple set off, Awan stared back, tears in her eyes. Cain kept his eyes forward so no one could see his tears. The couple walked off into the distance, leading the mule onward, toward the east.

Chapter 37

The Aftermath

As Cain and Awan disappeared over the horizon, the people of the community began to disperse. That was when Grigori returned. He was smiling.

"How is Abel?" I asked him.

"Wonderful! He is agog with the Holy City. I would've been back sooner except he insisted I show him every corner of heaven. What's happened here?"

I told him. He nodded gravely as I described the reaction of the community to Cain's sentence of expulsion. He seemed surprised when I told him Awan had been made to go with him.

"Poor girl," he said softly.

I was about to comment when my attention was diverted by Asher, running back toward the village center where most of the people still congregated. His face was red with anger as he stopped in front of Adam.

"What is it?" Adam asked him.

"Lasha is gone."

Enoch stepped closer to the two men. "Where would she go?"

"I don't know, but all her clothes are gone, as are our wineskins and the bread I made yesterday."

Tamir, who had been looking around, said, "Where is Jared?"

Asher made eye contact with Adam, and they both sprinted around one of the nearby tents toward the forge, Grigori and I following close behind. When we arrived, Jared was nowhere to be seen. The forge was cold, and his tools were missing. So was the cart he usually kept there.

"They're gone," Asher said, stating the obvious.

The group erupted into a gaggle of overlapping comments and questions, conjecturing about which way they might have gone and asking whether someone should go after them. Then I had a sudden realization of my own and turned to Grigori.

"Where is Belial?"

He looked around and replied, "I don't see him."

I nodded. "I haven't seen him since Cain came back into the village. In fact, that was the last time I saw Lasha and Jared as well."

Grigori gave me a look that indicated we were thinking the same thing. Together, we rose high into the air and scanned the horizon in all directions.

"There," Grigori said, pointing.

Peering in the direction he indicated, I spotted them, three small forms a long way off in the distance. Lasha and Jared were walking in front of a mule. They held hands, gazing into each other's eyes and laughing as they walked. Then they kissed.

We were there in a flash. Belial was lounging in the back of the cart, but he sat up eagerly when we approached.

"Well, well," he said with a laugh, "look who finally figured it out."

"What do you think you're doing, Belial?" I challenged him. His expression changed to one of mock disappointment.

"Oh, maybe you haven't figured it out, after all. Perhaps you are not as intelligent as I thought."

I made a move toward him, but Grigori grabbed me by the arm. Belial just cackled. Then his face took on a serious expression, menacing and intense.

"You have always underestimated me," he spat at us. "Belial is just a nuisance." His words were mocking in their tone as he imitated our assessment of him. "He is too lazy to cause any real trouble."

Then his tone changed again, back to the venomous antipathy born of his wounded pride. "Well, I fooled you both! While you thought I was merely tempting children to lie to their parents or steal sweet breads from Asher's ovens, I was worming my way into the hearts of these two."

The demon threw a thumb over his shoulder to indicate the pair of humans walking in front of the cart.

"I have been working on them for years, ever since Lasha was forced to marry that boar of a man, Asher! Her lust for Jared grew along with her contempt for her husband. Jared took a little more work, which is why I had to spend so much time with him, but as he grew older and realized he would never have the opportunity to wed, his growing resentment gave me the opening I needed."

I glanced at Grigori, knowing Belial was right. We had underestimated him and his influence. The small temptations he used on the people, the minor sins he succeeded in luring them to commit, had given him a foothold in their hearts. Over time, he had increased his influence along with their growing indiscretions until he was able to get them to abandon righteousness entirely.

"You thought Valac was the real threat, but he couldn't have accomplished half of what he did without my groundwork. Cain committed murder, true, but that only eliminated one troublesome human. My plan has torn the community apart. Asher will succumb to his anger and turn away from God altogether. All the others are old except for Sara, and who will she marry now that Abel is dead?"

The demon hopped to his feet and bobbed up and down in a crouching stance. He was reveling in his victory and wanted us to know just how badly we had been beaten.

"The community of Adam will wither and die while the offspring of Lasha and Jared will thrive. They will meet up with Cain and Awan, and between these two couples, we will grow a new community of humans, one that will not honor or worship the Lord. My community will be based on debauchery, deceit, fecklessness, and tyranny. It will be a city devoted to the destruction of souls. Mankind will turn from God to Lucifer. Eventually, the Lord will have no choice but to wipe them out. And when that day comes, we will have won."

I stared at him in stunned silence. I longed to wipe the smug grin from his face, to respond with some rejoinder that would crush his argument, but I had no such retort. He was right. He had split the community of Adam. All the marriageable people capable of conception were heading out into the world, away from the community and away from God. The forces of Satan had won a devastating victory here, and I had not seen it coming. Belial had fooled me.

But I could not concede defeat, to allow my silence to confirm his pronouncements of victory. I had to say something. I had to defy him.

"Jared and Lasha won't abandon God altogether. They will come back to the way," I said, knowing my response was a weak one.

The demon laughed. "I think not. See this?"

Turning his head, he indicated an object lying in the cart. It was made of gold and had been formed into the shape of a man. Belial turned back to us, the crooked grin growing on his face.

"What is it?" Grigori asked.

"It's me!" Belial proclaimed with glee.

I did not understand. "You?"

"Yes, it's me." The demon was growing smug now. "Jared made it. It's called an idol, a representation of his new god."

"What are you talking about?" I demanded. "There is only one God!"

"Not anymore," Belial shot back. "Jared has abandoned the Lord. I am his god now."

Grigori was incredulous. "That's absurd. You are no god!"

"I know that," Belial retorted, "and you know that. But Jared? He believes I am his god, the god of thunder and fertility."

"Nonsense!" I was aghast, unable to comprehend how this demon had managed to convince a human that he was a god.

"Not to Jared. I have told him there are many gods, that Adam's God is a stern and uncompromising deity. But not me. I am a kind god who wants him to be happy. I do not require Jared to meekly accept his lot in life. If he wants Lasha, and if she wants him, then they should be together. God would call that adultery. I call it seeking happiness. I have freed him from any moral obligation to respect the marriage vows that Lasha made to Asher."

"You can't do that!" Grigori said, "They are committing sin, and you do not have the power to absolve them!"

"I have no desire to absolve them!" Belial's eyes glowed red in utter glee as the full scope of his plan became clear. "I wish to damn them, damn them all! And the best part of my plan is that they will come into that damnation willingly!"

The demon roared with laughter. I looked at Grigori and he at me, and we knew Belial was right. He had presented the humans with a choice, one which allowed them to justify their proclivity to act selfishly. He had offered them an alternative. If they did not like the rigid morality required by God, they could follow a different god who did not hold to those same restrictions. I had to admit, it was brilliant.

"How did you manage this?" I demanded.

"Through whispers," he said, smiling. "I whispered to Jared in moments of aggravation, each time he saw Lasha in the company of her husband, this man who did not appreciate her or love her the way he could. I whispered to him in dreams about the life he and Lasha could have if only they could get away. I whispered to him that Adam had misled them all, that he had withheld from them the truth that there were other gods, gods who were not as unyielding as the Lord."

Belial's expression took on a grim intensity as he said the next words, "And then, I whispered to him my name."

"Your name?"

"Yes, my name. I whispered to him the name of his new god, who wants him to be with Lasha and be happy."

I could not believe it. "He knows your name?"

"Of a sort." The demon shrugged. "He didn't get it exactly right, but close enough. In fact, I think I like the name he has come up with for me, so I believe I will keep it."

"And what name is that?"

Belial smiled evilly. "He calls me Ba'al."

Part Four

Warriors Of The Spirit

"Put on the whole armor of God, that you may be able to stand against the schemes of the devil. For we do not wrestle against flesh and blood, but against the rulers, against the authorities, against the cosmic powers over this present darkness, against the spiritual forces of evil in the heavenly places." (Ephesians 6:11-12)

Chapter 38

Revelations

"Ba'al?" Paul gasped, "as in the Canaanite god, the one that Elijah denounced atop Mount Carmel?"

"The same," the angel confirmed.

All Jews were taught the story as children. The kingdom of Israel had been stricken with a terrible famine caused by a drought that lasted three years. God had withheld the rains in punishment for the people's worship of false gods, primarily Ba'al. The prophet Elijah confronted Ahab, the king of Israel, because he had allowed his wife, Jezebel, to not only sway him from worshiping the one true God, but also to encourage his people to worship idols.

Elijah challenged the priests of Ba'al to prove their god was more powerful than the true God, Yahweh. He had two altars built atop Mount Carmel, one for Ba'al and the other for God. Wood was placed on both, then oxen slaughtered and laid upon them. Elijah challenged the priests of Ba'al to pray to their god and ask him to send fire to light the sacrificial pyre. The priests did so, from morning to noon, but the altar remained unlit.

At noon, Elijah began to taunt the priests, saying, "Cry aloud! Surely, he is a god; either he is meditating, or he has wandered away, or he is on a journey, or perhaps he is asleep and must be awakened."

The priests did as Elijah bid, raising their voices loudly. They cut themselves and added their own blood to the sacrifice to entice their god to acquiesce to their entreaties. They prayed without result until evening, when Elijah finally put a stop to it. He ordered the sacrifice laid out for Yahweh to be drenched with water from four large jars. Three times the jars were filled and emptied over the sacrifice until the wood was soaked and the water pooled upon the altar. Then he prayed to God to accept the sacrifice and to send fire from heaven to light the wood.

Indeed, fire did fall from heaven, and so hot was it that it consumed the wood, the sacrifice, the water, and even the stones of the altar. No trace remained. At that moment, Elijah ordered the priests of Ba'al to be seized, and they were all executed, to a man.

"So, it was a demon who set himself up as a false god," Paul said.

"Yes, a demon who was once a legion-mate of mine, an angel who at one point I might have called friend."

"What happened to Jared and Lasha?"

"Grigori went with them while I returned to the community to watch over those who remained. Later, when Grigori and I reunited, he told me that Jared and Lasha had found Cain and Awan. Together, they founded a city in the east.

"Cain called the city Enoch. It was Awan who suggested the name, that of her beloved great-grandfather. It was also the name of their first child, a son. The city grew, and over time, the descendants of these idolaters spread across the earth. The wickedness of Belial, of Ba'al, spread with them until, finally, the day the demon predicted came to pass."

Paul's eyes narrowed. "God decided to destroy humanity."

Malachi nodded. "That was Satan's plan all along, to cause mankind to degenerate to the point that God would wipe them out."

"So, he sent the flood."

"Yes. But Cain and Jared were not the only descendants of Adam. After the tragedy of Abel's death, Eve had another child."

"Seth," Paul said.

"Exactly. Seth married Sara, and the two of them had children of their own. Their first son was named Enosh. Enosh had a son named Cainan, and he had a son named Mahalalel. You know the genealogy.

Mahalalel begot Jabel, Jabel begot a new Enoch, Enoch begot Methuselah who begot Lamech. Then Lamech had a son.

"Noah," Paul finished for him again.

Malachi inclined his head. "The same. By this time the world had grown so full of wickedness that God resolved to destroy mankind. Lucifer had won, or so he thought."

"But Noah found grace in the eyes of the Lord," Paul quoted the scripture.

Again, the angel inclined his head. "You are familiar with the story. God ordered Noah to build an Ark to carry his family and the animals of the earth while the Lord sent a mighty flood to wash away the evil spread by Satan and his minions. Mankind was destroyed, but Noah and his family were spared. From their seed, mankind would begin again."

Paul smiled triumphantly. "And yet again, Satan was defeated."

The angel's eyes narrowed. "Yes, but do not underestimate how close he came to succeeding. If it had not been for one righteous man, Satan might have accomplished his goal."

Paul let out a long, slow breath, contemplating humanity's narrow escape from destruction. Malachi continued the lesson.

"Even now, Satan strives for your destruction. This world has grown increasingly corrupt. His demons have been dispersed to spread Godlessness across the whole world, and they succeed more often than they fail. Every human soul is a battleground, and we need Christian soldiers, warriors in Christ, to fight alongside us in the conflict."

"So, it is indeed a war."

Malachi nodded. "Lucifer has been at war with mankind since the beginning of your world. He still believes if he can cause mankind to degenerate to a sufficient degree, God will finally give up on this creation and wipe out mankind altogether. He thinks that then, perhaps the Lord will relent, return the universe to the way things were before the creation, and restore him and his angels to glory."

"But surely, by now he knows the Lord will never do that."

"Perhaps. Perhaps he no longer cares. Perhaps now all he seeks to do is condemn as many souls as possible, to hurt God. Regardless of Satan's motives, his hatred and evil are focused on your people. He seeks your destruction."

Malachi leaned forward and spoke the next words softly, yet intently, "That is why I have appeared to you this night. You must understand, you are more than a teacher of the gospel. You are a combatant in this war. More than that, you are to become a great general in the Army of the Lord. Understand that while you strive to win souls for Christ, there are dark forces at work that conspire to defeat you and frustrate your efforts. You struggle not against flesh and blood, but against Satan and his demonic legion. You must put on the whole armor of God and equip others to do the same. Only through spiritual warfare can Lucifer and his horde be denied."

Paul nodded. "I will do as you say. I will teach others to fight against Satan and his forces. I will use the power of prayer and of praise to protect the brethren from demonic influence."

"And I will be there to guide and support you," Malachi said. "I have been the guardian of the family of Adam and Eve from the beginning. I have moved from one generation to another, and I follow the lineage of mankind from one significant personage to another. From Seth to Noah to Abraham to Jacob and his twelve sons, to David and eventually to Christ Himself, I have been there to watch, report, and protect. After Christ's ascension into Heaven, I moved on to watch over His disciples. I was watching over a young apostle named Stephen when I came upon you."

Paul was stunned, remembering how he had held the coats of the men who stoned Stephen.

"I have been with you ever since, and I will continue to walk with you until the day you go to be with the Father. Afterward, I will transfer to watch over those who come after you. That has been and continues to be my mission."

Paul was dumbstruck. "You have witnessed all the significant moments of the scriptures? Abraham, Isaac, Jacob, Joseph, Moses, Joshua, the Judges, Samuel, King David, Solomon, the Babylonian exile? All of it?"

"Indeed."

Paul was excited as he said, "In that case, there's so much more you can tell me! I know the stories of the scriptures, but not like you do, not with all the detail you can share. And then there's the story behind the story, of how you have contended with the agents of the devil, how your struggle has overlapped with our struggle. Will you tell me of Noah and the Flood?"

Malachi shook his head. "That is a story for another time. Midnight is at hand, and you must rest. Tomorrow they will come to call you before the council of magistrates."

"I don't feel like resting."

"That is your choice." The angel gave him a broad smile and added, "You do, after all, have free will."

Paul laughed, but then he saw the heavenly visage begin to fade, the auratic light diminishing by degrees as the seconds passed.

"Are you leaving me?"

"Of course, not," Malachi promised. "Know that although you cannot perceive my presence, I will always be nearby, watching over you. Whenever you sleep, whenever you eat, I will be there. When you minister to the poor, when you preach the gospel to the lost, I will be standing close. When you go through trials and tribulations, my sword and my shield will stand ready to protect you. For all the days that you walk this earth, I shall walk beside you. This is not goodbye, my friend."

As the angel spoke these final words, the auratic light faded until Paul was left in the darkness of the cell. But not total darkness. Paul was surprised to learn he could still see. A dull glow lit the room, like the gray light that precedes the dawn. Paul could discern shapes and some detail. He could see Silas and the forms of the other prisoners in the cell. It was as though some portion of the angel's light remained, a final gift from the angelic visitor.

He heard a noise off to his right. A groan, a long intake of breath, and finally a voice, the voice of his friend and missionary partner. Silas, at last, was waking up.

Chapter 39

The Earthquake

"Paul, are you there?" Silas asked.

"I am here."

"How long was I unconscious?"

"I don't know, but it is almost midnight. How are you feeling?"

"Not great." Paul could hear the groans of his friend as he struggled to sit up. "Still, for some reason, I have a distinct impression that I should feel much worse."

Paul smiled to himself, remembering the healing touch of the angel on his friend's back and head. The two sat and talked for a long time, discussing the events leading up to their imprisonment. They expressed their shared hope that Luke and Timothy were well and had not gotten caught up in the sudden anti-Jewish fervor. They began to pray, and to his surprise, Paul found himself doing so in a manner that was new, but now seemed necessary.

"Lord God," he intoned, "please place Your protective hand upon us. Banish any and all evil spirits from this room and remove their foul influence from the minds of those confined here with us. In the name of Jesus Christ, I pray, amen."

It was then that the remainder of the prisoners slowly began to awaken. As each one regained consciousness, they found the bowls left for them and began to eat. Paul had forgotten about the food and had not touched it. A sudden rumbling in his stomach reminded him of it now, so he picked up the bowl. There was nothing pleasant about the thin gruel that had grown cold in the coarse ceramic bowl, but it coated his empty belly and took away his hunger. With that accomplished, he was able to turn his attention back to more important matters.

"There is a guard here," he said to Silas, "who seems receptive to the gospel. I think he may even be the keeper of the prison. He is skeptical, of course, but he was asking me questions earlier. We should speak with him again if he is still on duty when we are released."

"Have you still not learned your lesson?" said a harsh voice from across the cell.

"What?" Paul asked, surprised and curious, for the voice sounded oddly familiar.

"You have been beaten and imprisoned, and yet you persist in your preaching. Will you not leave well enough alone?"

Paul was certain he knew the voice now, although he could not quite place it. He squinted in the darkness and stared at the gray figure who spoke the words. He was at least ten feet away and locked in stocks, just as Paul and Silas were. Although Malachi's gift allowed him to see enough to make out shapes and movement in the cell, it was not sufficient to discern facial features at any distance.

"Do I know you?" Paul asked.

The figure laughed, a rough, hoarse laugh. "I wish to the gods we had never met. You have brought me nothing but trouble, Jew."

Realization clicked in Paul's mind, and he said, "Epaphroditus?"

The figure laughed in acknowledgment. It was the Brute, the master of the fortune-telling slave who had brought him and Silas before the magistrates.

Paul frowned. "What are you doing here?"

"I will tell you what I am doing here, Jew," Epaphroditus said with venom in his voice. "I was arrested for inciting the mob. The magistrates were terrified by the disturbance that accompanied your arrest. There was almost a riot, for which we were blamed, and we received a night in jail as punishment."

"I see," Paul said simply.

"You see?" Epaphroditus was indignant. "Is that all you have to say for yourself? You have brought nothing but disruption and chaos to our city. I do not understand why you will not just leave us in peace."

"That's why I am here, to bring you peace, the peace of God, which passes all understanding," Paul said. "I am here to show you the light of the Lord so that through His grace, you might be saved."

Epaphroditus laughed again. "If your god is so powerful, why are you in here with me? Why were you beaten with rods? Your god could not even save you. How could he save anyone else?"

Paul smiled patiently as he said, "This is not the first time I have been beaten for His sake, and I am certain it will not be the last. But when we are reviled, we bless. When we are persecuted, we endure. Out of all my persecutions, the Lord has rescued me!"

"Will he rescue you now?" Epaphroditus challenged him.

"If it is His will," Paul said.

"Ha!" The Brute threw up a hand in dismissal.

"I will pray for you, Epaphroditus," Paul said. "I will pray for your heart to be softened and your mind to be opened to the truth of the gospel."

"I don't want your prayers!" he snapped. "And why would you pray for me anyway? I am your enemy!"

"The Lord has commanded us to love our enemies," Paul said calmly, "to bless those who curse us, to do good to those who hate us, and to pray for those who spitefully use and persecute us."

"Yours is a very strange religion. It is weakness to place yourself at the mercy of someone who hates you."

Paul shook his head. "To return hate with love is not weakness. To trust in the Lord is not folly. The Lord is my strength and my shield; my heart trusted in him, and I am helped: Therefore, my heart greatly rejoices; and with my song will I praise him."

"What is that you are quoting?" the ruffian asked, confused by Paul's song-like words.

"It is the Psalms," Silas answered him, "the Song of Songs."

Paul began anew in a language that Epaphroditus did not understand. "Adonai Ro'i, lo echsar."

"What language is that?" Epaphroditus demanded.

"It is the language of our fathers," Paul said. "It means; 'The Lord is my shepherd; I shall not want.'"

Silas took up the refrain.

"He makes me to lie down in green pastures;
He leads me beside the still waters. He restores my soul;
He leads me in the paths of righteousness for His name's sake."

Paul joined him, and the two finished the verse in unison.

"Yea, though I walk through the valley of the shadow of death,
I will fear no evil;
For You are with me; Your rod and Your staff, they comfort me.
You prepare a table before me in the presence of my enemies;
You anoint my head with oil; My cup runs over.
Surely goodness and mercy shall follow me all the days of my life;
and I will dwell in the house of the Lord forever."

"Amen," Paul whispered.

Epaphroditus opened his mouth to respond but hesitated. He had felt something strange as though the room had shifted. He was suddenly dizzy and disoriented. Placing both hands on the stone floor, he felt a shudder in the ground.

"What was that?" one of Epaphroditus' companions asked of no one in particular.

He did not receive an answer to his question. Instead, the two missionaries continued to sing their songs, to praise the Lord and exalt the power of His name.

"God is our refuge and strength, a very present help in trouble.
Therefore, we will not fear, even though the earth be removed,
and though the mountains be carried into the midst of the sea;
Though its waters roar and be troubled,
though the mountains shake with its swelling."

The rumbling began again, and fear struck the heart of the hardened ruffian. His companions likewise grew anxious and sought answers from their leader, but he had no explanation for them. As the two missionaries continued to sing and chant, the rumbling grew ever louder.

"Come, behold the works of the Lord,

Who has made desolations in the earth.
He makes wars cease to the end of the earth;
He breaks the bow and cuts the spear in two;
He burns the chariot in the fire.
Be still, and know that I am God;
I will be exalted among the nations,
I will be exalted in the earth!
The Lord of hosts is with us;
The God of Jacob is our refuge."

The room began to shake, the rumbling growing by degrees into a deafening roar. The prisoners began to cry out in panic.

"It's an earthquake!" one of them shouted.

The rumbling grew as the missionaries sang, and as their voices rose, the tremors grew in proportion.

"It's them!" Epaphroditus said to his men. "They are doing this!"

"Make them stop!" one of his men pleaded.

Dust began to fall from the tiles above, raining down on the frightened prisoners who all cried out, begging the missionaries to cease their praises.

"I acknowledge the power of your God!" Epaphroditus shouted, a faint whisper in the roar of the quaking earth. "Please, stop, and we will listen to you!"

But the two men did not stop. Undeterred by the rumble of the moving ground and the tumultuous roar all about them, they continued their songs of praise.

"Praise you the Lord.
Praise, O you servants of the Lord, praise the name of the Lord.
Blessed be the name of the Lord from this time forth and for ever more.
From the rising of the sun to the going down of the same the Lord's name is to be praised.
The Lord is high above all nations, and his glory above the heavens.
Blessed be the name of the Lord!"

With that final pronouncement, there was a loud crack and the wailing sound of rending metal. The two men ceased their singing at last and silence fell over the darkness of the prison cell.

"My stocks," one of the prisoners said, "they're loosened!"

"Mine too!" said another.

"They are all loosened," Paul informed them, standing. "The Lord God has freed us."

"Let's go," Epaphroditus said to his men. He made a move toward the door, only to have Paul step into his path and place a hand on his chest.

"No," he said. "We cannot leave."

One of the other men scoffed. "Do what you want, but we are going."

"No," Paul said, and there was steel in his voice. "You are not."

Epaphroditus remembered the rumbling of the earth and the terrible roar of the earthquake that had accompanied the singing of these two men. If they could cause the earth to tremble with their singing, what else might they be capable of? He stepped back and indicated to his men that they should wait.

Paul was still looking at them when he felt a hand on his left arm. Turning back, he did not see anyone, yet he was certain a hand had gripped his upper arm. Looking around, he saw Silas standing off to one side. His heart jumped as he realized who it must have been.

"Paul," he heard the disembodied, yet familiar, voice whisper urgently into his ear, "the jailer. He was asleep upstairs and awoke to find the doors opened. He thinks you have all escaped and is determined to die rather than face dishonor. Hurry! He has drawn his sword, and even now he bends over to thrust it into his abdomen!"

"Stop!" Paul shouted. Then thinking that he needed to be more specific added, "Do yourself no harm, for we are all here."

Silence resumed in the cell as the prisoners stared blankly ahead. Some of them cocked their heads to one side as though straining to hear. Paul remembered that they were all still in darkness. Only he had been granted the gift of sight in the blackness of the cell. They heard a sound, then a voice calling for light. There were footfalls on the stone stairs and soon the flickering glow of lamplight came into view, growing brighter as it descended the stairs. A few moments later the guard reached the bottom of the stairs and stepped into the cell which was now, thanks to the lamp, bright enough for all to see.

Paul recognized the guard. It was the same one who had questioned him earlier about the gospel. He was staring in open awe at the men who stood without their shackles.

"How did you know I was going to harm myself?" he asked.

Paul pondered the question, unsure at first how to respond. Malachi had instructed him not to divulge the fact that he had been in communication with an angel, but how could he explain his knowledge of the jailer's intentions? Thinking quickly, he came to an answer that was technically true, though opaque.

"I was given the ability to see."

The jailer considered his answer for a moment, then waving his hand, instructed him, "Come. Come with me."

He led the prisoners up the stairs and into an anteroom above. When they had all exited the stairwell, the jailer replaced the lamp in its holder and fell to his knees before Paul and Silas.

"Sirs, what must I do to be saved?"

Paul rested a hand on his shoulder and replied in a reassuring voice, "Believe in the Lord Jesus Christ, and you will be saved, you and your household."

"I do believe!" the jailer assured them. "Please, come to my house and minister to my family. I would have my entire household hear your words."

Paul nodded. "Lead the way."

As they walked out into the courtyard, the ruffians fled. But Paul noticed that Epaphroditus hung back, unsure of himself. He stepped up to Paul and asked him, "What should I do now?"

"What do you mean?" Paul eyed the ruffian who seemed perplexed by the question.

"I don't understand," he muttered.

"Are you asking me if you should go," Paul pressed, "or are you asking me something of greater import?"

"I don't know," he admitted. But as he spoke, one of his men rushed up to him and, taking him by the arm, hissed, "Let's go!"

He pulled Epaphroditus away, who looked back at Paul in wonder. The ruffians scurried off into the night, and Paul turned back to the jailer.

"Please, lead the way to your house."

Chapter 40

As For Me And My House

They did not have far to walk. As the keeper of the prison, the jailer's house was part of the prison complex, built against one of the interior walls. The jailer woke his entire household, his wife, his children, his aged mother, and two slaves. In Roman custom, the family consisted of all members of the household. That extended to any non-adults or un-married females and even included the slaves. The jailer was the Pater Familias, the head of the family. As such, he held the right to exercise authority over all the members of the familia, to reward and punish, and in theory, he even held the power of life and death over each.

Since Roman custom dictated that the Pater Familias made decisions for the family as a matter of course, there was no question as to their acceptance of Paul and Silas' teaching, but that was not the same as true belief. The pair had to be very careful to make sure each person fully understood the words of the gospel and truly accepted the gift of salvation for themselves. They spent a long time questioning the family members to be sure of their understanding and genuine desire to accept the gift of the Lord Jesus Christ. Once they were satisfied, they prayed with them and told them to prepare themselves for baptism. While they did so, the jailer took Paul and Silas to the nearby bath complex and personally washed their bodies.

He applied a salve to their wounded backs and dressed them in his finest clothes.

The family met them at the Roman bath, and Paul and Silas baptized them all in the name of the Father, the Son, and the Holy Spirit. Afterward, they returned to the jailer's house where he set food before them. They ate gladly, for they were very hungry after their ordeal. When they finished, the jailer made beds for them, and they slept in comfort and peace.

The next morning, the jailer came to wake the two men, but they were already up, engaged in their morning prayers. Not wishing to interrupt them, he waited a long time before Silas opened his eyes and saw the jailer in the doorway. Reaching out, he laid a hand on Paul's arm.

"Good morning," Paul said to the jailer when he saw him.

"Good morning!"

It was apparent from the jailer's expression that he was enthused about some important piece of news.

"I bring you word from the magistrates!" he gushed. "They have sent to let you go!"

Paul and Silas exchanged glances, but they did not rise. Paul pursed his lips and shook his head in irritation. The jailer's smile melted as he realized his new friends did not share his excitement.

"What is it?" he asked. "What's amiss?"

Paul said, "They have beaten us publicly, un-condemned Roman citizens, thrown us into prison, and now they would throw us out secretly?" Paul shook his head. "No."

The jailer took an involuntary step back and stammered, struggling to find words. Breathlessly, he said, "You are Romans?"

"Indeed," Paul confirmed.

The jailer blinked and his mouth fell open, the blood draining from his face to leave him pale. Paul was saying that he and Silas were Cives Romani, citizens of Rome. As Greeks, all the citizens of Philippi were members of the Roman Empire, but that was not the same as being a Roman citizen.

As citizens, they had the right to legal trial. They could not be imprisoned, tortured, or whipped. By beating and imprisoning Paul and Silas, the magistrates had violated the rights of Roman citizens, and he had participated.

"I did not know," the jailer said to them. "What should I say to the magistrates?"

Paul answered, "Let them come themselves to release us."

The jailer nodded and said, "I will. Please, wait here while I speak with them."

The jailer left the pair in his office while he went to confer with the authorities. Before long, he returned with the magistrates. The three elderly men stepped tentatively into the room, their fear apparent. Knowing their penalty could be death, they trembled and wrung their hands, sweat beading upon their foreheads. One of the magistrates, the same who had confronted them in the plaza the previous day, stepped forward and addressed them.

"Please," he said haltingly, "we did not know you were Romans."

"You never asked," Paul replied curtly.

The magistrate nodded his head nervously and glanced at his companions for support, but they appeared even more terrified than he.

"You are correct in what you say," he admitted in a small voice. "We did not question you properly to determine your rights. For that we are repentant."

It was not Paul's intention to humiliate the magistrates, only to make certain no stigma would be attached to his mission here. He did not want the brethren in Philippi to suffer because of the disturbance the prior day. It was important for the people of the city to know that they were innocent. Otherwise, the church here might suffer.

"We accept your apology," Paul said magnanimously.

The magistrates sighed in obvious relief and smiled weakly, but they asked the pair when they planned to depart the city. It was apparent they wanted them gone as soon as possible, so they could put this whole troublesome episode behind them.

"We will be leaving Philippi just as soon as we have seen our brethren and encouraged them," Paul said.

The magistrates clasped their hands and thanked the pair. They wished them well on their journey but stopped short of offering their hospitality should they pass through Philippi again. The missionaries did not press the matter. Instead, they said their goodbyes to the jailer and his family. Then they departed and made their way to the house of Lydia, with whom they had been staying.

When they arrived, they were welcomed enthusiastically by the faithful of the city who had all gathered there to pray for their deliverance. Luke and Timothy were present. They embraced Paul and Silas, then sat them down and brought them food and drink. When the small church heard of the miraculous earthquake that had freed Paul and Silas and that the jailer and his family had been saved, they rejoiced.

Spontaneous shouts and cries of gratitude and praise to God erupted from the gathered throng, and they all began to worship together. Singing broke out as the brethren praised God for the deliverance of the missionaries and for the wonderful demonstration of His power. The service was in full throat when, quite abruptly, people began to fall silent and look back toward the entrance of the house. Paul and Silas, deep in song, eventually noticed the interruption and turned to see what drew everyone's attention.

It was Epaphroditus. He had come into the house and now stood awkwardly in the doorway. His head was lowered with his hands clasped in front of him. As Paul and Silas approached, he glanced up at them, then back down again before taking a deep breath.

"Please sirs, would you tell me what you said to the jailer last night? What did he mean by saved?"

Indicating a nearby couch, Paul invited his guest to make himself comfortable. Paul sat down beside him and said, "Because mankind is sinful, we deserve eternal death. But God loves us as His children and has made provision for us."

Epaphroditus peered intently at Paul without blinking as he absorbed all the missionary said.

"The Lord God created the heavens and the earth, the animals, the plants, and mankind. In the beginning, man was innocent and enjoyed direct fellowship with God. But man disobeyed God. Because of that, because we are sinful, and we are doomed to die, not only physically, but spiritually as well."

Epaphroditus nodded as Paul continued. "But God loves us, and because of that, He sent His only Son to die and pay the debt we owed, to redeem us from sin. Those who believe in Him will not perish but have everlasting life."

Epaphroditus asked him, "What must I do to earn this favor?"

"There is nothing you can do to earn it," Silas interjected. "It is by grace we are saved, not of works. It is a gift of God, freely given."

Paul picked up on the thread, "The price has already been paid. All you must do is believe in your heart that Jesus Christ is the Son of God, that the Father has raised Him from the dead, and proclaim with your mouth that He is Lord."

"I do believe!" Epaphroditus proclaimed loudly for all to hear. "I believe that Jesus is Lord!"

A rush of excited voices filled the room as members of the fellowship began to cry out in praise at the ruffian's profession of faith. He glanced around at them, overwhelmed by the demonstration of shared joy on his behalf.

"Then you are redeemed," Paul said, smiling warmly, "and now you may be baptized."

"What is baptized?"

Silas explained, "We shall lower you into water and raise you up again. It is symbolic of our Lord Jesus Christ's death, burial, and resurrection."

Epaphroditus frowned, his eyes narrowing in confusion. "And then I will be saved?"

"No," Paul assured him, "that has already happened. The baptism is merely an outward sign, a proclamation that you have been washed clean by the blood of the Lamb."

"Then why do it?"

"We are baptized because the Lord commanded it and because we follow the example He set for us. It is an act of obedience and a testimony to others."

Epaphroditus nodded emphatically as his understanding grew. He pleaded with them, "Please, tell me more."

And so, they did. The congregation of believers of Philippi gathered around their newest brother and welcomed him into the fold, telling him of the life of Jesus and His disciples. They told him of how He lived, of the miracles He performed, and of His teachings. They recounted the story of His death, burial, and resurrection, and how even now, He sits at the right hand of the Father, hearing the prayers of believers and interceding on their behalf.

They prayed with him then. For the first time, Epaphroditus of Philippi spoke to God. He thanked the Lord for forgiving him his sins and redeeming him. He asked to be filled with the Holy Spirit and to be given the strength to preach the gospel. He committed the remainder of his life to the service of the Lord.

And his life would never be the same.

Epilogue

Thine is the Power

It had taken Epaphroditus all morning to locate the two men. First, he had gone to the prison to speak to the jailer, albeit over the objections of his men. They called him a fool, but he did not care. Throughout his life, Epaphroditus had sought happiness. He sought it in drink, in women, in gambling, and in danger. He had pursued power and wealth through violence and intimidation. He did what he liked when he liked, and no man told him what to do. Yet, he was not happy. None of the pleasures of this world could satisfy the emptiness that consumed him. The more he gained, the more lost he felt.

Then he had met this strange man and his friend who said they could save him and give his life meaning, even though they had been beaten and jailed because of him. At first, he had scoffed at their naïve notions. They possessed nothing but the clothes on their backs. What could they offer him? Then they had begun their prayers and their singing, and he had felt the power of their God.

Initially, it was fear that prompted him to acknowledge their Lord, fear and a desire that they stop before they brought the entire prison down on their heads. He would have been content to leave them to their fate and never see them again, but then the tall one received a vision of the jailer about to end his own life. It was the look on the jailer's face that had caused Epaphroditus to stop and reconsider. What he had seen in the eyes of the jailer was something he had been searching for his entire life.

Hope.

Epaphroditus so desperately wanted to experience that transformation, to gain what the jailer had found. He longed for the certainty of place and purpose that would give his life meaning. Now he knew what he needed to fill the void in his heart. The tall one had said the name, Jesus, in the cell, and the name had resonated within Epaphroditus' soul and started him on this desperate quest.

So, he had sought out the two men. First, he visited the jail, but the guard told him they had left, so he asked to speak to the keeper of the prison. He came out to him, and to Epaphroditus' surprise, he did not try to lock him back up. Instead, he answered his questions and suggested he visit the house of Lydia, the dye merchant where the two men had been staying. Epaphroditus ran through the streets of the city asking all those he came upon where he could find the house of Lydia. Eventually, he stumbled upon a tailor who regularly purchased purple cloth from her. He directed him to the house, and Epaphroditus hurried that way.

But he did not go alone.

Behind him, as though part of his shadow, lurked a dark form, unseen by mortal eyes. It hunched as it walked, trailing behind the hustling form of Epaphroditus. Red eyes glowed from within the sockets of its gray head while black leathery wings trailed behind, arching outward from its back.

It was Tannin, the same evil spirit who had possessed the girl and attempted to ruin the missionaries' effort to spread the gospel in this town. After he had been cast out by the one called Paul, he used his vile influence over Epaphroditus to goad him into seizing the two missionaries. Tannin had wanted them killed, but Epaphroditus resisted the temptation to execute the men on his own and instead handed them over to the authorities.

When the magistrates failed to land upon the right punishment for the missionaries, he put it into the head of Epaphroditus to start a riot. But the soldiers prevented the mob from laying hands on the two men.

Tannin had been thwarted at every turn. On top of that, his plan had the unintended consequence of landing Epaphroditus and his men in the same jail cell as Paul and Silas. At first, he thought that might be an opportunity. Perhaps if one of the ruffians got loose, he would throttle the two men. That would solve the problem quite neatly, and Lucifer would surely be pleased.

When Silas was brought into the cell, battered and bloody, Tannin thought he might be half dead already. He hoped Paul would be in similar condition. But then Paul had been brought in, and he appeared to be in good health, if a bit dazed and disoriented. Tannin had stooped over the sleeping body of Epaphroditus and was whispering venomous words of suggested violence to his unconscious mind when a blinding flash of light took him by surprise and he found himself shrinking backward toward a far corner of the cell.

It was Malachi.

The traitor had been assigned as the guardian angel of this apostle since before he was converted on the road to Damascus. Tannin's standing among the other demons had fallen steadily ever since. He had been given the task of frustrating the mission of this Paul, but instead, he was the one constantly frustrated. It seemed God had determined Paul would be someone of significance in the new church.

Malachi. He was the most hated of all the hosts, the traitor who had abandoned the Morning Star to stand against his own brothers. Nothing would have brought Tannin more pleasure than to humiliate the smug troublemaker. Still, every time Tannin thought he might win a victory, Malachi ruined his schemes.

Tannin brought up his arms to shield himself against the burning heat of the angel's intense aura, even brighter than it had been at the beginning of the war. He hissed through his pointed teeth and cursed the angel who only laughed.

"I told you not to taunt Paul," Malachi chided him, "but as usual, you did not listen."

"Damn you, Malachi!" the demon spat.

Malachi shook his head and clucked mockingly. "Haven't we been over this? I am not the one who is—"

"Yes, yes, I know!" Tannin shot back. "I'm trying to curse you!"

Malachi chuckled. "Oh Tannin, you are so easily agitated. Perhaps that's why you have been so unsuccessful here in Philippi. You lack," Malachi paused for a moment as though searching for the right word before saying, "composure."

The demon bared his teeth, hissing. He leaned forward to strike at his hated enemy but found himself shrinking back and screaming in pain, for the angel had intensified the white-hot power of his aura. It burned the leathery skin of the demon to be so exposed to the reflected light of heaven.

"Run along, Tannin," Malachi ordered the fleeing demon. "I have business here, and I do not wish for your company."

As the demon slunk away, he heard the angel speaking to someone, presumably the apostle. Defeated, he retreated to plan his next move. Of course, he could not have imagined that Epaphroditus would become enamored with the troublesome missionary or that he would seek salvation. This was disastrous! If Satan found out he had not only failed in his mission to stop the emergence of the Church in Philippi but that his own thrall had sought Christ, he would be flailed alive!

When Epaphroditus later escaped the jail, it looked as though Tannin's fears could be set to rest, for he and his compatriots fled into the night. But then Epaphroditus went back to the jail the next morning and was now actively searching for the missionaries! If he accepted salvation, Tannin would be through. He had to prevent it.

So, he followed Epaphroditus to the house of the woman, Lydia. Tannin had no idea how he was going to stop him from speaking to Paul and Silas, but he had to try. Scampering to keep up with him, Tannin whispered lies into the Brute's ear. He told him that the missionaries were charlatans who used parlor tricks to fool simple-minded townsfolk. He told him they were lunatics, and that others would say the same of him if he persisted.

When that line of persuasion failed, he switched tactics and began sowing seeds of doubt. Why was Epaphroditus even bothering to try and find these men? They would mock and ridicule him. They did not care about him, nor would they accept him. He was not worthy of redemption. What use could God possibly have with someone like him? He should give up on the entire idea and go back to his normal life before he embarrassed himself.

Inexplicably, that approach failed as well. As Epaphroditus rounded a corner, the demon realized the house he sought was at the end of the street. Epaphroditus took a couple of tentative steps forward, then paused, doubt clouding his face. He glanced back in the direction whence he came, then at the house, and back again.

Relief surged in Tannin. Epaphroditus was hesitating! His vile influence must have penetrated after all. Frantically, he scampered up beside the vacillating ruffian and hurriedly whispered words of discouragement into his ear. Epaphroditus shook his head violently as though trying to clear it of a fog. He peered down the street at the house, the object of his search and the realization of his hopes or potentially his fears.

Then clenching his fists with determination and fighting off the efforts of the desperate demon, he turned and strode toward the house at a deliberate pace. He leaned forward, willing his body to keep moving toward his goal. For good or for ill, toward victory or disappointment, he would see this through.

Tannin squealed with panic. He scuttled behind the determined man and prepared to follow him into the house. If he could not stop him, perhaps he could wreck things from the inside. If he sowed doubt in the minds of the believers, perhaps they would become suspicious and hesitate to welcome Epaphroditus.

Sometimes that worked. Sometimes, the followers of Christ could be corrupted and made to act callously toward new believers, particularly those who had been especially sinful or had harmed the believers in the past. This hypocrisy often had the effect of discouraging those seeking conversion, causing them to turn away from Christ. If the fears Tannin had been whispering to

Epaphroditus materialized, he might think better of his hopes and flee the house. It was worth a try.

But as Epaphroditus stepped through the gate of the courtyard and Tannin attempted to follow him through, the demon was suddenly jerked backward. He hit the ground with enough force to hurt even a non-mortal being such as he. He sat up to see what had assaulted him and found himself peering up into the face of the hated traitor, Malachi.

That face had changed. No longer smirking with sarcastic mirth, Malachi now glared down at the demon with intense, narrowed eyes. It was the face of a hardened warrior and Malachi was dressed as such. No longer wearing the simple robes of the angelic choir, he was now clad in the full Armor of God from head to toe with a sword hanging at his side. A long flowing white cape fluttered behind him, fanning out behind wings that were spread wide. He was a vision of heavenly power and Tannin cowered before him.

"You may not enter, Tannin," the angel proclaimed, his voice echoing grandly.

The demon scampered to his feet and objected. "You have no right to bar me! I have not broken the peace. Stand aside and allow me to work within the limits allotted to my kind!"

Malachi smiled, and the confidence of that smile brought a shudder to the demon. It was a knowing grin, triumphant and terrible to behold.

Malachi spoke in measured tones, "The rules have changed, Tannin. The people within have prayed to the Lord and asked that He erect a barrier around this place to keep out demonic influences. The Lord God has listened to their prayers and granted their request. You may not enter."

Tannin scrambled to his feet, glancing left and right for a way past the obstructing angel. Then the wings came down to reveal the scene around Malachi, and what Tannin beheld caused his eyes to bulge and his jaw to drop.

Malachi was not alone. Standing shoulder to shoulder with him, immovable as statues, were arrayed an entire company of angels of the legion of the Flaming Sword of the Spirit. They surrounded the complex like pillars of light, their auras merging to form a solid ring of heavenly power about the house.

Looking up, the demon saw hosts lining the roof of the home and even more angels circling in the air above. Tannin knew then that he had lost. The house was unassailable. He backed away, slinking off into the shadows of the nearby buildings. He would have to regroup and seek a new way to undermine the church in Philippi.

As he turned to head back down an alley, Tannin stopped abruptly in his tracks, gripped by fear. Looming over him stood a massive dark presence framed by towering black wings. Long curling horns, glistening like obsidian, rose from its forehead under which glowed two menacing red eyes. Those eyes were narrow slits that gave off a faint crimson glow, casting the face of the demon in eerie shadow. Tannin trembled and fell to his knees.

"Malphas!" the imp screeched. "What are you doing here?"

The slits on Malphas' face seemed to narrow even more, nearly extinguishing the red glow. The black lips curled back, exposing long white fangs and a black tongue that flicked in and out of his wide mouth.

"I have been observing your failure," the gravelly voice intoned.

"It isn't my fault!" Tannin insisted.

He would have said more, but he never got the chance. A clawed hand shot out and gripped him by the throat so tightly that he could not manage to utter more than a guttural choking gasp. Malphas lifted the smaller demon bodily into the air and brought his face up close to his own. Their pointed gray noses almost touched as Malphas bared his teeth.

"Lucifer wants to see you," Malphas said in a syrupy voice that promised pain and torment.

The squealing sound of Tannin's cries faded into the distance as he was dragged away to face his master. Standing next to his brothers, Malachi shook his head slowly. He almost felt sorry for the hapless demon. Almost.

The angel to the right of Malachi broke his discipline for a split second to jab an elbow into his side. Malachi flinched and reflexively glanced over at his neighbor who still stared straight ahead. A smile formed on the face of the robust host, and he offered Malachi a mischievous wink. Malachi grinned and winked back at his friend. He was glad he was here, for there was no one he would rather have at his side than Grigori.

The two angels remained there at attention amid their brethren, implacable and unmoving, a wall of heavenly might. The faithful had prayed in the name of Jesus Christ that no evil demonic forces would pierce this hedge, and so they would not. The Lord had answered their prayer. It was His will that Satan be denied.

And as it is the will of the Lord—
Let it be so.

Appendix

Source Scripture In Story Order

English Standard Version

Timothy Joins Paul and Silas
(Acts 16:1-5)

16 Paul came also to Derbe and to Lystra. A disciple was there, named Timothy, the son of a Jewish woman who was a believer, but his father was a Greek. ² He was well spoken of by the brothers at Lystra and Iconium. ³ Paul wanted Timothy to accompany him, and he took him and circumcised him because of the Jews who were in those places, for they all knew that his father was a Greek. ⁴ As they went on their way through the cities, they delivered to them for observance the decisions that had been reached by the apostles and elders who were in Jerusalem. ⁵ So the churches were strengthened in the faith, and they increased in numbers daily.

The Macedonian Call
(Acts 16:6-10)

[6] And they went through the region of Phrygia and Galatia, having been forbidden by the Holy Spirit to speak the word in Asia. [7] And when they had come up to Mysia, they attempted to go into Bithynia, but the Spirit of Jesus did not allow them. [8] So, passing by Mysia, they went down to Troas. [9] And a vision appeared to Paul in the night: a man of Macedonia was standing there, urging him and saying, "Come over to Macedonia and help us." [10] And when Paul had seen the vision, immediately we sought to go on into Macedonia, concluding that God had called us to preach the gospel to them.

The Conversion of Lydia
(Acts 16:11-15)

[11] So, setting sail from Troas, we made a direct voyage to Samothrace, and the following day to Neapolis, [12] and from there to Philippi, which is a leading city of the district of Macedonia and a Roman colony. We remained in this city some days. [13] And on the Sabbath day we went outside the gate to the riverside, where we supposed there was a place of prayer, and we sat down and spoke to the women who had come together. [14] One who heard us was a woman named Lydia, from the city of Thyatira, a seller of purple goods, who was a worshiper of God. The Lord opened her heart to pay attention to what was said by Paul. [15] And after she was baptized, and her household as well, she urged us, saying, "If you have judged me to be faithful to the Lord, come to my house and stay." And she prevailed upon us.

Paul and Silas in Prison
(Acts 16:16-24)

[16] As we were going to the place of prayer, we were met by a slave girl who had a spirit of divination and brought her owners much gain by fortune-telling. [17] She followed Paul and us, crying out, "These men are servants of the Most High God, who proclaim to you the way of salvation." [18] And this she kept doing for many days. Paul, having become greatly annoyed, turned and said to the spirit, "I command you in the name of Jesus Christ to come out of her." And it came out that very hour.

[19] But when her owners saw that their hope of gain was gone, they seized Paul and Silas and dragged them into the marketplace before the rulers. [20] And when they had brought them to the magistrates, they said, "These men are Jews, and they are disturbing our city. [21] They advocate customs that are not lawful for us as Romans to accept or practice." [22] The crowd joined in attacking them, and the magistrates tore the garments off them and gave orders to beat them with rods. [23] And when they had inflicted many blows upon them, they threw them into prison, ordering the jailer to keep them safely. [24] Having received this order, he put them into the inner prison and fastened their feet in the stocks.

The Creation
(Genesis 1)

1 In the beginning, God created the heavens and the earth. [2] The earth was without form and void, and darkness was over the face of the deep. And the Spirit of God was hovering over the face of the waters.

[3] And God said, "Let there be light," and there was light. [4] And God saw that the light was good. And God separated the light from the darkness. [5] God called the light Day, and the darkness he called Night. And there was evening and there was morning, the first day.

⁶ And God said, "Let there be an expanse in the midst of the waters, and let it separate the waters from the waters." ⁷ And God made the expanse and separated the waters that were under the expanse from the waters that were above the expanse. And it was so. ⁸ And God called the expanse Heaven. And there was evening and there was morning, the second day.

⁹ And God said, "Let the waters under the heavens be gathered together into one place, and let the dry land appear." And it was so. ¹⁰ God called the dry land Earth, and the waters that were gathered together he called Seas. And God saw that it was good.

¹¹ And God said, "Let the earth sprout vegetation, plants yielding seed, and fruit trees bearing fruit in which is their seed, each according to its kind, on the earth." And it was so. ¹² The earth brought forth vegetation, plants yielding seed according to their own kinds, and trees bearing fruit in which is their seed, each according to its kind. And God saw that it was good. ¹³ And there was evening and there was morning, the third day.

¹⁴ And God said, "Let there be lights in the expanse of the heavens to separate the day from the night. And let them be for signs and for seasons, and for days and years, ¹⁵ and let them be lights in the expanse of the heavens to give light upon the earth." And it was so. ¹⁶ And God made the two great lights—the greater light to rule the day and the lesser light to rule the night—and the stars. ¹⁷ And God set them in the expanse of the heavens to give light on the earth, ¹⁸ to rule over the day and over the night, and to separate the light from the darkness. And God saw that it was good. ¹⁹ And there was evening and there was morning, the fourth day.

²⁰ And God said, "Let the waters swarm with swarms of living creatures, and let birds fly above the earth across the expanse of the heavens." ²¹ So God created the great sea creatures and every living creature that moves, with which the waters swarm, according to their kinds, and every winged bird according to its kind. And God saw that it was good. ²² And God blessed them, saying, "Be fruitful and multiply and fill the waters in the seas, and let birds multiply on the earth."²³ And there was evening and there was morning, the fifth day.

²⁴ And God said, "Let the earth bring forth living creatures according to their kinds—livestock and creeping things and beasts of the earth according to their kinds." And it was so. ²⁵ And God made the beasts of the earth according to their kinds and the livestock according to their kinds, and everything that creeps on the ground according to its kind. And God saw that it was good.

²⁶ Then God said, "Let us make man in our image, after our likeness. And let them have dominion over the fish of the sea and over the birds of the heavens and over the livestock and over all the earth and over every creeping thing that creeps on the earth."

²⁷ So God created man in his own image,

in the image of God he created him;

male and female he created them.

²⁸ And God blessed them. And God said to them, "Be fruitful and multiply and fill the earth and subdue it, and have dominion over the fish of the sea and over the birds of the heavens and over every living thing that moves on the earth." ²⁹ And God said, "Behold, I have given you every plant yielding seed that is on the face of all the earth, and every tree with seed in its fruit. You shall have them for food.³⁰ And to every beast of the earth and to every bird of the heavens and to everything that creeps on the earth, everything that has the breath of life, I have given every green plant for food." And it was so. ³¹ And God saw everything that he had made, and behold, it was very good. And there was evening and there was morning, the sixth day.

The Seventh Day
(Genesis 2:1-3)

2 Thus the heavens and the earth were finished, and all the host of them. ² And on the seventh day God finished his work that he had done, and he rested on the seventh day from all his work that he had done. ³ So God blessed the seventh day and made it holy, because on it God rested from all his work that he had done in creation.

The Garden of Eden

(Genesis 2:8-14)

[8] And the Lord God planted a garden in Eden, in the east, and there he put the man whom he had formed. [9] And out of the ground the Lord God made to spring up every tree that is pleasant to the sight and good for food. The tree of life was in the midst of the garden, and the tree of the knowledge of good and evil.
[10] A river flowed out of Eden to water the garden, and there it divided and became four rivers. [11] The name of the first is the Pishon. It is the one that flowed around the whole land of Havilah, where there is gold. [12] And the gold of that land is good; bdellium and onyx stone are there. [13] The name of the second river is the Gihon. It is the one that flowed around the whole land of Cush. [14] And the name of the third river is the Tigris, which flows east of Assyria. And the fourth river is the Euphrates.

The Creation of Woman

(Genesis 2:18-25)

[18] Then the Lord God said, "It is not good that the man should be alone; I will make him a helper fit for him." [19] Now out of the ground the Lord God had formed every beast of the field and every bird of the heavens and brought them to the man to see what he would call them. And whatever the man called every living creature, that was its name. [20] The man gave names to all livestock and to the birds of the heavens and to every beast of the field. But for Adam there was not found a helper fit for him. [21] So the Lord God caused a deep sleep to fall upon the man, and while he slept took one of his ribs and closed up its place with flesh. [22] And the rib that the Lord God had taken from the man he made into a woman and brought her to the man. [23] Then the man said,
"This at last is bone of my bones
    and flesh of my flesh;

she shall be called Woman,
because she was taken out of Man."
24 Therefore a man shall leave his father and his mother and hold fast
to his wife, and they shall become one flesh. 25 And the man and his
wife were both naked and were not ashamed.

Lucifer Cast Out of Heaven
(Isaiah 14:12-15)

12 "How you are fallen from heaven,
    O Day Star, son of Dawn!
How you are cut down to the ground,
    you who laid the nations low!
13 You said in your heart,
    'I will ascend to heaven;
above the stars of God
    I will set my throne on high;
I will sit on the mount of assembly
    in the far reaches of the north;
14 I will ascend above the heights of the clouds;
    I will make myself like the Most High.'
15 But you are brought down to Sheol,
    to the far reaches of the pit.

The War in Heaven
(Revelation 12:7-9)

7 Now war arose in heaven, Michael and his angels fighting against
the dragon. And the dragon and his angels fought back, 8 but he was
defeated, and there was no longer any place for them in
heaven. 9 And the great dragon was thrown down, that ancient
serpent, who is called the devil and Satan, the deceiver of the whole
world—he was thrown down to the earth, and his angels were
thrown down with him.

The Fall of Man

(Genesis 3)

3 Now the serpent was more crafty than any other beast of the field that the Lord God had made.

He said to the woman, "Did God actually say, 'You shall not eat of any tree in the garden'?" [2] And the woman said to the serpent, "We may eat of the fruit of the trees in the garden, [3] but God said, 'You shall not eat of the fruit of the tree that is in the midst of the garden, neither shall you touch it, lest you die.'" [4] But the serpent said to the woman, "You will not surely die. [5] For God knows that when you eat of it your eyes will be opened, and you will be like God, knowing good and evil." [6] So when the woman saw that the tree was good for food, and that it was a delight to the eyes, and that the tree was to be desired to make one wise, she took of its fruit and ate, and she also gave some to her husband who was with her, and he ate. [7] Then the eyes of both were opened, and they knew that they were naked. And they sewed fig leaves together and made themselves loincloths.

[8] And they heard the sound of the Lord God walking in the garden in the cool of the day, and the man and his wife hid themselves from the presence of the Lord God among the trees of the garden. [9] But the Lord God called to the man and said to him, "Where are you?" [10] And he said, "I heard the sound of you in the garden, and I was afraid, because I was naked, and I hid myself." [11] He said, "Who told you that you were naked? Have you eaten of the tree of which I commanded you not to eat?" [12] The man said, "The woman whom you gave to be with me, she gave me fruit of the tree, and I ate." [13] Then the Lord God said to the woman, "What is this that you have done?" The woman said, "The serpent deceived me, and I ate."
[14] The Lord God said to the serpent,

"Because you have done this,
    cursed are you above all livestock
    and above all beasts of the field;
on your belly you shall go,

and dust you shall eat
    all the days of your life.
¹⁵ I will put enmity between you and the woman,
    and between your offspring and her offspring;
he shall bruise your head,
    and you shall bruise his heel."
¹⁶ To the woman he said,
"I will surely multiply your pain in childbearing;
    in pain you shall bring forth children.
Your desire shall be contrary to your husband,
    but he shall rule over you."
¹⁷ And to Adam he said,
"Because you have listened to the voice of your wife
    and have eaten of the tree
of which I commanded you,
    'You shall not eat of it,'
cursed is the ground because of you;
    in pain you shall eat of it all the days of your life;
¹⁸ thorns and thistles it shall bring forth for you;
    and you shall eat the plants of the field.
¹⁹ By the sweat of your face
    you shall eat bread,
till you return to the ground,
    for out of it you were taken;
for you are dust,
    and to dust you shall return."

²⁰ The man called his wife's name Eve, because she was the mother of all living. ²¹ And the Lord God made for Adam and for his wife garments of skins and clothed them.

²² Then the Lord God said, "Behold, the man has become like one of us in knowing good and evil. Now, lest he reach out his hand and take also of the tree of life and eat, and live forever—"

²³ therefore the Lord God sent him out from the garden of Eden to work the ground from which he was taken. ²⁴ He drove out the man, and at the east of the garden of Eden he placed the cherubim and a

flaming sword that turned every way to guard the way to the tree of life.

Cain and Abel
(Genesis 4:1-17)

4 Now Adam knew Eve his wife, and she conceived and bore Cain, saying, "I have gotten a man with the help of the Lord." [2] And again, she bore his brother Abel. Now Abel was a keeper of sheep, and Cain a worker of the ground. [3] In the course of time Cain brought to the Lord an offering of the fruit of the ground, [4] and Abel also brought of the firstborn of his flock and of their fat portions. And the Lord had regard for Abel and his offering, [5] but for Cain and his offering he had no regard. So Cain was very angry, and his face fell. [6] The Lord said to Cain, "Why are you angry, and why has your face fallen? [7] If you do well, will you not be accepted? And if you do not do well, sin is crouching at the door. Its desire is contrary to you, but you must rule over it."
[8] Cain spoke to Abel his brother. And when they were in the field, Cain rose up against his brother Abel and killed him. [9] Then the Lord said to Cain, "Where is Abel your brother?" He said, "I do not know; am I my brother's keeper?" [10] And the Lord said, "What have you done? The voice of your brother's blood is crying to me from the ground. [11] And now you are cursed from the ground, which has opened its mouth to receive your brother's blood from your hand. [12] When you work the ground, it shall no longer yield to you its strength. You shall be a fugitive and a wanderer on the earth." [13] Cain said to the Lord, "My punishment is greater than I can bear. [14] Behold, you have driven me today away from the ground, and from your face I shall be hidden. I shall be a fugitive and a wanderer on the earth, and whoever finds me will kill me." [15] Then the Lord said to him, "Not so! If anyone kills Cain, vengeance shall be taken on him sevenfold." And the Lord put a mark on Cain, lest any who found him should attack him. [16] Then Cain went away from

the presence of the Lord and settled in the land of Nod, east of Eden.

¹⁷ Cain knew his wife, and she conceived and bore Enoch. When he built a city, he called the name of the city after the name of his son, Enoch.

The Philippian Jailer Saved
(Acts 16:25-34)

²⁵ About midnight Paul and Silas were praying and singing hymns to God, and the prisoners were listening to them, ²⁶ and suddenly there was a great earthquake, so that the foundations of the prison were shaken. And immediately all the doors were opened, and everyone's bonds were unfastened. ²⁷ When the jailer woke and saw that the prison doors were open, he drew his sword and was about to kill himself, supposing that the prisoners had escaped. ²⁸ But Paul cried with a loud voice, "Do not harm yourself, for we are all here." ²⁹ And the jailer called for lights and rushed in, and trembling with fear he fell down before Paul and Silas. ³⁰ Then he brought them out and said, "Sirs, what must I do to be saved?" ³¹ And they said, "Believe in the Lord Jesus, and you will be saved, you and your household." ³² And they spoke the word of the Lord to him and to all who were in his house. ³³ And he took them the same hour of the night and washed their wounds; and he was baptized at once, he and all his family. ³⁴ Then he brought them up into his house and set food before them. And he rejoiced along with his entire household that he had believed in God.

Paul Refuses to Depart Secretly
(Acts 16:35-40)

[35] But when it was day, the magistrates sent the police, saying, "Let those men go." [36] And the jailer reported these words to Paul, saying, "The magistrates have sent to let you go. Therefore come out now and go in peace." [37] But Paul said to them, "They have beaten us publicly, uncondemned, men who are Roman citizens, and have thrown us into prison; and do they now throw us out secretly? No! Let them come themselves and take us out." [38] The police reported these words to the magistrates, and they were afraid when they heard that they were Roman citizens. [39] So they came and apologized to them. And they took them out and asked them to leave the city. [40] So they went out of the prison and visited Lydia. And when they had seen the brothers, they encouraged them and departed.

Nathan Crocker grew up in the Baptist Church, the son of a minister. He served four years in the US Marine Corps, achieving the rank of Sergeant and serving in the second Iraq war.

He lives in Belmont, NC with his wife and children. He enjoys writing, camping, and keeping his sharpshooting skills sharp.

Made in the USA
Columbia, SC
25 October 2020